EVER MARKED
SHADOW GUARDIANS BOOK 1

ELLE SCOTT

BOOKS BY ELLE SCOTT

THE INCANDESCENT SERIES
Ray of Light
Harbour of Light
Symphony of Light

SHADOW GUARDIANS
Ever Marked
… plus more to come

BE A PART OF THE TEAM
www.facebook.com/groups/ellescottstreetteam

For Jasmine and Jade.
For getting me through the teenage years unscathed.

TUESDAY

noon

A mark—the shape of a spiral—curved over her forearm, right below the crook of her elbow. Around it, a faint glow radiated beneath her skin, as though her blood was laced with sunshine.

She hadn't been dragged to a tattoo parlor... no one took a pen to her arm and drew their heart out while she was sleeping... no one cut her and implanted a glow worm under her skin. It was real and permanent and scary; and she wasn't sure she was equipped to handle such things.

Yes, seventeen-year-old Leila Belmonte was in trouble. It didn't help that her best-friend turned boyfriend was staring at her like she was lying on her death bed and had merely hours to live. She felt perfectly fine... well, apart from the mark on her arm. That damned mark.

"Can you remember?" Riley asked.

Leila tried to steady her breath, wondering if not remembering equaled doom.

"It was five days ago," she replied, tugging at the last hanging piece of her newly chewed fingernails. "How can I remember everyone I came in contact with on Friday? I can't even remember what I had for lunch yesterday."

"It was a salad roll, the same as today. Ham and cheese with tomato... but no mayonnaise."

She looked up. He always did that, recalling small pieces of seemingly useless information.

Riley's head was as low as his voice, and his brown eyes returned her stare. It took all she could do not to sweep his blond hair back out of his eyes, but she wasn't sure they were up to that part of their relationship yet — the part where they could touch each other whenever they felt like it.

He furrowed his brow. "You were complaining about the lack of said mayonnaise. You really can't remember?"

"Well, I remember now you've mentioned it. I've just..." Leila sighed. She rolled up her sleeve and began to peel off one of the band-aids on her forearm. "It's been a weird few days."

"Wait!" Riley covered his hand over hers. "Remember what I told you. You need to leave it covered. We don't know who's watching."

"Aw come on, who's watching? The lunch lady? Maybe she crept into my home and poured some squid ink on me while I was passed out?" Leila teased.

"Can you be serious for one moment, Leila, please?"

"Right, I forgot about the glow..." she continued, sarcasm in full force. "First the lunch lady painted me with that glow-in-the-dark paint, then she inked me."

"Leila!" Riley moaned, squeezing his temples with his thumb and index finger.

That, right there, was the kind of relationship they had. He was the serious one and she was the one who avoided any topic that weighed more than a sheet of paper.

"Sorry, but how else did this happen? Someone simply touched me and all of a sudden... *poof*... it magically appeared? I mean, come on. As if, right? Right?" Leila waved her hands around in front of her face and made a ghostly coo.

A few students in the cafeteria turned to see what she was doing. She dropped her hands and played with her barely touched lunch.

Of course, he believes in magic, she thought, *him and his obsession with all things supernatural.*

"Can you think back to who touched you on Friday? Just tell me about your whole day, I'll write a list. At least try and humor me." The crack in his voice, raspy and desperate, brought her back to reality.

Leila acted calm on the outside, but deep down she knew how serious it was. Of course it was — a freaky black spiral was imprinted on her forearm! Her throat suddenly felt void of saliva; she swallowed hard. She'd been marked by something and soon, according to Riley, she was about to become a shape-shifter.

FIVE DAYS EARLIER

FRIDAY

morning

Wild. Untamed. Un-freaking-ruly.

Leila tried to flatten the stray hairs that floated out from her temples but, no thanks to genetics, they had a life of their own. Some days her hair looked amazing, perfect tiny ringlets full of bounce and radiance, as though she'd been blessed by magic. Other days, like this particular Friday, it was a dark curly frizz.

Long statement necklaces hung from the top edges of a rectangular mirror, and tiny Polaroids of her friends and family were tucked into its white frame. She had an eclectic style, she adored accentuating the plain with bold patterns. Black jeans with floral shirts. White sheets with gold and pink striped pillowcases. Boring school uniforms with turquoise-painted nails.

It was a meeting of peace and chaos, a harmonious clash—humble yet vibrant, just like her.

"Hey Leila?" Kale, her brother, poked his head through her doorway. "Hurry up with that mane of yours, I don't want to be late again because of your vanity." He flashed a grin. There was nothing spectacular about him, an otherwise average-looking guy with great skin, but when he smiled he could melt the coldest of hearts... and he knew it. And so, he had a mischievous expression, permanently planted on his face.

"Gimme a break." She turned back to the mirror, pulling her hair up as tight as she could and tying it at her crown. "I don't care what it looks like, it just gets in the way sometimes."

"Yeah, right." Kale said, before flattening his lips into a pout. Leila wondered if he was annoyed or endeared, then decided on the latter because she was his sister and he had to love her, right?

"It's okay for you." She reached up and patted his buzz cut.

He ducked at the touch. "Don't mess it uuuup."

Leila laughed, then lunged forward to give his head an even bigger pat, but he was too fast—he threw his hand up and clutched her wrist. She cried out in pain.

"Damn, sorry." Kale let go immediately.

He didn't hurt her, he wasn't that rough. Irritating and boisterous, yes, but always gentle enough with his little sister.

A smile spread across her face. "Works every time."

"I didn't hurt you?" he asked, concerned.

She shook her head with delight and took fast advantage of his vulnerability, bouncing her fingertips over the top of his head. Before he had the chance to retaliate, she grabbed her backpack and ran downstairs, with his footsteps close behind her.

The house was a simple canvas: white walls, pale timber furnishings, with splashes of pastel colors in things like cushions, lamps shades, and watercolor paintings. Eclectic vases, candle holders, and other ornaments made of polished white or mint green, sat on pine shelves in every nook.

In the kitchen, two paper bags were lined up on the bench.

"Uhh, you know I don't need a packed lunch anymore, right? I'm twenty-two, plus I work at a cafe," Kale said, throwing his thumb up in their mother's direction and rolled his eyes at Leila, as if to say *get a load of the crazy!*

Their mom, Aileen, was sitting at the dining table with papers sprawled over it. A messy red-haired bun rested on the top of her head, she was wearing yesterday's makeup and hadn't changed out of her pajamas yet. She looked up with her mouth agape. "Oh yes, of course, force of habit. Sorry."

"How's the speech going?" Leila asked.

"Mmm?" Aileen looked at her with wide hazel eyes. Her freckles danced on her pale nose as she scrunched it upwards. "I'm not sure, I suppose what I've got will have to do."

Leila mimicked her mother's nose scrunch in sympathy. They didn't look the same doing it, though. Leila's skin tone was a mix of her parents'; her dad's earthy complexion, and her mom's freckles. It was the same with every part of her. Dad's dark hair, Mom's frizzy curls. Dad's eye shape, Mom's eye color. Dad's compassion and Mom's aloofness. They called Kale and Leila the perfect blend of cultures. Half Irish, a quarter Hawaiian, a quarter Mexican. Kids at school called her…

"Dad and I won't be here when you get home from school. I've organized your dinner for the week. It's all in containers in the freezer… labeled of course. I've put the number of the hotel into speed-dial, but you've got my cell in your phones anyway… so try that. I'll answer… I'll try to answer. If I don't answer, don't hesitate to call again, if you need. About anything. Kale will be here to make sure you'll be all right though."

Aileen took a breath, nodding to herself, making sure she remembered everything she wanted to say. As she turned back towards her papers, she flung her hand in the air. "Oh, and for the love of all things good in this world don't go into the woods. Did you hear about the latest poor soul? They say it's a cougar."

Leila winced, she was trying hard not to think about the attacks. There had been five of them in less than two weeks. One of them fatal. Most of the alleged attacks happened deep in the woods, but the most recent one happened on the outskirts of town by the old apple shed — way too close for comfort. Half the town were screaming for the animal to be found and taken out; and the other half called for calm, they considered it pointless to cull without proof of which animal it was.

Leila didn't know which half she belonged in, so she buried her head in the sand. "Mom, it's fine, we'll be fine."

"Yeah, go and do your thing, enjoy your fairytale convention. You're the freakin' key-note speaker, don't worry about us," Kale said behind them.

"It's folklore, Kale. I'm a professor in folklore." She shook her head and stood up to give Leila a hug. Nuzzling her face into Leila's shoulder, she whispered, "I am excited, though."

Me too, Leila thought, thrilled to have a whole week without the parents. She figured it would be a great trial run for when she went to college in two years. Plus, no bedtime limits, no hovering or nagging, no noise control — it was going to be bliss.

"Sorry to break up the farewell but we have to go, I can't be late for work again." Kale nudged Leila's back, but all it did was provoke their mom to grab his wrist and pull him in towards them.

Their dad, Tate, entered the kitchen, and not wanting to

12

miss out on the family embrace, wrapped his bear-like arms around them all. With his cheek resting atop of Leila's head, he said, "No parties, no alcohol, no strangers, no leaving the house after dark, no skipping school, no hormonal activities in this house, or any house... or anywhere. Say yes if you agree," he said.

"Yes," Leila replied honestly.

She had every intention to follow his rules, but intention goes out the window when you're trying to save your own life. She would break every single one of them over the next week.

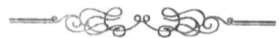

Kale pulled his car up to the curb, as the last trickle of students were making their way inside.

"Wait for me here after school, kiddo, I want to take you somewhere," he said, revving his beat-up Mustang.

"Okay. Bye." Leila slammed the door. As she ran down the path she could have sworn she heard Kale holler at her to be more gentle with his baby.

Her school was Cedar Falls Academy, the only private school in the district. As she made her way down the path, she opened her navy-blue blazer and neatly tucked the white shirt underneath into a blue and gray tartan skirt. Nylon gray stockings covered her legs. She was one of the only people she knew who preferred wearing a uniform to school, happy with not spending mornings trying to decide what to wear. The car park out front led to a long footpath surrounded by lush grass and sporadic cedars. The building had a red-brick facade that showcased two-stories of thin rectangular windows with arches on their tops. To the left, was an open football field and out-dated bleachers.

She ran up the five steps of the entrance and pushed both glass doors of the main entry with force, accidentally declaring her arrival to anyone inside. No one was around though, which was good because Leila wasn't the type to relish that whole grand entrance thing. Plus, she was late, as always. She didn't know why or how, it was just one of those things, like her internal clock was set five minutes behind the rest of the world.

She rushed past the major trophy display and hightailed it to her locker.

What class do I have first? Math? Or is it Earth Science? Ugh, my locker is a mess. Or, as she liked to tell her friends, her locker was an organized chaos. Yet, she could never seem to find what she needed — more chaos than organized it seemed. It was another one of her quirks. The locker mirrored her mind, everything she needed was in there, it just took a while to sort through the daydreams to get to the necessary information.

Leila found her science book underneath an old assignment on deforestation; for a second, she wondered if she forgot to hand it in, but then she remembered it was the old version with burn marks on the edges from Gabby's lighter.

I should really throw that out.

She pulled out her science book at the same time she realized that she did, in fact, have math. She threw it back in and grabbed her math book, which had been sitting nicely against the side of her locker all along. She slammed her locker shut and flipped through her book to make sure she had the right one.

An unexpected shadow to her side caught her eyes. As she turned to see who it was, fingers wrapped her arm.

"Riley!" she scolded, shifting back in surprise.

"Whoa!" Riley flung both his hands in surrender. "Sorry, I didn't mean to scare you."

He stood a head above her, his hair hitting the top of his black-rimmed glasses. Behind them, his brown eyes glistened with delight at Leila's muddled state.

14

"These fell out of your locker," he said, scooping up a few papers from the floor.

She snatched them from him and re-opened her locker.

"You're late," Leila said, throwing the book inside. She stared at her possessions, wondering when she had become so careless.

"So are you."

She could hear the smile in his voice and turned to face him. "Yes, but I'm always late. You… are not."

He smiled again. "No, I'm not. Mr. Robertson asked me to get these from the library for him and I saw you fumbling about."

"Great," she said flatly. And then, as she cast her eyes over the books on tectonics and crustal evolution he held, she realized she did have Geology. Sighing, she opened her locker and swapped the books around… again.

"Are you okay?" Riley held her arm, his thumb giving a slight stroke. His smile faded, his mood changing from teasing to concerned.

They'd been friends for a few months. The day they met, he'd just moved to town, and since she'd been late to class that day as well, they were paired together for a history assignment on Japan. He did most of the work while she sat back in awe of his knowledge and dedication… and maybe his looks. Crushing on his all-round goodness aside, to her, he was probably one of the best friends she'd ever had. Leila could tell him anything and she didn't think he would make any bad judgments, the kind of person who accepted her as she was—wild hair or muddled mind.

"You know me, my brain doesn't kick in until midday," she said, tapping her head.

"C'mon then, Miss. Scatterbrain. I'll walk you to class." A wry smile lifted the edges of his lips as he pointed behind her. "It's this way. You know, in case you forgot."

FRIDAY

noon

Boredom didn't take long to settle in.

Leila had to wait in class an extra fifteen minutes to catch up on the time she'd missed that morning, but the clock seemed to be broken. According to the time, it'd only been five minutes since she last looked. Yet, she could have sworn it felt more like thirty. As she imagined the cafeteria full of students scarfing their lunch, hunger pangs zipped through her stomach.

Mr. Robertson sat at his desk, shoulders hunched as he scribbled corrections on someone's completed essay. A hideous orange knitted sweater hung off his narrow shoulders. *He* wasn't hideous. Far from it, in fact. Sadie, one of Leila's closest friends, insisted that he'd be a teenage dream if he had a makeover—the kind where he got a whole new closet, hair style, and a dash of self-confidence to boot. Failing a full makeover, a simple haircut would have done him wonders—anything had to be better than the oil slicked hair that curled at his nape. In Leila's eyes, he was a good teacher, mostly unassuming, except when she was late for the fifth day in a row.

She stared at empty lines on a paper that was supposed to comprise an essay on the anatomy of an earthquake. Okay, it wasn't completely empty. She'd written a few words... the title at least. Instead of focusing on the task at hand, she let her mind wander to her plans for the weekend: Hang with the girls, photograph the basketball game, maybe even accidentally bump into Riley somewhere. She drew a dot at the edge of the paper and created a line that flowed from it, around and around —

Mr. Robertson cleared his throat behind her, tapping her shoulder with a pen.

Focused on her spiral drawing, the sudden interruption startled Leila. She gasped, her butt lifting off the chair about five inches. "Oh my Lord, you scared me!"

"You can go to lunch now," he said, glancing at the blank page in front of her.

Finally. She didn't wait for any further commands, she grabbed her belongings and turned towards the door.

"Leilani?" Mr. Robertson said, grabbing her arm.

Stopping on the spot, Leila looked down at his fingers curling around her forearm. She wasn't sure whether to be more offended that he called her by her full name or that he thought it was okay to touch her. Had she said those things about him being mildly attractive out loud and now he thought he'd make a move?

Promptly letting go, Mr. Robertson wiped his hand down his sweater. "Sorry, ahh... I want the finished product on my desk Monday morning."

Leila gave a sigh of relief. "Right, of course." Running out the door, she gave her best Yoda impersonation, "On your desk it will be!"

Sadie Sloan and Gabrielle Harper were doing what best friends do—waiting at Leila's locker for her.

Gabby leaned against the locker beside Leila's, twisting a pencil between her fingers as though it were a cigarette. She'd quit smoking, again, a few weeks earlier. God love her, it was the third time she'd tried. Her brown eyes flitted up as Leila approached; she pushed the pencil through her messy top-knot with one hand and waved with the other. Gabby was an understated beauty: eyes constantly lifting at their edges, and high cheek bones accentuated her heart shaped face. She was tall, yet always stood with more weight on one foot, as if she didn't care about her potential model-esque stature. Unassuming yet incredibly outspoken. She was also wildly unpredictable— having platinum hair one day and jet black the next. Currently, her locks were dark brown with month old tiny braids above her left ear.

Sadie hadn't noticed Leila yet. She was talking to Gabby half interestedly while watching people stroll through the halls. She loved everyone else's business… but it was more about compassion than defamation. Some people might have called her gullible, but Leila and Gabby knew different, they knew her trust was something to be admired. Long, bohemian-inspired, golden hair framed her petite facial features—she had small everything, except for her eyes, which were blue, round and surrounded by thick long lashes.

"Sorry I'm late," Leila said, opening her locker. "I had to stay a while to make up for lost time." She tried to say the last few words in a mock teacher accent, but it came out more like a bratty child who didn't get their way.

"I was just saying to Gab that Nicole looks like she's lost weight… don't you think?"

Leila looked at Gabby, who rolled her eyes, and said, "Umm, I guess, I haven't notic—"

"Wow," Sadie interrupted. "Your locker is a disaster.

18

Let me…" She pushed past to straighten books and flick through papers.

"No, it's fine. Let's go eat." Leila grabbed her lunch bag and closed her locker.

"Good, I'm starving," Gabby said, heading towards the cafeteria.

"Wait!" Sadie almost screamed.

Gabby and Leila stopped as though they might stand on a snake if they took one more step.

Sadie pulled Leila back and wrapped her arms around her. "I haven't seen you all day."

Leila hugged her back. When Sadie pulled away, Leila tucked her arms around Gabby. "One for you too then."

Gabby squeezed her tight.

"How was Earth Science?" Sadie asked, as they walked towards the cafeteria.

Leila walked in the middle and keeping a tight grip on her lunch bag, she linked arms with both girls. Giving Sadie a side eye, Leila answered, "Apart from being held back, you mean?"

Sadie returned a look that said, *I feel for you, but I'm also glad not to be you.*

"The more important question is, how was Riley?" Gabby elbowed Leila, her face a mix of sass and sincerity.

"Fine? Why wouldn't he be fine?"

"Damn fine," Sadie said as they turned the corner, entering the cafeteria.

Riley sat with his friend Damien. They were deep in conversation, but Riley looked up as Leila entered the room. Damien's long black hair hovered just above his shoulder, hiding parts of his face as though it was a shield.

"Let's guess what they are talking about." Gabby nudged Leila playfully.

"Quantum physics," Sadie said in a deep voice, spreading her arms out wide.

"Ugh," Leila moaned. "They're probably dissecting some book written in the nineteenth century."

"Hmm." Gabby rubbed her chin. "I'm guessing they are talking about Leila, and how Riley wants to *bang* her."

Leila quickly backhanded Gabby's ribs. "Shhhh."

Riley waved them over, eyes only on Leila. Even though she had her lunch, Leila walked to the counter with the girls anyway. It was bad enough they teased her about him when they were just friends, Leila didn't want to deal with what they'd do if she ran at his every beck and call.

"What did you guys have this morning?" she asked, changing the subject.

"I had French," Sadie said, leaning sideways to peer at the food on offer. Then, she plastered a smile on her face and waved her hand with a flourish. "Joie de vivre."

"Joy da what now?" Gabby asked, holding out trays for them. Leila shook her lunch bag, so Gabby kept the tray for herself.

"It means the joy of life, or joy of living, or something... I dunno but it's now my new favorite phrase."

"Joie de vivre." Leila attempted, liking the sound of it.

"I had advanced math. Lame," Gabby said over her shoulder.

"Well, if advanced math is lame, then I'm lamer than lame." Sadie's face scrunched in disgust. "I found out yesterday I have to take extra classes to catch up with the curriculum."

"That sucks, babe." Leila pouted, leaning her hips against the silver bars of the buffet counter.

"I can help you out over the weekend if you want?" Gabby pointed excitedly to the greasy tater tots and the lunch lady plopped a pile in the corner of her tray.

Sadie gave a sad nod.

"Who would have thought?" A taunting voice came from behind. "Gabrielle Harper, the bleacher kid, has become a tutor. Moving up in the world girlfriend!" The last word was said with a condescending lilt.

Leila turned to see Sebastian Weir. Basketball jock, arrogant with a capital A-ss, frequent detention getter. He was a grade above Leila and flaunted the seniority like it meant he was better than everyone. The kind of person they all tended to avoid.

Sebastian's perfect teeth glistened as he gave the girls a cocky grin. Within a split-second, his pretty-boy face became marred by an ugly attitude. He reached his arm between Gabby and Leila and grabbed a fist full of tater tots.

"She came to this school on a scholarship, you tool-bag," Sadie jeered.

But her words fell on deaf ears, Sebastian had already moved out and squeezed in again a few places ahead.

"He never used to be so... vile," Leila said, watching him cut in and out of the line, collecting food as he went.

Leila remembered when she moved to Cedar Falls in seventh grade, Sebastian had been selected to show her around. He taught her to avoid the bleacher kids—they were trouble. He'd even introduced her to Sadie because he thought they'd make great friends. But by the time Leila got to her freshman year, after Sebastian had been there for a year already, he'd changed into someone entirely different... someone cruel.

"Delayed puberty?" Gabby suggested, tapping the glass above the fried chicken on offer.

"Maybe," Leila replied half-heartedly, scrunching her nose at the almost raw chicken pieces landing on Gabby's tray.

"I see that judgmental face, Leilani Belmonte. Don't knock it till you try it!" Gabby said, shoving a tot into her mouth.

Once the girls got their lunch, they exited the line and fanned out for some space. Gabby's eyes were set on

Riley's table as she led Leila and Sadie across the room.

"She's relentless," Leila said to Sadie over her shoulder.

Gabby glanced back, smiling at Leila without any hint of an apology. Facing forward again, she jumped to the side to avoid a spilled cup of apple juice.

Leila wasn't that quick though, her shoe hit the liquid with a splash. She stopped to wipe her shoe along the dry ground. Out of the corner of her eye, she spotted Sebastian close in on her, walking backwards, calling for his friends to join him. By the time she thought to warn him, Sebastian had already slammed into her.

He spun around, his short blond hair sat gelled and untouched on his head.

Out of all the people Leila could have bumped into, it had to be him.

She opened her mouth to apologize.

"Watch it, Mutt," he spat.

As he took a step to storm off, his foot slid right through the spillage. Horrified, Leila watched on. As his tray crashed to the ground, he took a few quick steps to stop himself from falling with it. Stabilizing himself by grabbing the side of a table, his head spun around, blue eyes ablaze—a direct glare at Leila as if she pushed him into the trap on purpose.

"That's called karma," Gabby scowled. Trying to be intimidating, she puffed out her chest and her blazer opened to make way for her bigger-than-most breasts.

"I don't think that stance does you any favors," Leila whispered, grabbing her defender's arm and dragging her away.

"He's just mad that the basketball coach benched him," Sadie murmured, rushing behind them. "I heard he ditched school all last week and called the Principal a jerk when he asked why. Anger problems with that one."

Yeah, but why? Leila thought, watching Sebastian storm

back to the counter for a second helping. *What is it that turned Sebastian Weir from a thoughtful kid into a nerd's worst nightmare?*

Leila let the thought go as they took their seats opposite Riley and Damien.

"Are you okay?" Riley asked.

"Fine. Just fine." Leila brushed him off and placed her paper bag on the table.

"He'll get what's coming to him one of these days," Damien said under his breath, sweeping his hair behind his ear. It was one of the very few sentences he had ever said to Leila—he even looked her in the eyes when he said it.

Leila smiled softly at him, appreciating the effort. Damien was an enigma to her. She would never tell him, but Leila didn't even know he was a junior like them until Riley started hanging out with him. It wasn't an isolated case though, most people didn't know he existed. He had this knack of fading quietly into the background, which was quite a feat considering he was at least a head taller than Riley. He was thin and looked like he didn't get enough sunlight. But somehow, Riley saw something in Damien and there they were—apples and oranges—the best of friends.

It reminded her of her friendship with Gabby. They too were opposites, but Leila knew Gabby was special the first time they met in seventh grade.

Gabby took the title of *new girl* from Leila, along with a plethora of other mantles. *Loner, Fatherless Freak, Hillbilly.* People whispered about her, a lot. The day before she started, their teacher sat them all down and told them Gabby's dad had recently died and they were to be gentle with her. All that information did was fuel the rumor train. Did he die of cancer? Was it a random accident? Had he killed himself? And so, instead of talking to her, everyone talked about her. She seemed to prefer it that way though.

Well, until Leila decided to make it her mission to get to know her.

Despite Sebastian's earlier advice Leila followed Gabby to the bleachers one day, where she was smoking a joint with a boy who was soon to be expelled.

"Gabrielle, right?" Leila asked, trying not to look at the joint being passed between them.

Gabby eyed Leila while taking a long drag. As she puffed out smoke, she said, "Leave."

The next day, Leila went back, dragging Sadie with her. They were met with the same hostility. Day after day they continued going, until finally one day the new girl snapped.

"What do you want from me?"

"We just... do you..." Sadie stuttered, not prepared for the follow-up.

Leila stepped forward and smiled sweetly. "Wanna hang out with us?"

At first, Gabby looked at her with a scowl. Despite the overwhelming urge to run away, Leila kept smiling. Hopeful. Somewhere, in Gabby's piercing brown eyes, there was a hint of kindness where Leila had only seen sadness before.

They'd all been best friends ever since.

Leila looked over her shoulder at Sebastian, who waited in line with his friends, smiling wide and laughing as though he didn't have a care in the world. "You all talk as though he's some kind of monster. But somewhere underneath all that bravado has to be a little hint of humanity, right?"

Sadie twisted in her seat to see what Leila was looking at. When she connected the dots, her eyes lit up. "I smell a project coming on."

"Oh god, not again," Gabby groaned.

"Wait a minute, weren't you one?" Riley teased.

"I was... but I'm different than *him*. I was worth making time for."

"It's true. You're a gem in a mountain of dirt," Leila said, pinching Gabby's cheek. She returned to her lovingly-made salad roll and picked at the bun. "It's just that... maybe he is, too."

"Yep, she's got that look in her eyes," Sadie said, staring at her friend with awe. "Project Sebastian? Yikes, you've set your sights high this time."

Leila turned to get another glimpse of him as he sat on the edge of a table and belched.

When she turned back around, Riley was pointing a chip in her direction. He gave a tilted smile. "You, my dear girl, have the courage of a lion."

FRIDAY

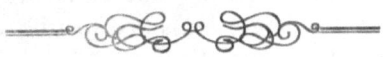

afternoon

Leila pulled at the bottom of her gym top. It had either shrunk, or she'd grown since last week. Reaching her arms toward the ceiling, she asked, "Can you see my belly button when I do this?"

"Yep." Sadie waited for her at the locker room entrance. "Come on, slow-poke, class has started."

Leila arms deflated along with her ego. "But it's too small."

"It looks hot, girl! Let's go!"

Leila wasn't so sure, but they were late, so she followed Sadie into the gymnasium.

"Line up girls, we're doing rounds of five versus five," Coach commanded, pointing to the edge of the court where everyone else waited.

Leila and Sadie slid next to Gabby, who promptly stepped off the line.

"I've got a note," she said, passing it to coach.

He looked at the note, pouted his lips, then looked at

her. He sighed before telling her to sit down.

She limped back on her fake injury and winked at her best friends on her way past.

"Any more excuses? Broken leg? Appendicitis? Brain tumor? No? Great. Teams of five… go!"

They were playing basketball… as usual. Coach was so predictable. He had his special squads and pandered to their every need. If they needed to practice, the whole class had to do it too.

Leila and Sadie reluctantly made their way to Riley and Damien. They didn't get a chance to find a fifth person before Coach blew the whistle.

"Team A and B, you're up."

Leila looked around to see who the teams were, wondering when they were allocated.

"We're Team B," Damien said, running onto the court.

Riley and Sadie were already there, ready to go. Riley smiled at Leila, his lips pursed as though he was trying not to laugh. Blushing, she kicked her heels to join them.

A sudden blow to her ribs knocked her off balance. Pain lashed through her torso and air whooshed from her lungs. As the room spun, she braced for the fall—but a strong hand clasped her arm and hauled her upright.

Leila stood hunched for a moment, trying to catch her breath.

"Are you okay, Leila? You ran right out in front of me, I couldn't stop in time," a caring voice said.

Wincing, Leila looked up to see Cap, the Coach's assistant, hovering over her, arms wide as though waiting for her to collapse again.

"Oh yeah, pfff," she said, waving her arm. "I'm fine. Just fine."

Then she coughed and her lungs sent a pain signal to her brain.

Danger, Leilani Belmonte, air levels low.

"I've knocked the wind out of you," Cap said, frowning. "I'm so sorry."

Leila smiled, trying to appease his guilt. His real name was Daniel, but he'd been the captain of the basketball team for so long, Cap became his second name. He was a senior and received extra credit for assisting Coach. Teachers loved him because he was effortlessly smart. And students loved him because he was inclusive. Everyone loved him, and Leila could see why.

"Well, it was probably my fault. I'm a bit vague today..." she puffed. "More than usual, anyway."

Cap took both her arms to brace her and turned to Coach. "I don't think she should play."

"Sit down, Belmonte," Coach yelled. As an afterthought, he added in a softer tone; "You could have forged a note like Gabrielle if you wanted to get out of gym so much."

***

Leila had study hall for the last period of the day. After mid-terms, the school had been fairly lax about study hall, so most people ended up doing whatever the hell they wanted. Some people went home, and some used it as an excuse to hang out on the field, or the court, or the cafeteria.

Sadie and Gabby left to go shopping but Leila told them she wanted to study for that damn earthquake essay with Riley. They saw right through her excuse to spend more time with him though, giggling and winking all the way out the door.

The girls were right, she did like him—a lot. She always had, but lately her senses told her he liked her too. The way he looked at her was different, a lingering gaze—more than friendly yet still apprehensive, like the boundaries of their relationship were blurring.

Riley and Leila huddled together at a table in the second-floor library. Orange coated walls and mahogany bookshelves gave the large space a rustic warmth that was perfect for quiet studies. Not too quiet though, as a group of freshman girls giggled from the set of velvety, maroon sofas sat at the end of the room—behind them, a giant window spanned almost the entire wall.

Riley's hand cupped the side of his face as he read from a book on tectonic plates. His mouth moved, but she wasn't listening. It was as though the words floated above his head and dissipated into the air. As she watched his lips move, she imagined what they would feel like against her own.

"… then the earth shifts and tiny fairies the size of dust-mites swarm out of the cracks and into the atmosphere."

"Huh?" She blinked.

"You're not listening, are you?" Riles teased, his smile blooming.

She bit her lip to stop herself from saying, *No, I'm thinking about kissing you.*

His smile faltered as his gaze lowered to her mouth, staring at her a moment too long.

As Leila wondered if she did in fact say what she was thinking out loud, the library doors swung open. She tore her eyes away from Riley to see Sebastian and his friends walk in, talking loudly among themselves. The librarian looked up and glared, but upon noticing Cap in the mix, she smiled to herself and went back to her computer.

Riley cleared his throat and started reading again, but Leila had already made her mind up.

"Wait a minute," she interrupted, jumping up.

Sebastian *was* going to be her new project. And she *was* going to find the good in him again.

With all the confidence she could muster, she walked towards Sebastian, chanting silently to herself.

You've got this, you can do this!

He was with Cap and two other friends from the basketball team, Don and Thomas. They sat on top of the table and chatted a bit too loud for a library.

When she reached them, she smiled, but no one acknowledged her.

"I mean, it sounds bad. But the rest of you have gotta try it." Thomas said, looking to Cap for approval, who grinned and raised his eyebrows.

Clenching her fists as if she could hold onto her bravery, Leila spoke up, "Hey Sebastian, listen, I wanted to apologize for earlier."

He propped a foot on a chair and squinted at her. His friend, Don, leaned around Sebastian and leered. Leila did her best to ignore him—they had a thing once, something she'd rather forget about.

"When I accidentally tripped you and Gabby called you a jerk..."

A slight sparkle appeared in Sebastian's eyes and he lifted his chin. "I've come up with another nickname for you. Wanna hear it?"

It's gotta be better than Mutt, right? Leila thought.

"Bitsa," he said, not waiting for her reply. Then, he pretended to point to different things in front of him. "You know? Bits of this and bits of that."

She sighed, fighting the urge to roll her eyes. "You'd be surprised at how many different ethnicities are running through *your* veins."

"Whatever. You got Mexican in there somewhere don'cha, Bitsa?" He leaned forward and looked deep into her eyes. "I love tacos, can you make us some tacos?"

Her nostrils flared despite her resolve to remain calm. "Actually, you're right, my Papa is Mexican, I'm sure he'll have a nice recipe that I can get for you."

Sebastian's eyebrows dropped. "What do you hope to

get out of this exchange exactly? Do you want to date me or something?"

"Be careful mate," Don sneered. "She's a kiss and runner."

Leila kept her attention on Sebastian and shrugged. "No, curiosity led me here."

"Oh yeah?" He stood up on the chair, a full two feet taller than her—his knees level with her eyes.

"Sebastian Weir!" the librarian scolded from her desk. "Don't make me send you to the Principal."

"I'm bored," he said, jumping from the chair. As he strode towards the door, he called for his posse, "Let's go."

His three friends followed, none of them looking back, not even Cap.

Watching him go, Leila crossed her arms. *He's going to be harder to break than I thought.*

Riley appeared at her side, chuckling. "That went well I see."

"I know, right?" she retorted, tearing her eyes from the door. "We're totally best friends now."

Riley gave her his best puppy dog eyes. "Hey! I thought *I* was your best friend?"

"Oh, you know how it is," Leila teased, letting her body sway close to him. "I have a selection of besties, depending on what I need them for."

"What do you need from Sebastian?"

Riley's serious tone turned the conversation.

Leila thought for a moment before replying, "To prove that there's good in everyone."

"And what do you need from me? As one of your best… *friends*?" he exaggerated the last word as though it was a question, as though he was asking if they were *just friends*.

His gaze was unwavering, lingering longer than most friends would allow. As Riley's eyes flitted to her lips,

Leila's heart fluttered like a butterfly was trapped in her chest, trying desperately to escape the tension. He slowly leaned in, so close she could feel his breath.

"Your smarts, of course," Leila blurted, turning on her heels and speeding back to the table. She inhaled deeply in an attempt to calm the butterfly causing havoc inside her. Waiting for him, she placed the paper in front of her and forced a grin. "Help me with this essay, Bestie."

Smirking at Leila's sudden retreat, Riley followed her.

"Hand it over," he said, taking the paper from her.

His eyebrows lowered as he flipped it over.

"I... uh..." Leila smiled sheepishly. "I haven't started yet."

With an endearing roll of his eyes, Riley shook his head. "Of course, you haven't."

FRIDAY

late afternoon

Under a tree outside the front of her school, Leila waited for Kale to pick her up after his shift at Belladonna's Café. She closed her eyes and rested her head back against the rough bark, swimming her fingers through lush grass.

"Leilani Bel-Barney, you're supposed to sleep at home, not school!" came a familiar male voice.

"Hey Taj," she said, without opening her eyes.

When she looked up, Leila found him standing above her. The afternoon sun created an ethereal glow around him, as if he wore a halo. His dark brown, almost black, hair was shaved at the sides and three-inch tendrils tumbled from the top like a fountain. The tie of his school uniform was undone—as it probably had been all day— and he wore ripped jeans instead of gray pants. He was probably the only student in the whole school that could get away with it, too. Most kids would get a detention for even a hair out of place.

He was currently juggling a pile of books and papers, holding them close to his chest so nothing blew away.

"Loved your pics of the rally. I had a difficult time choosing which ones to use for the Chronicle." He lifted his knee to help contain his stack of items as he flipped through them. "I swear it was on top... wait a minute... ugh, where the hell is it? Oh, wait... got it!"

He pulled out the school newspaper and passed it to Leila. *The Chronicles of Cedar Falls Academy* was displayed boldly across the top of the page, and underneath the title, one of her pictures was printed front and center.

"Thanks," she mumbled, dropping the paper in her lap.

"You okay?" Taj squatted before her.

"Rough day," Leila replied, wondering if she should go into details. First, she was late. Then, she had the wind knocked out of her. And finally, she finished the day by making an ass of herself when she reached out to Sebastian. Leila sighed. "Yup, rough day."

Taj gasped dramatically. "Leilani Bel-Monte Carlo, where's your positivity gone?"

She rolled her head to face him. "I took on a project that killed it. My positivity is now hiding behind disappointment and failure."

"Ah yes, good old disappointment likes to shadow positivity's limelight..." He shook his head in mock dismay. "Such an attention seeker."

Leila gave a small smile to her ever-cheerful friend.

"That's it: positivity, come out of the shadows!" Taj wobbled on his tip-toes and his knees knocked together to keep his balance.

"You're so weird," Leila chuckled.

She grabbed his shoulders, trying to help stabilize him. But all it did was serve as the tipping point. Taj tumbled back with a thud, his papers and books falling to the ground with him.

Taj snorted and scrambled to collect his papers and books. "Says one weirdo to the other."

Laughing with him, Leila helped him gather his things. As she picked up his Advanced Darkroom book, she marveled at its weight.

"Hey! Leila!" someone called.

She glanced around to see Sebastian jogging her way. As she gaped, the Darkroom book was snatched from her hands.

"Ugh, that's my cue to go." Clutching everything precariously under one arm, Taj patted Leila's arm. "Remember, Leilani Bel-ony, tomorrow's a new day. Whatever has disappointed you will pass, and your sickeningly sweet light will shine again."

Taj stood up, glanced at Sebastian, and rushed off.

"Leila!" Sebastian panted, stopping beside her. He raked a hand through his short hair, which didn't do anything to the non-existent style.

Curious, Leila stared up at him. He'd called her by her actual name. Hope rose inside her. *I must already be getting through to him,* she thought, pleased with herself.

"Hey there, cutie," he said, collapsing onto the ground beside her.

She inwardly cringed. It seemed she was too quick to get her hopes up — she went from Mutt to Bitsa to Cutie in less than a day.

"Uh, hi, how are you?" she asked, instantly on edge.

He lifted one knee and casually rested an arm over it while turning towards her. The movement opened his collar away from his neck. The black line of a tattoo poked out on the front of his shoulder. He noticed her looking and gave a sly smile.

"Wanna hook up?" he asked, lifting his hand up to stroke her cheek.

"Sorry, what?" she sputtered, too shocked to notice his hand as it lingered around her temple.

He lifted his chin and winked. "C'mon, I see the way you've been checking me out all day."

"No, I think you've got the wrong impression, I don't want to hook up with you." Coming to her senses, she shifted out of his reach.

A hissing noise flowed through his teeth. "Right. You're with that Riley dude, huh? God, I hate that guy."

Taken aback by the hostility in his voice, Leila asked, "You hate him? Why?"

Sebastian wriggled closer to fill the gap she'd just made. He danced his fingertips from her wrist to the crook of her elbow. Before he could go any further she pushed his hand away. If she wasn't so confused by his sudden change of behavior, she would've had the presence of mind to slap him, too.

"Aw, girl, relax. I won't bite…" He moved closer still and held one of her hands to the ground, while he snaked the other hand around her waist. As she tried to tug herself free, Sebastian dragged her closer to him. "… much."

Behind his head, Leila saw Kale's Mustang pull up to the curb.

"Stop!" she squirmed. "I said I don't want to."

Angry, Leila shoved her elbow into his chest. As he fell back, she jumped to her feet. Sebastian reached up and grabbed her arm, squeezing so hard that his fingernails nearly broke through her skin. With a whisper that wasn't quite a whisper, he sneered, "As if I'd want you anyway. I bet you'd be frigid and cold in bed."

"God. Sebastian," Leila almost laughed, yanking her arm free. "You think I don't remember who you used to be? Why do you try so hard to showcase this bully-like persona?" She snatched her bag from the ground. "I know there's a good guy in there somewhere, even if he's lost in the pit of your bitter soul."

She spun on her heels and walked away.

"Screw you, Bitsa Mutt," Sebastian shouted after her, his voice cracking.

Waiting for Leila at his car, Kale crossed his arms and glared over her shoulder. "Do I need to jack this kid up?"

"Nah, it's fine. I can take care of it."

Fine was fast becoming her most used word of the day.

FRIDAY

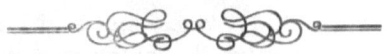

evening

They drove through the main street, not stopping at any of the local restaurants. Buildings became trees and they passed the sign that said: *You are now leaving Cedar Falls, Washington.*

"Are we going to the city?" Leila sat forward, knowing the answer already.

Watching him nod, she pulled at her school blazer. "In these clothes?"

Kale smirked and tapped his head. "Have a look in the back."

She twisted in her seat and found half her closet strewn across the back seat.

"Oh my god, I love you!" she cried.

With her eyes glued to the road behind them, scanning for any police cars, she climbed through. She found her favorite pants—black fake leather. Getting dressed in the small space required Leila to maneuver herself across the whole seat in order to squeeze into them.

"Be honest. This isn't just an 'I love my sister, so I'm going to treat her to a meal in the city' thing, is it?" Leila asked, sifting through the rest of her clothes. *Not the yellow camisole. Not the striped sweater.* Her eyes lit up at the leopard-print, satin blouse. Kale remained silent as she changed her top.

"Well?"

"I…" Kale sighed. "I want you to meet someone."

She looked at him through the rear-view mirror. He had a smile on his face that she'd only seen a few times before. And every time it was about a girl. Excited at the prospect of her brother finally having someone see him for the amazing human he was, Leila scrambled back to the front seat. "Oh yeah? What's her name and how serious is it?"

He glanced at her sideways. "Pretty serious."

In a little over an hour they reached the inner city of Seattle. The sun sat low as lights began sprinkling through the high-rise buildings.

As they walked across the street to the Northwest Grill, Leila glanced at her brother. Kale walked with his shoulders back and a huge grin on his face.

Oh lordy, it really is serious, Leila thought, smiling to herself.

They made their way inside and the sounds of the busy streets were replaced by quiet chatter. Candles lit every table and the low-light pendants hung from the ceiling. The clink of cutlery-to-plate together with the smell of well-cooked steak made Leila salivate.

"Table for Belmonte," Kale said to the Maître d'.

"Belmonte?" The Maître d' repeated. "Ah yes, your friend is already here." He whipped two menus from his station and turned on his heels. "Follow me."

Leila trotted on her tip-toes behind Kale, glancing around him, trying to spot an early peek at his new girlfriend. As they stopped by a table at the back, Leila's gaze landed on a woman who stared back.

She had long ebony hair, with blonde tips at the ends. She was elegant, from her six-inched heels to her tight-fitting, knee-length black dress. Leila thought she was the most striking and beautiful human she'd ever seen.

Leila eyed Kale as he greeted the woman. He was wearing a plain blue t-shirt and dirty jeans. As they kissed, Leila shifted her eyes to the ground, wondering how her average-Joe brother managed to score a stunner like this.

"Leila?" Kale said, bringing his sister's attention back. "This is Tsukiko, my girlfriend." He grinned at Tsukiko. "Babe, this is my sister, Leila."

"Hey there." Leila wriggled her hands in a shy wave. Then, after deciding that wasn't displaying proper manners, she threw her hand out in an official gesture of goodwill.

"Call me Kiko." Kale's girlfriend ignored Leila's outstretched hand and pulled her in close for a hug. As quick as Tsukiko grabbed her, she let go. "Are you feeling all right?"

Glancing at Kale, Leila shrugged. "Yeah, I'm feeling—.'

Without warning, Kiko slid Leila's sleeve up and lifted her arm to inspect it. She placed her palm over the crook of Leila's elbow, her top lip curling.

"What are you doing?" Leila asked, trying not to laugh —she'd seen Kale check for mold on week old bread like this.

"Huh?" Kiko glanced up. Noticing Leila's expression, she dropped her arm and waved a hand at the ceiling. "Oh nothing. It must be the lighting, you just looked a little flushed."

"On her arm?" Kale asked with a smirk. "That she had covered?"

Kiko flicked her silky hair over her shoulder and batted her long eyelashes. "Stop it, you tease. That's how we check temperature where I'm from."

As they sat down, Leila gave herself a mental note to search the internet for Japanese temperature-checking methods. Riley did most of the work on their project on Japan earlier in the year, but that certainly didn't come up during their research phase.

After they ordered their meals, Kale turned into an excited Kindergarten student at show-and-tell. He told Leila what Kiko did for a living, about her younger brother, where she grew up. As she munched on her steak and steamed vegetables, Leila struggled to keep up with his speed. And so, she drifted off into her own world, smiling whenever appropriate.

"He kept filling up my mug so I would stay longer," Kiko said, looking lovingly into Kale's eyes.

Kale brushed a hand across Kiko's cheek. "It worked didn't it?"

Leila propped her elbow on the table and rested her cheek on her fist. Glancing between the couple, she assumed they were talking about how they met. And going by the look on Kiko's face, she knew there was genuine affection between them. Leila was impressed that her own goofy brother managed to obtained the courage to even talk to Kiko, let alone ask her on a date.

"Leila?" Kale leaned forward as if only just noticing her presence.

"Mmm?" Leila blinked and turned to Kiko. "I'm surprised. He's a wimp when it comes to stuff like that."

Confused, Kiko glanced at Kale. "Stuff like what?"

"What you're talking about," Leila said, pointing between them. "Asking her on a date."

Kale's brow creased. "We were talking about that twenty minutes ago."

"No, you were just talking about how you met at Belladonna's Café, where you work." A sweet scent glided up her nostrils and she looked down to find caramel slice in front of her. An unsettling feeling surrounded her. "Dessert? Already?"

She didn't even remember finishing her main meal.

"Are you okay?" Kale looked at her with concern, the back of his hand finding her forehead. He turned to Kiko. "Maybe she is unwell."

Leila waved his hand off. "I'm okay, probably just tired from all the braining at school." Yawning, she glanced at Kiko, who stared back at her, lip curling again. It would have been weird if she wasn't so tired. Leila slumped in her chair. "I'll just close my eyes for a moment."

Kale sculled the last drop from his glass of water. "All right, I think it's time to take you home."

"But we haven't had dessert," Leila moaned. "Wait, where did it go? It was right here in front of me?"

"You've been asleep," he whispered. "And you look like death."

Leila shook her head trying to wake up, but something wasn't right. It was as though a fog had clouded her brain. Faces blurred in and out of focus. Their voices felt like a million miles away. As the lights flickered, she pushed to her feet. "Excuse me."

Kale stood too, his hands outstretched in case she fell.

"I'm *fine*," she hissed, shoving away from the table.

When Leila stumbled into the bathroom without any memory of walking there, she knew that she was, in fact, *not fine*. Gripping the sink to hold herself upright, Leila saw her reflection. Kale was right, she looked… awful. Sunken eyes, gray skin. Struggling to breathe, she pinched her blouse by the cuff and waved air onto her irritated skin. What was happening to her? It was more than tiredness.

"There's a horrible flu going around," Kiko said, behind her.

Leila span around. "When did you get in here?"

"Take it easy." Kiko rushed to Leila's side, putting an arm around to stabilize her. "The best thing for you is rest."

With Kiko's aid, Leila managed to take two steps out of the restroom before her knees buckled and everything went black. Within moments, she was in the car with Kale. She couldn't even remember saying goodbye to Tsukiko.

On the drive home, she passed in and out of consciousness, saying things like: "I'm sorry"; and, "I bet you'll never take me to a fancy restaurant again"; and, "I hope I made a great first impression"; and, "Do you have a fire extinguisher in the car? I think my arm is in flames."

"Your arm is fine." Kale kept his eyes on the road as he shook his head. "Mom and Dad will be so pissed I took you out like this. Why didn't you tell me you had the flu?"

But Leila couldn't answer as deep sleep finally took her.

FRIDAY

almost midnight

Leila's phone woke her. She rolled over in her bed and lifted it from the bedside table. According to the screen it was eleven in the evening. Leila stared at the time for a moment, wondering when she got from car to bed.

"Hello?" she answered, her voice groggy from sleep.

"Hey!" Riley's sweet voice echoed back at her.

"Hi you," she sniffed. "What's up?"

What's up? That the best I can do?

"You don't sound so good? Are you all right?" he asked.

She placed the back of her hand on her forehead. Warmth radiated her skin. "Mmmhmm."

"I was going to ask you if you wanted to meet up over the weekend."

Her cheeks flushed with heat as a bead of sweat trickled down her neck.

So hot, so so hot.

"Can we get ice cream?

Riley chuckled. "It's Winter. But sure, I like ice-cream."

"I like cats."

Leila blinked. *Cats? What's wrong with me.*

Riley laughed again. "I'm more of a dog lover myself."

"Well, dogs *are* loyal."

"And protective," he added.

"And funny." She smiled sleepily.

"How are dogs funny?"

"Well, they do chase their tails."

Isn't it obvious?

"Have you been drinking?"

A wave of nausea soared through her body as she racked her brain to remember the night. "What's today?"

"Friday."

"Then, yes. I drink Friday, just like every day." She paused to smack her lips together, her mouth suddenly dry. "Water is good for your skin, ya' know. Not to mention basic survival."

"You're a loch ness," he stated.

Leila didn't know what that meant. Was it a term of endearment or an insult? "A loch ness?"

Riley chuckled. Leila knew he was amused by her weird behavior, but she didn't mind though. As awful as she felt, his laugh brought a kind of peace.

"No, I said hot mess."

"I don't think that's better."

"I do." All teasing had left his voice.

A pause.

She threw the covers back and tried to sit up. Her head spun and a wave of heat swept down her body. She laid down again and fanned her face with her free hand, wondering what would help to cool her down.

Riley mentioned something about liking ice-cream before. "I like ice cream, too."

"We've established that, what *else* do you like?" he asked as if there was something specific he was waiting for her to say.

So, I'll just say it then.

"You."

Leila closed her eyes and smiled at his soft reply, "I like you, too."

They were both quiet for a while, until the phone slipped from her grasp and her eyes jolted open.

"I, uh, Kale says that I have the flu," she said, wearily. "I'm hot and itchy and… something else. I feel like I'm sleeping and awake at the same time."

Riley was quiet for a while before saying, "You should get some sleep."

He'd said it so softly that her heart skipped a beat.

SATURDAY

afternoon

The high-pitched trill of Leila's phone stirred her from sleep. She was relieved to not feel so hot anymore, but now, her head felt like it was being crushed in a vice. The longer her phone rang, the tighter the vice wound.

Without opening her eyes, Leila patted along her bedside table until she found her phone and brought it to her ear. "Riley, I thought you said I needed to sleep?"

"Hello?" not Riley said.

"Sadie?"

"Where are you?" Sadie shouted over a chorus of cheers in the background.

Leila rolled around, arching her back in a stretch. "What time is it?"

"The game's already started! Taj is freaking out. Where are you? It's ten past three."

"In the afternoon?"

Leila sat up straight, her eyes quickly darted to her camera on her dresser. She was supposed to photograph the basketball game.

"No, three in the morning—of course three in the afternoon. Are you all right?"

"I think I've got the flu," Leila muttered, scratching her arm. "I feel awful."

"Oh rats. We were going to hang out by the lake—you're not coming?"

"I don't think so."

Despite her constant digging, the itch on her arm wouldn't stop. Sadie said something in reply, but Leila didn't hear it as she rolled her arm around to get a better look at the irritation. A pink rash had spread from the crook of her elbow to half way down her wrist. Flakes of dried skin lifted at the edges.

Sweet biscuits! Leila thought, gawking at her arm.

"Sadie, I gotta go. I'll call you later, okay?" Leila didn't wait for her answer before hanging up.

Any lingering sense of lethargy had left her body, Leila was suddenly wide awake. She jumped out of bed and made her way downstairs to the laundry room where the first-aid kit was kept. Rummaging through the kit, she pushed bandages and various creams aside. She hadn't had eczema for over a year, she wasn't even sure if they had any cream left in the house.

A roar came from the living room.

Jumping, she hurried from the laundry room to follow the noise. Kale was playing a video game. He sat on the edge of the sofa with his elbows on his knees and a frown on his face.

"Do you have any eczema cream?" she asked, trying not to scratch.

Kale spun around as though a ghost had come back from the dead to haunt him. He rested his hand on his heart, realizing it was his younger sister... a normal human. Smirking, he raised an eyebrow. "She lives!"

"Hi." Leila grinned back, rolling her eyes. "Do you know where the eczema cream is?"

"Wouldn't have a clue." He shrugged and turned back to his game. "Do you have a flare up?"

She moved around the sofa to sit, but a chocolate-smeared wrapper was attached to the cushion. With the tips of her fingers, Leila picked it up and balanced it on top of the garbage pile Kale had already made on the coffee table.

"You're gross," she said, making sure nothing was left on the cushion before sitting.

"Since we're talking about gross things..." Kale kept his eyes glued to the television, slamming his thumbs repeatedly against the controller. "How bad is the flare up?"

"Who knows how eczema happens." Leila sat back and examined the rash. "Maybe I came into contact with something that I'm allergic to."

"It's probably just a heat rash. You've been sweating pretty bad."

Leila let her arm drop. "Probably."

Kale glanced at her sideways and paused his game. Sighing, he turned to face her. "Want me to call Mom?"

"No!" Leila blurted. "Don't tell her. It's her keynote today, I don't want to worry her."

"Wanna do a movie marathon? I've been dying to watch the last Incandescent film." He brushed his hand over the coffee table, knocking cans of soda to the ground, and revealed a pizza box. "Hungry?"

"Yes to the movie." Her eyes winced at the sight of the pizza. It had probably been sitting out for hours. The thought of it made her want to hurl. "No to the pizza."

As if knowing what she was thinking, Kale retorted, "It's not *that* old, only a few hours."

Repulsed, she leaned away and shook her head. "I'll have an apple or something."

"Cool." Kale threw the remote at her and picked up his phone. "I'll be right back, I just gotta do something."

As he ran off, Leila leaned back onto the sofa and buried her head into a cushion. She flipped through the channels until something caught her eye. She sat up straight, dread filling her body.

The screen displayed a photo of a cougar and the caption underneath it read: "Cedar Falls: a predator on the loose."

Leila turned the volume up.

"This is the sixth attack in under two weeks," the reporter said. "Regina Long, President of the Cedar Falls Horticultural Society and well-loved member of the community, was the first victim in what has gone on to see five other maimings and attacks."

Leila swallowed. When she found out about Mrs. Long a few weeks ago, she'd done her very best to push it to the back of her mind. How does one deal with death like that? Especially when it was so close to home. Mrs. Long lived in Leila's street. She was an elderly lady with a penchant for gardening — she was often out in her yard watering and weeding, always smiling. She died in hospital after a cougar jumped her on one of her walks up the mountain. She was fit and healthy, and no matter her age, still too soon to leave.

"There's been another attack!" Leila called out to Kale.

The photo on the screen switched from a cougar to a girl named Samantha. Leila knew her from school, she was the foster sister of someone in Leila's photography class. Only nine years old, apparently the animal had no age limit. The attack wasn't fatal, luckily, most of them were.

The image flipped to a reporter standing on the park side of Rattlesnake Lake, right on the edge of town. "Thank you, Clare. All residents are cautioned to stay on high alert. The local authorities advise to stay in the city bounds and avoid wooded areas. If you should see the cougar, please seek shelter and call 9-1-1."

"This is getting scary," Kale said, from behind the sofa. "Is there a shortage of deer or squirrels or something?"

The news feed returned to the lead anchorwoman. "A search for one adult male and one teenage male has begun. Both were last seen on Friday afternoon. It is unknown if their disappearances are connected." The anchor's face was replaced by a photo of a man with slicked hair and a woolen cardigan.

"Ugh, this is depressing. Put the movie on." Kale leaned over the sofa and snatched the remote from Leila.

"Wait!" Leila swiped it back and pointed it at the screen. "That's my Geology teacher, Mr. Robertson."

"Please forward any information you might have of their where-abouts to police…" The reporter's voice faded into the background as another photo displayed on the screen.

Shoulder-length black hair covered half the boy's face. But she would recognize those piercing blue eyes anywhere.

They belonged to Damien.

SUNDAY

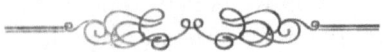

morning

Sharp flashes of pain pulsated through Leila's arm, jolting her awake. She took a hastened breath and rolled up her sleeve, hissing through her teeth as the material grazed her skin.

The pink irritation had turned deep purple like a burn, spreading from the crook of her elbow half way to her wrist. It stung like a burn too — raw and swollen.

As she sat up, her head felt heavy, like the brain fog from Friday threatened to return at any moment. Clutching the edges of her mattress a dark thought fluttered to the surface. Something was wrong. More than the pain, more than the fever, more than the light-headedess. Something she couldn't explain was coursing through her veins.

Leila pushed herself upright and lurched forward. She stumbled across her room, bypassing the mirror — lord knows, she didn't want to know what she looked like right then.

"Kale?" she called, leaning against her door frame.

A blurry vision of her brother shuffled out of his room, yawning.

"Mmm?" he asked, rubbing his eyes. When he finally looked at Leila, his mouth dropped. "Shit, Leila! Get dressed, I'm taking you to the ER."

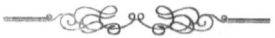

The emergency room was busy. Leila looked at the people at the end of the long line in sympathy. She couldn't remember when they arrived, or even when they were seen by the receptionist, but she was sitting now and that's all that mattered in that moment.

She peered around the last person in line to a middle-aged man, holding his hand. Blood dripped through his clenched fingers.

Kitchen accident, Leila guessed.

To her left, a little boy sat next to his stressed mother. He sniffled into her chest as she hugged him tight.

Infection.

Another person sat with their head back, studying the intricacies of the ceiling. Leila looked up, but only saw dirty-white ceiling tiles with strips of fluorescent lights.

"Drugs," she guessed out loud. *Oops.*

"Shhhh," Kale hissed, looking around to see if anyone heard.

Leila pushed her bottom back into the chair and folded herself forward until her head touched her knees.

"What are you doing?" Kale asked nervously.

"Comfy," she replied, her words muffled against her jeans.

"Sit up." Kale grabbed her shoulders and pulled her upright. "This is what you were like on Friday. What the hell's wrong with you?"

Leila rolled her head towards him. "Let me count thy ways, oh brother. Tired. Sore arm. Hot…" she trailed off, squinting as his face came in and out of focus.

And then there was Damien. She didn't sleep much. Aside from the flu getting worse, his face on the news last night haunted her. Every time she thought of him, she called Riley. By the time she finally drifted into slumber, she'd lost count of how many messages she'd left on his voice mail.

Diving her hand into her pocket, Leila pulled out her phone. Her screen was blank. No missed calls or messages. A thought: *What if Riley's missing too and no one knows?*

As quick as she could, Leila scrolled through. She couldn't find his name though; everything was blurry, like she was floating through an alternate universe. She lifted the phone closer to her face in an attempt to clear the fuzz. It reminded her of when Gabby gave her three shots of Vodka at her birthday last year.

"Did you drip feed me alcohol while I was sleeping?" She glanced at Kale, head spinning as she moved.

"Leila!" he moaned, turning to the woman next to him. "She's delirious, she doesn't know what she's saying."

Leila scowled and turned back to her phone. Squinting to see the letters on her phone, she pressed the buttons hard and typed her message. *Where are you?*

Kale snatched the phone out of her hands before she could send the message. He hit the delete button. "Don't be that kind of girlfriend."

"He's not my boyfriend," she muttered.

Rolling his eyes, he stuffed her phone into his jacket pocket. "Yeah and my car's a pile of useless junk."

"But you love your car," she said, watching her phone disappear.

Kale smirked triumphantly. "Exactly."

A nurse pushed through the swinging ER doors. The still waiting patients, shuffled in anticipation.

"Leila Belmonte."

As soon as she stood, the blood rushed from her head. Her knees buckled. Leila crashed into her brother, who clasped at her shoulders to keep her from hitting the floor. She swayed in his hold. Black circled the edge of her vision, until everything went dark.

SUNDAY

evening

Leila's eyes darted open and she threw her arms in front of herself to break the fall. Except she wasn't falling, she was snuggled under warm sheets and laying on soft pillows in her own bed.

She rolled her head around to see Kale hunched over in a chair beside her. "I mean, the doctor was slightly alarmed when she passed out in the waiting room. But she came to and they realized it was the same flu that has been going around…" He ran a hand over his short hair. "Well, apparently there's a rash that comes with it. Anyway, they wrapped her arm and sent us home." Turning to see Leila awake, he gave her a smile. "Yeah, she's been in and out of sleep the whole day. I'm sure she'll be happy to see you."

The whole day? Leila thought, unable to remember anything after she passed out at the hospital.

A sudden sense of time loss saw her reaching for her phone. Was Riley still missing?

On the bottom of her phone screen, a small text notification from Riley flashed. Resting a hand on her chest to ease her speeding heart, Leila exhaled and swiped on the notification.

"Hey there," Riley's message read. *"Sorry I missed your calls. Was away for the wkend. Everything OK? Call if you need."*

Before Kale could rip the phone from her, Leila tapped her reply: *Glad to hear you're safe. Talk soon.* She hit send, dropped her phone on the bedside table, and rolled back over, closing her eyes.

Kale cleared his throat and tapped her foot. "How are you feeling?"

Peeling an eye open, Leila mumbled, "Not dead."

Kale chuckled and sat on the end of her bed. "Rest up. I've taken the day off work tomorrow, so don't worry about setting your alarm for school."

Leila cringed; she hated causing this much hassle. "Did Mom freak out?"

"A little. *Oh, my poor baby. I should've been there.* The usual stuff. Then, she thanked me for being a hero and all." Kale smiled his normal halfway-to-arrogant smirk, like he did when he wanted to get a rise out of her.

"I'm sure." She smiled back.

"They'll be home tomorrow afternoon."

Guilt gripped Leila. They were supposed to travel around and do things after the conference—things that people with kids didn't get to do enough. Fall in love all over again… not come home early to tend to a sick child. She'd cut their week short. Whether she meant to or not, it still made her feel bad.

"I wish you'd told me before you called her. They haven't had time like this for so long. I'll be fine—"

"You're not fine, Leila. This isn't you being fine.' He pointed at her, eyebrows knitting together. "And honestly you scared the hell outta me. I'd kick a guy's ass for you. I'd run bare-foot through burning lava for you. I'd take the brunt of a damned animal attack for you. But I can't watch you suffer."

His words stabbed her heart. Not in a painful way, but more in the way that made her feel totally and utterly helpless. She made her brother scared, and that wasn't something anyone could do often. Leila didn't know how to respond, so she changed the subject. "Hey, did they find Damien and Mr. Robertson?"

Kale pressed his hands against his knees and stood. After a long breath out, he shook his head. "Sleep. I'll be downstairs or in my room. Text if you need anything."

As her protective brother made for the door, Leila quickly grabbed her phone and punched a text through. Kale's phone buzzed from his back pocket, stopping him in his tracks. He quirked an eyebrow in her direction as he reached for it. Leila watched his eyes scan over the message, a soft smile curling his lips. He strode back to give his little sister what she asked for. A hug.

MONDAY

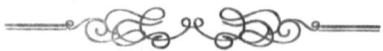

morning

Snow crunched under Leila's bare feet as they propelled her through the darkened forest. Trees reached up from the ground they shared, their icy tops silhouetted by the moon-lit sky. Lower branches, like giant fingers, seemed to reach for her as she ran.

And she was running for one thing only. Survival.

A growl rumbled in the distance and echoed all around. She couldn't tell which direction it came from, but she kept moving anyway. Anything was better than giving up.

Another growl, this time closer. Trees shook above her as a flock of birds scattered into the sky. A bleat she recognized as a deer came from nearby. Clutching her chest in fright, Leila scanned the forest until she caught sight of it—charging straight for her. The deer zig-zagged in panic, dodging her as it fled.

Calmly and oddly she thought, *Would anyone hear me if I screamed?*

It was in that moment Leila realized she was dreaming.

Then, all she could hear was the sound of her own feet against the cold earth, the sound of her heart as it pumped blood through her body, and her breath as it moaned out for her to stop. *I won't stop. I can't stop.*

In front of her, barely five meters away, two round lights appeared. They blinked at her in the darkness, like a pair of blue diamonds suspended in mid-air. *I was running towards it the whole time!*

She took a sharp right, willing her legs to go faster. Pounding footsteps behind her whispered imminent death.

It was a dream, she knew it was a dream. But it didn't *feel* like one. Her speeding heart burst through her chest, warning her not to let the creature catch up.

Something glistened on the path. Only then, as her foot fell through snow covered leaves, did she realize it was a trap. She crashed through snowflakes, dirt, and leaves, squeezing her eyes shut and waiting for impact. When it didn't come, she peeled an eye open. She didn't fall, yet she didn't find solid ground either, like she was floating between earth and her grave—hovering mid-air as though suspended like a puppet. Immobilized, her feet dangling above ground, Leila watched snowflakes fly upwards in reverse until they dissipated into the starry sky.

The air itself taunted her, carrying a low buzzing noise that seemed like the wind and a snarl combined. The sound was accompanied by millions of dark particles, as tiny as dust, tumbling towards her. She writhed against the invisible force that held her, but she was paralyzed. All she could do was watch as the darkness reached her and encircled the ground beneath her hovering feet. The particles continued to spin upwards until they buzzed around her like a mini-cyclone. Heaviness and agony surged through her body.

Wake up, she begged of herself.

As if by her own will, a small flicker of light appeared within the particles. Then another, and another—

minuscule beacons of mercy. They kept multiplying, kept spinning, until her whole being was encircled in a big blurry of light. She took a quick breath, and without warning the light soared into her mouth. It filled her lungs like water.

I can't breathe.

She tried to scream but no air could pass her lips. The only sound she could hear was the distant roar of a lion.

Leila sat up, clutching her throat. She was home, safe in her bed. Her head felt fuzzy as remnants of sleep dripped off her. In her head, she could still hear the lion, still feel the crisp air on her face. She wiggled her toes, as if surprised they were warm and not frozen numb. Then, she sighed, long and loud.

She took another breath and was surprised to feel better. Stronger, more energized, sprightly even. Placing her palm over the bandage on her arm, she noticed the burning had lessened. After giving it a quick tap to quench the itch, she bounded out of bed.

Her mirror let her know that she was definitely over the worst of it—and as each second passed, she realized, apart from the subtle itch and the fact her hair could do with some brushing, she was feeling better than she had in days… weeks… years, even.

After getting dressed, Leila ran down the stairs, skipping two steps at a time. She found herself humming while eating breakfast. When she was done, she grabbed her backpack and yelled up the stairs, "Kale! Call Mom and Dad. Tell them I'm all better. They don't have to come home."

"What?" Kale leaned over the top railing.

"I'm all better!" she repeated with a beaming smile.

As she opened the front door, Kale thumped down the stairs. "Wait! Where are you going?"

"Oh yeah." She laughed, coming back inside. She dug her hand into the loose-change bowl. "I'll buy lunch. Don't worry about the drive, I'll run to school."

"Its five miles away. You... you don't run!" Kale yelled as she slammed the door and kicked up her heels.

Taken aback by everyone buzzing about in the corridor, Leila wondered if she'd ever been that early for school.

As she opened her locker and threw her backpack inside, a blank piece of paper that was supposed to be her completed Earth Science essay flew out. Mr. Robertson expected it on his desk that morning. Leila's enthusiasm came to a screaming halt. She picked up the unfinished project, her heart aching at the realization that her teacher might not be alive.

Crumpling the paper in her fists, Leila looked down the corridor for any sign of Damien. People bustled about slamming their lockers, meeting up with friends, recalling their weekend activities. Leila was used to the halls being empty as she rushed to her first class. A gaggle of over-excited cheerleaders screamed with delight at seeing each other and rushed past her. As they separated to their respective lockers, Riley appeared. He was looking right at Leila, his head tilted in amusement.

Normally, she would be thrilled to see him. But in this moment, all she could think about was her missing friend and teacher. As soon as he was close enough to hear her, she asked, "Did you hear about Damien?"

Riley's face dropped. He rushed to meet Leila and clutched her elbows. "Oh God, Leila, look at you. He's okay, he's fine."

"He is?" Leila searched his eyes, hoping against all hope that his words were truth.

He smiled warmly. "You're really worried, aren't you?"

Frowning, Leila placed the paper into her locker and pulled out her history book. "Of course I am. His face was on the news."

"Yeah, the whole thing was a bit dramatic wasn't it?" Riley released his hands and waved one flippantly. "But, he's fine. He likes camping, he's out breathing nature in."

"Camping?" Leila scrunched her nose. "I took him for an indoors type of person. Anyway, why would anyone go camping with that man-hunting cougar out there?"

"Oh, he normally goes down past Enumclaw, not here. Now, that would be worrisome." Riley's left eye twitched. He looked over his shoulder and within a beat he turned back to her, smiling. "Anyway, who are you? And why are you at my friend's locker? Do you think that, because she's always late, you can use her things before she arrives?"

Leila nudged his shoulder. "Very funny."

Underneath her bandage, her rash tingled. She resisted the urge to scratch it. So instead, she tucked her elbow in and rubbed her arm against her ribs to alleviate the tickle.

His smile receded. "You look—"

"Careful with your words, Riley Jansen!" she interrupted before he could throw any cheeky insults her way.

"No, I was going to say that you look radiant." His eyes shifted to the floor as he rubbed the nape of his neck. "Is that a weird word to say?"

"Hmm... " Leila stared at his soft hair, falling over his brow. She watched him jab his foot on the floor, as though kicking an imaginary rock. He was nervous. And that made her nervous. So, she resorted to levity to break the tension. "Yeah, I think it is a bit weird."

"Well, then," he said, looking back up. His smile returned with a twinkle in his eyes. "You look divine."

A sudden rush of blood filled Leila's cheeks. "I think radiant was better."

"Yeah, as soon as I heard it, I knew I'd made the wrong word choice." He leaned against the locker next to hers and looked down at her with piercing eyes.

With one eyebrow raised, his eyes danced around her face and lingered at her mouth. Riley was flirting. Leila grazed her teeth over her bottom lip, trying to flirt back.

Riley sighed and leaned the side of his head against the locker. "Leila?"

The way he said her name felt different, like the weight of his heart came with it.

Her stomach flipped as she croaked, "Mmm?"

"Are we—"

The bell rang, signaling five minutes until the first period.

Riley cleared his throat and pushed himself away from the locker. He held out his hand for Leila. "I suppose we'd better get to class. Don't want to waste the early start you've given yourself."

Leila kept her eyes on Riley's outstretched hand while she closed her locker. They'd never held hands before. It seemed like a big deal. She glanced up to his face. His mouth twitched as he waited—body almost frozen in anticipation. Swallowing, she moved next to him and slid her hand into his. Their palms pressed together, fingers finding the spaces in between.

Riley smiled to himself as he took the first step. Leila moved with him, walking through the halls to their history class. And it would have been exciting and romantic, if it didn't feel like the most natural thing in the world.

The first half of the day was a normal Monday, minus Mr. Robertson. A substitute teacher took them through lessons they'd already learned, but no one told her otherwise. Leila spent most of the time doodling spirals and answering Sadie's questions about her sudden fever and equally sudden recovery.

By lunch time, Leila was starving. She distinctly remembered eating breakfast, but her body didn't seem to. Her stomach rumbled as soon as they entered the cafeteria.

"Where's your packed lunch?" Sadie asked as they lined up.

"Her momma's not home this week," Gabby teased.

"I'm being adventurous and trying new things." Leila rubbed her hands together, then added; "I ran to school this morning."

"You what now?" Gabby almost choked on her words. She shared a glance with Sadie.

"Are you okay?" Sadie asked, "Are you sure you're not still sick?"

"Nope, all better," Leila said, scratching her arm.

She grabbed a tray and turned her attention to what was on offer, but all she could think of was the raw chicken she saw on Friday. Regretting the decision not to bring a packed lunch from home, Leila asked, "Do you have any... salad rolls?"

The lunch lady looked at her expressionless before turning to the fridge. She pushed an open salami packet aside and reached for a roll with the same hand. Leila winced.

"A roll? Really? Do we live in Ireland or America?" Gabby asked, eying off the tater tots.

Leila lifted her tray and the lunch lady smacked the roll down. Facing Gabby, she smiled and said, "Baby steps!"

On her way to a table she made sure to pay extra attention to the ground — particularly for spilled juices, and for anyone who might be walking in her direction — particularly Sebastian. Riley waited at their usual table and a sudden pang of concern re-entered her mind. It was weird seeing him without Damien at his side. If he had been camping, like Riley had said, shouldn't he already be back at school?

Leila sat down, and before he had the chance to talk about anything else, she asked, "How can you be sure he's okay?"

Sadie and Gabby slid in next to her and stared at Riley, all three of them waiting for his reply.

Riley swallowed a mouthful of food and shrugged. "I just know."

"Well, you can't *know* for sure unless you've spoken to him." Gabby stabbed a tater-tot with her fork and wagged it in his direction. "And *if* you have spoken to him, then you've told the police, so his parents stop worrying, right? I mean, if he's run away or if he's doing something illegal, I'm sure they'll still be relieved to know he hasn't been mauled to death by a cougar."

"Gabrielle!" Sadie scolded. Her already large eyes widened at Gabby's callous comment.

"Just sayin'." Gabby shoved the tot in her mouth, scraping her teeth along the metal as she did.

Leila brought her attention back to Riley. He didn't seem fazed by Gabby's rant. "Have you spoken to him?"

"Mmhmm. Yeah, last night," his tone was casual, as though she'd asked him if he was enjoying the weather.

Leila sighed with relief. Although, it would have been good if he led with that information earlier.

"And you told the police?" Gabby asked, unconvinced.

"I told his parents," Riley was quick to reply. "And they told the police. I feel like I'm being interrogated here. If you watched the news this morning, you'd know they called off the search for him."

Riley's eyes darted between Gabby and Leila, a certain pain hidden behind his defensive glare. He rested his softening gaze on Leila and he gestured at her tray.

"Anyway, what's the go with Miss Healthy, eating from the school cafeteria?"

Leila shrugged as she took her first bite into the roll. The crust was dry, like week old bread. She could swear she tasted mold, even though she didn't know what mold tasted like. Leila opened her mouth, and globs of half-chewed roll fell limply on her tray.

"That's horrid, Leilani!" Sadie cried, shifting her seat a few inches away.

Gabby let out an almighty guffaw. The kind of laugh that was both shocked and delighted.

Riley covered his mouth, but the sparkle in his eyes revealed what kind of grin he hid underneath his hand; one that defined his chin and brought dimples to his cheeks. A smile that Leila loved.

"It's okay," Leila said, taking another bite. With a mouthful of stale food in her mouth, she chewed slowly, faking a smile. "Just a little dry, is all."

MONDAY

afternoon

Standing in front of her open locker, Leila was trying to decide what to do with the study-slash-free period that afternoon.

"Skip it," Gabby said. "Come shopping with me. I need some new boots."

Even though that sounded incredibly enticing, Leila's nose scrunched. "I would, but there are things I need to catch up on. Essays and projects, things like that."

Gabby looked at Leila as though she'd grown a second head. Beside Gabby, Sadie squinted. Then, the two of them shared a sharp glance before turning back to Leila.

"What?"

"You've changed." Gabby raised her eyebrows.

"No, I haven't. I'm still me. Only a little more focused, you know? My brain feels less fuzzy than usual. I don't know, I'm sure it won't last long. So, I want to make the most of it."

"I like it," Sadie piped up, smiling. "It suits you."

"Thank you." Leila rolled her shoulders back and nodded, grateful for the back-up.

"Ugh." Gabby loosened her tie with a scowl. "I don't suppose you want to skip school either?"

"Gabby, Gabby, Gabby," Sadie sighed, shaking her head. "Just because it's easy for you, doesn't mean it's easy for us. We have to work hard for good grades."

"Well, what are you studying?" Gabby asked, eying a large binder in Sadie's arms.

"Still with the math." Sadie waved the textbook in front of her, she needed to use two hands to hold it.

Gabby gave an exaggerated sigh, then said, "Fine, I'll stay and help you with it."

Leila watched her two best friends bicker with the familiarity of siblings. It made her smile. Behind every jab and sigh and roll of the eyes, there was warmth and safety and comfort.

Sadie tried not to smile as she lifted her chin to Gabby. "I never asked you to."

"That's because you don't have to. I'm an awesome friend." Gabby grinned.

"And you want to help me because *I* am an awesome friend!" Sadie declared. Her eyes were alight, glistening under the luminescent down lights above the lockers. She was waiting for the returned agreement with intense anticipation.

Gabby looked past her, distracted by something further down the hall.

"I'm awesome, right?" Sadie tapped Gabby's arm with her textbook.

Mouth agape, Gabby pointed behind them. "Look."

Damien walked, no, strutted towards them. His head was high, and his normally draping dark hair was swept behind his ears. As he moved, his shoulders remained back, causing his chest muscles to strain against a tight black t-shirt. He made eye contact with everyone he passed, even reaching forward to shake Cap's hand. The girls surrounding Cap stared at Damien as if they'd discovered their favorite shoes were on sale. Cap turned to his friends and asked, "Who *is* that?"

"Hey girls!" Damien said, stepping between Leila and Sadie.

The three of them stood silent, eyes and mouth wide. Leila couldn't remember the last time he approached them. Come to think of it, she couldn't even remember him being near them without Riley by his side.

He looked so different. Less slinky, more... bulky. Like a cornstalk turned into a redwood overnight.

Sadie craned her neck, looking up at the surprising visitor. She blinked once, and with wide-armed ferocity, proclaimed. "Oh my god! You're safe. We were so worried about you."

"Yeah, of course." He squeezed her shoulder, then looked directly at Leila. His gray eyes crinkled as he smiled. "All good, ladies."

"Wha..." Gabby started but lost her words when Damien winked at her.

Leila stared, unsure whether she was confused or surprised or amused. Her eyes drifted to his seemingly newly formed biceps and noticed a dark line of ink escaping from the edge of his sleeve.

"Did you get a tattoo?" Peering around, Sadie pulled his shirt up and revealed a large black spiral curving around his shoulder. She let out a little peep and dropped her hand, as though she touched something she shouldn't have.

"Don't tell my parents." He grinned wider than Leila had ever seen before. She'd never seen that much of his teeth before. She'd never seen so much of him at all. And there seemed be a lot of him.

"Are they blind?" Gabby blurted.

Damien laughed, and it wasn't his normal shy snicker. It was a hearty laugh, one that shook his shoulders and echoed around the hall. Leila's chest expanded, all at once utterly relieved. He was okay. He was more than okay. *Maybe I should get out and about in the wilderness more often.*

"It must have been one good camping trip," Leila finally managed to say.

His expression shifted, smile making way for a curious frown. "Huh? I don't like — "

"Damien!" Riley appeared out of breath, almost charging into them all. "Hey man! You're just the guy I wanted to see. Can we chat for a second?"

The three girls stood dumbstruck as Riley grabbed Damien by the wrist and dragged him down the hall. As quick as Hurricane Damien blew in, out he went again.

It was quiet in his wake for a long moment.

"What. The. Actual. Hell?" Gabby broke the silence.

"I didn't even know." Sadie stared after them, eyes as large as saucers.

Leila pulled her attention away from the now distant boys to look at her friend. "You didn't know what?"

"That he was hot."

In the library, Sadie and Gabby sat on the sofa in the corner going over equations. At a nearby table, Riley hunched over with his head in a book. Next to him, Leila looked on, amazed at how he could read so many books that weren't in the school curriculum.

He smiled, eyes still on his book. "What?"

"You look cute when you're reading." *Did I say that out loud?* She quickly moved her eyes back down to the paper she was pretending to write.

"Leila, can I ask you a question?" He placed his book on the table.

The tone in his voice sent alarm bells ringing in Leila's head. A warning signal that things were about to get serious. And so, she did what she did best.

"You just did," Leila teased, deflecting.

"Okay, I'm just going to say it then..." he stopped to take his glasses off, resting them on his open book. "What are we?"

Leila's heart sped up as warmth spread across her chest. Trying to make a joke, she croaked, "Besties?"

"Right." He rubbed the nape of his neck and gave a pained smile.

"What's up with Damien?" she said, changing the subject. "He's so different. Don't tell me it's just the mountain air."

Riley's eyes lit up. "Thanks for reminding me... wait here."

He rushed to the supernatural section and came back moments later, dropping a massive book on the table in front of her. The table shook under the weight, causing a few students to glance their way. Leila smiled apologetically, then peered down. The book's cover was brown with a golden spine and edges, and white lettering simply read; *The History of Therianthropy*.

"I literally just finished reading this book the other week and I freaked out when Damien came in today with that spiral tattoo on his arm... check this out." Riley remained standing as he flipped through the pages. He stopped on a drawing of a half-human, half-bear with a spiral mark on its arm. Leila leaned forward to get a better look. The bear-man stood upright, its open mouth showing large teeth—a severed head swung from its claws.

Gross. Leila inched back, hoping Riley would close the book soon.

"So, he got a tattoo to match an urban legend?"

"What if it's not a tattoo?" Riley said, sitting down.

"You're saying Damien is a man-bear?" She raised her eyebrows.

She'd known that Riley was into that kind of quirky stuff. She thought his love for science fiction and fantasy was so cute. Even the way he rambled about hidden worlds and paranormal things human eyes can't see was endearing. Sometimes she'd catch Riley and Damien arguing about random ideas, like who would win in a fight, a vampire or a werewolf. But, she didn't realize he actually believed in it.

"Could be, or an eagle, or a wolf, or a—" He stopped talking when he noticed her staring. "Bear with me, just listen… The spiral is a mark of a Guardian."

"A Guardian?"

Riley's eyes lit up. It reminded her of the time she wondered out loud what would happen if the moon stayed full the whole month long and he took great pride in explaining it. She knew from the look on his face, that things were about to get complicated. And fast.

"In recent times, humans have altered the actual facts. They've made them into fantastical myths. But basically, Guardians are Therianthropes, or in—"

"Theri-what? You're making words up, Riley Jansen."

Smiling, Riley continued, "Therianthropes… or in modern terms Shape-shifters."

"Shape-shifters? You mean people that can turn into animals?"

"You got it." Riley made a finger-gun in her direction, then tapped the book. "Like this bear. Or even a wolf."

"Oh, you mean werewolves? I know them. I've seen Teen Wolf." She leaned back in her chair, proud of herself.

"Ha!" Riley laughed. "I thought you said your mom was a folklore professor?"

73

Leila shrugged. "You know me, I don't listen."

"You're listening now?" He leaned forward, resting his elbows on his knees.

His proximity took her breath. That look was in his eyes again. Her eyes drifted to his full lips, pink and smiling. She nodded, forcing her gaze back up again. "And you're saying that Damien is a Guardian."

"Well…" He sat up, glancing at the book. "Yeah."

"Wait? What? I was just joking."

"I mean, it's obvious isn't it?" Riley said, running his hand over the large page. "To receive the spiral mark, he must have been touched by another Guardian, with the intent to transition them…" He turned to look at her. "Do you know what that means?"

"That you're a complete nerd," she smirked.

Riley opened his mouth to reply but nodded instead. He closed the book. Leila wondered if he was upset—she'd never seen him upset, so wasn't quite sure. It wasn't the first time she'd called him a nerd. He'd called her Miss. Scatterbrain or Miss. Healthy just as often. What made this moment different?

Watching him intently, Leila sat back in her chair. She ran her fingernails across the bandage on her arm.

"What are you scratching at? You've been rubbing your arm the whole day." Riley reached for the bottom of her sleeve.

"It's fine. A tiny rash." She turned her arm over and let him roll the shirt up.

He frowned at the bandage. "You were sick all weekend and now your arm is itching?"

"The sky is blue, my eyes are hazel, you wear glasses…" Leila's words faded as she noticed Riley frowning. "What? We're not stating the obvious?"

Riley let go of her arm and sighed with frustration. "Are you ever serious?"

"I can be," Leila replied, rolling down her sleeve. *I think.*

"Okay then, let me ask you a serious question."

"Go ahead." Leila settled back in her chair, expecting a question about why she wasn't taking better care of herself, or why she was so late all the time, or why she couldn't complete her homework on time like the rest of class.

"Are we just friends?" he asked, drawing out the last word.

Leila stared at him expressionless. Under the surface, her heart fluttered without bounds, pounding against her rib cage, begging for freedom. Her answer could have come in the form of a lame joke to bring levity, in fact, Riley probably expected it. But there was something about the way he made her feel—vulnerable yet comfortable—that made her want to be honest.

Leaning forward, she looked him square in the eyes and said, "No. We are so much more than that."

"Oh, thank god," he said, sighing the words.

His next moves were thoughtful and deliberate, as though the weight of them slowed him down. He clutched the sides of his chair, knuckles turning white from the pressure. He shuffled closer to her, air streaming through his nostrils. He looked up, eyes locking onto hers. From there, everything seemed to flow. He stroked the side of her jaw under her ear, and leaned in, mouth parted. His breath warmed her lips and she inched forward with every intent to bridge the minuscule gap between them. She forgot where she was, but only for a second.

"Get a room!" Gabby yelled a few meters away.

"Quiet!" The librarian hissed.

Slinking away from Riley, Leila glanced around to find everyone in the library looking at them.

"Meet me at the lake after school?" Riley whispered.

Leila could only nod.

He put his glasses on, picked up his book, and settled back into the chair.

MONDAY

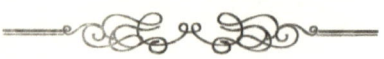

late afternoon

Small evergreen trees lined the main shopping strip of town. Cedar Falls wasn't a huge town, but it wasn't tiny either. It had everything its residents needed, and for everything else they had Seattle an hour away.

Leila checked her phone for the millionth time and her heart leapt. Fifteen minutes. She was meeting Riley in fifteen minutes.

"Lover boy can wait." Gabby grabbed her by the wrist and veered into a locally owned boutique.

A mixture of pastels and earthy darks lined the racks. Couture and well out of Leila's price range. Gabby shuffled through a collection of chiffon tops, gasping as she held up a white shirt with dark blue polka dots. She practically threw it against Leila. "Try that on."

"I don't have money," Leila said, pushing it back towards her.

"You go to Cedar Falls Academy, Leila Belmonte. Of course you have money." Gabby pushed it back.

Leila tilted her head. "My parents work hard for that tuition. I'm on a super strict budget. My brother works in a cafe, for heaven's sake."

"For heaven's sake," Gabby mocked. She forced Leila's fingers around the coat hanger. "I just want to see what it looks like on you."

Leila sighed. There was no point arguing with Gabrielle Harper. That's a fight she knew she'd lose. She followed her bossy best-friend to the change rooms. Gabby sneaked into the next one to try on some leather pants.

It was just the two of them. Sadie had to go home with her sister, Summer, because their parents both worked late on Mondays. It's not that fifteen-year-old Summer couldn't look after herself, it's more that she was going through a stage at the moment... a sneaking out of windows to parties kind of stage. And Sadie, being the poster-child for all perfect daughters across the Pacific North-West, was entrusted to keep her wild sister under control.

The dynamic shifted when Sadie wasn't there. The friends were like three parts of the same wheel. Sadie was the flight, propelling them in forward motion, as though she was lifted by the breeze. Gabby was the direction, steering them all, making sure they stayed true to themselves. And Leila was the anchor, she kept them all sane in the process. Although right then, it seemed Gabby was both direction and flight, because Leila was trying on clothes she couldn't afford.

"I wish I had a sister," Leila mused, pulling the top over her head.

"You do."

"Are you saying Kale is a girl?"

Gabby swung the door to Leila's change-room open. "You have me and Sades!"

Leila hadn't fully pulled the top over her stomach yet, but Gabby didn't care; she spun in a circle and kicked her back foot up. She was wearing a pair of tight black jeans with rhinestones down the seams. "Hot, huh?"

"Smokin'," Leila agreed.

"That top doesn't suit you," Gabby stated before going back into her change room.

Leila frowned at her reflection in the mirror. She didn't think she looked too bad. It didn't matter though, she couldn't buy it if she wanted to anyway.

Once Gabby had made her purchase, they left the shop. Leila followed Gabby down the main strip of Cedar Falls, quickly pulling out her phone to check the time. Ten minutes.

"Where'd you get the cash for shopping, anyway?" Leila asked, catching up.

Ignoring the question, Gabby stopped and peered through the window of a shoe store. Leila watched Gabby's eyes widen at the price ticket.

Spinning around, Gabby said, "Boots will have to wait, I want a jacket next. What time do you have to meet *him*?"

"*Gabby*." Leila scolded. If she knew Gabby as well as she thought, right now she was trying her best to deflect. Leila knew it because that's what she did—except where she used jokes, Gabby used random questions.

"I stole it. Is that what you wanted to hear?" Gabby crossed her arms across her chest.

"No. Because what I want to hear is the truth."

Gabby raised her eyebrows, and as though only just realizing what Leila said, she dropped them again. "You're too good, Leila."

Across the road, an old red Honda Civic caught Leila's attention. It was unmistakably Riley's car—three scratch marks lined the bumper right above the license plate. It was parked outside Jimmy's Italian restaurant, where Riley worked on weekends.

"I did steal it," Gabby admitted. "From my step-dad. He's so stupid, he won't even notice it's gone."

Leila heard Gabby's admission, but it didn't sink in. Her mind was too far away. She was too busy staring at a boy — *the boy*. Riley. A vision of All-American sweetness — the physique of a jock but the heart of a nerd. He was out of his school uniform, leaning against his car and talking to his boss. Head-phones were hanging around his neck and he wore a maroon slouch beanie, the ends of his hair poking out from the left side.

"Earth to Leila." Gabby waved her hand in front of Leila's starry-eyed face and followed Leila's eye-line. "Oh, you've got it so bad. I kinda wish I didn't interrupt your almost kiss in the library today."

"It's okay," Leila said wistfully, still watching Riley as he grabbed his boss' hand and gave it a strong shake. "We kind of talked about *us* today."

"And..." Gabby stood between Leila and the road to block the view.

Leila blinked. Someone ran past them and a rush of air fanned her face. Moments of time caught up to her, her lagging brain repeating words she failed to notice. "You stole the money from your step-dad?"

Gabby squinted. Moving sideways, she allowed Leila's eyes to find Riley once again. "Have you slept with him yet?"

"What? No. Gab, we haven't even kissed."

"You guys are so adorable." Gabby pouted her lips into a face Leila had seen many times before. It was a look that said: *I have an idea and there's nothing anyone can do to stop me.* One nod and she turned around, starting towards Riley.

Leila sighed and followed. Even when Sadie was at her flightiest, she was still much easier to anchor than steamroller Gabby. By the time they crossed the road, Riley had said goodbye to his boss and was already walking towards the turn-off for Rattlesnake Lake.

"I've still got a few minutes," Leila said, trying to slow

Gabby down. "I'll help you find a jacket with your stolen money."

"Don't be silly. He's your boyfriend, you should be able to talk to him if you bump into him down the street." Gabby marched ahead.

"This isn't technically bumping into him, Gab." Leila tried reason to help settle her friend down. "This is more like stalking."

"Shoosh." Gabby waved her hand, turned the corner, then stopped. "Who's the girl?"

Leila stepped out from behind her and saw Riley about ten meters away. His back was towards them as he talked to someone. Not just anyone. A girl. Blonde hair—smooth and straight—sat like silk on her shoulders. She was as tall as Riley and had curves in all the right places. Her eyes twinkled as they spoke, her head slightly tilted to the side, taking in his every word.

"I don't know," Leila replied, her eyes fixed on Riley. His arms were animated, flinging to the air one moment, and pointing a rigid finger the next. Whoever she was, they were familiar with each other. They knew each other well. "I feel like I'm spying."

"Where's a popcorn stand when you need one?" Gabby glanced over her shoulders as though looking for literal popcorn. "Shall we go and interrupt?"

"Noooo," Leila begged with horror. Then, she stood up straight, eyes unblinking as the mystery girl threw her arms around Riley. "It looks like she's leaving anyway."

Riley hugged the girl and they parted ways. As he put his head-phones on and jogged towards the lake, his model-esque friend walked directly towards Leila and Gabby. Her stride belonged on the runway.

As she got closer, Leila span in a circle and clutched at Gabby's wrist. "Oh sweet biscuits, what do we do?"

"Chill, babes. I'm here." Gabby took a step forward, adding, "And sweet biscuits, really?"

As the girl passed, she glanced across. Gabby lifted a hand and said, "Hello."

At first, she seemed shocked at the greeting. A moment later, she smiled warmly and tucked her hair behind her ear. "Hi."

Gabby gazed after the girl until she turned the corner. She gave a wry smile and turned back to Leila. "All right, this is where I leave you. Smooch that sucker like there's no tomorrow."

"It's not like that. We're just hanging out," Leila lied. To Gabby and herself.

"Yeah? And that almost library kiss was *just hanging out*." Gabby brought her hands together, twisting her fingertips against themselves and making a kissing noise.

Leila grabbed Gabby's hands to make her stop. "No thanks to you. Anyway, I like that we're going slow, it shows me he cares."

"There's slow and then there's you. It will be prom before you kiss at this rate."

"Is that so bad?" Leila defended herself.

Gabby raised an eyebrow. "Are you serious? Unless you're keeping secrets from me, your last kiss was exactly eight months ago. I actually feel sorry for your lips."

Leila shuddered. *If I was Gabby, I'd feel sorry for my lips eight months ago, not now.*

Long before Riley stepped foot into Cedar Falls Academy and stole Leila's attention, there was Don Brand. The fact that he was Sebastian's friend should have given her all the warning she needed to stay away—but she didn't, and now she had a memory she'd rather forget. Out of the blue one day, he walked up and told her she had nice eyes. Every day for a whole week, the creep winked at her in the corridors of school. She couldn't help but admit that the attention made her feel so good. And then one day, when he ask for a chat, she said yes. Within moments they were making out in an abandoned class room. It was sloppy and gross, his hands in search of damn near everything. When he got a phone call, she saw it as her opportunity to sneak out the door. She hadn't existed to him since, and she liked it that way.

"You're being pushy," Leila said, trying to get the image out of her head.

"I know." Gabby sighed. "I can hear it in my voice. I can't help it. I care about you and he's a nice guy—a really nice guy. And he's here, alone. Have you even spent time with him outside of school hours before?"

"Yes." Leila shifted the weight between her feet.

"Having him serve you and your family dinner on a Saturday night at Jimmy's doesn't count."

Leila looked towards the entrance of the Lake park. From the end of the parking lot, lush green grass blanketed all the way to the lake and around in a semi-circle. And in the middle, directly in front of them about twenty meters away was Riley. Gusts of white mist leaving his mouth as he slowed down and approached a bench.

She sighed. "You don't have to convince me. He invited me here, I said yes. It's not like I'm going to chicken out or something."

"I love you Leila, but sometimes you're ridiculously stubborn." Gabby literally pushed Leila in Riley's direction and turned around. "I'll see you at school tomorrow. I've got a girl to chase."

"Oh lord, Gab. Don't stalk her!" Leila called, but Gabby had already gone.

MONDAY

early evening

Leila took a deep breath and walked towards Riley, rubbing her fingers over her lips to make sure they weren't too dry. On both sides of the lake the lawn was interrupted by a forest that climbed up the mountain ledge overlooking the town. On the left was a playground where children played with innocent delight, always under the watchful eye of their parents. And on the right, was a walking track into the forest.

Riley was sitting on a bench in front of a muddy track. His hands supported the back of his head, one of his fingers tapping slightly on the nape of his neck. She'd noticed his hands before—long and slender, perfect moons, tanned. But she'd never allowed herself to imagine what he might do with them. They looked like they were made for combing through curly locks. As she made her way around to the front of the bench, she noticed his eyes were closed.

Laying her hands under her thighs, she sat down next to the book beside him. She bit her lip as she watched him exhale and move his hands down to smooth his shorts. He opened his eyes.

"Hi," she drew out the word.

He jumped and skidded along the bench, his usual cool decidedly not collected. Removing his headphones, he said, "Geez, Leila. You scared me."

She'd never seen him in fright before, actually, she'd never even seen him on edge. It made her feel like she had some sort of opportunity to step into the driver's seat, direct the meeting the way she wanted it to go... but all she could do was wipe her sweaty palms along her jeans and try not to unravel herself.

"Sorry..." She moved her hand in a slow arch. "Hi."

"Hello," he replied calmer, sliding back to his original spot.

"Sorry, I'm early." Leila checked her phone. She was, in fact, five minutes late. But she'd already started with the excuse, so she kept going. "I was shopping with Gab and saw you come this way. I thought I'd say hi... so hi."

"Hi." He smiled, clearly amused. "Again."

"Okay, I'll stop saying that now." Her knee bounced with nerves as she watched a little boy about four or five years old throw a piece of bread into the lake. He sat down, cross-legged, waiting for something to take his offering. She guffawed and pointed to him. "Does someone wanna tell him the ducks have gone for the Winter?"

As soon as she heard her voice say those ridiculous words, she knew she was being weird. She could feel Riley's eyes bore into the side of her face. Swallowing, Leila kept her eyes on the lake. It felt different. Being with Riley, there, it felt like something between them was going to shift in a big way.

Riley cupped her shoulder. "It's me, Leila." When she turned to face him, he pulled at his black sweater. "No tie, but it's still me."

She settled back, wincing and nodding simultaneously. Where were her jokes? Her sarcasm had all but zapped from existence.

As though sensing her unease, he flipped his book around, sacrificing himself to bring the regular Leila back. "I like to sit out here and read sometimes."

"Of course you do," she said. It was meant to be a tease, but as she drifted her gaze around his handsome face, she knew the tone had missed its mark. It had come off too heavy for a joke.

They sat in silence for a beat. Riley breathed in sharply through his nose, a shaky exhale followed. Without saying a word, he lifted his headphones over his head and held them out. She ducked her head and as he placed them on her ears, the soft tones of a Coldplay melody drifted through. He let his thumb linger at her temple for moment, giving her cheek a quick stroke before moving back.

Leila smiled, relaxing with the tune. "And, of course you love this band."

"Am I that predictable?" he asked with a straight face.

"Mmhm." She nodded. "But that's one of the things I like about you most."

An endearing laugh tumbled out of his mouth.

"What?" she asked.

He pointed to his ears. "You're shouting."

"Oh." Leila removed the headphones, resting them around her neck.

His eyes glistened as his hands mindlessly flicked through the pages of his book. "Do you want to know what I like most about you?"

There it was, the impending shift in their relationship. She could barely get the word out of her mouth. "What?"

"You're unpredictable."

Leila felt her brow descend. Honestly, she didn't know what she was expecting him to say. They liked each other and they were there to discuss what the hell that meant. But she was unpredictable? That's what he liked most—

"And funny," he continued. "And smart. And you always manage to see the best in everyone. And you never complain. And you're so self-assured. You're just you..." He smiled and arched his face to the sky, as if releasing the words into the world had freed something significant inside of him. Looking back down, he finished, "And. You're. Just. So. Beautiful."

Leila's mouth dropped.

"Sorry," he rushed. "I didn't want to say that. You're simple. No, I didn't want to say that either. I mean, you are... simple *and* beautiful. If Coldplay wrote a song about you there would be this glorious metaphor about the place where the familiarity of a leaf meets the surprise of a wildflower."

He cringed and lifted the book to cover his face.

A bubble formed in Leila's chest. All these things he thought of her? They were lovely. No one had said such verbiage to her before, not even her mother, who could ramble along with the best of them.

How would she reply?

In the Leila way.

She teased, "You could grow a harvest from all that corn."

Riley lowered the book with a grimace. "Yeah, it was bad, even for me. Sorry. Let me start again." He took a breath, looking at Leila with unblinking eyes. "I meant to say that you're the nicest person I've ever met. That's what I like most about you. You're out of this world kind."

Somehow he had inched close enough to her that a slight lean was all it would take for them to be kissing. All at once, an internal itch arose. It was a little niggle at first, a small thought in the shape of a tall blonde girl with perfect swaying hips. Then, it grew into something insatiable, a torment.

"Who was the girl you were with?" Leila cleared her throat and casually looked out to the lake. A few kids played on the crest a little way down, they giggled and threw rocks, causing splashes that rippled out all the way to the edge in front of them.

"What girl?"

"The model-looking one." She turned her face from Riley so he didn't see her cringe at herself.

"Leila?" Riley chuckled. "Are you jealous?"

She flung her head around and lifted her chin. "No." *Yes.*

"Good, cos she's my cousin. Her name is Odette."

"Your cousin?" Leila let out an audible sigh.

"Yeah, she lives in Enumclaw…" Riley's eyes drifted down to Leila's arm. "You should stop scratching that, you know. It will only make it worse."

Leila looked down at her fingernails grazing over the bandage. She didn't even realize she was doing it. "Habit," she replied.

"Mmm." He squinted and shied back away.

The gap between them lengthened, and in the middle, unresolved tension hung in the air. Leila scolded herself for ruining the moment with her sudden pang of jealousy. But the way he was looking at her, made her feel like she'd never done anything wrong at all. Her heart ached. How could he make her feel so wonderfully in pain? She'd never felt this way before, about anyone. And so, Leila did what Leila did best — deflect. She flashed a nervous smile and lifted the headphones back over her ears.

Out of the corner of her eye, she saw Riley nod. He swung his foot to rest on his knee and opened his book.

For the next while, they caught themselves stealing glances at each other. A sneaky turn of the head here, a quick peek there. At one point, Riley dropped an open hand by his side and Leila slid hers into it. He never looked up, but he smiled. He was so close but felt so far at the same time.

What's wrong with me? He is by far the best thing in my life, Leila thought, annoyed at her own bashfulness. She wouldn't have dared say that to the girls, but it was the truth. She arrived at school and looked for him, at lunch she looked for him, study periods were always spent with him. When she was with him, she never had to pretend to be anything else, she was free to be herself and he responded to it like she was a superstar. He made her feel like she was the only person in the world who had ever made him smile. And that smile? She wanted to see it all the damn time.

"Riley?"

"Mmm?" He tapped her knee with his foot, not looking up from his book.

She took the headphones off again, this time placing them on the seat beside her. He was so calm and sweet and patient, and she couldn't take it. Warm blood flooded her heart and flushed upwards to her cheeks.

"Maybe we should kiss and get it over with?" she blurted.

He looked over his glasses. "Get it over with?"

"Uhh... never mind, it was a stupid —"

His open lips found hers before she finished what she was saying. They closed over her mouth just once, soft and tentative. He moved back half an inch. "There. Now that's over with can we be normal again?"

Leila's eyes drifted to his mouth. His lips were round and they felt exactly as they looked — soft, like liquid candy. Leila couldn't speak, so she shook her head.

"No?" he whispered, shaking his head, too.

"No," she mouthed.

He grazed his knuckles along her jaw, right under her ear and spread his fingers, threading them through her hair. He opened his lips again and this time she parted hers, too. Then, they connected like magnets, as though that was where they were always meant to be. Leila's hand found its way to Riley's chest—his heart pounded as fast as hers. The movements he made with his mouth were slow yet purposeful. As he glided his tongue slowly along hers, the heat in her chest spread throughout her body. She burned in places she would never say. Kissing him was like eating hot butterscotch pudding; she wanted to savor yet devour at the same time. Riley closed his mouth once more and wiped her lower lip with his thumb as he pulled away.

Leila smoothed his collar back down, and said, "I don't think you and I will ever be normal again."

MONDAY

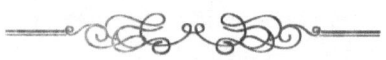

evening

Leila had the house all to herself. She thought she should invite Gabby and Sadie over—even Riley, considering they were now officially together—but instead, she blasted the stereo and danced around the house. What was Sadie's new French phrase? Joy of living?

She grabbed a frozen meal her mom had prepared, tearing off the lid like a magician revealing a bunny from a hat. She sang her own made up Coldplay lyrics about leaves and wildflowers as she watched the food defrost in the microwave. She ate while watching a re-run of Heroes. After dinner, she leapt up the stairs and made a bee-line for the bathroom. As the water warmed, she made a twirl just for the fun of it. She hummed as she folded her clothes into a tidy pile in the corner of the room. Normally, she would leave her clothes wherever she happened to be standing... maybe Gabby was right about her being different. Last to come off was the bandage. After all the cream Leila lathered onto it the night before, the rash should have been all healed up. White steam filled the room as she unraveled, round and round and round and —

This can't be right.

Leila clutched the sink and stared at her arm.

How?

Flinging the door open, she stepped into the hallway to get a better look. Her thumb rubbed where the rash once was, but it did nothing to remove what was there now.

Is this a joke?

She went back into the bathroom and lifted the bandage, running the length of it through her hands. She checked for any sign of black ink seeping through, looking for a rational sign to calm her speeding heart. But there was nothing. Not a damn thing, except that *thing* on her arm… a black spiral, just like Damien's. And behind it, however possible, there was a faint glow, like a flashlight sitting under her skin, shining onto the mark from below.

TUESDAY

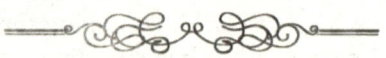

early morning

Even cold concrete seeping through her skirt couldn't make Leila move. She was frozen on the front steps of school, waiting for Riley. She'd ran to school again. Without taking the time to put her hair up, it hung over her shoulders in thick curls. Her knees knocked together with nerves, as she gazed out into the parking lot, waiting for a certain red car to arrive. There were still forty minutes before the bell. Students arrived in trickles here and there. A few friendly faces passed by, trying to strike up a conversation, but she brushed them off quickly. Riley was the only one she wanted to talk to, the rest of the world could dissipate into nothingness for all she cared.

As she bit into her already chewed fingernails, an overwhelming unease descended over her. Someone was spying on her. She whipped her head to the left. The fact that no one was there didn't stop the feeling. It was like an invisible rope had been tied around her waist and someone on the other end pulled at her relentlessly. She stood on impulse and without thinking, walked towards the corner of the building. As she reached the edge where a small pathway separated the school from the bleachers, a group of boys hurled around the corner.

Sebastian charged right into her, his arm bumping into her chest. They both stopped from the impact. His face softened for a second, almost as if he was about to apologize. Then, when he noticed it was Leila, he scowled, "Watch it, Bitsa."

"Right, because I was the one running around the corner a hundred miles an hour." Leila rolled her eyes and turned her back.

Behind him, his friends made "*ooooh*" sounds.

"Self-righteous bitch," Sebastian muttered, walking off.

It took everything within her not to turn around and rip his throat out.

Wait what? Why would I rip his —

"Hey!" Riley called, running over. "Are you okay? I saw the collision."

Leila looked at him, still confused by her murderous thoughts. "Have you ever felt like you could tear someone into pieces?"

"Project Sebastian isn't going too well then?"

Leila glanced to Sebastian, rubbing her collarbone where his elbow hit. "You could say something like that."

Looking over his shoulder, Sebastian eyeballed Riley. Surprising Leila, Riley glared back, his top lip curling slightly. He pointed his finger in accusation. "There's something about that overgrown toddler I don't like."

Remembering Sebastian saying a similar thing about Riley on Friday — albeit in a nastier way--Leila asked, "Has something gone down between you?"

"Why do you say that?" Riley turned his attention back to her.

"Oh, I don't know, the shared death stares that could melt the sun itself."

Riley licked his lips and his face softened. He ran a hand down her arm, sliding his hand into hers. "I don't like the way he talks to you. If you gave the project up, no one would blame you."

Leila squeezed his hand and took one more look at Sebastian as he walked into the building. Maybe she should give up the project. Considering there were more pressing matters at hand.

"Anyway." Riley took a deep breath and smiled. "You're early again!"

Nodding, Leila tugged at his hand and pulled him around the corner towards the barren bleachers. "Come on, there's something I need to show you."

"Wow, the bleachers? Classy," he teased, tapping on the peeling paint.

Ignoring his jab, she rolled her sleeve up. There was no preparing Riley for this moment. She'd have to do it quick — figuratively and literally. Leila lifted the edges of a large band-aid she'd covered the spiral mark with — the kind meant for knee gashes and burns — and peeled it off.

As soon as Riley's eyes landed on the spiral, he blurted, "Ha! Great prank."

"It's not a prank."

Riley's face dropped. "What do you mean?"

"I wasn't just sick on the weekend. My arm has been aching, burning and itching for four days." Her heart began racing and behind the black mark, whiteness glowed brighter. "And now this."

"Put it back on!" Riley snapped. He turned around in every direction, making sure no one was watching. He snatched the band-aid from her and placed it back over the mark carefully. Taking her hand, he said, "Come with me."

He pulled her in through the side door and up the back

stairs to the library. Weaving her around empty tables, Riley dragged her into the supernatural section. He tapped his fingers along book spines until he found a golden one. Riley opened up the book then looked at her. "This is serious, Leila, you know that, right?"

"I'm the one with a strange mark on her arm and no idea how it got there, Riley... I know it's serious."

He took a deep breath, but it was shaky, like he couldn't suck the air into his lungs properly. He sat down in the middle of the aisle, cross-legged and patted the floor in front of him. Leila gulped and lowered herself to face him.

"Remember yesterday when I was telling you about Guardians touching people to prepare them for transition?" He lifted his knees to hold the book as he flipped through pages.

"You want me to be honest?" Leila flicked at a loose edge of the band-aid.

"Yes."

"I really wasn't listening. It seemed so..." She pressed her palm down onto her forearm. "Unrealistic."

Riley took his glasses off and rubbed his eyes. His hair fell forward, and as he removed his hand, he looked at her through fallen tendrils of blond. His light-brown eyes transmitted fear. "It means you've been marked by a Guardian to be turned into—"

"I'm sorry," she interrupted. "Can we back track? What the hell is a Guardian?"

"Shifters, remember?" Riley's nostrils flared. He put his glasses back on and returned to the book.

"Right," Leila sighed, shaking her head. "Shifters."

Riley cleared his throat.

"It says Shadow Guardians are here to protect humankind. They keep their true selves hidden until they are needed to save a life or intervene in other ways, for the elevation of individuals or society. You may find them in great seats of power impacting those around them for the better." Riley paused and scoffed. "It fails to mention that not all Guardians are good. Some use their power for their own gain. They prey instead of protect, they tear down, instead of uplift."

Leila threw her hands behind her and leaned back, lifting her gaze to the ceiling. She wanted to show Riley because of his interest in Damien's mark. But, she thought he'd be more logical. She thought he'd give her an explanation that didn't involve humans that shifted into animals.

"They're called the Fallen. And they kill." Riley squeezed her foot. "Leila? Are you listening?"

She looked down,, staring at him blankly. "Of course. We've established that shifters are monsters."

"Pretty much," Riley said, not noticing her disdain. He traced his finger over the page. "Oh, okay, this is the part I wanted to tell you. If you have been marked for transition —which you have, the incubation period can last from 1-5 days—which it did. The incubation period can bring on fever, swelling, and irritable skin."

Riley glanced at her arm for a second before he continued to read. "Once the spiral appears, the full transition usually occurs immediately but can take as long as a few days; the exact length of time is determined by the Guardian and when they come back into contact with the marked one."

"Okay, I've had enough." Leila leaned forward and snapped the book shut in Riley's hands."Can we take a moment to consider possible causes other than what's in this stupid book?"

Riley looked hurt. "Um…" He lifted his gaze up and finally saw what she'd been trying to show him. She was scared. Petrified. Her eyes glazed with tears. "Yeah sure. Whatever you want, whatever you need."

"I need for this to be gone!" She ripped off the band-aid.

Riley slammed his hand over it. "You can't! Leila, you need it covered. The mark is like a lighthouse to all Guardians, True and Fallen. Do you have a bandage in your bag?"

"I've got a few more of these." She waved the used band-aid.

His brow scrunched down as he unzipped her bag and dug around. He retrieved a handful of band-aids and put one over the mark, then another, and another.

"Riley, is this necessary?" she asked as he put the fourth one on.

"You're a shining beacon! Whoever marked you will be waiting for your incubation period to be over so they can transition you! Just pretend you have a simple rash still. What's today? Tuesday... yeah, you might have a little time — just pretend."

She sighed as he put one more Band-Aid on. "This is ridiculous. There *has* to be an actual logical explanation."

"There is. This is it."

Leila tried to pull her sleeve down, but the bulk of the band-aids wouldn't let it slide. "For a paranormal freak-a-zoid, it's logical. For me, it's absolutely not."

"Thanks."

A single bell chimed — the five-minute warning that school was about to start. Leila couldn't jump to her feet fast enough. She grabbed her bag. "I'm gonna go get ready for class."

"Class?" Riley asked as she turned on her heels. "I don't think you should be — "

His voice faded out as she left him in the supernatural section and pushed through the library doors. As soon as they were closed behind her, she started ripping off the Band-Aids. The first one fell into the bin as a student rushed past, the air their run created tickled her arm. She started to peel the next one off and gazed around at people near their lockers. She saw Damien leaning against his locker talking to three giggling girls. He was all confidence. His *tattoo* was so bold and dark she could see it from there. He looked across the hall and gave Leila a one finger wave. Taking a shallow breath, she re-stuck the half-peeled Band-aid back on and forced her sleeve down.

I guess it won't hurt to cover the mark a bit.

TUESDAY

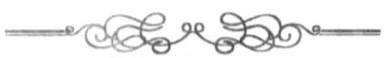

mid-morning

After everyone dispersed from the hallway into their classrooms, Leila sneaked into the photography darkroom. It wasn't her scheduled time, but no one else seemed to have booked in either. The room was only a little bigger than the janitor's closet, but the confined space was a welcome sight. It made her feel safe.

A red light-bulb hung from the roof, casting a deep scarlet across the enlarger on the left wall. Photographs were strung up along the back wall—an array of colorful abstracts and black and white candids of students. Leila dropped her bag on the floor and danced her fingers along the bench that held tubs of chemicals.

She hadn't made it to her locker after she saw Damien. She froze, stuck inside her own mind. School seemed so trivial, so unimportant. Instead of math or history, Leila was hijacked by thoughts she'd never entertained before.

In particular, one single question replayed over and over. *Is Riley right about Shifters?*

She felt numb. Turning towards the filing system tucked neatly beside the door, Leila flipped through to her folder and pulled out a sheet of negatives. She took them to the enlarger and settled herself on the swivel chair. The negatives were from the week earlier. After the pep rally, Leila went down to the lake and set up a few long exposure shots of the sunset. As she held the negatives up to the light, the door swung open.

"Leila Belmonte!" Taj exclaimed.

She gulped. Whenever he called her by her actual surname, he wasn't happy.

He closed the door, taking one wide step to stand over her. "Where were you on the weekend?"

"I was unwell," she replied, placing the negatives back into her folder. "I didn't realize you had scheduled time in here. I'll leave."

"Never mind. I'll only be a few minutes." Taj opened the filing cabinet and scrolled through the folders. He pulled one out with his name on it and slammed the drawer shut. Throwing his folder on the bench beside her, he added, "I mean, really? You were too unwell to call me and arrange a substitute?"

"Yes, actually. My brother took me to the ER."

Taj gave her a skeptical glare, tracing his eyes down the length of her body and back up. "Really? You recovered that quick?"

"It's a miracle!" Leila smiled nervously, lifting her arms into a shrug.

"I had to use my phone," he groaned.

Opening his folder, Taj pointed to grainy prints inside. "These awful crap photos for the Chronicle. Ugh, I could strangle you, Leila Bel..."

Leila winced, hearing her full surname come out of his mouth was unsettling. Taj often gate-crashed Leila's processing time in the darkroom. He said it was to use time efficiently, talking about what was needed for the Chronicle. But deep down, Leila always thought that he just liked spending time with her. She liked spending time with him, too. Not like this though, not being hounded.

As though noticing her discomfort, he abandoned his annoyance. With a gentle shake of his head, he held his folder to his chest and opened the door. "Bel-bitch, you'd better make it up to me."

"I will. I promise," Leila said, as he stepped out of the room.

Leila hung her processed photograph by its corner and stepped back to admire her work. She liked how whimsical the clouds looked, like smoothed cotton candy. Next time, she decided, she would reduce the shutter speed even more and see how silkier the clouds would become.

Absentmindedly, she rubbed her hand over the bulky band-aids on her arm and returned to her back-pack. Wondering what the time was, she fumbled through her bag. As she pulled out her phone, the screen lit up, showcasing a plethora of worried text messages from Riley.

One simple question popped into her mind, again: *Is he right about shape-shifters?* And, like a switch being flipped, a thousand more questions came flooding in after it. *Who marked me? And are they True or Fallen? Are they good or evil? Will I be evil? Will I become a monster? Is there a cure?*

With her back leaning against the door she dialed the number of the only person who could answer those questions.

"Sweetheart!" Leila's mom, Aileen, cooed down the phone.

"Hey," Leila said softly. "How are you?"

"Oh great, honey. It's been so great. It's like our honeymoon all over again. We didn't even get out of bed yesterday. Well, we did, and then Kale called and said not to come back, so we spent the day—"

"I don't need the details," Leila's voice was monotone, yet somehow, hearing her mom's voice lifted her spirits.

"Right, of course not. Eww gross. Parents and sex, how disgusting."

"Moooom!" Leila moaned, secretly loving her mom's candor.

"Sorry. How are you feeling?"

Leila rested her head on the door as she traced her fingers over a skull sticker on the filing cabinet. She wanted to tell her mom about the mark, Aileen knew everything about folklore and mythology after all. But something in the pit of her stomach told her to keep her mouth shut.

"Fine. How'd the keynote and conference go?"

"Beautifully, I couldn't have asked for a better crowd..." Aileen paused. "Are you sure you're fine? Is anything wrong, Leila?"

Leila stood up straight. "What? Why would anything be wrong?"

"Shouldn't you be in class?"

"Oh..." Leila slouched against the door again. She hated lying to her mom. "Study period."

"And you decided to call me? Aww honey, I love you too. It's so good to hear your voice and that you are all better. Kale had us worried there for a while."

"Yeah, it was just a quick fever I think..." she lied again, then she told the truth; "I miss you."

"I miss you too, beautiful girl. Are you sure everything is okay?"

Leila realized then, why she so desperately didn't want to tell her mom about the mark. Fear. What if she confirmed everything Riley said about the Guardians, and cemented the fact that she was doomed to become a shape-shifter? Leila bit her bottom lip hard. "Mmmhmm."

"Are you enjoying the meals I prepared?"

Leila sighed, relieved at the change of subject. "Of course. Thank you for doing that."

"Well, God knows Kale wouldn't cook." Aileen let out a light cackle. It was true, he worked in a cafe but he would never cook at home.

"I could've," Leila said, knowing she wouldn't have.

"I didn't want you to. You can blame me for being an enabling mother, but I do enjoy looking after you."

Leila disagreed with the enabling part, the reason why she was a well-adjusted teen was because of Aileen. Yet, most of the ways Leila was similar to her mom, were also the traits that made her feel less than awesome. She blabbered too much, was clumsy, and used sarcasm when she felt vulnerable. But Leila loved her mom, so she guessed she had to love that part of herself too.

Even though no one was watching, Leila flicked her hair over her shoulder dramatically. "Well, you are the reason why I'm so awesome."

"Oh, I know. No doubt about it." Leila imagined Aileen sweeping her own hair back. Like mother, like daughter.

They were quiet for one moment, then they both burst out laughing.

Through the door, Leila could hear a stampede of teenagers rushing from one class to the other. Louder than the footsteps, the bell rang for second period. She knew skipping two classes would be pushing her luck.

"It's been great to talk to you Mom, but I gotta go."

"Already?"

"Yeah, I have class."

"I thought you said you had study period?"

The lilt in her mom's voice almost broke her. Leila

hesitated, trying to think of an excuse. But she couldn't bring herself to say it, so she divulged a different version of the truth. "Well... a self-imposed one maybe. I just wanted to speak to you. I'm overwhelmed with essays and..." Leila glanced at the ceiling. "Other things. I needed to hear your voice."

"I'm glad you called. Now, get back to class!"

As soon as she ended the call, a sudden burst of laughter swept through Leila—a self-mocking jeer for entertaining Riley's theory for even a second. *Shape-shifters? Ha! He talks of them as if they're real.*

As she lifted her arm to grab the door handle, she noticed the band-aids bulging under her sleeve.

They can't be real, right?

Leila covered her forearm with her hand, just in case, and tip-toed down the hall to the English classroom. Entering the room as quietly as she could, she took her seat next to Sadie, noting that Gabby's usual spot behind them was empty. Out of the corner of her eye, she felt Riley staring at her from the other side of the room.

She let her gaze fall on him as he mouthed, "Where have you been?"

Quickly, she adjusted herself so Sadie's head blocked his dread-filled stare. The look rattled her. He truly believed she was in danger.

"Where's Gab?" she whispered to Sadie, hoping for a distraction.

"She's sick," Sadie whispered back as she innocently scrawled over a red C, turning it into a smiling sun. "She has a fever or something."

Leila's heart flipped. "What?" she said too loudly.

"Miss. Belmonte!"

Leila's name echoed around the room.

Past the sea of students looking at her, Mr. Robertson stood with his hands on his hips. Leila's mouth dropped open. Gone was his orange sweater and corduroy pants, his gel slicked hair and pimple scarred chin. Replacing them, were tight jeans and a leather jacket, wild unkempt hair on top with buzz cut on the sides. His blue eyes pierced through her.

As though reading Leila's mind, Sadie leaned over and murmured, "I know, right!"

"Yes, you've got me for English today. Miss. Carson decided it would be a fun idea to not show up without telling anyone." His dark stubble caught the light as he spoke. "Lucky me, huh? I get to fill in... can I have your essay please?"

"Uh..."

"Uh... Uh..." Mr. Robertson stuttered, mocking her. "Uh, you don't have it?"

She could've told him she'd been sick, but he was so damn intimidating that all she could do was shake her head.

Mr. Robertson rolled his eyes. "You can complete it in detention after school then."

A few students in front gave her sympathetic looks and watched him silently as he turned back to his desk. Leila's eyes wandered to Riley—expecting him to be laughing or rolling his eyes at her scatterbrain—but instead he looked panicked. He tore a piece of paper out of his work book and folded it into a paper plane. Without hesitation, he threw it. The plane hit the back of Mr. Robertson's head.

"Who's is this?" Mr. Robertson stared down the class. Some jerk in the back pointed to Riley. Confused Mr. Robertson asked, "Is it yours, Riley?"

"Yeah," Riley said, his chin an inch higher than normal.

"I'm surprised." Mr. Robertson frowned and placed the plane back on Riley's desk.

Just like that.

"Teacher's pet," someone snickered behind him.

Mr. Robertson swiveled on his feet and pointed directly at the taunter. "Detention!"

Riley was busy tearing out more paper, this time from an actual study book. He folded the paper plane and threw. Again, with perfect aim, it hit Mr. Robertson's back. His head pivoted almost the whole way, before the rest of his body followed. Riley sat back in his chair, feigning a careless attitude, almost as if it came naturally to him.

"Riley? Seriously? This is damaging school property." Mr. Robertson shook the paper plane. "I can't let this slide. You have detention."

Riley folded his lips into his mouth and nodded. Mr. Robertson glanced at Leila, squinted, and looked back at Riley, as if trying to piece a puzzle together. His fingers tapped a few times on Riley's desk before he walked to the front of the class.

"What are you doing?" Leila mouthed to Riley.

He glared at her, chewing on the inside of his mouth. Then, he sat forward and returned to his study book.

Did Riley get detention on purpose? Did Riley get detention for me?

TUESDAY

noon

They were in the cafeteria alone. Riley wanted it that way. He sent Sadie on a wild goose chase to find Damien, knowing she would be a while because Damien was in the boy's locker room having a shower. Leila rolled her eyes as soon as Sadie left, she didn't even need convincing—she would have taken any chance to spend time with Damien now he was attractive to her.

"Salad roll, please," Leila said to the lunch lady, watching Sadie run out the doors. She whispered to Riley, "Was that a good idea?"

Riley tapped on the glass for the slop that was supposed to be fried rice. "Why not?"

"He's got a mark like mine."

A quick smile flashed across Riley's face. While he balanced his lunch tray with one hand, he tucked a strand of hair behind Leila's ear.

"He's not a Guardian. Trust me, I'd know."

As soon as they sat down, Riley asked Leila who

touched her on Friday. She did a lot of deflecting, her sarcasm in full force. After a while, and a fair amount of coaxing from Riley, she slowly resigned to the fact he may be right, after all. And once she gave in to the possibility of his theory being truth, a hunger took over. She needed to know all she could about the thing she'd been cursed with.

"What does it mean to be transitioned? When they turn you?" Leila asked Riley, remembering what he'd said earlier that morning.

"You become a Guardian... a Shifter."

"Yes, I know that, but how?" Leila asked, even though she was pretty sure she already knew the answer.

"Bite." He said it so casually, as if he didn't actually understand how terrifying the notion was. Riley had spent a lot of time trying to convince her of how serious the situation was, and then, like an unexpected hailstorm, he became cavalier with powerful words. Like bite.

Leila shuddered and squeezed her hands together between her knees. "Of course."

Riley rested an elbow on the table and let his hand drift to Leila's face. His thumb glided down her cheek. "Sorry. But that's the truth. Don't worry though, I'm going to be with you the whole time. I won't leave your side. I won't let anyone hurt you."

A sweet gesture yet an albeit useless one. If Guardians were as powerful as he said they were, he'd have no chance against one.

Riley continued, "That's why it's important to pin-point who touched you on Friday. So, I can get to them before they get to you."

Leila grimaced. She didn't want to say it, but she wasn't sure how the heck *he* could protect her from something so... primal. He was into books and music, not fists and blood-shed.

"What are you going to do, negotiate? Tell them: hey, thanks for the offer, but no thanks?"

"Whatever it takes." Riley flexed his jaw and pulled a piece of paper from his back pocket. Sliding a pencil out from behind his ear, he added, "But first, that list. Who touched you on Friday?"

Leila took a deep breath. "Kale, Mom, and Dad."

Riley scrawled down the names. His hand writing was nice. Small and round; slanted to the left a little.

"You."

Riley stopped writing. He chewed on the inside of his mouth until it created a dimple on his cheek. Then, he wrote down his name.

"Mr. Robertson, Gabby, Sadie, Taj—"

"Who's Taj?" Riley frowned, a hint of worry flashing across his face.

"Taj. You know. He runs the Chronicle. He gives me alternate surnames all the time." She paused, waiting for realization to click. Noticing Riley's confused face, she continued, "He made a stand against the school's homophobia at Halloween by bringing his boyfriend to the Nightmare Ball...?"

Riley stared at her with a blank expression, blinking slowly. Leila sat up straight and glanced around the cafeteria. She spotted Taj at a table alone, wobbling a pen between his teeth. "There!" She pointed at the same time Taj noticed her. His eyes turned to slits and he dropped the pen to make a thumbs down signal.

Leila suppressed a laugh.

Riley frowned, not understanding that Taj's scowl was harmless. "And he's a friend?"

Leila wiggled her fingers in a wave. "For as long as I've been here."

"Who else?" Riley asked, adding Taj to the list.

Leila scrunched her nose. She tried to forget that nausea-inducing moment under the tree. Leila cringed at the memory. "Sebastian."

"Sebastian?" Riley looked horrified. "When?"

"After school, on the front lawn. He was being weird."

"And how…" Riley hesitated. He scratched his hairline with the back of the pencil. "How did he touch you? What did his eyes look like?"

"Umm, like this." Leila shuffled her chair closer to Riley. She rolled his sleeve up and danced her fingertips from Riley's wrist to his elbow. "I can't remember what his eyes were like."

A low rumble resonated in Riley's throat as he wrote down Sebastian. He put an asterisk beside his name. As though fighting the words, he clenched his teeth and asked, "Anyone else?"

"That's it," Leila said, resting her back against the chair. As soon as she relaxed, she sprung up again. "Oh, wait! I forgot that lady-friend of Kale's."

"Lady-friend? What's her name?" Riley asked.

What was her name? Leila thought. *That night was a blur.*

"I can't remember."

Riley exhaled loudly. "Try. This is important."

"I know!" Leila snapped, more annoyed with herself than Riley. "You're lucky I can recall everyone else."

Riley stared down at the list and with a gentle tone, asked, "What did she look like?"

"Found him!" Sadie yelled across the room. She scuttled behind Damien, her legs taking twice the steps as one of his long strides.

As the two of them lined up at the end of the buffet line, Leila pointed to Damien. "You know what? We should be looking for people with a mark like that."

"What? Who?" Riley snapped his head up.

"Damien," Leila said, wagging her still-pointed finger. "He's one of them right, he's a Guardian?"

Riley stared at Damien for a while. He opened his mouth to say something, but a moment later he closed it

111

again and turned to Leila.

Leila met his gaze. "You can't tell me I've been marked by something, but it's just a coincidence the exact same symbol is on his body. Plus, he's so completely different. You'd be lying to yourself if you didn't notice it... I mean, come on, you're the one who showed me the picture."

"Yeah," he drew out the word, looking at her like he'd created a monster.

"It's settled then. We'll find the person who did this by the mark." Leila tapped her arm.

"Leila, let's slow down a bit." Riley held his hands up. "It's best if you don't do anything. I'll handle it."

Leila shifted in her seat, frustrated. She swiped Riley's piece of paper and tore off the unused bottom half. "I can't do nothing. I can't sit by on the side-line, letting you lead the way. It's me who's been marked..."

Riley sat in silence as she drew a spiral, leading the pen around in circular motion until it became dark and thick and obvious.

"It's me who's been cursed," Leila muttered.

"Whatcha got there?" Damien asked, sliding into a seat opposite them. He looked at the drawing and automatically pulled his shirt to cover his mark.

Sadie sat beside him, snatching the paper off Leila. She looked at it, made a *"that's weird"* face, and passed it back. Looking at Riley, she asked, "You thinking of getting a matching tattoo?"

Riley lifted his face to the ceiling and groaned.

"Not him. Me," Leila stated.

"You want a tattoo? I think you could go with something a little more... *feminine."* Sadie whispered the last word as though she was swearing.

Leila stared at Damien as she peeled all her band-aids off at once. She placed her arm across the table for him to see.

Damien choked on his roll.

"Why doesn't your mark glow like mine? You've already turned, haven't you?" Leila asked.

"Oh, my god! Leila, you didn't? Tell me you didn't!" Sadie grabbed Leila's wrist and pulled her arm closer. Leila's ribs slammed against the edge of the table. "How did they get it to glow like that?"

"It's not a tattoo." Leila wriggled her arm away, still staring at Damien, who was looking everywhere else but at her.

"Oh, thank the heavens in the beautiful blue sky above!" Sadie raised her hands.

"Damien?" Leila demanded. "Tell me how you got yours."

He finally looked at her, his left eye twitching. "I don't know."

"Do you know who else has a mark like us?" Leila asked, this time softer.

"I said I don't know, all right?" Damien swung his legs around, taking an aggressive bite out of his roll. He glanced at Riley, before storming off.

Leila turned to Riley. "Have you talked to him about it?"

Riley watched Damien charge through the cafeteria doors and step outside. "He won't say much."

"Have you even tried to get any information? I mean other than asking him if he's a shape-shifter?" She knew she sounded like a brat, but this was her life on the line. He couldn't drop a life-changing bombshell like that and not expect her to want a deeper explanation.

A slow sigh left his mouth as his hands fell limply onto the table. "I can try again?"

"Please." Leila nodded fervently. "And I can look around for the spiral anywhere."

Riley brought his fingers to his temples and rubbed in

circles. He closed his eyes. "I think it's best if we stick to the list."

Leila understood his reservations—he'd read that book and he thought he knew how to deal with the situation. Problem was, the situation was one that could only be handled by someone with experience. And Leila wasn't the kind of person to sit back and not do anything, she'd already told him so.

"Look, Riley. If you want to be a knight in shining armor, you'll have to find another princess to save. I'm not about to hang back and let you do the protecting. Because whether I become a Guardian, or whether I can stop the transition from happening, I still need to know what I'm in for. Do you get it? I'm not going to hide in my tower."

He chewed on the inside of his mouth, a dimple flashed and then disappeared. "I'm not stopping you. Can you let me speak to Damien first, though? Before you go looking for others with the mark? I'll find out all I can and then we will re-assess. Whether we go through the list or show the spiral around for information."

"Yes, fine," Leila said, realizing her idea seemed a bit ridiculous anyway. She settled back in her seat. "I'll stay here and do nothing."

Riley grabbed her hand, letting his fingers weave through hers. With his eyes still on her, his other hand tapped across the table until they found her removed band-aids. He dangled them between two fingers.

Leila sighed and held out her arm. He stuck them back over the mark. Then, he stood up and went where Damien fled.

Sadie watched him until he was out of sight. She turned to Leila, her wide blue eyes never looking so innocent. "What the hell is happening?"

Leila slid the spiral drawing closer and traced her finger around it. "It's complicated."

"Try me." Sadie crossed her arms, trying to look tough. But Sadie could *never* look tough.

Leila wracked her brain to come up with some kind of excuse. A lame drama project maybe? She could claim dehydration. Or residual effects from the fever. But nothing stuck. Sadie was her best friend, and Leila couldn't lie to her.

"Okay, well," Leila said, leaning forward. "You've noticed how Damien is different?"

"Did I notice? Of course I noticed." Sadie's mouth twisted into a smirk.

"Wipe your drool," Leila teased. "Don't you think it's weird?"

"Yes, and you're different too. Not in a drastic way like him, but more subtle like... well..." Sadie raised her eyebrows. "You've run to school two days in a row."

"Exactly." Leila lifted the spiral drawing. "Something's happening to us. I didn't choose this mark. Someone gave it to me and I want to know who."

"Gave it to you?" Sadie stared, somehow her eyes became wider.

"There's a book that Riley has read. It's about—" Leila paused as a group of students walked past their table. She lowered her voice, "Shape-shifters. It says they choose people to turn and touch them using some sort of magic. First, they get sick, then this appears." Leila tapped her arm. "Then, they turn them."

Sadie was quiet for a moment. She stared at the spiral drawing, her eyes circling around the lines.

She's taking this a lot better than I did, Leila thought.

Then she asked, "Do you believe me?"

"Why wouldn't I believe you?" Sadie looked up and frowned, as if there was no doubt in her mind that her best friend was telling the truth.

"Because, it's crazy." Leila almost laughed.

"Well… yeah, but *you're* not crazy, so…"

Before Sadie had the chance to finish her sentence, Leila hugged her. "You have no idea how much that comforts me."

As she pulled away, Sadie nodded. "I'll do it."

"You'll do what?"

Sadie took the spiral drawing from the table and waved it. "I'll ask around."

Leila stared at her for a second, deciding whether or not she was being serious. "You'd do that?"

One tilt of Sadie's head was all Leila needed to know the answer. It was true, Sadie Sloan could never *look* tough, she was all too pixie-like on the outside. But on the inside? She was an Amazon warrior.

"Okay." Leila looked around the cafeteria and pointed to the Goths at the back table near the exit. "You should start with them… or is that cliché? Maybe the debate team, Riley did say that Guardians like places of power."

"Leave it to me." Sadie tapped her fingertips to her forehead in a salute. "I'll report my findings in T-minus… however long we have left of lunch break."

As Sadie jumped to her feet and headed towards the gymnasium door, Leila settled back in her chair, and dragged her lunch towards herself.

After five minutes, and only a few picks at her salad roll, Leila bounded up. A sudden realization in the error of her ways. In her urgency to find answers, she'd put her best-friend on the front line.

Riley is right, what if the person who marked me is a Fallen?

Without wasting another second, she ran to the gymnasium and swung the door open. Eyes darting across the basketball court for any sign of Sadie. A few boys from the junior varsity team stared at her as she entered.

Don Brand, that one-time kiss, glowered at the sight of her. The movement of his snarled lips made her stomach churn. She wanted to leave immediately, but she needed to know where Sadie went. Despite her mind screaming at her to get as far away as possible, she moved towards them.

"Leila!" Cap called, running over. The others followed him. And soon she was surrounded by four sweaty senior boys.

"How are your ribs?" Cap asked at the same time Don said, "He's not here."

Leila avoided eye contact. "Who's not here?"

"Sebastian," Don answered. She caught a glimpse of his scowl from the corner of her eye.

"Uh, no." Leila tried to step away, but they had closed in so tight around her, there was no gap to escape through. "I'm not looking for him."

"Then why are you asking about his tattoo? Stalker much?" Don taunted, digging the ribs of the person next to him.

"I wasn't." Leila turned in a full circle. It was a good thing she wasn't claustrophobic.

"Come on, we know you got your sexy little friend to ask for you."

"Don't call her that!" Leila snapped, locking her eyes on Don. It was one thing for him to make her feel uncomfortable but lord help him if he tried something on Sadie. Leila was feeling bad enough about sending her on such a stupid mission.

"Sadie, right?" someone else said. "Man, she's a minx — she came in here with those bright eyes that can lull any hot-blooded man into a deep sleep. I'd take a bite out of her any day."

Leila spun until she found the face that matched the voice. Brad: with his ear-length, curly brown hair that looked like it hadn't been washed in weeks. Leila's nostrils flared at the sight of him.

"Calm down, boys," Cap said, calmly raising his hands.

"All right, all right. Your friend was asking about this spiral thing, if we'd seen it." Brad paused to laugh. "I've seen —"

"Didn't that dorky kid copy Seb's design?" Another guy interrupted with a scoff. Leila recognized him as one of Sebastian's friends from that morning. Thomas, she thought his name was. "One tattoo and suddenly he's God's gift to women."

Leila faced him. "Damien? His tattoo is a spiral... wait, Sebastian has the same one?"

Thomas lifted his chin, half-nodding, as though he was too cool to finish it. "On the front of his shoulder."

Leila's heart lurched out of her chest. It was all too obvious. She covered her mark with her palm. *Sebastian marked me.*

"Are you okay, you've gone pale?" Cap grabbed her shoulders to steady her swaying body. The four boys stood shoulder-to-shoulder, staring down at Leila. She could feel her knees buckling as they hovered over her. Shimmying her shoulders between Cap and Brad, she created a space big enough to squeeze through.

"I gotta go," she blurted, running across the gymnasium and into the corridor. She didn't stop running until she reached Riley's locker. He was right to put a star beside Sebastian's name. As she waited, she planted her forehead against Riley's locker and took three slow breaths through her nose.

"You went searching, didn't you?" Riley crept up, making her jump so high she scraped her head on the vent in his locker door.

She turned to him with wet eyes and a bleeding eyebrow.

"Leila! I'm so sorry." He lengthened his sleeve over his hand and pressed it against her brow.

Leila gave a small smile. "And it seems I'm all out of band-aids."

Riley shook his head, eyes twinkling as he pressed against her wound. "Forever with the jokes."

Shrugging, Leila took his hand and pulled it away from her face. She leaned in and closed her eyes, awaiting his kiss.

"I found something," Sadie said, panting. She was holding the hand of Morgan Wakefield, senior cheerleader and debate team extraordinaire. "Show them!"

Morgan's round gray eyes darted between Riley and Leila with fear. She wiped her hand against her perfectly pulled-up hair, which cascaded in ringlets from a high ponytail. Her pointed chin quivered.

"Go on," Sadie urged.

Morgan swallowed and turned around. She lifted her top at the side. There, on her waist, was a glowing spiral.

TUESDAY

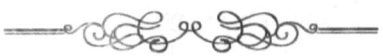

afternoon

By the end of the day, half the class had made it into detention.

Mr. Robertson pressed his back deep into his swivel chair, while his feet were propped on his desk. He rolled a pencil between his fingers, and looked at the clock. Leila stared at him, trying to make sense of the changes in him. Her teacher was different, that's for sure. Rougher than normal. Cleaner than normal. Much more confident, and a little bit arrogant. But why? Could he be a Guardian? If he was, would he be True or Fallen? And if he was True, could he help her?

Riley had told her that he couldn't get anything out of Damien, only that he felt great and not at all murderous. After they found out about Morgan, Riley made her promise to meet them as soon as detention was over. Morgan, who'd been sick all weekend just like Leila, was scared. She'd found the mark that morning while changing into her uniform—and again, just like Leila, she had no idea where the mark had come from. Riley told Leila that everyone on her list was a suspect, but Leila knew it was Sebastian. He'd obviously marked them both. And how convenient for him to not show up at school all day.

If he's not here he can't turn us, Leila thought. *At least not right at this moment.*

She looked over her completed essay. She wasn't sure how legible it was, but it was done, and that's all that mattered. She raised her hand.

"Yes, Miss. Belmonte?" Mr. Robertson sighed, still rolling the pencil.

"Um, I've finished the essay."

Mr. Robertson flipped his hand and the pencil spun in the air. While it careened toward the floor, he motioned for her to come to him. Then, as smooth as a cat, he caught the pencil right before it hit the ground.

Out of the corner of her eye, she saw Riley move. He edged forward in his seat, one foot angled back as though ready for a quick take-off. Meeting Leila's eyes, he gave her a reassuring nod as she passed by.

Leila reached the side of Mr. Robertson's desk and handed him her paper. As his bored eyes swam over the words, she searched his body for any sign of a spiral. But there was nothing she could see on his bare skin.

About one paragraph in, he tossed the paper to the edge of his desk. "Okay, good. You can go then."

"I can?" Leila was shocked. After his unpredictable behavior all day she was half-expecting him to give her another essay to write. Maybe he really was a True Guardian.

He rolled his eyes in her direction and said dryly, "Or, if you want to stay for the next half-hour…"

"Oh, heck no… I just…" Leila looked back at Riley. His hand clutched the edge of the desk; his glasses hanging between his thumb and index finger. His head gave the slightest shake as if he knew what she was about to ask.

Mr. Robertson sighed. "I just — I just — spit it out."

Leila shifted on her feet, hoping to God he didn't tear her to shreds. *He wouldn't do that though, would he? Not in front of everyone.* Leila gulped, pushed the thoughts aside before saying, "Can I ask you something random?"

In the back of her mind, she knew he couldn't possibly be the one who marked her. When he'd touched her on Friday, he wasn't, well, like he was now. He was still oily and nervous, not confident and ripped. He hadn't transitioned, yet.

As Leila dug into her back pocket to grab the drawing, Mr. Robertson stood. He took a wide step around his desk, standing between her and the rest of the class. He stretched his arms high over his head, making a groaning noise as he arched side-to-side. Behind him, a noise of papers scattering and a chair scraping along the floor echoed around the room. Leila leaned around to see Riley waving at her. He pointed to the list, Mr. Roberston's name circled in red.

"What's the question?" Mr Robertson said, taking a seat again.

Leila glanced at Riley. He shook his head again. His mouth made a long oval as he mouthed the word, "Noooo."

"Um, can Riley leave early too?" She shoved the drawing back into her pocket and gave the sweetest smile she could without being creepy or improper.

"No." He picked up his pencil and began rolling it over his knuckles. "Leave or sit down."

She left.

Morgan was waiting on the bleachers, where they told her to meet. Leila had no idea what to do next, but they were in this together now, they both had someone who was going through the same thing. It was dreadful yet comforting.

As Leila got closer, Morgan stood up.

"Come on!" a rough voice called. Across the yard, a shiny sky-blue Nissan idled in the middle of the parking lot. Sebastian leaned through the window, waving Morgan to him.

"Wait!" Leila yelled.

Morgan's head twitched slightly in Leila's direction, but her eyes remained on Sebastian as she continued to walk towards him. Sebastian scowled at the sight of Leila as she began running. He looked back to Morgan, eyes turning to slits. As if by his will alone, she picked up speed.

"Morgan!" Leila yelled.

"Hurry up, hurry up, hurry up!" Sebastian banged the side of his door, watching Leila gain ground. Yet, all the renewed energy in the world, couldn't make Leila fast enough. As she crossed the lawn towards the parking lot, Sebastian pulled away with Morgan in his car.

Leila, furious and confused, tore after them. She chased his car all the way down Murray Street, and around the corner into Hudson Avenue. She passed intersections and street lights. Everywhere he drove, she followed. Slowly, the distance between them lengthened. But she kept running until her breath was shallow and she couldn't feel the ends of her toes. As she saw his car take a left turn at the west-end of the town, she stopped. He could've gone anywhere from there.

"Dammit!" she cried into the wind.

The breeze was stronger down there in the gully. The tops of the pine trees swayed in harmony. It was the side of town where mansions rested on rolling hills. Horses. Million dollar barns. Gated driveways. Leila realized how far she'd run. Her home was on the other side of town. She'd have to double back.

She took a deep breath and set off again. Almost an hour had passed by the time she got back to school. Not surprisingly, Riley's car had gone. She swiveled her bag around and fished for her phone. Five missed calls and two texts. All from Riley.

The first one simply said; *Where are you?*

The second one was more urgent; *Leila? Are you okay? Call me now!*

Sighing, she pressed the call button.

"Where the hell did you go?" Riley's voice echoed through her phone.

"It's Morgan," Leila puffed, not wasting time on apologies. "Sebastian's got her. Thing is, he told her to get in his car and she did. Why would she do that?"

Through the phone, Leila heard the sound of a car screeching.

"Are you talking while driving?" she asked.

"Just did a u-turn, I'm going to Sebastian's…" Riley paused, then said, "At least, if he's got her he doesn't have you."

Leila winced. "She can't be turned by him Riley!"

"I know, I didn't mean it like that. Just go home, I'll call you soon." Riley hung up.

Leila's legs hurt from running so far, but at the same time it was a good ache, like her body was saying thank-you. She needed more, like the wild was calling her. The idea of circling around Rattlesnake Lake before going home invigorated her. Surely, a short detour wouldn't hurt?

After sending a quick text to Kale to tell him she'd be late, she took a right into Main Street. Picking up the pace, and feeling her pulse through each of her limbs, she ran. Air whipped along her cheeks and whooshed through her hair. A wide smile stretched across her face.

Half-way around the lake though, it didn't seem like enough. She needed more air in her lungs, more blood through her veins. More. More. More. Seeing the sign for the lookout—two miles return—Leila grinned. She didn't think twice about tearing up the gravel track.

She zoomed past trees, and the increasing incline didn't slow her down. Opposite to its normal bustle, the track was mostly unoccupied. She dodged a few runners on their way back; they looked at her as though she had two heads. Leila figured they didn't see many school kids running in their uniform with their backpack on. She admitted to herself, she probably looked ridiculous, but this feeling... she'd never felt it before. There was nothing she'd rather be doing, or nowhere she'd rather be, than to be charging through the wilderness with her heart pounding. She felt strong, she felt powerful, she felt unstoppable.

As the edge of the forest made way for clouds, and the gravel made way for a rocky ledge, Leila finally slowed down. Fresh air streamed in through her nose, a small smile lifted the edges of her mouth. She crept to the edge that overlooked the town of Cedar Falls. The Lake looked like a small pond from here. In the distance, on the other side of town, she swore she could see the clearing for the actual waterfall of the town's namesake. It was the first time in the whole day she felt, that maybe, being marked wasn't so bad. As her heart-rate dropped, the feeling quickly passed. Being marked? Becoming a monster? What was she thinking? It was bad. Very bad.

She plonked herself on the ground and unzipped her bag to find her phone. Swiping past Riley's text messages and missed calls, she scrolled through until she found the name she needed. Someone who may be experiencing the same thing.

"Mmmm?" a noise resembling a dying bird echoed down the receiver.

"Gab!" Leila puffed. "How are you? Sadie told me you weren't well. You missed a helluva day."

"I bet I did, always the way... What are you doing? And should you be calling me while you're doing it?"

"I ran up to the lookout... wait, what did you think I was doing?"

"You don't..." Gabby stopped to take a strained breath. "Run."

"It's a new thing." Leila shrugged even though she was alone. "How are you, really?"

"I'm okay, just a fever I can't freakin' shake. I feel like death to be honest, you'd be wise to stay away." Gabby breathed out long and loud.

"Are you itchy anywhere?" Leila prodded.

"Huh?"

"Well, I had that same sort of fever and was crazy delirious on the weekend, I was itchy, too. Just wondering if it was the same thing." Leila bit her lip, waiting for Gabby to tell her she had it wrong, that she hadn't been marked too, that one of her closest friends in the world wasn't cursed.

"Oh right... I'm not, uh, itchy."

"Really? Because, uh, you, uh, always hesitate when you're uh, lying." Leila's voice was light, but on the inside her heart sank deep.

"Listen, babes, I love ya but I'm—"

"Sorry," Leila blurted. "I'll let you rest. Talk soon."

Leila placed her phone into her bag and sighed. Closing her eyes, she took a moment to fill her lungs once more. With her head lifted to the sky, she thought two things at once: *I don't come up here often enough* and *This whole town is cursed.*

A branch snapped behind her, startling a flock of birds into the sky. Leila's eyes sprung open. She spun around, searching through the trees for the cause of the noise. It was hard to see though — speckled golden light hit one side of the trees and created dark shadows on the other. The sun's glow was cut in half by the mountain top, threatening to leave her in darkness at any minute.

Leila realized those people weren't looking at her strangely because she was in her uniform, they were looking at her like that because she was heading into the forest at the edge of night... alone. They would have been hurrying back into their homes, safe from cougars or bears. But man-hunting animals weren't the only predator Leila had to worry about. Somewhere out there, a shape-shifting Guardian was waiting for her mark to appear.

The urge to get home panicked her, she leapt to her feet and ran with wide leaps back down the track. A pounding flooded her ears, like she was surrounded by a thousand woodland drummers, beating sticks against the trees. She couldn't tell whether it was her own heart beat or footsteps — and if it was footsteps, did they belong to her or someone else? She didn't stop to find out.

Down, closer to town, stars began scattering across the darkening sky, mirroring a few shimmery ripples the last sun rays left on the lake. The early evening brought cooler air — it rushed into her lungs and she gasped at the sting.

Street lights begin to flicker on as Leila made her way onto Main Street. She clutched her back-pack straps and slowed to a walk. Being back in suburbia relaxed her. She stayed close to the street lamps, walking faster in each gap. Medium-sized cypress evergreens lined the middle of each street; in the day time, they were beautiful, but at night, Leila tried not to imagine creatures out of their shadows.

There weren't many people around, house lights shone behind drawn curtains — after the recent animal attacks, no one liked to be out after dark. She was the only one crazy enough or stupid enough to dare. It seemed ridiculous to her though, she didn't know why that made any difference, considering all the attacks had taken place in broad daylight. Still, there was a level of fear the darkness brought—more shadows to hide things. When the sun rose again and light filled in the shadows, nothing could stay hidden for long.

Leila instinctively rested her palm over the mark. In the chaos of the day, she didn't realize she hadn't scratched her arm for a while.

A circle of thoughts. What did that mean? Was the mark gone? Maybe the Guardian who touched her on Friday, touched her again to remove the mark. If they can put it there, surely they can remove it, right? Or maybe, because she hadn't turned in a certain amount of time, it had simply disappeared?

All she had was hope in that moment.

Leila tugged at the band-aids and tore them off. Her heart sank at the sight of the spiral. Disappointed, she scrunched the old band-aids into her blazer pocket and told herself to put some fresh ones on when she got home. It was only two blocks away, and every street that bought her closer to her home, gave a little bit more peace. The sign in the distance read Miller Ave, her street. She let out a quick sigh and then sucked in her breath again.

A tightening in her stomach came, an overwhelming urge to stop. The feeling she had experienced in the morning when she bumped into Sebastian returned. She was being watched.

She slowly looked behind her. Nothing but motionless cars and occupied houses. The feeling lessened.

Leila turned back and quickened her pace, eyes fixed on her street. Ten meters away… five meters away. When she reached the turn off, she glanced back. The moon was low in the sky, almost full yet not quite bright enough to make out the moving silhouette. Someone ran from behind a tree to the car right beside her. They were fast, and she didn't hear their shoes on the cement, but she knew they were there.

Again, a tug from the pit of Leila's stomach told her to get closer. And no matter how much her brain wanted to run home, her body couldn't obey.

She walked towards the car and placed her hand on the hood, stretching her neck to get a better look around it. But nothing was there. She walked a full circle around the car and stood on the road, confused. Her eyes searched every other car, tree, and garbage-can someone could have hidden behind. In her mind, she felt crazy, but the tug was a force stronger than fear.

A warm gust of air blew across her arm.

"Hello?" she asked, turning around.

A low growl answered.

TUESDAY

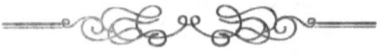

early evening

Thick tufts of silvery-white fur shimmered in the moonlight. Its eyes—blue like tourmaline—were as bright as the sun. Its head was low as it stared at her, paws prodding the ground eagerly. A wolf. Bigger than any Leila had ever seen.

Leila felt her blood freeze as she stepped back. The wolf's mouth opened into a snarl, baring flesh-cutting teeth. Every step she made, it took one forward in return.

Then, as if it couldn't stand the anticipation any longer, the wolf lunged. Leila's heart leapt but her feet didn't move like she needed them to. She stumbled, falling hard onto the pavement. The wolf rushed forward. It's face leveled with hers, shading the rising moon with its body. The fur on its legs tickled her shoulders as it stood over her helpless body. She closed her eyes, waiting for it to crush her neck. With clenched teeth she braced herself for the impending blow. Instead, a drop of saliva landed on her arm. Slowly peeling her eyes open, she found the wolf sniffing at the mark.

This isn't an animal, she thought, *it's the Guardian who marked me… it's here to turn me.*

With the wolf distracted by her arm, Leila shuffled herself out from under it. She stood up, pulling her sleeve down. It growled and lowered the front half of its body, ready to pounce.

"Not yet!" she screamed. "Please Sebastian, wait."

The wolf's head tilted as though it understood her.

Leila felt like she was going a little crazy. She let out a short, almost manic chortle. "I'm just a girl, standing in front of a wolf, asking it not to kill her."

The Guardian remained pensive, hind legs bending to sit. She took the pause in its hunt to back away. The wolf watched her, eyes somehow squinting when her feet hit the sidewalk. As she kept moving backwards, her gaze never wavered from the animal. It exhaled, a puff of mist circling from its nose, then darted off in the other direction. Feet at once frozen, Leila didn't blink until the wolf was out of sight.

When she was sure it had gone, she turned on her heels and ran as fast as she could. Her heart thumped so loud in her eardrums, she couldn't tell whether the wolf started to follow her again. She didn't stop to find out.

Sweeping the corner into her street, Leila swung her backpack around to find her phone. She fumbled through the contacts until she found Riley's name and pressed the call button.

"Leila?" a sweet voice answered.

"Riley!" she huffed, as she leapt over the gate to her yard. "Come to my house. Now."

She dropped her phone into her bag and skidded up to the front door. The sound of footsteps echoed behind her. *Oh god. It's back.* Leila pushed the door open and jumped inside. She flung the door behind her as hard as she could. Breathing fiercely through her nose, she waited for the slam, but it never came. She spun around to see long slender fingers with two-inch claws curving around the door, pushing it slowly.

"Kale?" Leila yelled.

As the door opened and Leila got a glimpse of who the hand belonged to, she gasped. It was Kale's girlfriend. She couldn't remember her name earlier, when Riley was writing his list—but now it was too late, the name flashed in her mind like a bright neon sign. Kiko.

"Leila! Nice to see you." Kiko stepped over the threshold, her eyes glowing red.

"What are you?" Leila demanded, knowing full well what she was.

Kiko's movements were slow. Her iridescent eyes dropped to Leila's marked arm, her top lip curling. Then, she looked up and smiled.

Leila didn't have time to think before Kale rested his hand on her shoulder. "Kiki!" he beamed.

"Kale don't…" Leila raised her arm in front of him to stop him from getting any closer.

Kiko drummed the door with her claws. "It's okay, Leila. I won't bite."

"What's wrong?" Kale asked, brushing Leila's hand off.

"Can't you see that?" Leila cried, pointing at the monster in their doorway.

"Can I see what?" Kale stepped past his sister to embrace his girlfriend. As they hugged, the red in her eyes dulled to their regular brown, and resting on his back, her claws retracted into painted fingernails.

Leila squeezed her eyes shut and opened them again. What was happening? Leila felt the blood drain from her face.

"Are you okay, Sis? You look pale," Kale asked.

"Something's spooked her," Kiko said, reaching for Leila. "You look like you've seen a ghost."

Leila flinched as Kiko's hand landed on her arm. She pulled away and took a step back. She began to think she was going crazy. Maybe it was the after effects of her being sick. Maybe it'd all been one long hallucination. "Sorry..." she stuttered. "I think I spooked myself. It got dark quick... there's been a few animal attacks recently."

"Yeah, well, you need to take better notice of the time. Where did you run? To Seattle?" Kale gave an easy laugh and reached for the door.

Before he could close it, Leila caught sight of a red car pulling into the driveway.

"Wait! That's my ride." Leila burst through the doorway, only stopping mid-point to say, "I'm staying at Gab's tonight."

She shut the door behind her and ran across the lawn. Riley was already stepping out of his car when he spotted her, his face a mixture of fear and relief.

She threw herself into his car. "Let's get out of here!"

He slid back into his seat. "Where?" he asked, as his key found the ignition.

"Somewhere safe... your house?" Leila buckled herself in and nodded at Riley, urging him to hurry up.

"Sure." He waited a few beats before asking, "What's going on?"

"Just go!" she demanded, lifting her knees up to her chest. Leila watched her house as they drove away. "I think I'm going crazy. I'm seeing things."

"Hallucinations?" Riley whipped his head between the road and Leila.

When they turned the corner onto the street where Leila saw the wolf, she dropped her knees and leaned forward on the dash. Her eyes were wide, searching for any hint of her assailant.

"Leila?" Riley gently prodded, as he turned onto Main Road. "Are you sure?"

Leila thought of the wolf, its glowing eyes and tilted head. Then, she thought of Kiko. Kale didn't see her sharp claws or red eyes. Maybe that's because they weren't real. "I had to have been. There was a wolf. I mean, it could have been a regular one, but then I saw these glowing—"

The car came to a screeching halt. Riley grabbed her arm and rolled up her sleeve.

She pulled away. "I only had it off for a few minutes."

"For God's sake!" he muttered, reaching over her to open his glove-box. He pulled out a first-aid kit and passed her a bandage. "Put that on"

Leila didn't object. As she wrapped up her arm, he started driving again.

"You really need to cool it with the searching for whoever marked you." Riley squeezed the steering wheel until his knuckles turned white.

"I wasn't... I was... running." Leila didn't know how to explain it. She felt scared, but also free; determined yet helpless.

Riley's foot weighed down on the gas. Street lights flickered across his face as they passed the main shopping strip. A red streak glistened from his mouth to the bottom of his chin as he spoke, "You were lucky tonight."

"You're bleeding!" Leila exclaimed.

Riley lifted his fingers to his lips, then said, "Oh yeah, by the way, Sebastian didn't mark you."

"What?" Leila sat up straight. "How do you know?"

"I found him. He's only just been turned." Riley licked his bottom lip as fresh blood poured from the cut.

"You're kidding?" Leila asked, swimming through the first-aid kit still in her lap.

"I wish I was."

Leila tucked her knees under and leaned over to dab an antiseptic wipe across the cut on Riley's lip. He turned his face towards her, trying to pay attention to the road, but every now and then, his eyes flitted to her. Leila held his chin still, making sure to be gentle.

"All better." She moved back to her seat.

"Thank you, Nurse," Riley said, smiling.

"So, Sebastian..." Leila packed the kit back into the glove box and relaxed back into her seat. "Was he turned by a Fallen?"

Riley's face dropped. "I think so. He punched me even before asking what I was there for. He's as scared as you are though, he has no idea what is going on. If he was turned by a True Guardian they would have trained him and guided him through it."

Leila frowned. "And Morgan?"

"I..." Riley hesitated. "I don't know. She wasn't there."

Heart skipping, Leila sat upright again. "Well, we should go back and find her, make sure she's safe!"

"Listen, I don't care if she's safe... well, I do care she's safe, but my priority is you now. I can't risk my life for her. I need to keep you safe and if that means not worrying about her, then that's what it means."

Leila looked at him in disbelief. "But you'd risk your life for me?"

Riley parked his car alongside the curb. He sighed and reached across, taking her face in his hands. His light brown eyes hooded over. "Whatever it takes."

Looking past Riley, Leila gaped. They had stopped outside a white weather-board house with cracked paint and a dented tin roof. The fence was crooked and rusty hinges rested where a gate should have been. There was no garden bed, but the lawns were at least mowed.

Riley cleared his throat. "Welcome to my home!"

TUESDAY

evening

"Can we put a pin in the whole Guardian talk until after dinner? I don't want my mom to get caught up in any of this," Riley asked as they walked through the non-existent gate.

His mom? Leila gulped at the dawning realization. She was about to meet his mom.

Taking his hand, Leila smiled nervously, "Of course."

He gave her hand a quick squeeze. As if reading her mind, he said, "It's okay. She'll love you."

Riley led her to his front door and held it open while Leila stepped through. The inside was slightly better than the outside. Wallpaper along the ceiling edge was beginning to peel back, but apart from that, it was clean. Maybe too clean. Borderline stark. A few pieces of furniture adorned the living room; a checkered futon with a small wooden side-table, a tall lamp with black shade stood in the corner, and a television mounted to the wall.

"Mom, this is Leila," Riley said behind her. "Leila? This is my mom, Abigail."

Leila spun around. A woman in her late forties stood behind a bench in the open plan kitchen. Abigail's short gray-blonde hair bounced over her ears as she looked up. Spotting Leila, Abigail's eyes widened with delight. She marched around the bench, passed the dining table and walked into the living room. As soon as she approached them, the whole room became warm and inviting.

Abigail looked at her son as though he'd bought home thousands of dollars to renovate and decorate the house. She wiped her hands on her apron and brought Leila into an embrace. "Call me Gail. I've heard so many wonderful things about you."

Riley had never spoken to Leila about his mom. She glanced at Riley and lied, "You too."

His teeth clenched into a tight smile.

"Are you hungry? Stay for dinner." Gail clutched at the bottom of her apron, looking between the two.

"Actually Mom." Riley rubbed the nape of his neck. "We were wondering if she could stay the night. Her parents are out of town and her brother is busy."

"Oh..." Gail thought for a moment, looking over her new house guest. She eyed the grazes on Leila's legs, the tears through her skirt and stockings, even her blazer had tiny holes in the sleeve. "Sure, of course. Would you like to wash up before dinner?"

"Mooom!" Riley moaned.

Gail lowered her voice, "Well, I don't mean she's filthy I just mean, she might want to..."

"It's okay," Leila interjected. "I *am* filthy... it's a long story."

Gail gave Riley an *I told you so* look and patted Leila's shoulder. Returning to the kitchen, she called over her shoulder, "We're having spaghetti."

"So, that's my mom," Riley whispered, pressing his palm against the arch in Leila's back. "I'll show you where to go." He took a few steps out of the living room, stopped at the end of a short hall, and opened the bathroom door.

Inside, he grabbed the shower curtain with both hands, gently holding it from the top and the side. Pulling it across, he revealed an off-white bath tub with a shower head above. He leaned over to adjust the faucet.

"They're a bit touchy," he said, testing the water with his fingertips.

Leila stood in the doorway, picking at the holes in her blazer. She felt weird watching him near the shower, as though she was getting a glimpse of the part of him only meant for private. Her fingers became entwined in navy blue thread. "I don't have anything to change into."

Riley turned around and swallowed. He nodded and hastily stepped away from the shower, as though he too was thinking what she was. His voice cracked as he said, "I'll find you something."

"Okay." Leila held her breath as he walked past her.

When he was out of sight, she closed the door. She got undressed, folding her ruined clothes into a neat pile on the floor. The bandage came off next. Leila unraveled it quickly and threw it onto the floor. Without looking at the mark she stepped into the bath.

As the water streamed over her she tried not to think of the afternoon's events. The water pressure switched every few seconds from a few sharp lines of water, to slow fat droplets. Riley's house had a few parts that could use a fix up, but she would rather be there than home. Especially if the hallucinations returned, if that's what they were.

A few minutes later, Riley tapped lightly on the door. On instinct, Leila grabbed the curtain and wrenched it shut. With a pop, pop, pop, three rings fell of the rail.

"I'm not looking," Riley said as he stepped into the bathroom and dropped some clothes on the floor.

"I broke the curtain." Leila kept a hold of it against the wall, so he couldn't see past it.

"Oh, that always happens."

Leila could see his shadow as he moved into the room. He stood an arm's length away from her naked body, with a only a sheer piece of material to separate them. Leila's heart raced at seeing his fingers poke over the top of the rail. He hooked the rings back together and sighing, Leila let go of the curtain. Quickly, as if the small gap was too much temptation, Riley pulled it across to meet the wall again. His hand lingered at the edge for a moment, still clutching the curtain. Leila resisted the urge to touch his fingers, her hand dripping with water as it hovered an inch away from his.

"I'll see you in a bit," he whispered before leaving.

With her heart in her throat, she turned the shower off. At least he took her mind off the day's events, if only for a little while.

A pile of clothes awaited when she got out. A light blue t-shirt that smelled like Riley, and some denim shorts that fit her perfectly. As she got dressed she could hear Riley and his mom talking through the thin walls.

"We left Seattle to get away from this and you've found it again? Why do you always get involved?" Gail scolded.

"I care about her." Riley's voice was deeper than normal.

Leila hovered inside the bathroom, trying to find the best moment to open the door.

"You always care about them."

Leila frowned.

"She's different," Riley replied, only slightly appeasing Leila's new concern — he always cares about who?

"Mmm, well, be careful."

The house became silent. Seeing it as her opportunity, Leila crept out of the bathroom. As soon as she stepped into the dining room, she felt the tension in the air.

"Oh look," Gail said, spotting Leila walk in. "I told you

the shorts would fit. I'm glad I didn't throw all of *her* clothes out."

"Who's clothes?" Leila asked.

Gail raised her eyebrows and quickly brushed off the question. "Oh, no one important. You can keep them if you like."

"Thank you." Leila smiled. She turned to Riley, tugging at the bottom of his t-shirt that draped over her. "What do you think?"

He smiled softly, and said, "It suits you."

Riley pulled a chair out for Leila. She looked at him with contemplation as she sat down. She had known him for months, but never knew his living conditions, and he'd never even mentioned his mom. What were their reasons for leaving Seattle, anyway? A messy relationship? Was there more about him she didn't know? Had she even scratched the surface?

"What happened to your arm?" Gail asked, carrying a large pot to the middle of the dining table.

A crinkle formed between Riley's eyebrows.

"Oh." Leila gave a quick glance to Riley before throwing her hand in dismissal. "Just a rash. The bandage stops me from scratching it."

Relieved, Riley began dishing up their dinner. He scooped thin pasta and sauce into three bowls. As soon as he placed Leila's meal in front of her, she began slurping the spaghetti as though she hadn't eaten in weeks. It was delicious, like heaven had been diced into perfect mouthfuls just for her. Moments later, after the bowl was empty, Leila looked up to find Gail and Riley staring in amazement.

"Sorry." Leila lifted the back of her hand to her mouth. "But that was the best meal I've ever had."

"Would you like seconds?" Gail offered, amused.

Leila nodded feverishly.

Riley chuckled. As he scooped another helping into Leila's bowl, he said, "So, Mom. Leila is a really talented photographer. She takes these fascinating ethereal landscapes."

Taken aback, Leila blinked rapidly at the compliment. She'd never talked about her art, even to Riley. But then again, he always paid attention to the most important things.

Gail's eyes lit up. "Do you? I love photography. Although, I haven't picked up my camera since..." She paused, her eyes lifting to the archway between the dining and living rooms.

Riley twirled a fork around his spaghetti. "A while... you should start again."

Leila opened her mouth to ask Gail what she liked about photography, but after seeing her company suddenly retreat within themselves, she shoved a lump of food into her mouth instead. It felt like she was thrown into a conversation where she didn't belong. That was a later question for Riley. She'd ask it along with why he left Seattle... and what makes her different to the other girls he's cared for.

After dinner, Leila stood to help clean up. As she reached for Riley's plate, Gail swiped it away first. "Don't mind about that, love. Go, do teenage things. But remember, I can hear through walls."

Riley's face lit up. He took Leila's hand and grinned. "Come on."

He led Leila to his room, which was right next to the lounge room. His room was small—a bed took up most of the space under the window, and a large wooden chest of drawers sat opposite. Apart from a pile of books on his bedside table, he had hardly any other possessions. Leila wondered why Riley never mentioned he lived like this.

"At least no one would get lost in here," he chuckled, reading her thoughts, again.

"You don't come across as..." She struggled to find right words.

"Poor?"

Leila shook her head much more ferociously than she needed to. "That's... No... I just..."

"It's okay." Riley pinched the side of his drawers. "We never used to be."

Leila perched herself on the edge of his bed. "What happened?"

"It's a long story. What matters is that the rent is cheap and we have a roof above us, right?" He plonked himself next to her.

"Absolutely! For sure. Who needs things? Having more things doesn't mean you're a better person. Of course not..." Leila took a breath. She hated it when she rambled. Calmer, she said, "When you're with family, that's all you need."

Riley cleared his throat and stood up.

Did I say the wrong thing?

"Where is it?" Riley said to himself, looking around his room. He shuffled the books next to his bed and a small speaker revealed itself.

"What was your mom talking about?" Leila whispered, looking at the open door.

He threw a hand up in her direction, as if to say *don't worry about it*. Then, he lifted the speaker up and flipped it around, checking the bottom for batteries.

"She doesn't want me here, does she?"

Riley, still holding the speaker, walked two long steps to the door and closed it.

Getting frustrated with his dismissive non-verbal answers, Leila stood up.

"Remember yesterday when we decided to be more than friends?" she asked.

With his back to her, Riley swept his hair back. He looked over his shoulder with a stiff mouth but smiling eyes. "I remember."

Leila pouted. "Well, mostly, people in that kind of relationship tell each other things."

Riley nodded once. He placed the speaker on the floor, facing it towards the door, and pressed a button—music came billowing out. His shoulders lifted as he sighed, and he stepped closer to Leila.

"We can talk now, without her hearing." He ran a hand along her arm and sat down.

"Oh," Leila said, embarrassed at her loss of temper. She sighed and sat beside him, crossing her legs.

Riley stared at the floor, chewing on the inside of his mouth. He inhaled through his nostrils and turned to face her. "When we lived in Seattle, I lost a bet."

"A bet?" Leila tried not to smile. It sounded like the start of one of those dirty teen flicks where someone ends up eating dog crap instead of chocolate.

Riley's eyes lowered and Leila scolded herself for being insensitive. He was opening up to her, the least she could do was listen without making a joke. She placed her hand on his knee, urging him to continue.

"There was this girl who claimed to know where a werewolf pack lived." He swallowed, eyes glazing over at the memory. "I didn't believe her at first, so we made a bet. She was right. But by the time I realized it was real, and the pack were Fallen Guardians, I was already being hunted by them."

"What?" Leila gasped. Riley hadn't just read about Guardians, he'd seen them firsthand. No wonder he'd been so protective of her.

Riley met her gaze. "They tore through our home, literally, damaging everything we owned. My mom used her savings on the bills to the rental company. We had to move... quickly. This was the only place we could afford at the time. We're slowly building it back up. My weekend job helps."

The missing gate, the broken shower curtain, the peeling paint—it all made sense. And Riley, his fear for her life. That made even more sense.

Leila inched closer. "What was the bet?"

"I don't even remember. None of that matters now." Riley lifted his hands to his head, scrunching his fingers through his hair.

Even though she could see the agony that played across his whole face, Leila needed to know more. "What happened with the girl you made a bet with?"

He winced, as though it pained him to remember.

Immediately, Leila moved back, knowing she'd overstepped the mark. Changing the subject, she asked, "Why didn't you tell me this before, when you showed me the book?"

Riley shook his head and his hands fell limply onto the mattress. "I didn't want to scare you."

The words broke her. They came with a knife and pierced through her very core. She wanted to take him in her arms and hold him close. She wanted to tell him that she was okay. Thanks to him.

She wondered if it would be bad timing to kiss him. The care she had for him in that moment, it warmed her whole body. Her heart felt like it was going to explode.

All at once, the truth of her fate weighed on her. She'd brought this mess into his life again. Just like his mom said. Beneath her bandage, the mark pulsated.

Arm aching, Leila stood. She turned to face Riley and started to unravel the bandage. She felt shackled. Trapped like a lion, pacing along the border of its cage. Riley watched her, his eyes following her movements intently as she hastily spun the bandage around and around. Once it was off, she shook her arm, freeing it from its constraints.

Riley rose to his feet, his face hovering just inches above hers. He ran a knuckle from her shoulder, down her arm to the spiral. His skin was cool and it soothed her rising temperature. As he traced the mark, she closed her eyes, enjoying the touch.

Next, he moved one hand to her waist. His other hand lifted to her face and slid through her hair behind her ear. He breathed in deeply as his fingers dug into her skull. Leila swayed under his hold, the beat of his heart against her chest eased her anxiety.

His cheek grazed hers, as he whispered, "I'll keep you safe. Whatever it takes."

Leila couldn't remember the moment between his warm breath on her neck and his mouth on hers. But there they were, his lips pressing hard—slow and desperate at the same time. She let out a whimper, a light exhale resounding in the back of her throat. He tasted like honey and Leila couldn't even imagine how that was possible. She grasped his shirt, feeling his toned muscles beneath it. She'd never seen him without a shirt, but now, that's all she could think of.

Riley moaned, a quick gasp for air. Leila opened her eyes to find him throw his glasses onto his bed. He grazed his bottom lip with his teeth before he clutched both sides of her face and brought their lips together again. It was forceful yet delicious, like that time she stole her dad's bourbon to taste.

The door clicked open and the speaker tumbled backwards with a crash.

Riley immediately grabbed Leila's arm right where the mark was. He tugged it behind his back. Then, they both sheepishly turned towards the door.

Gail picked up the speaker. She walked to the bedside table, trying not to let her anger show. She placed it down with both hands, taking a moment to collect her thoughts.

"Mom. I swear, nothing was—"

"I've made up the futon for you to sleep on, Leila. I hope it's comfortable enough for you." Gail let go of the speaker and faced them, smiling.

"I'm sure it will." Leila smiled back, nodding suspiciously fast.

Riley and Leila shuffled around, trying to hide Leila's mark as Gail walked past. She stopped at the door and looked over her shoulder. "Keep this open, won't you?"

As soon as she was out of sight, Leila rushed out an exhale. Riley picked up the bandage and threw it at her. Stifling a laugh, he said, "Better keep it on."

TUESDAY

almost midnight

Moonlight streamed sporadically through a gap in the drapes. Every now and then, a slight breeze lifted them and light flickered across the room. Leila sat up, swearing she saw something move near the lamp in the corner. Before he went to bed, Riley told her the window was broken—permanently slightly open. She stood up, stepping over the jean shorts on the floor, and slowly walked to the window. Just a quick peek to make sure the gap wasn't large enough for a wolf to fit through. Cool air trickled in through a tiny sliver at the bottom of the sill. Leila sighed.

As she shuffled back to the futon she saw something she hadn't noticed before. Photos. Four of them in a row along the wall opposite the television. The first photo was Gail and two adolescent children, one boy and one girl. The girl was slightly older than the boy, her arm draped over his shoulder as though she was his keeper. The boy was definitely Riley, blond hair and a dimpled smile.

The next photo was the same, yet the children were older — the girl had braces and her wide grin showed them off with pride. The next photo was just the two of them, much younger — around five and seven years old. They were laughing at each other, both covered in mud. The last photo was obviously the most recent, but with one difference... there was no girl. A simple shot of Riley and Gail, his arms wrapped around her and his head tilted down in a most protective embrace.

Leila looked around the room for any more signs of the girl, but it was bare, like they'd just moved in. She turned back to the photos, to the grinning faces and the bond only siblings could share. *Riley has a sister*, Leila thought, before looking down at the shorts on the floor. *Had a sister.*

She tugged at the bottom of Riley's t-shirt, making sure it covered her underwear and crept into the hallway. The first door on the right, Riley's bedroom, was open. Leila tip-toed in, all too aware of his mother sleeping in the next room. She walked to the side of Riley's bed. With sleepy eyes, he lifted the quilt, and she rolled in, tucking the back of her body against the side of his. He put the covers down, his arm coming with it, encircling her curved body.

"Can't sleep?" he whispered to the back of her head.

"No," she whispered back.

Riley wriggled closer, pressing his chest against her back. "Me either."

How far they'd come in one day. From first kiss to sleeping in his bed. There was no way she could sleep then though, not with all the questions she needed to ask him.

"Riley?" She rolled over to face him.

He lifted a finger to his lips and grinned. "Shhh, Mom will kill me if she knows you're in here. She's nice but strict with... girls."

"Any particular reason why?"' Leila lowered her voice again, trying not to be a jealous girlfriend.

"It's a long story." He shifted onto his back. He wasn't wearing a shirt, and the top of the quilt rested right below his upper chest. The dips of his pecs were deeper than Leila had imagined.

"How can someone who reads more than he talks, have such a strong body?" As soon as the words were out, Leila covered her mouth, eyes wide. She didn't mean to say it out loud.

Riley pulled the quilt up to his neck horrified. "Nerds can work-out too, you know?"

"Yeah, of course, pfff... I didn't mean to stereotype, I know not everyone fits in a perfect little box... you're just..." Leila stopped herself. Sighing, she figured she might as well tell him exactly what she was thinking. "You're smokin' hot."

"Well, if we're being honest?" Riley propped himself up on his elbows, his biceps bulging even further. His eyes scanned along her body. "Then, so are you."

He tucked his hand under the quilt and curved his palm around her hip. He squeezed, pulling her closer to him.

Leila's stomach leapt to her throat, then all the way down to her feet and back up again. When his lips found hers, her heart was already pumping a million miles an hour. She ran her hand from his chest to his torso, letting her fingers fall in every divot they found. They ran down, counting each ab muscle and even when she'd counted six, she didn't stop.

"Wait!" Riley grabbed her wrist and groaned. He placed her hand on the bed between them and sat up.

"Ugh, Leila. Not like this."

"What's wrong?" she asked, sitting with him.

He took her hand again and cupped it between his palms. "I like you so much." He lifted her hand to his mouth. "So much, Leila. Dammit, I hope you know that?"

Leila held her breath as he kissed her fingers. The touch was so light she could barely feel his lips. She swallowed. She wanted to tell him that she felt the same, but somehow words escaped her.

"I know you heard my mom and I talking earlier." Riley squeezed her hands and let them go. The corner of his mouth twitched and he rested his arms over his raised knees. "The shower had stopped a long time before you came out. You weren't meant to hear that. It's not at all what you think. There are no other girls I care about, only you." He looked at her sideways. "You don't have to prove yourself to me. We don't have to rush into anything."

"I like you too, Riley." Leila tugged at the outside edge of her bandage. Feeling vulnerable wasn't her thing. Not with the mark and definitely not with him. The pressure of tears began to rise as they scrambled from her heart to her eyes. "But would it be a bad thing if this happened? What if tomorrow I'm turned and I'm evil? What if tomorrow I try to kill you? What if tonight is all we have?"

Riley shook his head as he slid off the mattress. He stood to face her, his hands finding the top of his head. "I can't be distracted right now. If I'm distracted, then you'll be hurt. What if I'm so caught up in you, I make a choice that ends up seeing you turn? I need to stay focused, I need to be alert."

Leila mimicked Riley's movements and stood on the other side of the bed. A gaping space between them. "Is that what happened in Seattle? With… that girl you made a bet with?"

Riley took a few steps backwards and his shoulder blades slammed into his closet. The sliding doors banged against their rails. Both Riley and Leila paused, eying Riley's bedroom door. Through the walls, a loud snore erupted. Leila sighed with relief.

Riley slid down the closet and sat on the floor, his knees lifting to hold his bowing head. Without missing a beat

Leila jumped over his bed. She knelt beside him. "Riley, what happened in Seattle?"

He looked up, tears streaming down his face. "It wasn't an ordinary girl… it was my sister. She was obsessed with supernatural things. She began staying out late, sometimes not coming home at all. She started wearing all black, stopped talking to us, even went as far as being arrested for theft. Mom was worried she was caught up on hard drugs, but instead, she'd been marked by a Fallen Guardian." Riley blinked, forcing fresh tears to coat his cheeks. "I didn't even notice the change. My sister was out hanging with shifters, meanwhile I'm the high school jock and couldn't care less about anything other than being MVP every game. And by the time they came to turn her, there was nothing we could do to stop it. She tried to turn me, but I refused and her clan destroyed our house. I haven't seen her since."

Leila tried to find words, but nothing seemed good enough. So, she draped her arm across his shoulder and rested her head against his. Underneath her hold, Riley shuddered. In that moment, Leila knew why he was so fixated on finding who marked her. Because he'd seen it… the devastation a Fallen Guardian left behind.

"What's her name?" Leila's voice fell onto Riley's ears like audible silk.

Riley sniffed. "Tessa."

"Did you try looking for her after she fled?"

"Why would I?" Riley clenched his jaw. "She clearly didn't care about us."

Leila thought about Kale; how painful it would be to lose him in such a traumatic way. "I'm so sorry."

"Don't be sorry. I'm not. I would never have met you if we didn't move here," Riley said.

He scooped his hand through Leila's and stood, tugging gently for her to follow. She complied and followed him to the bed. He waited for her to hop under the covers before he laid down and faced her. Leila didn't dare move, transfixed by Riley's gaze. His tears had dried and his light brown eyes smiled as he stroked the side of her arm.

"I have one more question," Leila whispered.

"Mmm?" Riley mumbled, absentmindedly tucking a stray hair behind her ear.

"Was she the same?"

Riley tensed, his hand suspended in the air above her temple. "What do you mean?"

"I mean, Damien is different, but Sebastian isn't really... did Tessa change? Will I change?" Leila didn't know what she was asking. Maybe somewhere deep down she had hope that Fallen Guardians didn't change but True Guardians did, and she felt a little different already, so...

Riley let his hand rest on her shoulder. "I think... According to that book, when you're turned, no matter if you're True or Fallen, your innate nature is enhanced — you become a bigger, better, smarter, bolder, badder version of yourself. So, for Damien, it made him more confident. He was already awesome to me, but he just needed to believe it, too. For Sebastian, maybe there's something we haven't seen yet? But to answer your question, yes, my sister changed; she opened out of her shell, she talked more, she stood up for herself more."

Leila lurched up. Being a bigger, better version of herself didn't sound so bad. Sure, the Fallen part sounded a bit nasty, but there were things she would definitely upgrade if given the choice. Less frizzy hair, for example.

"Leila?" Riley said, waving a hand in front of her face. "Where'd you go?"

She turned her head and smiled at him, resting her chin on her shoulder. "I wonder what will enhance with me."

Riley let out one clear, "Ha!"

"I wasn't being funny." Leila pouted. Although she couldn't blame him if he thought everything she said was an ill-timed joke.

"I know." Riley grinned. Then, his face softened. "I can't imagine you being better than you already are."

"Smooth answer," Leila said, drifting her head back down to the pillow.

"I thought so, too." Riley leaned over. In one swoop, his lips covered hers, and anything she was thinking about floated out of her mind like flour through a sieve. He pulled away, smirking. "I love being able to do that, I've wanted to kiss you forever, you know?"

"Me too." Leila tucked a hand between her face and the pillow. She could get used to him whispering sweet nothings. His lingering gaze seemed to be the only thing that could distract her from the black mark of death on her arm. "And thank you."

A cute line creased between his eyebrows. "For what?"

"Helping me forget." Leila swooped her hand through Riley's hair, amazed by how soft it was.

Riley gave her a quick kiss. "Oh."

Kiss. "You know."

Kiss. "I do what I can."

Kiss.

WEDNESDAY

early morning

"Nothing happened, I swear." A low vibration rumbled beneath Leila's head.

For a moment, she thought she was dreaming, until she dribbled out one side of her mouth. Her eyes darted open as she hastily wiped her saliva off Riley's chest.

"Good morning." He smiled.

"Hey," she whispered in reply.

"Oh. No need to whisper, love." Leila jumped at the sound of Riley's mom's voice. Gail stood in the doorway, arms crossed. "I didn't think you'd stay on the futon the whole night. As long as no funny business went on."

"No, absolutely not. No funny business," Leila said, sitting up straight.

"Hmm." Gail looked between the pair, squinting as though she was having trouble believing them. She turned towards the hallway. "I hope not. Bad things happen when you aren't paying attention."

Gail pushed the door further open as she left.

"She believes in Guardians, doesn't she?" Leila swung her feet over the edge of the bed and looked down at her turquoise toenails.

"Yes, why?"

Leila folded her hands in her lap, suddenly self-conscious of her bare legs. "Does she know about me, is that why she's worrying?"

Two strong hands smoothed across Leila's shoulders and criss-crossed along her collarbone. "Nope," Riley said quickly, before kissing her cheek. Leila watched him scramble off the other side of the bed. As he walked backwards to his closet, he pointed at her. "It's just you and me against the world."

"That's so clichéd." Leila scrunched her nose.

Riley lifted his fingers to his chin in contemplation. "Always together, despite all odds?"

"Same thing." She rolled her eyes, trying not to smile.

"How about, it's our dirty little secret?"

"Please stop!" Leila threw her head back onto the bed and covered her face with a pillow.

"We'll have breakfast and I'll take you home to find a clean uniform," Riley said, closing his closet.

"School? Really? Do we have to?" Leila sat up on her knees to find him buttoning up his shirt.

Nodding, Riley swung a tie around his neck. "You don't want to draw attention. If you're at home, there's an open opportunity for them to find you. At school, they can't do anything with so many civilians present."

"I suppose this stupid bandage stays on too, then?" Leila asked, even though she knew the answer.

Riley lowered his eyes, clearly unamused by the question. "You don't remember last night with the wolf?"

"We still don't know if that was a Guardian, or if it was a real one." Leila leveled both her hands out like scales. "Or... if I was seeing things." She dropped her hands to the mattress.

Riley picked up his glasses from the bedside table and pointed them in her direction. "An actual wolf, in the middle of suburbia? I think we both know exactly what it really was."

Leila's brows furrowed to her eyes. "Can't these last few days just be a crazy dream? Where reality doesn't have Shifters or Guardians or any of it."

"Any of it?" Riley asked, one eyebrow raised.

"Well, *we* are real, of course. I just wish I could wake up from this nightmare without this mark... but still be kissing you."

"So..." Riley smirked, rolling his shoulders back. "It *is* just you and me against the world?"

"Ugh, stop being cheesy." Leila picked up a pillow. She hurled it across the room, a white ball of feather and fury. It landed square on his face and he stumbled backwards. Only his head colliding with the closet could stop the momentum.

Leila gasped. "I didn't mean to throw it so hard, I didn't even think it would reach you."

"Maybe that's you're enhancement." Riley winced, rubbing his head. "Super strength."

"Is it supposed to happen before you're turned?"

"No."

"It specifically says there is no way to turn unless through a bite. You are still completely human, just marked," Riley said, flipping through the book.

Once again at school early, they huddled in the same spot as the day before—in the supernatural section of the library, sitting on the floor between the book aisles.

"So, I haven't been turned? You can say that confidently?" Leila stared at her hands as she clenched them into fists and released them. There wasn't anything physically different, but she could feel it, a power waiting on the sidelines.

"Your mark would have stopped glowing. Besides, you wouldn't be asking that question—I'm sure you'd definitely know if you were a Guardian." Riley slammed the book shut, and a surge of air blew the hair from his eyes.

"Right," Leila said, still confused. How did she have super strength then? She looked at Riley as he stood and placed the book carefully back on the shelf it came from. She wondered how he could be so sure about everything.

As Leila stood, a dim light lit the edges of her dirty blazer pocket. She dug her hand in and retrieved her phone. Reading the text, she began heading for the door. She looked over her shoulder to make sure Riley was following. "Sadie's here. She has the spare uniform I asked her to bring."

"Wait up," Riley said, chasing to catch up with her.

On their way to school, he made her promise she'd stay close to him all day. After what he told her about his sister, Fallen Guardians sounded ruthless. But deep down she knew that the place she was heading, Riley couldn't follow. She cared about him too much to put him through it all over again. For the mean time though, she'd let him think he was helping.

Sadie was waiting for them outside the girls' change room. Her long blonde hair was twisted into a messy knot at the nape of her neck. Leila wondered how much effort was needed to make it look effortless.

"Holy heck!" Sadie exclaimed as soon as she saw the two of them approach. Her lips curled almost to her nose. She looked like an innocent mouse, tasting off cheese. "What on earth did you do? Fall down a ravine?"

Leila cringed and covered her tattered uniform as best she could. But there were too many holes and not enough hands, she ended up looking like she was trying to stop water from leaking through a net. Dead-pan, she said, "I wrestled with a wolf."

Sadie laughed. She pulled a plastic bag from her backpack and passed it to Leila. "I hope it fits."

Inside the change rooms, Leila discovered it was a tight squeeze. The tartan skirt showed too much thigh, and the knitted stockings wouldn't quite go over her hips. Pleased with the decision to wax her legs a few weeks ago, Leila resigned that she would have to go bare-legged. She bent over in front of the full-length mirror beside the showers, just to make sure her underwear didn't show. Next, the cuffs of the white shirt sat too far away from her wrists, so she rolled up the sleeves like it was on purpose. After she'd forced the buttons through and put the blazer on to hold everything in place, she looked in the mirror. *It will have to do.*

Riley was waiting when she left the change room. As she hurried into the corridor, his eyes lowered. "Nice legs."

"Shhh," Leila hushed, backhanding his chest. "No one was supposed to notice."

Riley threw a hand in her direction. "Hi. I'm no one, pleased to meet you. I notice everything."

"Har. Har. Har." Leila mocked laughter as they turned the corner into a bustling corridor.

Hordes of teenagers talked above each other just to be heard. Lockers were slammed, and insults were hurled. Leila tucked her body behind Riley to avoid any collisions.

Everyone seemed so carefree, so innocent, so... oblivious. Leila felt anything but. Not just because of the shrunken uniform hugging her curves, but because of the literal target on her body. She started looking at students with an altered perception. Who else was a Guardian? Who planned to make her one?

As she passed a group of sophomores, Leila glanced over their bared skin. Any hint of a spiral or glowing eyes and… well, she didn't know what would happen. Cedar Falls Academy was a private school, a costly private school. A simple scratch on the floor boards and there'd be an uproar.

"Riley?" she asked, staring at all the ironed collars and faultless ties.

He took a wide step to dodge two freshmen, carefully balancing a giant papier maché volcano between their wiry arms. Meeting back in the middle of the corridor, he said, "Yeah?"

"You're poor, yet…" she picked up the end of his tie and dropped it again.

He ran his palm down the tie, flattening it against his chest. "Scholarship."

"I should have known." Leila smiled and jumped back behind him in time to avoid a basketball flying past.

On her tip-toes to see over his shoulder, she saw Sadie waiting at her locker, which was right next to Leila's. She was talking to someone in a cheer uniform, with platinum blonde hair curled into a high pony. As they got closer, the girl turned her head, searching the corridor with widened eyes.

"Morgan!" Leila proclaimed, pushing out in front of Riley. She jogged to them, glaring at Morgan as if an unwavering stare would reveal if she was a Guardian yet. "What happened yesterday?"

Morgan's face dropped.

"It's okay." Sadie wrapped an arm around Morgan and squeezed her warmly. "You can trust her… And him… you can trust all of us."

Morgan nodded reluctantly, looking everywhere but into Leila's eyes. "I'm sorry for running away on you, I can't explain what happened really. I was drawn to him."

"Like a magnet?" Leila asked.

"Yeah." Morgan looked up.

"I've had the same feeling." Leila smiled in reassurance. She turned to Riley, quickly adding, "Not to Sebastian, just the tug."

"It *is* like a tug," Morgan agreed, her gray eyes relaxing. "My brain was saying *don't go*, but my body had other ideas. I just got in the car with him."

"I totally understand," Sadie piped up, resting her elbow onto her closed locker door. "I get like that with chocolate."

"Book shops." Riley raised his hand in confession.

Leila sighed, amused yet not. "Uh, it's a little different than that. There is no control or choice."

"Uh, exactly." Sadie furrowed her brow. "Didn't you hear me say chocolate?"

"Anyway." Leila turned back to Morgan. "Then what happened?"

"We got to his house out back of Crescent Road. He has this large barn with a huge paddock, horses and stuff. He threw me in the barn, showed me his mark and demanded I tell him who marked me. I have no idea, so I couldn't tell him. He was furious, I've never seen him like that before. I mean he's a jerk but once you get to know him, he's nice... well, he used to be."

"Ha!" Riley guffawed behind them. He cleared his throat, waved his hand in the air, then said, "Sorry. Carry on."

"Well, then you showed up," she said to Riley. "While he was distracted, I ran out the back of the barn and went home."

"I'm surprised you came to school," Sadie said.

Morgan glanced at Leila and then Riley. "I have no idea what's going on and you both seemed to genuinely want to help me."

"Yes, we do." Leila clutched Morgan's shoulder. "I'm so glad you're okay. We're in this together."

"Against all odds?'" Riley dug his elbow into Leila's ribs with a cheeky smile.

Rolling her eyes, Leila threw a thumb in Riley's direction. "He's been doing these awful one-liners all morning."

"All morning?" Sadie raised her eyebrows.

Leila's mouth dropped open. "Uh—'" she hesitated and looked to Riley for help, but he just stood there smiling, waiting to hear what wonderful explanation she'll come up with. But she had none.

"Hey guys." Damien approached with a confident stride and a twinkle in his eyes.

"Damien!" Riley smacked his hand on his friend's back. "You have impeccable timing."

Damien spotted Morgan in the middle of their huddle and flashed a grin. "Morgan, right? I'm Damien."

"I've seen you around. Sadie says you're one of..." Morgan looked up and down the corridor before whispering, "*Them.*"

Damien's eyes narrowed. "If by *them*, you mean good guys. Then, yes, I am."

"Who turned you?" she asked.

Damien cleared his throat and dug his hands into his pockets. Darting his eyes to Riley and back, he shrugged. "Uh, turned me where?"

"She has a mark, too," Riley filled him in.

"Oh, right." Damien exhaled. "Sorry, I can't help. I didn't see a person, they were in their animal form."

Leila looked at Damien. He was standing there so damn casually as if he'd always been this way, as if last week he wasn't walking down these halls with his head low, hoping no one would speak to him. To Leila, he was the key—the one who could fill in the blanks. Riley said he didn't find out much yesterday, but there had to be more Damien knew.

And she wasn't going to rest until she found out exactly what that was.

WEDNESDAY

morning

"Was it a wolf?" Leila blurted, still staring.

"Uhh, yeah." Damien frowned, eyes moving around the group. "I think so. I really can't remember much."

Keeping her gaze on Damien, she pressed further, "Why did you disappear for a few days?"

"Is this an interrogation?" Damien asked, half-smirking.

"Maybe," Leila huffed, crossing her arms.

"Fine." Damien sighed. "I'd just turned. It was confusing. My body needed time to adjust, so I got some alone time until I felt more in tune with it."

"There were animal attacks over the weekend." Leila's eyes hurt from staring too long, but she couldn't blink—she needed to see every facial twitch, every held breath, any sign of lying.

Damien grimaced. "That wasn't me."

Leila flit her eyes briefly to Riley. He was looking at Damien, his lips pressed into themselves in an apologetic smile. Riley believed Damien, but she couldn't let it go that easily. She stood on her tip-toes to get a better look at his eyes. "That's what a Fallen would say."

He returned her accusation with a snicker. "I'm not a Fallen."

"Leila, take it eas—" Riley started.

"What if you are?" She tapped his chest with her finger. "What if you're a Fallen and you don't even know it? You shift and kill people and then you return to human form with no memory?"

She stared harder, her nose flaring with every hasty breath. She scrambled for air, like someone was pushing her under water but she couldn't see their face. Beside her, Sadie and Morgan stayed silent, hanging on every word of the interrogation.

Damien nodded as though he knew what she wanted from the exchange. He reached forward, and clasping her by her shoulders, he lifted her up. Her feet dangled a few inches above the ground as he brought her face level with his. He let her stare into his eyes, to find the truth she was after. With a voice as low as a heartbeat and equally as powerful, he said, "I wish I could tell you more."

Leila couldn't explain why, but in that moment, staring into his harmless eyes, she knew he was telling the truth. He lowered her down and she straightened herself.

"I'm just thinking," she said with a softer tone. "If Damien doesn't know who marked and turned him... and Morgan doesn't know... and Riley said Sebastian didn't mark me... "

Her voice faded out, not liking where she was saying.

"We're back to square one, searching for who did it." Sadie finished Leila's sentence. Eagerly, she offered, "Want to draw me the spiral and I can ask around again?"

"*No!*" Riley snapped. Then, he followed with a quieter, "No. Leila almost got attacked last night. This is getting out of control. I won't have anyone putting themselves in harm's way. Morgan, wrap your mark in something to stop the beacon to all other shifters. We should get to class, we don't want to look obvious."

Leila gaped at Riley. He was often cautious, but never bossy. She wasn't sure what she thought of it.

"Taking charge," Sadie said in a deep voice. She wagged her finger at Riley. "I like it."

Riley gave a smug smile. "Why, thank you, Miss Sadie."

Right on cue, the first bell rang, warning them that class was starting in five minutes. Everyone dispersed to their lockers, except for Riley.

"Ugh," Leila moaned, opening her locker. "Are you always right?"

Riley held her locker door open. With a glint in his eyes, he said, "Yeah, pretty much. It's a heavy burden to carry."

"Carry this!" Leila shoved her study books against his chest.

His feet stumbled back upon impact. He reached for her locker door to steady himself. Missing, his hand swiped the air and Leila's books crashed onto the floor.

"Sorry." Leila covered her mouth, trying not to laugh. "I forgot about that super strength thing."

"Did you say super strength?" Sadie peering around her locker door.

Riley scrambled the books together and straightened his glasses. "Yeah, you'd better keep that under—"

The P.A. speaker crackled. "Riley Jansen, please come to the office, Riley Jansen."

He hesitated for a moment, eyes scanning along the locker wall. Spotting Damien, he took off, turning around for a second to say, "Wait here!"

Leila watched him as he spoke to Damien, pointing to her and then to Morgan as she walked back. She could just hear him as he said, "Don't let them out of your sight."

As he made his way to the school office, Leila rolled her eyes. She really didn't think she liked the bossy version of Riley.

Once Damien had returned, the four of them began walking to class.

"I was wondering," Morgan said. "What did Riley mean by Shifters, I thought they were called Guardians?"

Leila shrugged. "Either, or. It seems none of them are True Guardians."

"Hey!" Damien croaked, offended.

"Except you... probably," Leila teased.

"Okay, wait!" Sadie held her hands in the air. "Can we backup a little?"

"To which part?" Leila asked. When she looked at Sadie, she found a bony finger pointing at her face.

"Something is different with you and Riley. I've got a sense about these things."

Leila laughed. She took a deep breath in preparation to divulge everything—the kissing, the sleepover—but when she opened her mouth to speak a hand touched her shoulder. She whipped her head around.

"Miss Belmonte. Can I see you in the Science Theory room for a moment please?" Mr Robertson waved Leila's essay in front of her and walked down the hall. He stopped a few meters away and glared, impatiently waiting for her follow.

She glanced at Damien and without her having to say a word, he nodded. "I'll come with you."

"You don't have to—" Leila started.

"Yes, I do." He made a point of the words *I do*, as though it wasn't a choice at all. "I'm a Guardian now... a True one. It's my job to protect."

"I'll see you soon." Leila said to Sadie and Morgan, before jogging to catch up. She trailed her teacher, Damien accompanying her close behind.

As Mr. Robertson opened the classroom door, Leila looked at the paper in his grasp. A clear A+ was written on the top corner in bold red pen. Leila baulked. She'd never gotten an A+ before, she was more of a B kinda girl.

Oh god, he thinks I've cheated, she thought, walking into the room.

Mr. Robertson closed the door behind her. As Damien hunched down to peer through the door window, Mr Robertson pulled the blind shut. He turned around and passed Leila the paper. "Impressive work."

Leila waited for the accusation, but it didn't come. She asked a timid, "And?"

"Take your blazer off." Mr. Robertson took a step back and crossed his arms, eyes glaring.

"I beg your pardon?"

"Show me your arm," he urged, annoyed that she hadn't already.

Leila curled her palm over the hidden mark. "I... I can't, the doctor told me to keep the bandage on."

With wild eyes he lurched forward. He grabbed her shoulders and pushed her backwards. She felt her shoulder blades hit the wall with a crunch.

"Wait, please," Leila begged, arms raised in defense.

Her teacher stood in front of her, breathing heavy and fast. With one hand, he held her against the wall and with the other, he pawed at her blazer until it fell off. Mr. Robertson eyed her bandage. Instinctively, Leila pressed her hands against his chest.

"I said, I can't!" she declared, pushing hard.

His face lifted in shock as he careened back, knocking down a desk. He tumbled over it and scrambled to his feet. Huffing, he clutched the fallen desk and pushed it out of his way. As he walked towards Leila, he began peeling his own clothes off. First his jacket and then, his shirt. Half naked, Mr. Robertson stopped a meter away.

"I'm...I'm not that kind of girl." Leila glanced at the door, wondering how many steps it would take her to get there.

"Settle down," he said, cringing.

He filled his cheeks with air, then exhaled loudly and turned around.

On the top of his shoulder blade was a spiral.

Facing Leila again, he motioned to her arm. "Now, show me yours."

Leila's heart raced. She knew it. He was a Guardian. And going from his behavior, he was a Fallen.

"Did you call Riley over the PA? To get him out of the way?"

"Eh." He shrugged. "That kid is stuck to you like glue, what else was I to do? Now, show me."

She shook her head, bringing her arms across her chest. "I'm not ready to turn yet."

He squinted at her, confusion crossing his face.

"I should get to class." She turned for the door.

He moved forward, reaching for her wrist. He tugged her backwards, spinning her around. "So, you're saying you've definitely got a mark?"

She took a shaky breath in, and exhaled, "Yes."

Satisfied with that, Mr. Robertson pulled his phone from his back pocket. Still grasping her wrist, he pressed the call button and lifted the phone to his ear.

"It's me. I have her here... She's marked... Yes, for sure... No, I haven't seen it." He rolled his eyes and let go of her wrist to point at her arm, motioning for her to take the bandage off.

Leila began towards the door.

"Shit, she's leaving... how do I?... okay..."

A magnet-like force squeezed her stomach, forcing her to stop in her tracks. Her legs became lead as she turned around, unable to fight the pull. Seeing her do his bidding,

Mr. Robertson's eyes lit up like a kid's on Christmas morning.

"Right. She's staying put... You want me to sight it? Ugh, for god's sake. Hang on." He put the phone into his back pocket and lifted his hand in a stop sign. "Not gonna hurt you, okay?"

Slowly, he twisted his hand, and claws grew where his fingernails had been. His eyes turned green—bright green, like a neon sign. In one emphatic strike, he tore through the bandage, and it fell to the floor in shreds. His head tilted as he retrieved his phone. "Visual confirmation coming right at you. Are you happy... No, well, I didn't mean it like that..."

His brows lowered and Leila could have sworn he looked at her with sympathy. The tug in her stomach disappeared. Leila dropped to the floor and scrambled to collect the pieces of her bandage.

"I'll do my best. Her boyfriend's very leech-y. Bye Tsukiko." Mr Robertson hung up and said, "You're a wanted girl, Miss. Belmonte."

As Leila fumbled to tie the ripped bandage back together, she tried to make sense of what was happening.

Tsukiko? Did she mark me? Are they Fallen or True? Are they helping me?

But the only words she managed came out as a squeak. "Can I go now?"

Mr. Robertson knelt with her. "Listen, you can't hide forever. You know that, right? They'll sense you, eventually. And if you refuse transition, your face will join the newsreel, added to the growing list of animal attack victims. Do you get that? You'll be the one the Fallen will hunt."

Leila gasped. "Are you threatening—"

The door sprung open. Leila looked up to see Riley standing in the doorway. His eyes were panicked, as were Damien's behind him.

169

Mr Robertson looked at them with indifference. He casually stood up and put his shirt back on. "Don't you kids have class?"

"What's going on?" Riley's chest rose as he stepped with aggression towards the teacher-turned-shifter.

Leila looked at the 'new' Mr. Robertson, he was huge... and tall. Tall and huge. If Riley got a split lip from Sebastian the day before, he'd be no match for this guy. She covered her arm as best she could and leapt to stand between them.

"It's fine," she said, pushing Riley towards the door. "Let's go."

WEDNESDAY

late morning

Leila re-read the first paragraph of the last chapter for what seemed like the sixtieth time, but the words on the page made little sense. Letters became blurry as they jumbled together into a sea of spirals. She blinked and the letters snapped back into their rightful place. Even black ink couldn't break through the cycle her mind was on.

She hadn't been seeing things the night before, the glow in Tsukiko's eyes were as real as Mr. Robertson's. If her calculations were correct, she began incubation the moment Kale introduced them to each other on Friday night.

She dragged the open book back towards the edge of the desk and lifted it upright. Looking up at Mrs. Wilson to make sure she wasn't watching, Leila slipped her phone into the crease of the book.

Kale! She began texting, wondering how to word the next part...

Stay away from Kiko, she's a shape-shifter.

No.

Has your girlfriend given you a mark?

No.

Don't let that bitch bite you.

No.

How was your night with Kiko?

Sent.

"Okay guys," Mrs. Wilson broke the silence in the room. A collective thump of books closing echoed around the room. Leila carefully shut the book and slid her phone onto her lap.

"If you haven't finished, that's your homework. Next time, I want to discuss what you think Orwell meant with the phrase: 'Some are more equal than others'."

Leila felt a waft of air on her neck. She imagined Taj had just flung his hand into the air behind her.

"Next time, Taj, we'll discuss it next time." Mrs. Wilson sighed.

Leila smiled to herself as Taj said, "You know me, Mrs. Wilson, eager as a beaver."

Mrs. Wilson looked up at the clock, there were still a few minutes until the end of class. As Leila kept her eyes on her teacher, hoping for an early reprieve, her phone buzzed in her lap, making one loud *ding!* Mrs. Wilson pursed her lips together, causing the lines around her mouth to deepen. She stared in Leila's direction. Leila looked at Sadie beside her, and Sadie returned with a 'don't-you-dare-throw-me-under-the-bus' glare.

"It was yours, Leila Bel-busted," Taj said, behind her.

Leila spun around in her seat and glowered. Was this his quirky attempt at payback for missing the game on the weekend? Her annoyance didn't last long when she noticed a row of Care Bear badges lining his lapel.

"It's in your lap," he added, pointing cheekily.

"Thanks, Taj." Leila pushed her chair onto its back legs

172

and leaned over his desk, whispering, "Are we even now?"

He smirked and lifted his chin. "Welcome. And nope, not even close."

"All right, you can all—" Mrs. Wilson didn't finish her sentence before chairs scraped along the floor and students began racing for the door.

Leila took the chance to check Kale's reply.

Kik went home. Nite = boring. Talked 2 mom 4 hr… think she misses us. Boys comin to watch game 2nite. Hope u dont mind.

Relieved, Leila tucked her phone into her blazer pocket. Now she knew that Kale was safe and that Kiko had gone back to Seattle, she felt the pressure drop a little. A small win. She strode towards the door and as she was about to step out, Taj darted out in front of her.

"Wanna know how you can make it up to me?" Taj gave a lop-sided smirk. Without waiting for her reply, he said, "Get me a scoop. A sordid photo. Something so juicy, it will make even me blush. Until then, you're on my black-list."

He glanced over Leila's shoulder, sucking in his breath. He fanned his face as he left. Wondering what he was looking at, Leila turned around to find a sheepish Riley right behind her. She jumped back, hand to her chest.

"Dude! Give me a heart attack, why don't you."

Riley squinted.

"You forgot about me? Leila, did you forget about your…" he lowered his voice, "You know, mark? Did you forget about the fact that someone is waiting to turn you? You can't just forget. And that was Taj, right? He's on the list rememb—"

Of course she remembered, it was all she could think about. She was sick of thinking about it, sick of hearing about it. Someone was waiting to turn her, and according to Mr. Robertson, if she refused they would kill her. Either way, she was toast.

She looked at Riley's earnest face, and a hollow feeling took over the place where her feelings for him lived. Since he told her about his sister becoming a Fallen, the more she thought of him in a romantic way, the more selfish she felt. No matter how much she wanted to be with him, she couldn't shake the fact that she was dragging him back into a world he tried so hard to escape.

Considering what happened with Mr. Robertson that morning; considering Morgan, Damien, and Sebastian; and considering Kiko, she knew she needed more than Riley showing her pictures in an old dusty book from the library.

She needed someone with knowledge. She needed an adult. She needed her mom.

"I'll see you in the cafeteria. I'm going to the bathroom," she stated, giving him no time to object before running off.

In the girls' restroom, she locked herself into a stall at the end of the row. She stared at her phone, her finger hovering over the call button.

"You're not skipping school again Missy, are you?" Leila's mom teased as she answered the phone.

"It's lunch," Leila replied, sitting down on the closed toilet seat.

"I know, I know. You must miss your momma, calling two days in a row."

Leila squeezed her eyes to stop the tears and said, "Yeah, I do."

"I miss you, too."

Leila thought about the day before, how she wanted to ask her mom about Guardians but was too afraid of it all being real. At the time, she had only heard the theory of them... but now, she had experienced them—in all their glowing-eyed and sharp-clawed glory. It was time to involve an expert.

But how would she do it without actually telling her mom about the mark on her arm? That was the tricky part. Because she couldn't really tell her mother everything. It was bad enough her friends were involved, it was bad enough how close Kale was to Kiko. She couldn't live with herself if something happened to her parents. She'd have to get the information some other way.

"Mom?"

"Yes, honey?"

"Can I ask you a weird question?" Leila's voice was soft like a mouse.

Aileen was fun and quirky and all things whimsical, but when her children showed any hint of distress or pressing need, she switched into protective mother mode with ease. "You can ask me anything, you know that."

Leila swallowed, trying to think of how to word it without sending her mother off the hotel bed and into a speeding car. "Right, well, this is for a project I'm doing on folklore."

"Ha! What are the odds? They give you a project on a topic your mother is prolific in! Lucky you."

"Actually, we were asked to choose our own topic." Leila covered her eyes with her palm, glad her mother couldn't see her lying face.

Silence.

"Mom?" Leila dropped her hand, could her mom tell she was lying by voice alone?

"I can't believe you'd choose that," Aileen finally said. "I didn't know it interested you. Oh my goodness, I'm so honored. Leila, this is so incredibly amazing. What do you want to know? Where shall we start? You've actually always loved mermaids… well, not always, but when you were three you asked me if you could be a fish when you grew up, it was adorable. Do you still like mermaids?"

Leila let out a half laugh, half exhale. Having her mom

distracted by her passion was a good start, maybe she could get away with being more direct? "So, I'm focusing on shape-shifters?"

"Ooh, yes, what about them? It's a very wide topic, you know."

"And the spiral mark," her voice lifted at the word mark.

"Spiral mark?"

Trying to sound casual, Leila elaborated, "Yeah, there's a book here that shows a picture of a shifter that has a spiral mark, like a tattoo."

"Hmm. I've not come across this in my studies. I can tell you about shape-shifters but not the spiral. What is this book? Do you think your information is wrong?"

Leila glanced to her covered arm and cleared her throat. "I hope so."

"What was that?"

"Nothing," Leila snapped and quickly veered her mother back on track. "So, shape-shifters? What do you know?"

"Well, the most commonly known shape-shifters are werewolves and vampires, although there is a popular upturn in curiosity for the metamorphosis from human to animal—"

"Yes, that's it, they're what I'm studying! Human to animal. What kind of animals?"

"Any really. Birds, carnivores, fish… the mermaid myth is an example of a half-human half-animal type. My grandmother used to tell me the Celtic stories of a lady who turned her step-children into swans because she didn't want to take care of them… that's what started my interest in mythology and folklore." Leila cringed. This was why she never talked with her mom about her work. Verbal diarrhea at it's finest. Leila spun the almost empty toilet roll, wondering when her mom was going to take a break. "There are so many different versions of where the mythology of shape-shifting from humans to animals started. I think you have to pick one avenue and run with it. There's the legend of Dracula, and then there's Jekyll and Hyde, but that's not animal shifting is it? What about the Armenian lore of the Nhang..."

We're in Armenia now? Leila rolled her eyes.

"But then the Native Americans have their own stories that are intriguing, too. Oh, I almost forgot, the Japanese have Kitsune's that are very interesting. They believe that all foxes have the ability to meta-morph into humans."

As her mother paused for breath, Leila took it as her chance to reel the topic back in. "What about the mythology of Guardians?"

"You mean Greek mythology? Athena and Zeus? They aren't shape-shifters."

"No, I mean Shadow Guardians."

"The what? Shadow Guardians?" Aileen cleared her throat. "Are you sure you've researched properly, spirals and Guardians, where did you hear that, Leila?"

The hair stood up on Leila's neck. How could her mother not know what she was talking about? "What *do* you know about them?"

"Well, nothing honey, they aren't a part of anything I've studied."

Leila recalled Riley telling her that the history of Shadow Guardians had been hidden in stories and legends. But were they hidden so much that even an expert didn't know anything about them at all? "Do you believe in vampires and werewolves and the nan and things you have studied?"

"Nhang."

"Whatever," Leila growled, annoyed at the pointless conversation. Her mom couldn't help her after all. Not if she didn't believe in it. "Do you think they are real, or do you study it just for fun?"

"I… I find it interesting, obviously."

Leila stood up, running her hand through her hair. "Just tell me," she said, voice shaking. "Do you believe it?"

"Leila, you're being weird. Are you sure everything is okay?"

Leila kicked the door, causing the top half to break off its hinges. The door hung, twisted, pulling at the bottom hinge. Leila caught a glimpse of her reflection—glaring back at her were wild eyes she didn't recognize.

"I'm fine. I gotta go." She hung up before Aileen had the chance to respond.

Immediately, Leila dropped her head, horrified at what she'd just done. She'd never hung up on her mother before. Her fingers tapped hastily as she sent a text.

Sorry for being rude, I'm just stressed over the workload. Love you.

WEDNESDAY

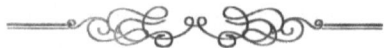

noon

Taking a long breath, Leila moved to the basin. She wet her hands and splashed her face, looking up in time to see the door swing open. Morgan and her friends walked in laughing.

One was Crystal—the head cheerleader, with perfectly coiled brown hair. Leila had never spoken to her before, but Crystal glared at her as though they'd been long-time enemies.

Leila couldn't remember the other girl's name. Bridie or Brittany or Bianca. Her hair was almost identical to Morgan's and Leila wondered who was mimicking who. Now that she knew Morgan a little bit, she couldn't imagine her being someone who cared much for trends. But that may have been because she'd only seen the vulnerable side—the side that had forgotten about what it took to be popular and focused on survival instead.

"Whatcha doin', Mutt?" Crystal asked before turning to her friends for approval.

"Don't call her that." Morgan shot Leila an apologetic glance.

The girls stood on either side of Leila to fix their hair and run gloss over their lips. Morgan's doppelganger eyed the way Morgan tucked a stray hair back into her pony tail and did the same, even though she had no strays. Leila smacked her lips together to hide a grin.

Noticing Leila staring, Crystal pouted and said, "I don't know how you do it."

Leila turned her attention to Crystal. "Do what?"

"I mean, I might positively die if my hair was such a weird mass of dry curls. I love how upbeat you are about the un-fixable situation."

Leila squeezed the sides of the basin, and bit back, "That's fascinating I was just about to ask how someone who has such a shriveled black heart still manages to have friends."

"What did you say?" Crystal scowled.

Leila pushed away from the basin and grabbed a paper towel. She turned to face the cheerleaders. "I said..." she stopped talking when a searing burn ran through her mark.

"That's what I thought," Crystal scoffed. "You know nothing about me, you tight-clothed cow. So, it's best if you keep your mouth... what's wrong with you?"

Leila dropped the paper towel and covered her stomach. A pull, stronger than any of the times before, yanked her backwards towards the restroom door. She stumbled under her feet, as they moved against her own volition.

"Answer me, Mutt. What's your problem?"

Ignoring Crystal, Leila grasped Morgan. "You feel that?"

"No, is it the magnet?" Morgan whispered, holding onto Leila.

Leila nodded. Fear gripped her, but it had nothing on the pull. She opened the door. Morgan rushed through, holding it open.

"Where are you going, Morgan?" Crystal demanded, grabbing her by the wrist.

Leila surged past Morgan, turning back to see her try and break free from Crystal. "Wait, I have to—"

"What you *have* to do, is tell us about your time with Seb. We saw you leaving with him yesterday. Is he everything we imagine him to be in bed?" Crystal tugged her back into the bathroom and the door swung shut.

Leila stared at the closed door, but she couldn't wait for Morgan, she needed to go… now!

As she walked, the distance between the cafeteria—and Riley—widened. With every step the tug grew stronger, and soon her walk turned into a run. She blasted through the entrance doors and hooked a left towards the bleachers.

An orange blur darted across the field.

Is that a fox?

She ran around the bleachers, the pull dragging her closer. The fox stopped between the goal posts and slowly turned around. It's burnt orange fur stood on end, shimmering like silken strands in the breeze. Two large ears sat on its head, twitching. It had a bushy tail that swished side to side as it contemplated its next move. It stared at her for a moment, eyes glowing as bright as the sun, then it spun around, ran under the scoreboard, and leaped into the edge of the forest. Leila ran across the field, straining her eyes to see where it went. But every step closer seemed to reduce the pull in her stomach. When the feeling had subsided, she knew the fox was gone.

"Leila?" a voice called behind her.

Startled, Leila span on her heels. Cap strolled across the field toward her as his team mates sat on the bleachers, staring.

Glancing back to the forest edge, Leila saw something along the tree line... a person. They had long black hair with blonde highlights at the tips, and her eyes were glowing red. Tsukiko. She flattened her hair as her eyes went back to normal. Her head tilted, and a saddened expression fell over her face. Leila swore she could see Kiko mouth the words, "Oh, Leila." Then, as quick as the fox did, she turned and ran deeper into the forest.

"Leila, are you okay? You ran out across here like you saw a ghost?" Cap said, reaching her. His band of friends now stood at the side of the field in front of the bleachers, whispering to each other. Sebastian was with them, and Don. Leila cringed, trying to avoid their stares.

She looked at Cap, his dark blue eyes had a sense of kindness to them, and in that moment she saw why he had been Captain for so long. A gratefulness flooded over her. If he hadn't been there, what would Kiko have done? It didn't feel as straight forward as death anymore though. She didn't know what to think.

It was a little odd though. That Leila's well-being was his first comment? Did he not see Kiko in her fox form? Leila didn't want to risk bringing it up.

"Um, yeah," she replied, throwing a hand in the air. "I run now."

"Okay," Cap laughed. His eyes twinkled in the midday sun.

"Yep," she nodded, itching to get back into the building and surround herself with people... a whole lot of people.

The bell for end of lunch rang out.

As they walked back towards his friends, Cap asked, "Are you going to the waterfall?"

"The waterfall?"

Cap gave her a look that was a cross between thinking she was crazy and genuine pity. "It's that time of the month."

"Excuse me?" Leila gasped, appalled that he would mention such a thing. "That's personal."

Cap's brows met his eyes, he smiled in amusement. "Ha! No... it's the first Wednesday of the month."

He could forgive Leila for forgetting the occasion, she'd only been a couple times, mostly dragged out by Gabby. It wasn't her favorite scene—a forest full of horny teenagers not knowing how to hold their alcohol, meeting for an unsupervised party at the waterfall, in the middle of Winter. No monthly tradition could persuade her.

Her not-so-enthusiastic face must have shown. Cap upped his game. His hand slid down her arm and squeezed her wrist.

"Please come, I'd love to see you there. Bring your friends."

Leila blinked a few times, taken aback. Not because it his action was sleazy, quite the opposite really.

The girls in the bathroom would be horrified that he's out here talking to me, little ol' Mutt, Leila thought, gleefully. *But it doesn't matter anyway... I won't be going.*

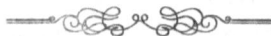

Leila's knuckles hovered an inch away from the Earth Science door. The whole Kiko experience changed everything. What did she know? Kiko asked Mr. Roberston to get proof of her being marked. Then, she came to school just to test it for herself by calling Leila with her fox Guardian. But did either of those facts mean she marked her? And if she did, was she a Fallen? As scary as they all seemed to be, maybe they were truly concerned for her. Plus, if Mr. Robertson wanted to hurt her, he had plenty of opportunity that morning. If Kiko wanted to turn her, she would have pulled her all the way into the forest.

Only one way to find out. Leila pulled her arm back

and as she thrust it forward to knock, a smooth palm caught her hand.

"What are you doing?" Riley huffed, dragging her down the corridor.

"I thought that he might give me some answers. If—" Leila stopped when she felt Riley's grip on her tighten.

He halted mid-stride and huddled her against the wall. "Where the hell have you been?"

He placed his hands on the wall behind her head, boxing her in. His eyes were hooded and deep as he stared down at her. His breaths were short and fast.

"It's okay, I'm fine," Leila whispered, trying to placate him. "I was on the phone to my mom. You know she's a folklore fanatic, I wanted to see what she knew."

"This stuff isn't in normal folklore. I told you that the mainstream has diluted, manufactured, embellished and separated the truth," he hissed back.

Riley had upped his game since morning. He'd gone from endearing and bossy to downright hysterical. Leila decidedly did *not* like it.

"Well, it was mainstream enough in that book in the library, so why wouldn't she know about it?" She ducked underneath one of his arms and stepped out of his barricade. She marched down the hall towards the art studio. "I have to get to class."

Riley frowned, following her along. "And what did she say?"

"She didn't know anything."

Riley raised his arms to the heavens. "You're driving me crazy, Leila. I thought we made a deal to stay together. You were being turned on the roof for all I knew. Keep me in the loop from now on. Tell me where you are at all times."

Stopping outside the art studio entrance, Leila held onto the door frame. He was right, and she hated it. She'd been taken all the way to the edge of the forest by Kiko against her will. Next time, she might not be so lucky. Knowing that sort of thing could happen at any moment was disconcerting to say the least. Worse still, it could happen when he was nearby and he could get hurt in the process.

She felt his eyes bore into her as she looked over her shoulder and said, "I'll see you in biology."

"Wait!" That wasn't the end of it for Riley. He followed her into the room. Students were hunched over tables working away on clay sculptures. They were oblivious to Riley's abrupt entrance, all except Damien, who swiveled in his chair at the front of room.

Leila took a breath and turned, staring at the black frame of his glasses so she didn't have to look into his terrified eyes. He took her hand and lifted it to his mouth, giving her knuckles a tender kiss. "Look, just don't wander off anymore. You're scaring me."

She fought the urge to tell him about Kiko being a fox Guardian; about the fact if she didn't transition she would be hunted by the Fallen. She fought the urge to tell him about how the instinctual pull could lure her away at any moment. Was it because she didn't want to scare him even more? Or was his over-protectiveness actually bothering her? Maybe a bit of both.

"It's going to be okay," she lied, sweeping his hair off the rim of his glasses.

Riley's breath quivered as he kissed her hand again. "I don't know if I could live with myself if something happens to you."

I could say the same thing.

"Mr. Jansen, I don't believe you're in this class," Miss Little said, strolling into the room.

Riley dropped Leila's hand and pointed to Damien. Then, he pointed to Leila. Damien nodded as Riley backed out of classroom.

"You're in trouble," Damien stifled a laugh as she sat next to him.

"He's just scared." Leila ran a hand over her stomach. Remnants of the fox's call still lingering. "If I'm honest, I'm scared, too."

"It's not so bad you know, this whole Guardian thing. He acts as if it's death." He nudged her with his elbow.

She looked at him. His chin was up, his shoulders were back and chest risen. Confidence oozed from the tip of his new hair-style to the phallic looking clay between his palms.

"What. Is. That?" she asked disturbed.

"It's a beak, you know, of a bird. Do you like it?" He held it up on display, mocking pride for his creation. "Wanna help me finish the rest of it?"

As she laughed at how untalented he really was, she hoped to God that whoever marked him, marked her too.

WEDNESDAY

early afternoon

A deformed clay sculpture of an eagle's head later, Leila was slow to gather her things. She had tried her best not to think of Kiko and her fluffy orange tail, but those ominous red eyes kept flashing on repeat. Should she ask for her help or not? That was the question of the moment.

Her next class was biology, which she found ironic after everything she'd learned about some humans not being humans but something else entirely.

She glanced at her phone to see a message from Sadie lighting the screen; *I'm at my locker.* Leila smiled. Sadie was the perfect person to break the cyclic visions of a fox turned human. All she had to do was make a few comments about anyone at school, and Sadie would begin rambling about who that person had a crush on, a breakdown of their eating habits, and somehow lead into what college they'd end up at.

"What's with the turtle mode?" Damien asked, waiting at the side of their table. "Is this why you're always late?"

"Sorry, my mind is preoccupied," she said, standing up.

"I know. But don't worry, Riley's on the case." With a wide smile, Damien swung his arm in front of him as though he was about to sidestep into a chorus line and belt out a theatrical number.

Even though it was obvious he was a True Guardian, his jovial attitude confused her. Couldn't he see that Riley being on the case was decidedly not ideal? In fact, it was downright dangerous. She wanted to tell him so, but he was distracted by his phone.

She glanced at him sideways. "That's him, isn't it? He's probably telling us to meet him somewhere *immediately*."

"Give the guy a break, he really cares about you."

"Yeah," she sighed. "That's the problem."

Damien smiled sympathetically as he showed Leila his phone.

I've got to go do something. Watch her with your eagle eyes.

Leila sighed again and rushed towards the door. "I think I'll be okay to walk to the lockers without my own personal bodyguard."

Damien ran, beating her to the corridor. He stopped, wagged a finger in front of her face, and said, "Uh uh."

One last sigh from Leila — an inhale that gave up on the small window of escape, and an exhale to accept that this was her life now. At least if something went down, he had the strength to fight. "Come on, then."

They found Sadie at her locker with her phone to her ear. As they approached, she let out a loud, "Ugh." Locking her phone, she said, "No answer. I've called Gab five times since last night."

"It's day three incubation, she'd be at her worst," Damien stated.

Leila swung her head so fast in his direction she almost snapped her neck. "What did you say?"

Damien's eyes widened. "Uh, I mean—"

Side by side, the girls glared at him.

"Should you be telling us something?" Leila questioned.

"Freaking hazelnut fudge on a salty cracker, you girls have a killer vibe going on." Damien nervously laughed at his own joke while taking a few steps back. "I, uhh, I don't know. I just assumed, everyone else has the mark, why not her too, y'know?"

"Baloney!!" Sadie cried, flinging her arms into the air.

Leila followed Damien, her finger tapping hard on his chest. "You'd better tell us now, or I swear to god, Damien!"

"What?" he said, trying not to smile. "You'll what? Stare at me? I'm a Guardian, Leila, have you seen my muscles?"

One side of her mouth stretched into a menacing smirk as she spread her fingers across his chest. She pushed, showing him exactly what she was capable of. He skidded along the ground, bending forward at the waist for stability—legs, arms, and eyes wide. As he came to a stop, his head lifted and a tiny golden sparkle flickered across his eyes.

Leila charged towards him. By the time she reached him his eyes were completely golden. He lowered his head so no one could see. She grabbed his collar with both hands and forced his chin up. "Tell me what you know about her."

"How are you doing this? Have you turned?" He lifted a hand to her wrist, trying to make her let go—his fingers circled around, talons growing from their tips.

Leila scrambled to the nearest empty class room and kicked the door open. She pushed him inside. "Talk. Now!"

Sadie ran in after them and closed the door. "What the hell is happening?"

Damien raised his hands. "Seriously, I don't know if Gab has been marked. I'm sorry for scaring you but come on, it's pretty obvious, right? Has she been itchy?"

"She told me no," Leila said at the same time Sadie said, "Yes."

"She has?" Leila turned to Sadie.

"Mmhm, she told me her symptoms on Monday night."

Damien gave Leila an *I told you so* look. The way his irises shimmered—bright yellow like a sunflower—it should have scared her. But it didn't. He wasn't the one out to get them. He wasn't the one marking people against their will.

"Oh god!" Leila fell back onto a desk as the door swung open and a stream of freshmen filed in.

"Let's go." Damien turned to the door.

Before he could get anywhere, Leila grabbed him and he jolted from her strength. She tugged him down until his ears were level with her mouth. "Your eyes and... talons."

Damien turned his back to the freshmen and stood up straight. He glanced at Leila's hand on his arm, blinked, and met her gaze. His yellow eyes returning to gray, he said, "Seriously, how are you doing that?"

"We'll worry about that later." Leila shrugged, a nervous smile on her face. She stormed out into the almost empty hallway. "In the meantime, let's go visit Gabby."

Damien rushed to keep up, Sadie close behind him. "I don't think that's a good idea. We don't want to raise suspicion. We should stay here until the end of school."

"They sound like Riley's words," Leila moaned, slowing down.

Damien shrugged. "He's annoying, but still smart."

Leila shook her head and muttered, "Terrible combination of traits."

"Ugh, we've all got biology," Sadie said, pointing to a classroom a few doors down.

They came to a stop outside the biology lab. Leila turned to Sadie. "I thought you loved this class?"

"That is so last week."

Leila stared at the door as her body began to sway. Around her the walls crowded in. Voices became distant. Lights dulled. She needed to get out of there. It wasn't the pull this time. It was the sudden lack of air. Stepping back, she said, "I'll see you guys in there."

She charged down the corridor and swung to the left. As she expected, Damien followed. Coming to a stop outside the female restroom, she pointed to the sign. "You can't go where I'm going."

"Oh, right." Damien settled himself against the wall and crossed his ankles. "I'll wait."

Without objecting, Leila pushed the door open and stood at the mirrors. She didn't need to be there, she just wanted some space to breathe.

She stared at her hazel eyes, wondering what color they might turn. Her fingers clenched the basin—her fingernails were nice... not perfect, a little bit chewed, just... nice. She wondered what it felt like to grow talons or claws. She turned the faucet and splashed cold water on her face. Visions of the wolf from the night before flooded her mind. Kiko, as the fox with red eyes, soon joined. Then, Mr. Robertson, Damien... and Gabby, all their faces swirled with the water as it ran down the drain—around and around in a spiral, just like the mark.

I'm running in circles, Leila thought, *should I just accept my fate?*

Taking a deep breath, she steeled herself to step away from the basin and opened the door. As she stepped out, her gaze drifted to Damien still leaning against the wall. His eyes were closed and he had a talon out, scraping it between his teeth.

"Damien!" she scolded.

His talon retracted and when he opened his eyes they were normal. "Sorry, I had some meat caught up in there, it was annoying me." He cleared his throat. "Ready for class?"

Leila nodded slowly, gazing up and down his body.

If this is going to happen, if I'm going to be one of them, I need to know what will happen.

WEDNESDAY

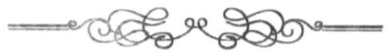

afternoon

Leila grabbed his wrist and hauled him down the hallway. Strutting right past the biology door, Leila led them down the hall until they reached the photography darkroom. She quickly checked over the schedule but knew that afternoons couldn't be booked, the door was always locked for ink drying.

Damien's arm writhed in her grasp. His free fingers tried to peel her off, but all that did was make her grip tighten. "Can you stop doing that please, it's making me feel very emasculated."

Shoulder first, she threw herself towards the door, and it clicked open. She pulled him inside, closed the door, and tapped the swivel chair for him. "Not until you tell me everything."

Damien sat down, his Adam's apple bobbing up and down in a hard swallow. "That's a loaded question. What do you want to know?"

She opened a low cupboard and pulled out an empty crate, flipping it upside down to sit on.

Everything, she wanted to say. But she couldn't give him an easy way to skirt on any details, she had to be specific.

"Who turned you?"

The darkness of the room gave extra gravity to the question.

Red highlights from the bulb above casted across Damien's cheekbones and shoulders. He sighed. "I told you already, I don't know."

Leila squinted, as if her slitted eyes could sense a lie. He stared back at her without blinking.

"You said it was a wolf," she pressed.

"Yeah, it was a wolf."

"A white one?"

Damien's head twitched slightly. "Yeah."

"Bright blue eyes?"

A smile spread across his face. "White, with blue eyes? Check, and check. Twice the size of a normal wolf, as fluffy as a kitten, freaking epic? Triple check."

"Were you scared?"

Damien's face dropped as he said, "Terrified."

"What happened when it bit you?"

With high eyebrows he leaned forward, yellow shimmered across his irises. "Magic."

Leila shuffled back. "What's with that? The glowing eye thing and... talons? Are there stages of shifts?"

He nodded with glee. "Three of them. The first stage is nothing really, I'm just a dormant Guardian, waiting... the second stage, the one where my eyes glow, this is a preparation..." He leaned forward, as if excited to finally be able to talk about it. Then, his mouth moved into an upside-down frown. "Kind of... I'm still learning, I really don't know how to describe it well."

Leila resettled herself on the crate. Hearing him get passionate about his transformation stirred something inside her. "Just try."

"It's like half way between the veil and here." Damien grinned, pleased with his explanation.

"The veil?"

"It's a spirit world."

"Oh," Leila said, still not quite understanding. "Like heaven?"

Damien's smile waned. "Are you going to butt in with questions the whole time or can I explain?"

"Sorry." Leila moved her fingers along her lips, zipping them shut.

Nodding, to say thank you, he continued, "It's not heaven. It's here all around us, but it exists beyond the human eye." He looked around the room. Spotting the enlarger he pointed at it emphatically. "Like that. The lens helps you see the picture. That's what the second stage does, it gives us sight into the veil. You can see everything in this stage—other Guardians mostly. I can even see who is marked… when the mark isn't covered."

Leila's heart skipped a beat. She unraveled her bandage, looking up to Damien with half-worried, half-hopeful eyes. "What do I look like?"

At first Damien glared, as if hesitating. Then, with a grin, his yellow eyes flitted from her arm to above her head and down the other side of her.

"Damien?"

"It's waiting for you," he said, smiling.

"Tell me what you see."

"You look similar to a Guardian in their dormant stage," he said vaguely, eyes still circling her body. She wrapped the bandage back around and he shook his head as though coming out of a trance. "Your animal stands behind you. For Guardians in the first stage, the dormant stage, the animal stands beside them. That's what it looks like. I mean there are colors… and they're real pretty."

"And the other stages of the shift?" Leila leaned forward, suddenly not so afraid.

"The second stage is where the animal aligns with you, like they've stepped into your body—which is why we grow claws and talons, and our eyes show the veil colors. Some even grow fangs, if their animal has them."

A rising thud slammed against Leila's chest. It seemed like nonsense and perfect sense all at the same time. "I'm guessing the third stage is when the full shift happens?"

"Yep. The third stage is where the animal steps forward for us. To a human eye, this looks like the actual animal, but it's not really there. When I shift I'm still me, it's only my Guardian that shows itself to the real world. It's energetically attached to me, moving for me, but it isn't really me."

"So, the animal isn't real? It can't hurt me?" she asked, hopeful.

"Sure it can. I told you, it's hard to explain. You kind of have to see it for yourself."

"I don't want to." At least, she didn't think she wanted to. "Show me!"

He nodded once—giving her request a moment of honor. As he rolled his shoulders back, the glimmer of color brightened in his eyes, and long talons arched out of his fingernails. He smiled as a yellow shimmer trickled over his body, from the top of his head to the soles of his feet.

With one blink of Leila's widened eyes, he transformed, and standing before her was an eagle the size of three men. His wings folded in on themselves in the cramped space, large feathers knocking prints as they hung to dry. The eagle crept forward, sharp talons making indents in the linoleum floor, and lowered his head to Leila. A light brown hue covered his body, the edges of each feather bright yellow. She lifted her hand, sweeping it through the bottom of one of his bent wings. He let out a loud screech, sending shock-waves through the room. In an instant, a yellow shimmer fell over his body and he returned to human form.

"Sorry, I forgot that our language gets replaced. What I said was: 'that tickled'."

"That was... that was..." Leila lost the words she wasn't sure she had to begin with.

"See, it's not all bad, is it?"

She gave a soft smile, comforted by his peaceful expression. "For a True Guardian."

Damien swung his elbow on the bench behind him. "What if you were marked by a True too?"

Leila recoiled, thinking about the number of animal attacks on innocent people.

"What if I wasn't?" she said.

Damien lowered his eyes and took a long inhale. Leila's mind whirled. She considered everything she'd just learned.

"So," Leila pondered. "Apart from me, you've seen other Guardians?"

"Only when I'm in a shifted state..." He quickly shook his head. "But I can't just go around with my shining eyes, staring at everyone to see if they are one or not."

"Yes, but you've seen one? You described them in detail, so I'm assuming yes." She inched forward.

"Uhhh..." he hesitated.

"Sebastian?" Leila offered.

"Sure."

"Who else?"

Damien squirmed on his seat, eyes darting to his feet. His inability to answer the question only made Leila press further. "Damien, why do I have to beg? This is my life!"

"Well..." Damien winced. "I kind of knew Mr Robertson was one. I saw him a couple days ago."

Leila folded her arms across her chest. "You could have

warned me."

"Riley didn't want you to walk into something that could have put you in a... situation."

"Well, that's stupid," Leila scoffed. "I could have been in a situation because of not knowing... like this morning."

"You know now." Damien shrugged and offered a smile that looked more like a grimace.

Something felt off. Why was he being so secretive? Yet, at the same time so cavalier. "You're so different, like nothing bothers you. Are you sure you're not a Fallen?"

"Ouch." Damien clutched his shirt at the heart, then threw a wrist to his forehead.

"This isn't a joking matter." In her head, she could hear Riley saying the same thing.

"Well," Damien said, resting his elbows across his knees. "I don't want to rip people's throats out, if that's what you're getting at? And there's an urge to protect... like with Morgan and you."

Leila sighed. "I thought you are protecting me cos Riley told you to."

"A little bit of coercion." Damien brought his thumb and index finger an inch apart. "But to be honest, it's more of a overwhelming desire to keep you out of harm's way. It sounds corny to say it, but there it is."

Somewhat satisfied that he was telling the truth, Leila was ready to move the conversation in a different direction. "Why am I stronger than you?"

"Again, ouch. You know how to bruise an ego."

Leila lurched forward and grabbed his leg, right above his knee, and squeezed.

"All right, all right. I concede." Damien raised his hands in surrender. "Honestly, I don't know. My strength has been amazing since I turned, but I felt like a child when you were dragging me down that hall... I'm just as surprised as you are about it."

Leila let go and sighed. She sat up straight, staring at Damien, hoping against all hope that it didn't mean she was destined to be a Fallen. If worse came to worst and she had to be turned, being what he'd become didn't sound so bad after all. In theory.

"Have you drained me of enough information? I actually like biology," Damien asked, standing up.

Leila threw a hand in dismissal. "You can go."

"*We* can go." Damien clutched the door handle.

Leila swiveled around and looked up at her sunset photo, still hanging at the back of the room. The darkroom was always a place of quiet safety for her, a place where she could go and forget about the rest of the world. One step outside of the room and she knew the real world would come flooding back. "I thought I'd stay here and sit for a while... I won't go anywhere, I promise."

"So stubborn," Damien teased, sitting back down.

Leila flung her head at him. Half of her was offended he didn't trust her, and the other half was strangely grateful. "Are you really going to stay with me?"

Damien pouted. "Afraid so."

Then again, maybe it wasn't the room that made her feel safe. Maybe it was the Guardian she was with.

"Ugh, fine," Leila groaned. "We'll go to class."

"Well, that was pointless," Damien said, as they walked out of class. Their biology teacher was off sick, and the relief teacher handed out books on the nervous system to read.

Riley would've loved it, Leila thought. *Where is he?*

"At least you only had to sit in there for half the class." Sadie rolled her eyes and followed it up with a snoring sound.

As they walked down the corridor, a hoard of seniors bumped the girls away from Damien. Leila scuttled to the side wall, watching them steam-roll everyone in their way. On the other side, Damien glared, and Leila swore she saw a flicker of yellow flash across his eyes.

"Are we going to Jimmy's Italian before the Falls Party again?" one asked.

"Abso-freaking-lutely," another answered.

"Hey!" Cap began walking backwards, pointing to Leila. "Come tonight!"

In front of Cap, Sebastian's head poked around. Noticing Leila, he scowled and swung his arm around Morgan beside him. She didn't flinch at his touch, her attention placed hypnotically on the floor in front of her.

"Morgan?" Sadie called, hastening her pace.

But Morgan kept facing ahead, rushing along with the rest of them.

"Wait!" Damien ran after her.

Leila clutched Sadie's wrist, willing her to slow. They stayed behind the group, watching Damien catch up to Morgan. He leaned over and whispered something. As he spoke, she barely looked at him, her eyes staring through him as though he was a figment of her imagination.

Leila was too far back to hear them, but she most definitely saw Sebastian's mouth make the shape of a curse word, followed by the word "off". And immediately after, Damien stopped walking with them.

"What are we going to do?" he asked when the girls caught up to him.

"We're going to save her," Leila replied emphatically.

"Urgh, of all the stubborn ideas," Damien mumbled. Despite the negative tone he nodded as though he knew it was the right thing to do. "Riley won't agree."

"Why not?" Sadie scoffed.

Damien rolled his eyes. "He says it's too risky to go after any Fallen."

"Yes." Leila nudged him with her elbow. "But what do *you* think?"

"Well, I want to help her." Damien threw an arm across her shoulders and pulled her close to him. He whispered, "But if she is turned by a Fallen and hurts someone, I most likely will have to kill her."

Leila was taken aback. She knew True Guardians were there to protect, but she didn't think they killed.

Seeing the look on her face, he dropped his arm. "Who do think did all those animal attacks and murders? The Fallen. As a True, I *have* to stop them."

"Well." Sadie squeezed herself between them. "We'll just have to get to her first."

"You're right," Leila said, hooking her elbow through Sadie's arm. "And Riley won't like it, but regardless, we are *going* to save her."

Sadie clapped her hands twice. "I'm all in."

"Me too," Damien agreed. As he peeled off to his locker on the left, he pointed across the hall.

Leila followed his finger and spotted Riley waiting at her locker.

"To tell or not to tell?" Sadie muttered as they weaved through the crowd. Then, getting closer, she beamed, "Hey Riley!"

"Hi Sades." Riley grinned, knocking her shoulder gently with his fist.

He looked at Leila and with a softer voice, he said, "Hey you."

Leila opened her locker and shoved a book inside. "Where have you been?"

"Oh, you know. Boring scholarship stuff. Anyway, I'm your chauffeur, here to take you home." He lifted his hands and pinched the brim of an invisible hat.

"To your home or her home?" Sadie peered out from her open locker, teasing.

Riley cleared his throat. His eyes flitted from side to side before landing on Leila, hopeful and wide. "Whatever she wants."

Thinking of Morgan, Leila blurted, "Let's hang out… all of us. We'll go to the Falls party."

Riley grimaced. "Are you sure that's a good idea?"

"Sounds great to me," Damien said behind them.

Riley glared at him.

"The seniors will be there… Morgan will be there. She wanted our help." Leila knew he'd be hard to crack. Appealing to his kindness seemed like the best way to go.

"Not at your expense," Riley spat, slamming his palm against a locker. "Remember the wolf last night? That's because you've put yourself out there too much. You need to cool it."

Leila glanced at Damien, who gave an apologetic smile. That's why Riley wouldn't tell her that Mr. Robertson was definitely a Guardian until it was too late. He didn't trust her to help herself. "Tell me, Riley. What's the alternative? Twiddle my thumbs while I wait to be turned… or worse?"

Riley moved his hand from the locker to her arm. His thumb gently tucked around her elbow. She watched fear replace anger. "The alternative is to go home… I can stay with you if you want company, if it's okay with Kale?"

Leila grabbed her backpack and closed her locker. "I don't want to go home."

"Why not?"

Why didn't she want to go home? She was in two minds. Did she want to save Morgan from Sebastian, an innocent senior with a promising life in front of her? Or was it because Kiko knew where she lived, and she wasn't quite certain what her motives where?

Maybe both.

Her answer was neither though, instead she was shocked to hear another truth spill from her lips. "I just... I've been thinking and I know it sounds morbid, but it really does feel inevitable that I'll be turned soon, right? Can we hang out for a while together, all of us? We don't have to go the Falls."

Sadie shuffled next to Leila and slid her arms through her backpack straps. "I like the sound of that."

Riley lifted his hands to his head. His face screamed uncertainty, yet there was something else too, a hint of resignation.

Leila was so close to convincing him, she could feel it. With the best pleading look in her eyes, she said, "The three of us are going, are you?"

Riley shook his head, a small smile on his lips. "Has anyone told you how stubborn you are, Leila Belmonte?"

Without hiding her own smile, she looked behind him to a winking Damien, and said, "Never."

WEDNESDAY

late afternoon

"I'm kinda glad you're busy tonight, I was starting to feel guilty about having the boys here," Kale said over the phone.

Leila stood in Sadie's room with clothes strewn around her feet on the floor. Trying not to mention Kiko, she asked, "Just the boys?"

"Yes, are you sure that's okay?"

Leila glanced at Sadie, who was in her under-wear, slipping dresses off their hangers and throwing them over her shoulder on the floor. "Of course it's okay. Hey, weird question... are you itchy at all?"

Sadie pivoted on her heels, her mouth in a perfect O shape. Grasping some black jeans, she shuffled towards Leila.

"Why would I be?" he asked.

"No reason, I just wondered." Leila hoped he would think his crazy sister asking bizarre question was normal. To be safe, she added, "That cream the doctor gave me didn't work, so I thought my rash wasn't eczema, maybe it was something... you know, contagious. But if you're okay, then good."

"Oh, right. Nah, I'm all good."

Leila sighed with relief. Kiko wasn't there nor was she going to be AND he wasn't itchy, so he hadn't been marked. She gave Sadie the thumbs up, who in turn dropped the jeans in Leila's lap, went back to her closet and continued to sift through clothes.

Hanging up the phone, Leila crouched and began searching through Sadie's tops in the hopes of finding something that fit.

"What do you think?" Sadie asked behind her. She was wearing a gold sequined mini-skirt and matching crop-top that barely covered her breasts.

Leila baulked. "Sweet biscuits! You can't wear that."

"Is this what you wanted to wear?" Sadie replied innocently.

"Heck no. It's Winter, Sades. You'll freeze your nipples off. Plus, can you even sit in that?"

Sadie ran her thumb around the bottom of the crop-top, wincing. "It's a little tight, but I like it."

"It's... it's... your body, wear it if you want." Leila conceded, picking up a pastel blue chiffon blouse.

There was a light tap on the door, followed by Riley's voice, "Are you ready?"

Sadie jumped over her pile of clothes and opened the door. She held the door half-open, other hand on her popped-out hip. Riley gaped at the sight of her.

Behind him Sadie's sister, Summer, walked past. Even though she was two-years younger than Sadie, they could have passed as twins. Summer was only an inch shorter than her older counterpart, but her body was slightly curvier. As much as they were alike in looks, they were opposite in personality. Where Sadie was super-friendly, caring, and respectful; Summer was stand-offish, self-centered, and rebellious. Catching a glimpse of her sister, Summer gave a brutal scoff, said "Try hard", and continued onto her own room.

"One moment." Sadie closed the door in Riley's face. She picked up a pair of ripped jeans and a pastel yellow sweatshirt. "I'll wear these instead, yeah?"

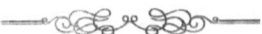

They pulled up outside the Burger Lounge, which despite its name wasn't a lounge but a diner. Stepping out of the car, Leila could smell the grease already—her stomach churned at the thought. But desperate times called for desperate measures. As they all walked towards the front door, she glanced across the road at Jimmy's Italian Restaurant. She would have much rather eaten there, but that would have been too obvious. Three cars—Cap's, Sebastian's, and another senior's—were in the parking lot right beside the building.

"You comin'?" Sadie called.

Leila rushed to catch up to them. Riley held the door open for her and she gave him a thin smile as she walked inside. A sliver of guilt panged at her heart. As much as he was being overbearing, deciding to go to this particular place felt like she was betraying him.

After they ordered, they filled their cups at the soda dispenser and found a booth by the window. Leila made sure to get a seat with full vision of Sebastian's car.

"We need to talk about how to keep you safe." Riley crunched his straw through his frozen cola. "The Guardian who marked you must know your mark is ready by now."

Leila smacked her lips together, she had all but given up on her own safety, but she knew if she said that to him, he wouldn't tolerate that stance. At that stage, he cared more about her not becoming a shifter than she did.

"Wanna stay at my house?" Sadie offered.

Damien let out a hearty guffaw. "Yeah? And how would *you* protect her?"

Sadie threw a sugar packet in his direction. "Shoosh, you overgrown grunge head. You don't have to be mean about it."

"Ugh," Leila mumbled. The fuss they were all making was starting to grate on her. She peered out the window to make sure all the cars were still there. "Why do I get protection but not Morgan?"

"Because—" Riley began.

Leila turned to him and pointed her dry straw at him. "Because her life is no less important than mine, you know!"

He opened his mouth to reply, but a phone call interrupted him. He slid his phone from his pocket and clicked the reject button. "It's only my mom."

Sadie gasped. "Mr. Jansen! You did *not* just reject a call from your own mother."

Riley put his phone back into his blazer pocket, eyes on Leila the whole time. "My attention is needed elsewhere."

"Oh, you're cheeky," Damien proclaimed, staring out the window.

A whole group of seniors piled out of the restaurant. Cap, Thomas, Don, Sebastian, Morgan, Crystal—the basketball team and all their cheerleaders. The pit of Leila's stomach flipped.

Think of something, quick.

As Riley turned his head to the window, Leila pushed her straw into her drink. She threw her hands back, and the force tilted the cup off balance. It toppled quickly—half spilling on the floor, half rushing across the table towards Riley's lap. Cold lemon soda dripped off the edge like a waterfall.

Riley stood up immediately, pants soaking wet.

"Oh my god! I'm so sorry, Riley," Leila gasped, dramatically covering her mouth with her hand.

"It's okay, it's okay," he reassured her. He nodded at Damien, before rushing to the bathroom.

Damien tutted, head shaking and finger wagging. "You're terrible."

"Listen, I feel bad about the drink." Leila stared out the window to see the Seniors pile into their cars. "But he makes it next to impossible to make a single move without his approval."

"Not that!" He said, flicking the puddle of fizzing liquid. "That was genius. But you knew they were gonna be there, that's why you wanted to eat here."

"And, I knew he wouldn't like it." Leila pushed to her feet and turned to Sadie, "Wait here."

Damien was close behind her as she ran outside. Cap was the first to drive off with a full car, and another soon followed. Sebastian and Morgan were the last ones remaining.

Morgan looked nice. She wore black, ripped jeans and a black satin cami to match. To keep warm, a red jacket with large brown buttons hung over her shoulders.

"Can you do your thing?" Leila asked, waving a hand in Damien's direction.

"She hasn't been turned yet." A quick shimmer of yellow flashed across Damien's eyes. He started running across the street, looking over his shoulder to say, "We'll cut them off at the exit."

Leila bounded after him, her eyes locked on Sebastian as he climbed into his car. Spotting the two of them bounding over, Sebastian hurried to start his engine. As wheels spun and the car steamed forward, Damien stood in the middle of the exit to block them in. The car screeched to a halt, its nose stopping inches from Damien's looming body.

Sebastian revved the car loudly. Leila took it as her chance, sneaking beside his open window. Like lightning, her hand reached through and grabbed his shirt.

"What the fuuu—" he started, but she'd hauled him out of the car before it even stalled.

Damien rushed to Morgan in the passenger seat, as Leila dragged Sebastian through the window. She pinned him to the ground, pressing her forearm against his collar. Through gritted teeth, she demanded, "Leave. Her. Alone."

"Get off me, Mutt." As he spoke, Leila pushed again, forcing his back to grate against the pavement. He shook his head violently, groaning under the pressure. "Stop, you don't know what you're doing."

"Tell me who turned you."

"You think that's what matters?" A smile spread across his face. Then, he frowned. "But you've gotta let me try."

His words confused her. She released her hold slightly. "Try what? To turn her?"

"To save her, you idiot." A low guttural moan rumbled from his throat. Squeezing his eyes shut, he writhed under her as though he was having some kind of fit. When his eyes opened again, they shone bright blue, just like the white wolf's did. He lifted his hips and threw his legs in the air, Leila tumbled onto the sidewalk. By the time she adjusted her focus, he was standing above her—eyes glowing, claws growing. "You'd better back off. I'm not the one you're after."

"Stop it!" Morgan screamed, running around the car to Leila's side.

Damien stayed close to her. He crossed his arms, showing off his biceps in the process, and stared at Sebastian with yellow eyes. "If you're trying to save her why are you here? Why are you out in the open instead of hiding?"

"Why are *you* here?" Sebastian ignored Damien,

looking at Leila instead. "Why do *you* go to school? Don't you get it? Because being in the open is safer than hiding alone where they can take you with no one else knowing."

Leila sat up. He was scared—it was written all over his face. She understood now, she believed him. Riley was wrong, he wasn't a Fallen.

"Morgan." Sebastian moved towards his car. His hands hung straight by his side, claws digging into his palms. "I've already told you, you need to stay with me. I don't want anything from you, I don't want you to end up like this."

Standing up, Leila said, "Let us help. Tell us who turned you, who marked us. We can figure it out together."

Sebastian took a leap forward, fangs inches from her face. "You have no idea what you're getting involved with. Leave. Me. The. Hell. Alone, Mutt."

He turned to Morgan and held out his hand. She stared at the half-moon blood marks dripping from his palm and took a small step closer to Damien.

"Come with me, stay away from them." Sebastian pleaded, throwing an arm out in Leila's direction.

"Stay away from us?" Damien scoffed, eying Sebastian over. "*We* aren't the bad guys here."

Sebastian let out an unnerving laugh. He shook his head and cranked open his car door. His fingers lingered on the handle as his claws retracted and his eyes lost their shine.

Leila swallowed, her throat drying up. He couldn't just tell them he was protecting Morgan and then leave, not like that. Didn't he understand there was safety in numbers?

"We want to help, we need help," Leila begged.

"Help?" Sebastian spun around. His eyes were normal but the fury in them remained. "Gimme a break. You were running around the school asking about the spiral to everyone. You're reckless, I'm surprised you haven't been turned already. And this guy?" He pointed at Damien, while taking small steps towards Morgan. "Do you know what he'll do to you if you slip up just once? He won't be trying to protect you then, he'll rip you apart limb from limb until you're nothing."

Morgan looked sideways at Damien.

He reached for her, shaking his head wildly. "No, I won't. I promise."

She flinched and stepped closer to Sebastian.

"Wait." Leila held her hands up—heart and mind racing. "We've got more chance if we team up. We need to stay together."

Morgan stayed by Sebastian, her head hanging low. "I'm sorry."

"Get in," Sebastian demanded.

Without a pause, Morgan rushed to the passenger door. Sebastian slunk into the driver's seat and revved the engine. Neither of them took a second glance at Leila and Damien as they drove away.

The food had arrived while Leila and Damien were gone. By the time Riley returned, the two of them were sitting innocently in the booth—mouths full of fries. He slid beside Damien, one leg of his pants stained in a light-yellow color.

"Sorry. It took a while to dry," he said, grabbing a fry. "And, my mom called again. I forgot to tell her I wouldn't be home for din..." He looked between his three friends and pointed his food at every face he turned to. "What's happened?"

"*She's* convinced he's not a Fallen," Damien stated, glaring at Leila.

Riley frowned, eyes darting from Damien to Leila and back again. "Who?"

"Project Sebastian is back!" Sadie declared, rubbing her hands together.

Riley opened his mouth but closed it without saying a word. He opened it again, croaked out an, "Ugh." Then, bit the fry.

"Hear me out," Leila piped up. "You, yourself, said that he didn't mark me. He hasn't actually hurt Morgan either. He keeps taking her away... but she always shows up unharmed." Her hands waved about, trying to explain the unexplainable. "I just feel it, okay? I think he needs help."

Two disturbed eyes stared at Leila. "How do you know this?"

She motioned outside, and with a wince, said, "We may have bumped into them."

Riley glanced at Leila's empty cup and back up again.

She quickly shoved an onion ring into her mouth, something she wouldn't normally eat, and looked everywhere but at his distressed face. Beside her, Sadie stifled a laugh. And, Damien made a weird grunt in an effort to keep himself from doing the same.

Ignoring his immature friends, Riley finally said, "I wish you'd stop putting yourself in harm's way."

At that, Leila met his gaze. "But isn't it better having more of us together? To keep Morgan safe? To keep Gab safe? To keep me safe?"

Riley tilted his head. "Why Gabby?"

"Isn't it obvious?" Sadie said, dabbing the side of her mouth with a napkin. "That girl has never been so sick she doesn't answer her phone or messages. She's like a sister to us, we know something isn't right."

"Well, I mean." Riley gripped the edge of the table. "I doubt she's been marked though, right?"

No one replied. No debate, no laughter, no hope.

"We need to check on her." Leila pushed her food across the table and stood up abruptly. "Now!"

As she started for the door she heard Riley hiss to Damien, "You were supposed to keep her under control. This is getting out of hand."

Damien shrugged. "That girl's got a mind of her own."

WEDNESDAY

early evening

Leila shivered as Sadie knocked on Gabby's front door. Not because of the cold, even though it was, but because of what might wait for them inside. Riley and Damien stood behind them, like two bodyguards, ready and waiting to step in if needed.

The door opened and Gabby's step-dad, Michael, appeared. Sweat pooled at the arm-pits of his grubby, blue t-shirt and he stared at them as though they were strangers. He held the door with one hand and a beer with the other, taking a sip before asking, "What do you want?"

"Um, to see Gabby," Sadie said softly, tugging on the cuffs of her blazer.

"Rosie!" he shouted over his shoulder.

While they waited he guzzled his beer, his eyes tracing down Leila's body. She shivered, but again, not from the cold.

Soon, Gabby's mom rushed down the hall to the foyer. She placed a quick hand on Michael's shoulder. He huffed and gave her a scowling glance. "Sorry," she said, averting her eyes from his stare.

"Hi girls." Rosie was barely audible. She winced as Michael sulked down the hall. When he was gone, she relaxed a little. "I'm really sorry but Gabby can't come down to see you. She's not well. I don't want anyone else to get this nasty flu that's spreading around."

"Like wildfire," Damien sneered.

"Well, if it isn't the Terrible Twins!" A familiar voice thundered through the house and out the door. Gabby's brother, Benjamin, peered out from the archway at the end of the foyer.

He was two years older than Gabby, and as hot as a chili soaked in lava sauce. Square jaw, dark eyes, broad swimmer's shoulders. He went to the University of Washington, studying Mechanical Engineering—which was a feat in itself, considering throughout all of high school he was practically a delinquent that lived in his friend's basement. He proved anyone could change.

Sadie waved enthusiastically, cheeks turning bright red. Leila gave her a quick nudge, which was fervently ignored as Benjamin waved back. As fast as he appeared, Benjamin retreated.

"Rosie?" Michael boomed with an acidic tone. "Shut that door, it's cold."

Rosie began to close the door. "Best to stay away."

"Wait! I..." Leila hesitated, trying to find the right words. "I had the same thing, I thought..."

"Sorry," Rosie mouthed, closing the door.

Well, that was a wasted trip.

Leila turned to Riley. "I think we need to go to the falls party. We'll find Sebastian, really talk to him, no fists, just talk." And to think, a day earlier she was mocking him for wanting to do just that.

Three sets of hopeful eyes were on Riley, waiting for his

response. He looked directly at Leila. "I just find it hard to know who to trust. My sister made sure of that. The Fallen are great at deception. Sebastian could be setting this all up to turn you all, like some kind of sick game. I won't play along, I won't let you become one of them. We need to use our brains, we can't go on feelings alone... don't look at me like that, I don't mean *those* feelings."

The door opened. Benjamin slipped outside and closed the door without a sound. He rubbed his hands together and exhaled, a thick cloud wafted out his mouth.

"Hello Winter." He hugged his arms across his own chest. "Hey guys. Listen, she's really sick—she has had a fever and the sweats. She keeps talking about feeling like ants are running over her whole body. I've begged Mom to take her to see a doctor, but she's worried about how that will look on our family's history. She thinks Gab has overdosed on something."

Leila cupped his shoulder in sympathy and shook her head. Gabby's family history. Leila didn't know much, only what Gabby had told her. Some vague telling of how her father had really died.

"Let me get this straight," Damien said. "Your mom thinks Gabby overdosed but would rather save face than her daughter's life?"

Benjamin glared at Damien. "Who are you?"

A hint of the old Damien showed as he sunk his head to his shoulders. "Nobody."

Benjamin sniffed and turned back to Leila. "You said you had the same thing?"

"Yeah." She nodded, wondering how much she should tell him. On her back, a light tap, tap... Riley was warning her. "It didn't last long, she'll be fine... sort of."

"Oh, thank god." Benjamin ran a hand over his face, as though the movement physically removed all concern.

"Keep an eye on her," Leila said as three loud thumps came from inside.

"I will." Benjamin looked over his shoulder. "Anyway, I better go. The step-douche is a live wire when he drinks." He leaned into Sadie and wrapped an arm across her shoulder. She giggled, almost melting on the spot. "It was good to see you both."

When he returned inside, Damien nudged Sadie. "You right there, Sades? You look like you're turning into a giant blob of mashed potatoes."

Sadie's face transformed from love-sick puppy to displeased kitten. "Have you seen yourself in the school corridor, lapping up all the girls' attention?"

Damien averted his eyes, a wry smile lighting his face. Sadie glared at him, scanning him from his feet up. By the time she'd reached his head, her face had softened into a smile.

Leila was still staring at the door, trying to come to terms with the truth. She received the answer she was searching for. Gabby had been marked. She ached. For herself, for her best friend, for the town. How was it going to end for them all?

"Anyway," Riley sounded aggravated. He threw a hand to the second-floor window. "Gabby is safe, for now. So, let's do the same for you."

"Okay, enough!" Leila declared, spinning around. "You're not the boss anymore, Riley. I know your whole goal is to keep me safe, and I appreciate that, I truly do. But in case you haven't seen the news reports lately, people are dying. And this mark..." she waved her arm in the air, "... is showing up on everyone. I need to help Morgan and Gabby. I need to stop the Fallen from turning innocent people into murderers. To do this, I need to find the person who marked us, who marked me." She resisted the urge to tell him she was pretty sure she knew who it was—her brother's girlfriend. "I know you're scared of history repeating itself, but I think I need a lot of backup for this, so are you in or out?"

Riley crossed his arms. "And what do you propose we do when we find the person who's been marking everyone, hmm?"

With a strange glint in her eyes, Sadie suggested. "Kill them?"

"Maybe," Damien agreed.

"No!" Riley glared at them both.

Leila poked her finger into his heaving chest. "Now who's being stubborn, Riley Jansen?"

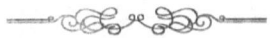

Riley pulled his car up to Sadie's house. Leila had decided to stay there the night and didn't give Riley the option to agree or not.

Walking them to the door, he resigned, "I suppose this will be all right. Messing up the routine will keep the Guardian who marked you a step behind. Plus, this house is closer to mine than yours." For good measure and to regain some type of control, he added, "Promise me, no party."

Sadie slammed her legs together and saluted. "Boring night in for us."

Riley didn't buy it. He lowered his chin, looking from Sadie to Leila. His bottom lip rolled out. "Please?"

"Okay," Leila resigned, rolling her eyes in jest. "No party."

Riley pulled her into his arms and hugged her, tight and lingering. He tore himself away and walked to his car, glancing back every few steps. As he opened the door, he said, "Call me if you need."

She nodded and stood on the front step, watching him take off. Once his car was out of sight, she turned to Sadie. "Your parents are out for the night, aren't they?"

"Not the whole night, but they're at a work dinner..."

Sadie fiddled with the keys in the lock. She peered over her shoulder with a grin. "For a few hours it'll be just you, me, and the terrible fifteen-year-old. Don't worry I didn't mention it to Riley, he's a bit testy lately."

"Tell me about it." Leila rolled her eyes.

Sadie pushed the door open. "Only cos he cares."

"I know he cares, but that's not the problem." Leila lingered outside, foot tapping on the ground. "The problem is, he only cares about me, not about Morgan or Gabby."

Sadie closed the door and sighed. "We're going to the falls party, aren't we?"

WEDNESDAY

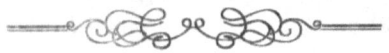

evening

At the end of the five-mile gravel road to the falls, cars were crammed alongside each other in a make-shift parking lot. Sadie parked her parent's second car behind Cap's—half on the gravel, half on the grass. There was no sign of Sebastian's sky-blue Nissan.

Between towering pines, the two girls walked in silence down the narrow path, distant laughter leading the way. In her heart, Leila knew she was doing the right thing, but her head kept scolding her for being exactly what Sebastian knew to be true: reckless. Leila smiled to herself, thinking, *at least that's one thing Riley and Sebastian agree on.*

Gravel crunched close behind them. On high alert, Leila clenched her fists and swung around.

A boy, taller than most, threw his arms up in surrender. "Whoa! Keep your super-strength for the bad guys!"

Relaxing, Leila sighed. "Damien? What are you doing here?"

"I had a hunch." He shrugged.

"In other words, Riley didn't trust me, so he sent you to spy?" Leila's eyes turned into skeptical slits, a small smile lifting her pout.

With a sheepish grin, Damien shrugged again. "Something like that."

"Hmph," said Sadie, arms crossed. "I'd like to think he'd give me more credit than that."

"But you are here though, right? You're not at home, sipping on soda having pillow fights in your underwear."

"Okay." Sadie lifted a finger. "For one thing—eww! And, secondly... whatever, I'm just being a good frien—"

"Shhh," Leila hissed, grasping Damien's shoulders. A wave of nausea careened through her stomach like a rogue wave. *Not nausea though*, Leila thought. The tug. She peered behind Damien. "Is someone with you?"

"No," he replied, checking over his shoulder, just in case.

It was definitely the magnetic pull she had felt with the wolf the night before and Kiko earlier that day. It wasn't compelling though—a weaker signal—not enough to control her, but still there, a faint warning that a Guardian was calling.

"Are you okay? I'll call Riley." Damien helped Leila regain her balance and lifted his phone.

"Wait!" Leila demanded. She knew her time left as a human was limited. She needed to act fast. "It's nothing, I'm fine. Don't call him yet. Let me find Morgan first."

"Okay." Damien swung his arm towards the party like a butler would, and Sadie marched ahead.

Before following, Leila quickly scanned the shadows of the forest.

Water cascaded, like white lines of paint dripping down a canvas, into a circular pool. In Summer, when the surge of water became a trickle, the natural watering hole was the place to be. In Winter, on the first Wednesday of every month, teens huddled and drank in secret. At the edge of the pool, a clearing the size of a basketball court housed a bonfire and more than half the high school.

Music blared from a portable blue-tooth speaker, fighting to be heard above flowing water, crackling flames, and intoxicated students. Cap, Don, and other seniors stood at the edge of the clearing closest to the waterfall. No Sebastian or Morgan in sight.

Stepping off the path onto the grass, Leila lifted her gaze. Above, a vignette of tree tops perfectly framed the clear night sky. And, as if the moon and stars weren't enough, fairy lights hung low on branches around the border of the clearing. She took a deep breath in, surprised to feel her spirit rise.

Sadie flipped her phone open and tapped on the message that lit up the screen.

"Who is it?" Leila asked.

A coy smile flashed over Sadie's face. "Benjamin."

"You messaged him? Oh, Sadie!"

If Sadie was blushing, Leila couldn't tell. But she could see Sadie's pearly whites as she looked over the message. "He says she's still tucked up in bed but feeling a little better." She locked her phone. "And don't *Oh, Sadie!* me, my crush on him is long gone."

"Speaking of Gabby," Damien piped up, a glint in his eye. "Is she dating anyone?"

Leila glared at him. Ever since he'd turned, it was like his testosterone had tripled. Once a shy introvert, now a lady's man.

"Well, you're not *her* type for starters," Sadie teased, adding a smirk that would suggest that he was hers.

"Really?" Damien looked down his body. "Even now?"

Sadie peered up at him, moonlight glistening off her

round eyes. "Don't worry, there are plenty of girls out there."

Leila moaned under her breath. Good old Sadie, no shame when it came to boys. Leila watched on, intrigued to see which direction the conversation would go. Sadie could talk the talk, but she was too chicken to walk the walk.

Damien cocked his head to the side, a cheeky smile lifting his cheekbones. "Are you flirting with me, Sadie Sloan?"

Her mouth fell open. "What? No!"

"Oh, thank the wild unknown, because you are definitely not *my* type."

"Of course not," Sadie muttered, looking away.

"Damien!" Leila chided, pushing his bicep. "That was a bit rude."

Damien took a step back. "Bu-but, she literally just said the same thing to me. How come she gets to be offended but I don't?"

"You can't be offended." Leila pat his shoulder in sympathy. "Because no male is Gabby's type."

The information took its time to register. He asked slowly, "She's gay?"

"Yup."

"Completely gay, like there's no chance at all?"

"Not. A. Single. One," Sadie snapped, satisfied to see him squirm.

Damien hunched his shoulders, black hair falling out from behind his ears. He squeezed her forearm, sliding his thumb along the inside of her elbow. "Aww, Sades, don't be mad at me. I can't think of you how I think — thought — of Gabby. You're too pure for those thoughts."

Sadie sighed, waving her hand in dismissal. "It's okay, I get it all the time. She's gun-powder and I'm pixie dust."

"Exactly." Damien sighed with relief.

Leila smacked her lips together. Damien may have suddenly been gods gift to Cedar Falls Academy but he truly still had no idea. Unsurprised, she watched Sadie brush his hand off her, and turn her back.

Damien turned to Leila and mouthed 'what?', his palms facing the sky in confusion. Then, a moment of realization. Dropping his hands, he whispered, "I wasn't supposed to agree, was I?"

"Don't worry," Leila whispered back. "She only likes you for your new-found muscles and jaw-line. It takes someone really special to get her full attention — you know, depth of personality and things like that. She's probably already over the idea of you."

While Damien stood silent, possibly deciding whether to be insulted or not, Leila searched the crowd again. With knees bouncing nervously under her, she said, "Morgan was supposed to be here."

She glanced at Damien, who — still dumbfounded — shrugged in return.

"What is *she* doing here?" Sadie exclaimed.

Damien perked up and nodded. "Well, Riley would agree with that. Leila, you probably shouldn't be here."

"No." Sadie pointed across the clearing. "Look."

Towards the other side of the fire pit, surrounded by a bunch of freshmen, was fifteen-year-old Summer Sloan with a drink in hand. Her long blonde hair flickered orange against the flames, her outfit none other than Sadie's gold midriff top and skirt.

"I'm gonna kill that kid!" Sadie proclaimed. Through smoke and dancing bodies, she weaved towards her sister, Leila and Damien close behind.

"Oooh, this will be good!" Damien said, gleefully rubbing his hands together.

"What the hell do you think you're doing?" Sadie boomed before they even reached Summer and her friends.

Summer stared at her older sister indignantly, as though she was the one who shouldn't be there. "Go back to the basement and play dungeons and dragons or whatever it is you do with your nerdy pals, and pretend you didn't see me." Turning back to her friends, proud giggles fluttered from her red lips.

Sadie grabbed her shoulder and twisted her back around. "Are you wearing Mom's favorite lipstick?"

"So, what?" Summer scowled.

"So, you're already grounded. I don't think you sneaking out of the house to go to a senior party will go down well, despite the fact you stole *my* clothes and *her* makeup."

"Yeah, but it looks so much better on me than it does on you." Summer threw a golden ringlet over her shoulder, then drew a fingertip across her collarbone and over the curve of her chest.

Leila looked at Damien as he watched on like he was about to receive a puppy for Christmas. "You want some popcorn with that inappropriate excitement?"

"You're so judgy tonight!" he replied, eyes still on the place where Summer's finger lay.

Overcome with either jealousy or protective mothering, Sadie grabbed Summer's wrist. Turning to Leila, as they passed, she said, "Sorry, I'm going to have to go."

Sadie dragged her flailing sister away from the party. On the way to the path, Summer whisked a plastic cup from the drink station. As she lifted it to her mouth, Sadie swatted the cup to the ground.

"You are so uncool." Summer groaned to the sky.

"See you tomorrow," Leila called to the back of Sadie.

A hand, quickly flung head-height, was all that Sadie could manage in return as she hauled her grounded sibling down the path back to their parents' car.

"Sooo..." Damien stepped beside Leila with his hands

clasped in front of him. "What now, boss lady? Partaayyy or business?"

"Well, for starters," Leila said, staring at the back of Sadie still struggling with her sister. "Don't call me boss lady—it's just boss, I wouldn't call you boss man. Anyway, I'm not the boss. Except of my own life." She spun around the face the fire, shoulders slumping. "Actually, not even that. So, cut me some slack."

Damien rolled his hands around each other as though unraveling a rope. "What? I'm giving you some slack... a whole ton of it. Have all the slack I've got." He rolled his hands some more before spreading them out wide, bowing slightly. Leila raised her eyebrows as he took a giant step backwards, still only two meters away. Shrugging an apology, he settled into a wide stance.

He's like a damned bodyguard, Leila thought, not realizing the smile on her face.

He'd changed in appearance and confidence, but he was still a complete dork and that made her feel eerily calm.

All this time, he's been blasé about my mark, as though it doesn't matter, as though turning into a Guardian isn't a big deal. Maybe it isn't.

WEDNESDAY

late evening

They sat under fairy lights on the edge of the clearing—Leila, on a large rock with grass growing from its crevices, and Damien, on the ground with his back firmly against a tree. In front of them, a drink station was set up with a keg and a pile of plastic cups stacked beside it. People would come to fill up their cups and then leave with either a smile or a cringe.

"It's never going to be the same again is it?" she mused.

"Wouldn't want it to be." His gaze was lifted to the starry sky, head settled on bark.

"It's okay for you, knowing you're a True..." She stopped talking, sick of contemplating the possibility of becoming a Fallen.

She watched the swim team dance haphazardly to faint music and the constant pounding of rushing water. She watched Don's and Cap's faces as they made obnoxious chatter. She watched Morgan's cheerleader friends worry about the decision to drink or not. What she wouldn't have given for *that* to be her choice, instead her only choice was to hide or accept her fate.

The cheerleaders hovered at the keg, giggling as their captain, Crystal, poured cheap beer into their red cups. As she carefully passed the full-brimmed drinks to each girl, a sudden movement at the end of the path caught her eyes. She dropped the last cup onto the ground and let out a high-pitched squeal. On alert, Damien jumped to his feet, ready. With gravel crunching beneath their feet, two people stepped into the clearing: one walking with purpose, his shoulders back and face stern; the other, clutching his arm, her timid body half a step behind.

Sebastian and Morgan.

The cheerleaders rushed over in a giddy excitement, breaking the two late-comers apart. As he passed Leila and Damien, Sebastian gave a sideways glance. Doing a double-take at the sight of them, he shook his head. Then, he quickly pushed through the crowd to Cap and Don.

"I'll call Riley," Damien said, stepping away.

Morgan's friends led her to the keg, bombarding her with statements like: "I can't keep up with your boyfriends", "I hope you used protection", and, "Tell us everything!"

"He's not my boyfriend, I didn't sleep with him," Morgan said flatly. She looked across the drink station to Leila.

Standing up straight, Leila gave a small wave and mouthed, "Are you okay?"

Morgan nodded once and lifted a cup to her lips, sculling the fermented liquid in one gulp. Crystal took her hand, trying to pull her towards the boys. Slipping out of Crystal's grasp, she said, "I'll be there in a sec." Morgan poured herself another drink and walked towards Leila, leaving Crystal and the others to look on in disgust. She passed the cup to Leila. "You look like you need this."

Within a second, cold beer tickled Leila's throat,

making her eyes water. She crushed the cup and spluttered, "Are you… sure… you're okay?"

"Yes. I don't think he wants to hurt me." Her eyes flitted to Damien, as though wondering if the same could be said for him.

"What was he saying?" Leila cleared her throat, still feeling the effects of the fizz. "Did he tell you who has marked us?"

Morgan shook her head. "He didn't tell me. He thinks I'll tell you and then you will cause a scene and put everyone in danger."

Leila's eyes drifted across the clearing and zoomed in on Sebastian. She watched his every move—searching for any tell-tale sign that would prove she could trust him. He laughed when his friends laughed, was animated and loud, yet every so often, he glanced over his shoulder to her and Morgan. There was something else about him too, something anyone could miss if they weren't properly looking. Up top, he was cool and collected, doing all the right moves—yet below, his heels twisted side to side, digging grooves into the soil, as if his nerves had been pushed all the way down to his feet.

Earlier, he told Leila she was reckless, that she dug too much. *Is that what I am?* she thought. *A reckless shining light of desperation.*

"Can I be honest?" Morgan asked, bringing Leila's attention back.

"Of course."

"We're doomed." There was a finality in those words, as though she had long since accepted her fate.

"No," Leila drew the "O" sound out while she searched for a reason why that couldn't be true.

"We are. And I'm tired of hiding, aren't you?" Without waiting for a response, Morgan continued, "But at least we can have fun. Have you been to a kicker like this before book-girl?"

"Sure..." Leila replied, hoping she didn't have to say how many times because the answer would be dismal. She quickly added, "But I prefer movies to books."

Morgan raised her eyebrows in disbelief. Then she clutched Leila's wrists and leaned in close. "Leila, I'm scared... like outta my mind scared. After spending so much time with Sebastian while he's running around in this controlling, paranoid, cloud of darkness... I'm not that kind of girl."

"Sounds like Riley," Leila replied, even though she knew that wasn't fully true. Riley wasn't *that* controlling. Was he?

She knew Morgan was right though, all the running and searching was prolonging the inevitable. If they were going to be turned, why shouldn't they spend their last moments as humans, enjoying life instead of hiding in fear? What would finding out who marked them change? Do they kill them? How? And if they try to and don't succeed, will they be killed? Was it better to be turned than to be dead?

"Riley's on his way," Damien said, returning.

"Change of plans," Leila said, marching to the keg.

Damien followed hesitantly. "What kind of plans?"

Morgan skipped beside them, rubbing her hands together. "The fun kind!"

"Really?" Damien smiled, then frowned. "Riley will be here soon, he'll bust you and then he'll bust my lip!"

In reply, Leila fixed herself a drink and lifted it to her mouth, staring at Damien as she gulped. She passed the half empty cup to Morgan, who took a quick sip, scrunched her nose, then took a longer sip. After it was gone, Morgan reached across for more, bopping her knees to the beat of the music.

Leila filled another cup and passed it to Damien. He sniffed the contents as he asked, "So what, in fact, is the new plan?"

She floated her hand at everyone around them. They were having fun, like they hadn't a single problem in the world — like they were seventeen and life was great.

"I want to feel like them."

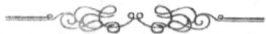

The three of them were dancing by the fire when Riley arrived. He didn't look happy, but Leila was too wasted to care. She sidled beside him at the keg. "Hello, super cute boyfriend." She giggled as she poured a drink. "Boyfriend... have I said that before?"

He covered the lip of her cup with his hand, but she slid it out from under him and drank it anyway.

His brown eyes darkened. "You're no good impaired."

"Oh, haven't you heard? My fate is sealed, Riley. It's inevitable. I may as well have fun as a human one last time."

"Can we talk?"

She glanced over her shoulder at Morgan, who was currently mimicking the flames with her dance moves. "Prob shouldn't leave her alone."

"Didn't you just say your fates were sealed?" Damien teased.

Leila shot him a glare.

He raised his hands. "All right, all right. It was a joke. She'll be fine, I'll watch her."

"Okay," Leila agreed. "But not for long, I'm on precious time here."

Riley led her down a small pathway framed by lanterns. It was short and took them to the edge of water, where the pool became a river. The spot was called *Make-out Lane*, but she knew they weren't there for that. Standing under a twinkling lantern, she mused, "This is pretty, they should put them closer to the party like the fairy lights."

She danced her fingertips over it before lowering her gaze to meet Riley's. He stood still, staring at her for a while, his eyes flitting between hers. He chewed on his bottom lip and a dimple flashed in and out of sight. The low-lighting made him look oh, so, cute.

Leila's heart skipped a beat. Blushing, she glanced away. "What?"

"It was a mistake coming here. I don't want to force you, Leila, but if we don't leave soon I'm going to have to..."

Leila snapped her eyes back to him, warmth disappearing from her chest. So much for him not being as controlling as Sebastian. "What? You're going to have to what?"

Riley sighed and lifted his chin to the sky. "Don't you care about yourself?"

"Of course I do... I care about Morgan, too... And Gabby. That's why I'm here."

Riley dropped his head back down. "You look like your here to drink your troubles away."

The way he looked at her made Leila feel both guilty and defiant. "So what if I am?"

"Well, what is it?" Riley said, raising his voice. "You say you're here for Morgan and Gabby, but here you are drinking and dancing. Geez, Leila. Last night you were scared for your life. Today you were chasing Sebastian. And, now tonight, you're pretending all is fine."

She blinked, surprised at his spiteful tone. "I'm not pretending anything. I told you before, if we get us all together we've got a chance to stop..."

"Enough!" Riley snapped. "Stop kidding yourself with this ridiculous notion that you can all be saved."

"Riley?" Damien appeared behind them. "Keep it low, brother."

"Go watch Morgan." Riley pointed towards the fire's glow, reeling at Damien with an unwelcoming glare. He turned back to Leila with softer eyes, and with a voice barely audible, he said, "Please, come with me."

The fact was though, dancing by the fire — as distracting as she knew it was — felt amazing. Free. Not tied by fear.

"I want to stay. I want to pretend." She brushed past him to let him know that was the final decision. But as soon as they hit the clearing, Riley took her hand. He pulled her down the path to the parking lot.

"Let me go," she demanded, writhing under his grasp. Riley tightened his hold and hauled her so fast her arm socket threatened to pop out of place. "Ow, Riley. You're hurting me."

But he didn't let her go. He held on, until they reached his car. As he fumbled to fetch his keys from his back pocket, Leila took it as her opportunity. In one swift movement, she spun on her heels and launched herself back towards the party. She wasn't quick enough though, Riley caught up before she even hit the tree-line. His arms wrapped around her like a boa constrictor, weighing her down as she wriggled under his strength. She felt weak, confused at how he could man-handle her so easily when her super-strength had almost knocked him out twice already. Clenching her jaw, she lifted her arms to create some space around her chest. Riley loosened his hold far enough for her to duck out beneath him.

"Don't you *ever* do that to me again!" she cried.

"I'm sorry." Riley lowered his head, peeking up through a strand of hair, his eyes glazed with tears. "I don't know what else to do. I don't get why you want to be here. Why you would want to pretend that your life isn't in danger."

"I..." Leila froze, her voice getting lost between the desire to feel the crisp night air on her face as she danced, and the overwhelming urge to find the Guardian who

233

marked her and rip their claws off their fingers one-by-one. "Because it's the nicer option."

"Nice won't save you." Riley ran his hand through his hair, stepping slowly towards her. "I know firsthand how serious this is. You can't pretend forever."

Leila rolled her eyes, sick of him comparing her to his sister. He thought he knew everything about shape-shifters and Guardians and the mark. But what he failed to know, that small detail he missed, was that Leila didn't want him to see her the way he saw his sister—she didn't want to be the one hurting him again. She was about to change, that much was true, and he couldn't follow on that journey.

"You think I'm like Tessa, don't you? Tell me, was she reckless like me? Was she stubborn and careless and stupid like me? Is that why you're so afraid, because of how similar we are? If she's a Fallen, I must be too?"

Listening to her, Riley winced like her words were a knife, cutting deep into his psyche. His chest heaved in and out. "You don't know what you're talking about."

"*My* life is about to change, Riley. Don't you get that? I'm about to become something other than *me* and this is my last chance to be a normal seventeen-year-old." She thrummed her palm onto her chest. Grieving for the person she didn't know she wanted to be. The person she won't get to become. "It's okay for you. You don't have a mark on your arm, you're not about to turn into a monster, you're normal."

He pressed his fingertips across the back of his neck. "I get you must be feeling like you're alone in this, but—"

"Anyway, how is being here any different than being at school? They're the same people."

Riley looked at her as if she suggested they jumped into the fire... naked... while singing Christmas carols. "Uhhhh, the trees, the night, the lack of supervision, to name a few!"

Leila let out a sharp giggle and was quick to cover her mouth. He was funny when he wanted to be. She tilted her head. "It seems I'm being supervised plenty."

"Yeah?" Riley eyed her from her feet to her head, eyebrows high and righteous. "Maybe you need it."

Leila tried not to laugh again as his expression deepened. In the pale moonlight, he looked a little like a cartoon character. Aladdin, maybe, but with blond hair... and a stern teacher face. She shook her head, reminding herself she needed him out of the picture. She needed him safe. Scoffing, she hissed, "What are *you* going to do to keep me safe? If a Fallen Guardian comes, no offense dude, you'll just get in their way. And, what do you think they'll do to things that get in their way? Actually, you know what? It's probably better *without* you around."

"I know what you're doing, and it won't work. I'm not going anywhere. So, if you want to throw your life away, you're going to have to do it with me by your side."

She looked at his unwavering body—arms crossed against his chest, feet planted hip-width apart—he wasn't budging. Nothing she could have said would have made him want to leave. She didn't know whether to be frustrated or adored. Inside, her head was screaming "no", but her heart filled with warmth. It bubbled through her body, overtaking any ambition to push him away. Endearment won, or maybe it was alcohol—either way, hearing his profession bled excitement to her limbs. She flung her arms above her. "Au contraire, Riley-boo. I'm not throwing my life away, I'm making the most of it. Join me, for tonight, we celebrate human Leilani Isidora Belmonte."

With a resigned spirit, Riley looked to his car once more. When he turned back again, a slight shift in expression lit his face. "Just... don't do anything stupid."

WEDNESDAY

almost midnight

Leila swung her hips side to side, her arms bending over her head in fluid sync with the music. After her heated conversation with Riley, she made him take a photo of her and Morgan "to commemorate their last night as normal teens", and they created their own dance floor between the fire and the pool. It was easy enough to ignore her mark as it burned hotter than the rest of her body, but no matter how hard she tried, she couldn't quite dance off the faint tug in her stomach. She was half free; so close to the sky, yet completely tethered to the ground. She danced wistfully, as though trying to touch something just out of reach.

Riley was never more than a few meters away, watching her every move. Feeling his eyes bore into her, she bit her bottom lip and ran her hands down her body—from the sides of her neck and around the shape of her torso, reveling at his face as it grew angrier with every twist she made.

"You came!" A voice bellowed behind her.

She blinked, annoyed at the distraction. Cap stood between the girls and threw his arm across Morgan's shoulders. "My girl! Wanna walk with me?"

"Um, I'm actually hanging with Leila," she said, shimmying out from under him.

"A girl thing, huh? I can appreciate that." He turned to face Leila, held his finger up, and ran away. He returned within a minute, holding two cups, one for each of them.

Leila sculled the drink. The beer didn't seem to touch her throat, she didn't even taste it. She crushed the empty cup and threw it into the flames.

"Whoa!" Cap reached forward and pulled her back a few steps. "Take it easy, girl. You don't want to fall in the fire."

"I'm already burning," she replied, looking past Cap to Riley. He was talking to Damien, hands flying, nostrils flaring.

"Okay. I'll leave you beauties to it, then." Cap's eyebrows knitted together for a second before he winked at Morgan. "See you later."

As he meandered away, Leila gushed, "He's so nice."

"Meh." Morgan shrugged. "He's not *that* great."

Leila wondered if she meant as a person, or in bed.

Morgan finished her drink and stepping closer, she pointed across the fire. "Look at my friends over there, such bitches."

Leila followed her pointing finger all the way across the other side of the clearing, where Crystal and ten other cheerleaders stared at them in disgust. Wait, not ten, five. Leila felt her body sway, the last drink catching up with her. She quickly lowered her gaze and steadied herself into a wide stance. In front of her, flames flickered and shone, orange sparks fluttering into the sky. Embers mesmerized her as they drifted down—dissipating before landing—

except for two that hovered in the distance, as though suspended by string. Not embers though. Eyes. Leila blinked, forcing herself to focus, but nothing was there.

She cleared her drying throat and squeezed Morgan's shoulder. "I don't expect anyone to understand our new friendship. But we're the same, you and me. So, we have to stick together."

"Like sandpaper to Velcro... is that right?" Morgan said, flattening her nose like a bunny.

"What about peas and carrots?" Leila grinned. "Or Shrek and Fiona... I'm Shrek of course."

Morgan laughed for the first time ... ever. She clung to Leila and giggled. "You are most definitely *not* Shrek. Why don't you come to more of these? We should have been friends ages ago."

"Don'know." Leila giggled back. She grasped Morgan's hand and led her around the fire.

"What ah'we doing?" Morgan asked, letting her free hand move up and down, as though preparing her wings for flight.

"A rain dance." Leila bent her knees and jumped twice. "Let's make it rain!"

They spun and laughed, and the fire became swirls of glorious orange-red. Stretching her hands as high as she could, Leila gazed to the heavens and twirled. She watched her fingers as they moved through the air, a faint glow lit their edges. Was that what Damien was talking about—the veil? She smiled. Her loose sleeves fell to her elbows and the end of her bandage flapped as she spun, undone by her wild dancing. *Let it fall*, she thought, considering that it wouldn't be a bad time to become a shifter.

And then, in a flurry of light and shadow, hands wrapped around her wrists and dragged her arms downward. She observed Riley as he frantically tightened the bandage up again, tucking the end so it couldn't undo.

"That's enough," he scolded, dragging her away from the crowd.

She looked over her shoulder for Morgan, relieved to find her hanging off Damien's arm as they weaved close behind. Morgan craned her neck, gaping at Damien. "Where'w'go?"

Just outside the clearing, the boys found a spot away from the party; isolated enough to give the girls the space they needed, yet close enough to make them not turn into four helpless teenagers alone in the forest.

Riley lowered her to the ground. "Just sit for a while."

Morgan's head weighed onto Leila's shoulder as she mumbled, "Wish had frienzzz like y'guys."

Leila stroked her new friend's head and rested her own onto the tree. Her mark still burned, as though it had absorbed all the heat from the fire. It clung to her, reminding her of what was soon to come.

"Should we take them home?" Damien asked.

"I don't know." Riley sighed. "I don't know what to do. She wants to be here."

Damien peered at girls over his shoulder. "They're also very drunk."

Silence for a bit and then, "They've got the right to be."

Riley's voice, saying those very words, made Leila's heart sing. He cared about her enough to respect her decisions, no matter how much he disagreed with them.

"Lighten up," Leila piped up, slumping forward. She wanted to help him understand how she felt but it came out all wrong. "Can't I celebrate my last day as a huu..." hiccup "as a..." another hiccup "a huuman." As soon as she got the word out her body lurched sideways.

Riley was by her side within seconds, sweeping his hands through her hair. As he held the curly strands behind her head, her body tightened. She convulsed as if she was retching, but nothing came up.

Her stomach churned, and it took her a second to realize she didn't need to vomit... a Guardian was calling her. It was the pull, strong and compelling.

She sat up, forcing Riley to move back. *Fight it, girl,* she told herself. She closed her eyes, breathing in time with the slow rhythmic bass that bellowed out the speaker and echoed through the leaves.

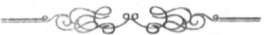

When Leila opened her eyes, the beat was different, a hyper-fast electronic sound. A breeze drifted across her right shoulder and she realized Morgan wasn't there anymore. She sprang forward.

"Where's Morgan?" Forcing her eyes wider, all she saw was a blur of bodies dancing in front of flames.

What have I done? she thought, Riley's fear becoming her own. She'd brought herself out there to the forest, at night... a sitting target.

A mumbled voice said something, and her eyes fluttered as Riley gently pushed her back against the tree. "Rest a bit."

"No. Wait! We have to help her." As soon as the words fell out her mouth she knew the truth.

And so did Damien. "It's like she's resting her fate on the fate of Morgan's. If Morgan is safe, she feels safe."

"Mmm," Riley agreed, shuffling next to Damien in front of her. He rested his elbows to his knees and looked out at the fire. "It makes sense I guess, she feels connected to her. Both of them are marked, both still not turned."

They talked about Leila as though she wasn't even there, and she began to think she may as well not be. They didn't seem to care about Morgan, it was up to her to find her. If Sebastian wasn't going to turn her, someone else would. It was fact, she wasn't safe. In a decisive moment,

Leila rolled to the side and shimmied around the tree slowly. And when she knew Riley wasn't looking, she crept into the forest.

After she'd walked a few meters into the forest, she swung back around and looped towards the fire. She glanced through the gaps in trees, willing her eyes to adjust. Blonde haired girls were everywhere—at the drink station tapping out the keg, sitting on the ground holding joints, dancing by the fire, standing at the lake. Seeing one with a red jacket laughing, Leila took a step closer.

She stopped, dead in her tracks. The magnetic pull was back, more powerful than ever.

"No, not now," she begged, covering her stomach. Despite her mind's protests she turned away from the party and—as though hypnotized—she began walking deeper into the forest.

Disconnected from her own body, Leila surged forward, pulled by a force stronger than her own will. She covered the bandage with her hand as she walked, surrounded by dark branches and menacing thoughts. Underneath, crunching leaves echoed around.

Is this where I die? she wondered, overcome with guilt for drinking so much. All this time she'd fought for survival and now her fight was going to end while intoxicated. She shook her head to contain an ill-timed bubble of laughter. *At least I'll find out who marked me.*

Not too far away, leaves crunched out of time with her step. She tried to stop walking but only managed to slow her pace a little.

"Morgan?" she called out into nothingness, avoiding leaves as she went.

Silence replied.

She took a few sharp breaths as her legs picked up speed. She stomped between pine trees, at least half a mile from the falls now, being led further from her friends and closer to transition. On reflection, she congratulated herself for lasting this long. Two full days with a mark and no Guardian had tried to turn her, until now.

And then, unceremoniously, the overpowering tug ceased.

She stopped walking—her weakened knees crashing together like jelly—and used a tree to keep her shaking body upright. The laughter she held in earlier, bubbled up again, but this time she didn't contain it. Was the whole thing a false alarm? Had the Guardian given up?

Inhaling the crisp night air, she turned to return to the party. Ahead of her, about ten meters, two glowing red eyes blinked.

She quickly squeezed her eyes together, hoping they would see clearer once opened again. The red eyes were moving closer, a dark silhouette taking shape around it.

"Wait!" Leila begged. "I'm not ready. I thought I was, but I'm not."

The woodland stalker stepped forward, out from the shadow of a tree into speckled moonlight. Standing there, half-shifted, was Tsukiko. Long pointed teeth poked out from her curled lips.

This is it, Leila thought to herself, *she's the one who marked me, and she will turn me right here in the forest, or worse, kill me.*

She readied her lungs to scream but Tsukiko lunged forward, covered her mouth and hushed. "I won't hurt you, Leila. I promise. I'm here to help."

Behind Kiko, stood a man with a small mo-hawk, his hands clasped in front of him. He wore a black leather jacket that made his dark eyes stand out. He looked around Leila's age, maybe a little younger. His skin was flawless.

"This is my brother, Ren," Kiko said.

His face remained stoic as he gave a quick nod to say hello.

"You must be so scared." Kiko's tone was gentle as she placed her hands on Leila's shoulders.

Leila replied with silence.

Kiko smiled softly, nodding. "You were marked on Friday."

Leila fought back tears. "Why did you do it?"

"Me?" Kiko cocked her head. "No, it wasn't me. On Friday, I had a slight hunch that you'd been marked but I couldn't see it on you. It wasn't until last night that I was almost positive. I could sense your mark in the air."

Collapsing to the ground, Leila was both relieved and tormented. Kiko didn't mark her, but who did? She looked up. "Are you a True Guardian?"

"How do you know about that?" Kiko asked, crouching down. Behind her, Ren crossed his arms and winced. Leila observed how uncomfortable he looked, as though he wanted to be anywhere else but in the middle of the forest, looking out for her.

"My boyfriend, he… he's good at research. Kind of a nerd like that."

"Right. And you obviously don't know who marked you, because you thought it was me." Kiko rolled back on her heels, eyes flitting in the air beside Leila's face, thinking. "If I knew who it was, then I could know if we can help you remove it."

"That's an option?" Leila's eyes lit up.

"Of course." Kiko smiled, baring more razor-sharp teeth. "Especially if someone from my clan marked you, they'll give you the choice. We won't turn you, unless you agree."

Leila used Kiko's shoulders to push herself up to her feet. "Well, I don't agree. How do I get rid of it?"

"Vervain, Himalayan salt, and the blood of the one who marked you—or their Alpha." Kiko pointed to her fingers as she counted ingredients.

She stood up slowly. "Melt the salt, crush the vervain, drop in the blood. Mix those together and you have your cure."

"That's it? That's all?" Leila looked between Kiko and Ren. "I've been in torture since last Friday and the cure is three stupid ingredients... wait... what's vervain?"

Kiko smirked and suppressed a chuckle. "It's a herb, and yes, that's all. The blood will be the hardest thing to find, especially if you don't know who marked you."

"Oh!" Leila's eyes widened, suddenly grateful for Riley and his appeal to know who touched her on Friday. "I have a list."

"A list?" Kiko asked.

"Of everyone who touched me on Friday," Leila explained. Then, her face dropped as excitement turned into gloom. "But, it's mostly full of dead-ends. The people who seemed most guilty have all come up clean, still Guardians, but clean."

Kiko lifted her delicate fingers to her chin as she thought. The few seconds of silence felt like hours of torture to Leila. All she could think about was the cure. Her chance for a normal teenage life was back within reach.

"Who are the other Guardians on your list?" Kiko finally said.

"There's Sebastian, this boy at school—he says he didn't mark me and hasn't tried to turn me. Then, there's Mr. Robertson, my geography teacher." Leila stopped. Then, she smiled. "You turned him?"

A glint of pride shimmered across Kiko's eyes. "Yes, that was me. I can't account for that Sebastian person, but your teacher? What can I say? I needed someone at the school to report to me about—"

"Me?" Leila interrupted.

"Kale means a lot to me, Leila." Kiko cupped her hand

around Leila's jaw. "I would do anything for him. That includes keeping his sister out of harm's way. That's what Guardians do."

Leila instantly thought about her eagle-eyed companion. "You should probably know, there's another Guardian. His name is Damien. He never touched me on Friday, but he was transitioned by a white wolf over the weekend."

Kiko spun wildly to Ren. He returned her movement with a pressing glare. "Do you think it's..." his voice drifted off.

Turning back to Leila, Kiko demanded, "Is there a William on your list?"

Leila furrowed her brow and shook her head. "I don't even know any William."

With a soft smile, Kiko settled. "Sorry. Just when you said white wolf... anyway, it doesn't matter, he's long gone. Now, that list?"

Leila closed her eyes, visualizing Riley scribing down names. She honestly didn't think any of them were capable of hurting her like that. She peeled her eyes open again. "They are all my friends, I can't imagine any of them doing this to me. Maybe someone else touched me and I didn't realize or can't remember."

"Maybe... possibly." Kiko took Leila's hand and gave it a reassuring squeeze.

The touch comforted Leila. It reminded her of when she was sitting in the darkroom with Damien. Like she was safe... protected.

She clenched her teeth into a nervous grin. "At least I know about the cure now. As they go to turn me I'll simply say, *hey can I have your blood*?"

"Any True Guardian would comply with that. But listen," Kiko's voice lowered. She took a breath before continuing, "If they aren't, they *will* come after you. Friends or not, Fallen Guardians don't take lightly to refusals. And, even if you've been marked by a True, the Fallen will see you as a threat and do everything they can to remove not only the mark, but you with it. They are great at deception, you'd be wise to remember that."

"I know." Leila hung her head, worried Kiko was implying that a friend was deceiving her.

Kiko and Ren exchanged sympathetic glances. Then, they looked at Leila as though she was already dead. Both eerily silent.

Leila lifted her chin, trying not to think of her friends still on the list. "So, where can I get vervain? And how do you melt salt?"

"Um, right," Kiko said, snapping out of her sorrow. "Kale has it. I've already made the ointment. You just need to rub the solution onto your mark. Or, you can tip it into a bath and let it soak around you. Whatever you are comfortable with. I put my blood in it, which will cover my clan—everyone I've turned, and anyone they've turned and so on."

Leila didn't want to say what she was thinking. But, for some reason she knew it's what Riley would ask and that meant it was a smart question. "And, what's the chance of one of them marking me? How many Alphas are out there?"

Kiko tucked a silken strand of hair behind her ear. Leila noticed a row of piercings all the way from the lobe to the helix, the lowest one was a silver spiral. "Ren and I are two of the earliest Guardians... ever. He is more selective with marking, but I have turned countless Guardians all over the world, and they are free to turn any more they see fit. If I saw a Guardian down the local street, I wouldn't even know if they came from me or not. To answer your question, yes, the odds are good."

"Leila?" Riley's voice echoed through the forest.

Leila whipped her head, heart soaring. She couldn't wait to tell him. But before she did, she needed to cover all bases. "What if the cure doesn't work?"

"Then things get serious... but don't worry. I'm in your corner, we'll sort it out no matter what." There was a comforting warmth in Kiko's voice.

"Wow, and I thought things were already serious. Can't wait to see what real serious is," Leila teased.

Smiling, Kiko said, "Ah yes, there it is. Kale told me you like to joke when you're afraid."

Leila pouted. "Oh, did he? Well, he's afraid of the dark, you know? He used to sleep with teddy bears until he was fourteen."

Ren let out a snort.

"I suppose that dear brother of mine also told you I was here? However he knew."

Kiko raised her brows. "He used to be your age too, once."

"Leila?" Riley sounded closer.

Kiko's head tilted. Leila imagined that if she were her fox, her ears would be twitching on high alert right now.

"That's my boyfriend," Leila said, motioning into the dark. "He will be worried, I should go."

"Go straight home." Kiko reached forward and hugged Leila, quick and tight. "Be careful."

After the short embrace, Leila felt lighter. She waved goodbye to Kiko and Ren, and turned back towards the falls. Kicking up her heels, she ran through the forest. Towards Riley.

Towards hope.

THURSDAY

after midnight

Distant flickers of raging flames turned the edges of leaves golden as she ran through the trees towards the sound of Riley's voice.

"Leila?" he cried desperately.

His silhouette came into view and she made a bee-line for him. "Riley. I'm here."

He came barreling towards her, zig-zagging around trees. Leila couldn't wait to tell him the news. He could stop being so worried for her, he could stop being so controlling. Things could go back to normal. They could argue about science essays and he could tease her for her tardiness and she could whip out sarcasm that he'd actually smile at. But most of all, they could be together without a dark cloud following their every move.

Riley crushed her in a fierce embrace, murmuring into her hair, "Thank God!"

With her cheek to his chest, she collapsed under his hold. She lifted her head at the same time as a cool drop of water landed on her forehead. It rolled down, catching on her eyelashes and collided with a forming tear.

His breath was short as he tilted his head down, lips closing in on Leila's. She awaited his soft kiss, but instead, he pulled away and tugged on her arm to study her bandage. "What happened? Are you okay?"

A few more droplets fell on Leila's head. Yelps and shrill cries echoed through the forest. The rain sounded like an unwelcome visitor to the party, partly because of the wet but mostly because of the cold.

"Yeah, I'm fine," Leila replied, smiling. As the rain landed on her, she enjoyed the refreshing coolness seep through her bandage.

Riley stepped back and exhaled loudly. Then, once his relief moved out of the way, his face changed. "What the hell were you thinking, wandering off like that? I knew this was a bad idea. I don't know why I let you talk me into this. You're completely out of control. It's like you don't even care." His arms flung in the air, eyes wild, breath heavy. "Well, guess what? I do. I care! And I can't take this..." He let his arms fall to his sides. A quieter, "I can't take it."

"First off." Leila frowned, hurt by his annoyance. "You haven't *let* me do anything. And secondly, I'm not your responsibility. If I turn, it's not your fault, there's nothing you can do."

"Of course it is!" He raked his fingers through his hair and started pacing. "It will be all my fault, just like before. All my fault."

"What do you mean before?" Leila watched him pace, every step bringing more pain to his face. He spun around, so she could no longer see him fall apart. "How was your sister turning, your fault?"

With his back to her, he stopped. "Let's go, let's get out of here. Damien and Morgan are waiting in the car."

Before he could take a step, Leila reached for his hand and tugged at him to face her. "Tell me why it was your fault."

Riley shook his head, avoiding eye contact. "I can't."

The more Leila pushed, the more he hid. There was something he wasn't telling her, but she'd had enough of his inconsistent behavior. Sighing, she brushed past him, and headed towards the dwindling fire.

Leila stepped into the deserted clearing by the waterfall as the last two seniors were running down the path. They precariously held the keg between them, as fairy lights dangled off their necks like boas. Nothing but sparkling ashes and scattered cups remained.

She turned to wait for Riley, but he was already right behind her, as usual. He gave her a bashful smile, his damp hair sticking to his brow. A rush of guilt flowed through her—she had ignored his feelings. She couldn't imagine what it was like for him, to watch someone he cared about being tormented like she was. She knew if it were him with the mark, she would do anything to keep him safe.

"I'm sorry for being a brat," she said.

He was silent as he walked right up to her, stopping barely an inch away. Looking at her through his darkened hair, he whispered her full name, "Leilani." His hand grazed her cheek, the light touch sending her heart into overdrive. "I know you want to pretend everything is normal but—"

She seized his hand. "I'm going to be all right, Riley. I can feel it.'

"I hope you're right."

Leila laughed. He didn't realize she meant it as truth, not simple hope. "I *am* right. I found a cure."

His eyes turned down at their edges. With sorrow, he stated, "There is no cure."

"Yes, there is." She cupped his face with both hands, willing him to believe her. "It's some witchy concoction, blood and everything. That's where I was just then, with a Guardian. She says an ointment removes the mark."

"What Guardian?" Riley's sadness swiftly turned to fear.

"Kale's girlfriend." Leila said it as though he should've known, but then she remembered she never told him about seeing Kiko shift. "She's on the list of people who touched me, but she didn't mark me... or so she said."

"Right." Riley looked at her skeptically. "You never told me her name."

"Tsukiko... I don't know her last name. She said she's one of the first Guardians ever." Leila held her arms across her chest, starting to feel the cold. But not even the temperature could dampen her spirits. She smiled eagerly, enthusing, "So, if she says there's a cure... I mean, it can't hurt to try right?"

"A cure," Riley said the words as though trying them on for size. He stepped back. His fingers weaved through soaked hair and his eyes searched the muddying ground for an answer.

Leila watched him as he retreated. "Riley?"

They were both silent for a while. Him hunched and brooding, her bright and confident. When he looked up, drops of rain streamed from his hair down his face, and one lone tear sat in the corner of his eye.

On the edge of hope, he gasped. "Leila, if this works..."

"I know." She stepped closer, clasping both of his hands. He spread his fingers and thread them in between hers. With the most serious face she could muster, she said, "We're going to get through this together."

His glistening lips opened and a chuckle tumbled out. "Stop being cheesy," he teased.

Releasing one of her hands, he swam his fingers

through her hair. He clutched the back of her skull, pulling her closer to him. One forceful kiss against her lips, and one tender kiss at the side of her temple. He pressed his cheek against hers. And squeezing her tight, he said, "I hope to god this works."

Damien was in the back of Riley's old Honda, humming along to the song on the radio. Next to him, resting on his shoulder, was Morgan—bleary-eyed and far from sober.

Leila leapt into the car and they melded into a jubilant embrace.

"You scared me!" Leila exclaimed.

"I was here the whole time," Morgan cooed, lifting a strand of Leila's hair. "You're so fluffy, like my Labradoodle when he's been bathed."

Leila settled into the front seat and resisted the urge to tell Morgan about the cure. She wanted to make sure it worked before she got her hopes up. She'd grown fond of her and, even though Morgan was a year older, Leila felt responsible for looking after her... for making sure she would survive this, too.

Riley stopped at Morgan's house and after they saw her safely inside, Leila blurted the cure news to Damien. His response was much of what she'd expected. "Are you sure it's something you want? I mean, you're giving up this awesome-ness." He motioned his body as though showcasing a prize on a game show.

Riley shot him a glare through the rear-view mirror.

"Uh, I mean, that's great news," Damien said quickly.

"Isn't it?" Leila settled into her seat. "I can't wait to get back to normality. No more looking over my shoulder. No more feeling like a puppet on strings." Leila flicked at the wet, dirty bandage. "Mostly, I can't wait to get this thing off my arm."

Behind her, Damien began humming again, tapping his palms against his thighs in time with the music. The beat ripped through Leila, too. She bopped her head to the bass and peered out the window, watching letter boxes blur as they drove.

"I hate to be the voice of reason." Riley turned the volume on his stereo down. "Let's take it one step at a time. The cure has to work first."

Damien leaned forward and patted Leila on the shoulder. "It will work, I can feel it."

"Oh but Damien," Leila said in a mocking deep voice. "We can't go on feelings alone."

Damien guffawed, thwacking Riley's seat. "I see what you did there. Did you hear that Riley? She used your words against you."

"Very funny," Riley said, shaking his head. A small smile hit the corners of his lips.

Leila grinned at him as they stopped at the curb by Damien's house. She looked out the window and rolled her eyes. Her house was actually closer to the falls. But, for once, she didn't blame Riley for wanting to drop her off last.

"I'll see you both tomorrow," Damien said, slinking out the car. With one arm holding the top of the door, he leaned down and pointed to Leila. "You, without the mark."

Riley looked at her with a smile. As soon as Damien closed the door, Riley put his foot down—water spinning off the back wheels as they went. There was a pep to his actions. He had let hope in, Leila could sense it.

As they approached the spot where Leila saw the white wolf with blue eyes the night before, Riley's hand crept across the car. He slid his fingers between hers. She closed her eyes for a brief moment.

Like the rest of the town, her street was quiet, apart from one house with its porch light on—hers.

Riley pulled up. He left the car running as he waited for a moment, staring at his hands around the steering wheel. Finally, turning to her, he asked, "Are you sure you don't want me to stay?"

Leila unbuckled her seatbelt and shuddered at the though of her brother interrogating her boyfriend. "I'm not sure Kale will like that."

"Stay with me, then," Riley urged. "Grab the ointment and tell Kale you're at Sadie's."

Remembering how uncomfortable his mom was with her there, Leila scrunched her nose. "I will be fine, I promise. Kale's a good protector, besides I'll put the ointment on right away."

Riley turned off the ignition. She opened her mouth to tell him he didn't have to walk her, but he had already opened his door. Rolling her eyes at his relentless and unnecessary gallantry, she exited his car and stepped into the rain. A biting chill was in the air, colder than before.

Riley rushed to the gate, opening it for her to walk through.

"Goodnight," she said, shivering.

He traced his fingers over the white rounded timber, as though prolonging the need to leave. Clearing his throat, he looked up. "I should get mom a nice gate like this."

The sides of Leila's eyes crinkled up. "Do you ever stop thinking about other people?"

Riley shook his head. "I can't."

"Of course you can." Leila pushed his bicep playfully. "You should do something for yourself… and I don't mean reading by the lake. Think of something exquisitely selfish, something you've always wanted to do but can't seem to bring yourself to. Just one thing. And then do it without second guessing yourself."

"One thing?" Riley smirked, stepping forward.

Leila watched him as he gleamed over her, his cedar-brown eyes hooded and hungry. She held her breath and whispered, "Anything."

He leaned forward and their silky lips, bathed in icy sleet, crashed together. He pushed his body against her, holding her lower back with one hand and the nape of her neck with the other. She grasped his shirt at his waist, bringing him closer still. Their mouths moved together, smooth and slippery—a mixture of hot breaths and greedy tongues. On the outside, Leila's skin was bumpy and purple, but her bones were far from chilled—warmth spread from her center all throughout her body. Taking a breath, Riley rested his forehead against hers, and scraped his teeth along his bottom lip.

Leila exhaled, a puff of white mist plumbed out. "You've done that before."

"It's the only thing I want." He ran a hand down her cheek. "You're the only thing I want."

She tried not to gasp, but her lungs expanded anyway. "I should go inside." She turned hastily towards her house before she did something reckless, like inviting him to climb up the lattice to her room, Romeo and Juliet style. She paused, one hand still clutching his shirt. Without looking at him, she said, "You could come in with me?"

Riley shook his head. "Now, you're asking me for the wrong reasons. It *would* be exquisitely selfish. But I can't be selfish right now, there are more important things to take care of first."

"Voice of reason, as always." She didn't mean for it to come out so callous.

She let go of his shirt and turned towards the house. After she took a few steps, Riley's shaking voice tumbled into the air, "I could have stopped it."

Leila spun around to find him right behind her. His face was wet but Leila couldn't tell whether it was just from the rain or his tears as well.

"It was my fault. Tessa's a Fallen because of me." A droplet escaped the corner of his eye, different from the other drops—thicker, denser, full of pain.

She took his hand and led him to the porch. They sat on the top step of the stairs, barely covered by the awning. Out of the rain but still in the storm.

"Tell me," she whispered.

He winced.

"Please."

Taking a deep breath, Riley ran his hands over his hair, slicking it back. He took another breath, quicker and decisive. "I could have saved her. I told you my mom was suspicious, but I didn't tell you that she asked me to follow her one day. I didn't want to, I was meant to hook up with some girl, I can't even remember her name..." He paused to wipe a tear from his cheek. "I'm not who you think I am."

The rapid strumming on the roof gave way to light splatters. In front of them, intermittent snow flakes fell with the rain. It was a subtle change, like a hushed breath, straining to hear a secret.

"What happened?" she urged.

Riley shook his head and craned his neck to the sky. "You won't look at me the same."

"Try me." Leila twisted around, squaring herself to face him.

He met her gaze, his brown eyes darker than their normal cedar shade. "My sister was marked that same day." He swallowed. "While I had a girl I didn't even know in the back seat of my car, my sister decided to become a Fallen Guardian." He tore himself away, unable to look her in the eyes. "If I hadn't been selfish and followed her that night, I could've stopped her from—"

"It's not your fault," Leila interrupted.

Riley winced. "How can it not be? I was so caught up in myself and my own conquests that I missed what was happening to someone I love. I won't do the same with—"

Leila interrupted him again, but this time with a kiss.

"You're distracting me," Riley said in a half-scolding, half-delighted tone. He held her head a few inches from his face, as though aching to kiss her back but resisting out of respect.

"I'm not your sister." Leila placed her hands over his. "And I'm not some random girl. I don't care who you *think* you are, I only care who you *actually* are. I know the real you, who you are now."

Riley let her go and shifted around. Leaning forward, he rested his elbows on his knees. He watched the snow settling on the small rose bushes that lined the stairs to the porch. Glistening white covered blood red. "I've lied about that time in my life so much, sometimes I forget who I really am."

"I'll remind you, then." Leila pushed herself up and stepped in front of him. Splatters of snowfall stuck to her hair. "You're someone who's caring, and who'll stop at nothing to keep those he cares about safe. No matter how annoying." She kicked her toe gently against his boot. "You're someone smart and goofy and super-cool at the same time—I don't even know how that's possible, but it is, because I've seen it. You're someone who makes me feel accepted with a smile, and weak at the knees with a glance. Whose kiss obliterates my fears..." she paused as her mark throbbed under the soaked bandage. Reaching down, she ran her fingertips over his ear, feeling how soft the shaved side of his hair was. "And guess what, Riley? I'm afraid. I want to be a normal seventeen-year-old, for just another moment. It would kinda be selfish of you not to kiss me."

Still slumped with his arms across his knees, Riley let his fingers fan out towards her. She knelt down at the same time he glanced up.

"Well then," he said with a sad smile. "I don't want to be selfish."

Clutching the collar of her shirt, he pulled her towards him, and planted a soft kiss onto her lips.

THURSDAY

very early morning

The warmth of the house engulfed Leila as she closed the door. Her face was flushed, her heart was full. She closed her eyes as she heard the sound of Riley's car driving away.

"Hey sis," Kale said tentatively.

Jumping a few inches, Leila clasped her chest. "Sweet biscuits!"

Kale gave a small smile, but his face was much more solemn than usual. He held a small clear bottle that had a violet-white cream inside it, black blobs swirling through the mixture. "Umm, Kiko dropped this off earlier. She said it was for your rash?"

"Oh great, yeah," Leila said, snatching it off him. "I bumped into her earlier and mentioned it. She said she had just the thing for it."

He studied her face, as if waiting for something. There was no way she could tell him the truth, though. One overprotective male was enough.

"Thanks!" Leila pushed past him and bounded upstairs.

"Okay... cool," he called after her.

In the bathroom, Leila turned the taps and poured the ointment in. As it churned through the running water, her heart skipped every few beats. She was quick to undress, sliding herself in the water before the bath was even full. She took the empty bottle and held it under the faucet, making sure all the solution was in the bath. Wiping her finger inside the bottle, Leila collected the last remaining drops, and wiped it onto the mark. She followed the spiral with her finger until the cure had all soaked in.

Sinking into the water, she let out a long sigh.

Blue eyes. Bright, blue, glowing eyes. They hovered in between trees, staring at her as though seeing through her very soul. She tried to run but she couldn't move, her feet dangling a meter off the ground. *I'm dreaming again,* she thought.

A wolf, as white as the snow it walked on, approached. It circled around Leila's floating body, sniffing the air around her. In the distance, a low growl rumbled through the forest. The wolf's ears perked. It glanced at Leila, then scampered towards the noise, leaving her alone.

The sky was dark blue; an orange hue shone near the horizon, promising daybreak.

If I hold on, Leila thought, *I can make it... I just need to last until morning.*

The unseen animal growled again, this time loud enough to shake the snow off every tree branch in sight. Flakes sprung into the air, tumbling as though inside a snow-globe. But instead of settling, they gathered— swirling together with increased momentum, until they became hundreds of white tornadoes, all heading for Leila.

Her stomach tightened; a Guardian calling her. It was heavy and desperate, as if even the Guardian couldn't make her move. She screamed out in pain, torn between her world and one much darker. As the storm careened towards her, an eerie howl fought to be heard above the whistling winds.

And then, a flash of lightning hit the ground in front of her. Another hit behind her, then another beside her. Countless flashes, one after the other, continued to hit — and when they stopped, a spiral of fire marked the soil below her.

The hurling snow storm, now upon her, met the burned ground and, like a force field, a blaze of golden light beamed up to protect her. It was bright and hot and dense. Her mark stung, like a thousand needles were digging into her arm. She closed her eyes, gasping for breath.

Two animal cries surrounded her, one like a howl and another more like a roar.

She shot her eyes open. It was still bright, but a lucid wave covered her vision and stung her eyes. She lurched forward, her wrinkled fingers clutching the side of the tub as her brain began separating the dream from reality.

Air, crisp yet humid, filled her lungs.

Surrounded by cool water, she sat up in the bathtub, gasping for breath. She held her arm out and inspected the mark. It was still there, bold and dark with a faint glow underneath.

Maybe it takes a while to work, she thought.

Leila climbed out of the tub. She wrapped herself in a towel and opened the cabinet to find a new bandage. After she covered her arm, she got into her pajamas and wandered into Kale's room.

He sat on his bed, eyes glued to a video game. "Hey kiddo."

"I fell asleep in the bath," she said flatly.

"You must have needed it." Kale smiled, turning off the TV. "How's your rash?"

"Rash?" Leila was confused for a beat. When her brain caught up, she waved a hand in the air. "Umm, yeah. The cream was soothing. I'll give it a while before I see what the effects really are."

Kale nodded and patted the mattress. "And how have you been? I feel like I haven't seen you much this week."

"I've been busy, sorry." She sat on the edge of his bed.

"Mhm." He raised his eyebrows, as if waiting for her to say something else. Just like before.

Leila wondered if Kiko told him about the mark. But quickly dismissed the idea. Kiko probably didn't want him to know about what she was. And Leila couldn't blame her, dragging Riley into this mess was bad enough.

"You've seemed pretty off." Kale pushed her knee with his knuckles. "What have you been busy with?"

"I have a boyfriend," Leila blurted, cringing at her use of distraction.

"Really?" Kale's eyebrows lifted. "When can I meet him?"

"Never!"

Kale lowered his bottom lip dramatically. "Aww, come on. I'm going to have to give him the once over, it's my brotherly right."

"No!" Leila cried, jumping to her feet.

"Pretty please?" He rolled up onto his knees, hands clasped together. "I'll only ask him a few questions. Like, *is he a murderer* and *does he love you*, things like that."

Leila cracked a smile. "Definitely not then."

"Okay, no questions." Kale sighed in defeat. Then, his face lit up again. He leaned forward eagerly. "Can I at least do the whole *you hurt her, and I'll kill you* thing? I've always wanted to do that."

"Fine, you can do that one," she relented.

"Yes!" He said, fist-bumping himself.

Leila shook her head and turned towards his door.

"You know I'd do anything for you, right?" A serious tone replaced the moment of levity.

With a timed smile, she glanced over her shoulder. "I know."

"Good, so that boy better watch it!"

Even though she trusted Riley, it was nice to hear her big brother's promise. Walking out the door, she raised her middle finger over her head. "Goodnight boof-head."

"Goodnight turd."

THURSDAY

morning

Leila woke up feeling like she'd had the best sleep since she was five years old. Remembering the snow fall, she swung her legs over the edge of the bed and peeked her head behind the drapes. A light sprinkle of white covered her front yard and plants. Looking further, she noticed the road was wet, but the snow hadn't been thick enough to settle. School would still be on as per usual. She watched a bird land on the rose bush out front, it sent a dust of snowflakes to the ground. It reminded her of something, a foggy memory just out of reach. The sudden pang of de ja vu was interrupted by her phone message trill. She dove across her bed and retrieved her phone. A message alert from Riley lit up the screen, *did it work?*

She sprung to her feet and unraveled the bandage with excitement. It crumpled to the floor as she stared at her arm. Her heart leapt at the sight.

Returning to her phone, she typed a speedy reply. She hovered her finger over the send button, a moment of hesitation. Was it too early to tell? Should she lie? She deleted her message and wrote a new one.

Yes! The mark's gone.

"Kale?" she cried, racing out of her room.

He opened his door, wearing nothing but black boxer shorts. Rubbing his eyes, he yawned. What's up?"

"Can you give me Kiko's number?" Leila demanded, her arm already extended.

"Why?" He blinked slowly, eyes still adjusting to the light.

"I want to thank her for the cream." She wiggled her fingers, urging him to hurry.

His tired eyes drifted to her arm. "Is it gone?"

Leila's mouth fell open and she instinctively pressed her arm against her torso. He knew? How long has he known?

"Is it gone, Leila?" he pressed.

Leila stared at him, dumbstruck. "She told you?"

"Of course she did. She told me about what she was weeks ago... is the mark gone?" he said it so casually, as though he was merely asking her if she liked donuts.

"But... but the other day at the... at the door," Leila stuttered. "You said that you couldn't see her red eyes or claws or..."

"Yeah, about that..." Kale winced and rubbed his neck. "I lied. Sorry, but you were freaking out and I didn't want you to be afraid. I wanted her to be one hundred percent sure before coming to you, I didn't want her to bring you into that world."

Leila glared at his grimacing mouth and earnest eyes. "Well, I'm in it. I'm freaking in it! Get me your phone."

"Okay, crazy-pants. Hold on." He rushed to his room and returned with his phone.

She snatched it off him and started scrolling through his contacts. Would he have put her name under T? Or

maybe K—

"Uh wait." He hovered over her and pressed A. Scrolling through, he stopped on the word *Angel.* "That's her."

"So corny," Leila muttered, hitting the call button. She began pacing along the hall between her room and the top of the staircase. Every ring out felt like hours.

"Hey there," Kiko cooed. "How's my love muffin?"

"It's Leila," she panted as though she'd walked miles not meters.

"Leila! Did you get the ointment?"

Heart pumping, Leila asked, "How long does it take to work?"

"It should work immediately."

"Immediately?" Leila swiveled on her heels and stared at Kale. When he noticed the look on her face, he lost all color from his. She wiped a falling tear. "Then no one in your sire line marked me."

Kale paced in the kitchen. He waved a soup ladle into the air, freaking out that a Fallen Guardian may be stalking his little sister to turn her. Kiko was sitting on the island bench and had just told Leila she needed to stay at home.

"Can my boyfriend come over at least?" Leila asked. "I kinda lied to him that the mark was gone."

Kiko smiled sympathetically. "He's a civilian, Leila. I'm sorry, it's too risky."

Leila stood at attention. It was time to stop running. It was time to be brave once and for all. "Okay, give it to me straight. What will happen to me?"

Kiko pressed her lips together, as though considering whether or not to divulge the whole truth. She stepped closer to Leila. Her eyes were low as she said, "The person who marked you will come for you. Honestly, I'm surprised they haven't already. I guess they've gotten themselves too busy."

"And?" Leila knew Kiko was holding back. She didn't want half-truths anymore. "Then what?"

Still pacing, Kale threw his arms in the air and muttered to himself, "I was supposed to be looking after her. I'm supposed to be her protector. Instead, here I am listening to my angel girlfriend prepare my baby sister for the worst-case scenario."

Ignoring him, Kiko answered Leila's question as emotionless as possible. "There's Guardian DNA hidden in our fangs, it works like venom. It needs to be inserted into the mark for activation. That DNA determines whether you're a True Guardian or a Fallen."

Leila licked her lips, forcing the sinking feeling in her stomach away. "After I'm bitten, what next?"

"You will align with your spirit animal. I know it sounds hocus pocus, but every human has one. A Guardian just has the ability to bring them forth and become one with them."

Leila nodded, remembering what Damien told her yesterday. "And I'll be in control of it?"

"Yes, even the Fallen have control..." Kiko gave Kale a side-eye as he began tapping the ladle on the top of his head. She furrowed her brow and turned her attention back to Leila. "Yet, their ruthless intent is often magnified. Their humanity is lessened, so they aren't empathic like a True guardian is. The line between animal and human is gone. They kill with no remorse."

Being something so rotten sounded worse than death to Leila. "When I'm bitten—"

Kale slammed the ladle onto the edge of the kitchen sink. "If, Leila," he cried. "If.".

Leila looked at Kiko, who dropped her eyes to the floor. She continued, "*When* I'm bitten, if I'm Fallen, will you stop me?"

Kiko lifted her head. "There is another way."

"What is it?" Kale spun on his heels, and leaned over the bench, eyes fixed on Kiko.

"I turn you," Kiko stated, her eyes on Leila.

Silence, not even a hitched breath could be heard. The offer sounded so final. The curtain call at the end of a long and tedious play. An end though, and not a terrible one.

"Is that what you want, Leila?" Kale asked.

She didn't know. Last night, she wanted to make the most of her limited time as a regular human, but now she'd had a taste of a cure, it's all she could think of. "What if I can find who marked me and get their blood to you to make another serum?"

Kiko tilted her head, a soft smile lit her face. "It's your life, I won't force you into anything. But it's an option."

"Don't be stupid Leila," Kale said, sliding across the bench, legs first. He grabbed her shoulders. "You've got a True Guardian here, offering you a lifeline. What if you don't get the chance to find who marked you? What if they turn you first? What if they... *kill you*?" He whispered the last two words, as if saying them out loud gave them power.

An unrelenting helplessness loomed over her, like she was waiting for that very thing... death. Her eyes filled with tears. "I don't know."

In divine timing, her phone vibrated in her pocket. Wiping her face, she took out her phone to see a text from Sadie. *Where are you? Gab is here... she has the mark.*

Leila glanced at the time, it was nine-thirty. With pleading eyes, she said decisively, "I'd like a day to think."

"You might not have a day!" her hysterical brother wailed.

"Okay, it's up to you." Kiko squeezed Leila's shoulder encouragingly. "It's always up to you."

Kale threw his arms in the air and sighed.

"But..." Leila winced, knowing she was pushing her luck. "Not spent here. I'd like the day at schoo—"

"Oh my god!" Kale began muttering to himself again. "She's crazy. She's actually gone crazy."

"Gabby's been marked." Leila lifted her phone, showing Kiko the text message. "Can I have just one day to find who did this to us—to save not only me, but my friends, too. Please?"

Sympathy flashed over Kiko's face. Nodding once, she said, "I'll call Luke... Mr. Roberston. I'll ask him to keep an eye out for you."

"Thank you." Leila didn't waste a moment to wrap her arms around Kiko. Pulling away. She turned to Kale. As she hugged him, his arms remained at their sides in defiance.

"You're a pain in my butt, you know that?"

"Yep, it's part of the little sister job description." She danced her fingertips over his head, grabbed a handful of coins from the loose change bowl, then ran upstairs to get into her uniform.

THURSDAY

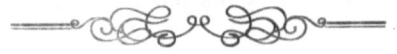

late morning

It almost felt like a normal school day to Leila. She arrived late and stuffed her bag into her locker. As she pulled out her English study book, she glanced at her math book, wondering if she did, in fact, have algebra instead.

"Hello there, Leilani Belladonna."

Leila's heart leapt at the voice. It belonged to someone on the list... someone who touched her on Friday. She closed her locker and slowly turned around.

Taj stood behind her, a wide grin on his face. His hair was properly unkempt as usual, and he had a row of care bear badges lining his blazer collar. Perfectly normal, if it weren't for the looming sense that she still had no idea who'd marked her.

Leila gave a nervous smile to the boy who'd been her friend for over a year now. Their unlikely pairing began when they accidentally scheduled the same time in the dark room and had to share space. It took them no time to bond over their mutual love for documenting the mundane and finding beauty in it—and, of course, Reese's Peanut Butter Cups.

"I've been waiting for you," he said, grin disappearing.

"You have?" Leila glanced up and down the empty hall.

"Yeah, I'm in the dark room this morning and wondered if you had those negatives from the pep rally still? I left my copies at home."

Leila looked at him for a moment, wondering if he was telling the truth or being a great deceiver. Still unsure, she replied, "Um, yeah, they should be in my file in the dark room."

"Can you come with me and get them?" He pored over her, his eyes flitting between her face and her still bandaged arm.

She cleared her throat, even though she didn't need to. Taking a hasty step forward, she brushed past him and said, "You're welcome to search through it."

He jogged to catch up, bumping her with his shoulder. "You may as well skip class and hang with me…"

Leila looked at him sideways, hoping for him to do or say something quirky, anything to show her that he was still himself and not what she was suspecting him to be. A broken fluorescent light flickered above them, a glimmer ran across his eyes.

"I've got these…" He dove his hand into his bag and pulled out a packet of Reese's. The rustle of the bag resonated against the stark walls in the hallway, illuminating the fact that she was all alone with him.

"I, ah, gotta…" She ran before finishing her sentence.

As she reached the end of the hallway and flung the classroom door open, she heard his voice echo down the corridor. "You still owe me a paparazzi style photo, remember?!"

"Hello, Miss Belmonte. Take a seat." Mr Robertson kept

his eyes on the board as he spoke.

She panned the room; knowing Gabby and Damien had different classes, she searched for the faces she knew best. Riley was smiling wide and Sadie waved ecstatically. They looked so happy, it was a welcome sight—and it took all her strength not to burst into tears right there in the doorway. She bypassed her normal seat next to Sadie and stopped in front of Riley's desk. Slamming her hands on his desk, she leaned forward and planted her lips hard against his. He pulled back at first, then when she followed him, he gave in and kissed her back. The classroom erupted with cheers. As she pulled away, she wiped the bottom of Riley's lip with her thumb.

"All right now," Mr Robertson yelled. "Who wants detention?"

Leila didn't care though. If that was the last time she ever got to kiss him, then it was worth a lifetime of detentions. Besides, she imagined Kiko to be a kind yet ruthless Alpha. He wouldn't want to mess with Leila or there'd be hell to pay.

"I'm glad you're okay," Riley said, glancing at the bandage.

She kept her hands on Riley's desk, still leaning close. She whispered, "I figured it would be best to keep it, so no one asked why it was suddenly better."

"Okay, good idea," Riley whispered back. He cupped his hand around her bandage and dragged his thumb across where her mark was.

"Miss Belmonte." Leila could hear the frustration in her teacher's voice. "Get to your seat."

She held her hand up in an apology, and tip-toed to her seat next to Sadie.

"Riley told me about the cure." Sadie was practically beaming. She looped her arm through Leila's. "Just in time, too. Did you hear about Miss Carson? Her body was found near the lake not two hours ago."

"What?" Leila baulked, horrified.

Sadie nodded, her eyes lighting up, as though taking pleasure in Leila's shock. "From what people are saying, it was pretty gruesome."

Leila slid her arm out of Sadie's hold. She looked across to Riley. His chin rested lazily on his hand as he stared at her with a goofy smile. Leila frowned. The news of a teacher's death should have elicited a different emotion than the ones her friends were giving her.

"So." Sadie moved her head forward, blocking Leila's view of Riley. "Did you bring the cure for Morgan and Gabby?"

"What?" Leila blinked a few times, slowly realizing what they were so happy about. They thought she'd been cured.

The space between Sadie's eyebrows wrinkled. "Is that the only word you can say today?"

"Ugh, come on girls. Can you at least pretend to listen?" Mr Robertson scoffed in their direction.

Leila sunk into her seat but as soon as he turned back to the board the PA crackled. "Leila Belmonte to the office, please."

Mr. Robertson glared at her, as though she was the one who made the noise. She knew he was on her side, but he still intimidated her. He swung his arm to the door.

"Well, go then, Missy."

At the office, the receptionist tapped her pen on her head while sorting through papers. "I swear I just had it... where... oh, here it is, Leilani Belmonte. Oh yes, how could I forget? There's a phone call for you." She slid her chair across the floor to the other side of the desk and picked up the receiver, pressing a button that was lit up red. "Are you there? Yes, I have Leilani here for you..."

Leila smiled to herself, it was kind of sweet for her brother to check up on her. She took the phone. "I'm fine, Kale."

"You want to know who marked you?" a male's voice that definitely wasn't Kale's croaked through the receiver.

The hair on the back of Leila's neck stood on end. "Who is this?"

"Meet me in the library," he demanded, then hung up.

Leila practically threw the phone at the receptionist and took a step back. She didn't recognize the voice, but it felt familiar at the same time. Was it Taj, trying to get her alone again? She didn't want to find out.

Determined to go straight back to class, Leila high-tailed it out of the office. She sped through the corridors, feet slipping on newly waxed floors. There was no way she'd go into the library. No way at all.

But the closer she got, the slower she ran. By the time she reached the library doors, she couldn't help but stop. Staring at the handles she took a moment to catch her breath.

She thought of Gabby, who must now feel as she did when she first discovered the mark. And Morgan, too, who had been through the ringer right beside her. This may have been her only chance. Taj might be reasonable, give her a drop of his blood, and let them all carry on with their lives.

As she turned the handle and pushed the door open, she scolded herself. *Don't be stupid. Go back to class and get Mr Robertson to go with you.*

Despite her own common sense, she stepped through into the library. The door swung shut behind her, closing her in.

It was deathly quiet. She took her time to stroll through the middle of the room, one tentative step after the other. She weaved past the tables and chairs, peeking down all the aisles as she went. When she reached the sofas at the back of the room, she released a breath that seemed to echo through the room.

There wasn't anyone else in there, not even the librarian. Was it all just a prank? On her way back through the aisles, she came across a section she had become well acquainted with that week. She trailed her fingers over spines until she got to a large brown book with its gold-foiled title. She pulled it out, and even though there was no dust on it, she brushed her palm over the cover. Riley said there was no mention of a cure in it, but she thought maybe he missed it.

She balanced the book on her forearm and opened to the contents page. The paper was thin and rough, crinkling as she turned the pages. As she read the first chapter title: *The Origin of The Myth*, a low snarl came from next aisle.

She snapped the book shut. On high alert she spun around in a full circle, clutching the book her chest, as though it could protect her. Through a gap in the shelf beside her, two neon blue eyes stared through.

The eyes belonged to Sebastian. He hid in the medieval section, breathing deep. Blood dripped from his fangs and splattered on the shelf.

Leila stepped back, her fingers releasing their grip on the book. As it crashed against the linoleum beneath her feet, Sebastian moved swiftly between the aisles. He stood in front of Leila, hunching over, not blinking—his eyes wide and manic. Scarlet stained his claws and mouth. He was silent aside from a deep rumble in the back of his throat, like his own breath was choking him.

Leila wondered if the vampire myth began from someone seeing a half-shifted Guardian like this. It was then she knew that she was wrong about him. He was a Fallen, the stench of someone else's blood on him proved that.

Heart pumping into overdrive, she kicked the book at him and sidestepped out of the aisle.

"No, no, no," he said, raising his hands and shaking them in surrender. "I'm not going to hurt you... I promise."

Leila eyed the doors over ten meters away. "What do you want?"

"Help." There was a twinge in his voice, meek and desperate.

Leila swallowed. Both Riley and Kiko said the Fallen were good deceivers. She stared at the blood around his mouth, globs of red stuck to his chin.

"Help me," he gasped.

"How?" She took another step back and braced the table's edge behind her.

Sebastian stepped back too, his hands still raised. "You found a cure? That's the word around."

Confusion soared through Leila's mind. His face said that he was a monster, yet his eyes screamed that he was scared. She felt a pang of guilt as she said, "I lied, it didn't work."

"What?" He could barely get the word out. He blinked rapidly as his arms fell to his sides. "There is no cure?"

"There is... but not for those who have already turned."

A small whimper left his mouth.

The shadow of Sebastian Weir stood in front of Leila. A lost puppy—vicious, but still in need of love. She eyed the blood all over him. "Is anyone hurt?"

He studied his hands, and as though seeing the red for the first time, he furrowed his brow. He looked up. Tears streamed down his face, sliding through dried blood. "I don't want to be this."

Leila's heart sank. Sympathy rushing through her, she stepped back into the aisle towards him. "Me neither."

"I was trying to save Morgan, you know that right?" He clenched his hands into fists. "This thing I am, that others are... it's bad."

Her bottom lip dropped, saddened by his confession. A Fallen had turned him, but he wasn't what she was expecting. He was an arrogant pig most of the time, but Leila would never say he was evil, not even now.

Sebastian's neon eyes dulled to their regular shade and his fangs began to retract, but the shameful stains remained.

"Wait!" Leila urged, unraveling part of her bandage. She lifted it up to him. "Would you mind?"

He bowed his head, glancing up at her with tear-glistening eyes. He slowly raised his hand and tipped his finger towards the lengthened piece of cloth. His razor sharp claws sliced through the bandage before they returned to normal fingernails.

Leila took another step forward, dangerously close to him and held out the broken piece. "Here, let me."

He jutted his chin out as she dabbed the torn bandage over his lips. White cotton now streaked with dark red. When he noticed how much blood was coming off his face, he grimaced and averted his eyes. Looking up at the ceiling, he said, "I lied to you, too."

"When?" she asked, wiping harder through the stubble on his chin.

"About who turned me."

Leila paused. As if afraid of the answer she whispered, "Who turned you?"

"Cap."

A sudden flashback to Friday; bumping in to him at basketball, him helping her up. He touched her. Cap touched her.

Leila scrunched the dirty bandage in her fist. "Do you think he marked Morgan and Gabby too?"

Sebastian nodded, bringing his gaze back down. "He's crazy. He turned all the team, every single one of them.

Then, he marked half a dozen girls around school for each of us to turn. And then, he marked another half a dozen people for us to kill. It's like some kind of sick initiation."

Nausea hit. Leila crossed her arms over her churning stomach. Had she been marked to be turned or killed? Then, she remembered what Sadie had told her. A sudden realization followed. "Mrs. Carson was killed today."

Sebastian lowered his eyes, searching the ground between their feet. He picked at the blood under his nails. A shudder ran through his body.

"Was that you?" she probed.

He shook his head, looking up with fresh tears in his eyes. "I didn't want to. You have to believe me. I refused. But Cap, he…" Sebastian anxiously squeezed his hands together. "He threatened my family. He told me if I didn't kill her that he would kill me, then her, then move on to my family. I'm not saying I made the right choice, but what would you have done?"

Leila couldn't understand it. The Fallen were painted relentless and demon-like. But how he acted—remorseful, and decidedly not ruthless, she knew it wasn't so black and white. "You made a difficult decision, one I can't judge."

"You've probably guessed that Morgan was my assignment to turn? I don't know how long I can stall before Cap does it himself."

A shiver ran down her spine. "Who was assigned to me?"

Sebastian lifted his shoulders.

It didn't matter anyway, she only needed one thing. "I can get a cure for her, for us—I just need his blood."

He straightened. "Leave it to me."

Curious with his change in loyalty, Leila asked, "Why would you help us?"

"I don't want this for anyone, let alone people I care about. Yes, Leila, I care about you. I'm not a complete monster."

Leila knew how that felt. She nodded and passed him the already stained bandage piece. "You should probably finish cleaning up in the bathroom." She took a step to hug him but changed her mind at the last second. "Be careful."

"I will, Mutt..." he cleared his throat. "Leila."

THURSDAY

noon

As soon as the class was dismissed for lunch, Leila was first out the door. On her way back from the library earlier, she'd called Tsukiko and gave her the locker number to leave the serum in. All she had to do was put a drop or two of Cap's blood in and the treatment should work for all three girls.

By the time she got to her locker, Riley had caught up with her. He wrapped his arms around her waist. "What's the rush?"

A smile spread across his face—Leila hadn't seen his eyes sparkle like that since before she was marked. She couldn't tell him what the rush was, not yet. If she told him, he'd be worried all over again, he'd go after Cap, he'd start something he couldn't finish.

"I'm meeting someone," she said, wracking her brain to come up with any excuse.

Sadie swished in beside Leila and opened her locker. "You were gone a while earlier, what were you up to?"

Leila glanced at Sadie and opened her own locker, swinging it in front of Riley's face. She sighed with relief to see a bottle of pink ointment sitting nicely on all her screwed up papers. Sadie peered around her locker door. Leila tucked the bottle in her blazer pocket.

"Sadie?" she said, closing her locker. "Can you bring Morgan and Gabby to the library? I'll tell you what I was up to when you get there."

Sadie nodded gleefully. She slammed her locker door and started running towards Gabby. Turning around to run backwards, she called, "I love your missions!"

"What have you gotten yourself into?" Riley crosses his arms, smile waning.

"Library?" Leila walked on without waiting for his reply.

Leila led the way to the library and he followed her in silence. Glancing at him every now and then, she caught him chewing on the inside of his mouth. His fear was returning and she hadn't even told him the truth yet. *Ugh, what a horrid feeling.*

When they entered the library, Leila slid her hand into his and pulled him to the sofas at the back. She plonked herself down in the middle of the sofa that faced the window. He sat opposite her, dimples flashing with every nervous lip bite.

"You want to know where I've been?" Leila dug her hand into her pocket. Cupping the bottle into her fist, she leaned forward and opened her hand. "I've been getting a cure for everyone else."

He stared at the bottle and the ointment inside. Looking up, he grinned. "You're relentless. You would have made a great True Guardian."

Leila cringed at his use of the words *would have*. As though all of it was behind them. How was she going to tell him? "What kind of Fallen Guardian would I make?"

He took the bottle out of Leila's palm and lifted it up to the light, casually saying, "A terrifying one."

"Don't joke about it." She snatched the ointment back.

"Sorry, I thought that's what you like." He winked and flashed his teeth in a cheeky smile.

"Jokes are for pretending everything is okay when it's not..." She tucked the bottle back into her pocket. "But I don't need to pretend it's okay, I know who marked us all." Without a moment of hesitation, she declared, "Cap."

Riley's eyes widened. "Cap, really? Shit."

Leila let the information sink in. She watched Riley get lost inside his own mind, piecing it all together. For effect, she added, "And, he's a Fallen."

"Oh my God." Riley collapsed back into the sofa, his palms running down the sides of his face. A second later, he sat up. "How do you know this?"

"Sebastian." Leila shrugged as if it were no big deal.

"You've been talking to Sebastian?" Riley sighed. "Leila, he's dangerous."

So definite. If it was up to Riley, he'd have everyone categorized into nice little boxes. Leila knew better. Or at least, she'd hoped for more.

"I know... but then, he's not... I mean, how do you know there are Fallen Guardians for sure? Everyone who has turned seems normal, just enhanced a little. Mr Robertson, Damien, Sebastian... they are different but still themselves. Not overly bad or overly good."

Riley frowned. "My sister."

"But was she completely out of her mind? I know you said she tried to kill your mom, but surely —"

"She wasn't herself, okay?" he snapped in a harsh whisper. Like he was mad yet not at the same time.

Leila wistfully looked out the window. From the second floor, she couldn't see anything but sky, overcast and gloomy. "But there has to be good in everyone,"

"What if there isn't?"

"There is!" she stated, turning her attention back to Riley. "There has to be."

A worried crease appeared between Riley's brows. His eyes flitted to her arm. "Why is it so important?"

"It just is," Leila said, placing her hand over the bandage.

She glanced back to the supernatural section, where not even two hours earlier, Sebastian came to her. He was scared, there was no denying that. And he felt guilt, not like what Kiko said.

Maybe she wasn't completely doomed. Maybe if she was turned by a Fallen, she would still end up mostly human? She held onto the small glimmer of hope, as though it was the very air that kept her alive. Who would have thought that Sebastian would be the thing that gave her hope?

She leapt to her feet and jogged to the supernatural section. The big book was still on the floor where she dropped it. She picked it up and returned to her spot on the sofa opposite Riley.

He reached for the book. "Let me see."

A double thud, fast footsteps, and loud whispers caused Leila to turn. She watched Sadie, Gabby, and Morgan walk towards her. Seeing Gabby made her heart ache. Leila jumped to her feet and hugged her tightly. Sitting back down, she said, "We'll fix this."

"They say you are cured?" Morgan leaned on the edge of the sofa, a hopeful glimmer in her expression.

More aches, this time guilt. Leila grimaced. "I'll have a cure for you too, soon."

"Morgan?" Riley leaned forward. "Did Cap touch you at all recently?"

"Uh." Morgan shifted her eyes to Leila and back. "What do mean by touch?"

Sensing Morgan's discomfort at Riley's poor choice of words, Leila interjected, "He marked us. He's also the one who turned Sebastian, and Sebastian was trying to prevent you from being turned, too."

Morgan dug her teeth into her bottom lip. "I thought maybe I was over-thinking it, but I had a feeling it was him. We slept together on Friday night. He seemed off..." Morgan glanced up, realizing her confession. "Not that I had slept with him before."

She shook her head at herself. "Anyway, he was controlling and forceful. Oh, don't get me wrong," she spluttered, grimacing. "I wanted to do it, it was just—not what I thought I wanted. Afterward, he told me I needed to go home and rest because he was coming back for me. I didn't really know what that meant until right now."

Gabby slumped next to Riley, letting herself sink into the grooves of the sofa. "He sounds like a charmer."

"What time is it?" Leila anxiously looked over her shoulder.

"It's lunch," Sadie replied, propping herself in between Morgan and Leila. She frowned. "Why are you so edgy?"

"I'm waiting on one more ingredient." Leila pulled the top of the ointment bottle out, giving them only a split-second glance before dropping it back into her pocket again.

"But what if I don't want to be cured?" Gabby asked, twirling the dyed-green ends of her hair.

"Pfft," Leila scoffed. "Of course you do."

"Uh, hello. Have you seen Damien? He is metal, a freaking force. That's not so bad," Gabby tried reasoning.

Leila sighed and reached for the book that Riley had placed beside him. He slammed his hand on the cover, squashing it between the sofa and his muscle. Leila frowned and yanked the book out from under him with ease.

She glanced at Gabby. "I'll show you what it says about Guardians and the mark and what happens when you transition... and what happens if you are turned by a Fallen. Just trust me, you don't want the torture they go through."

"Torture for who? The Fallen or those they hurt?" Riley huffed, reaching for the book.

Shimmying back, Leila glowered. "What's wrong with you?"

She flicked through the book until she found the picture of the man with the spiral tattoo—the page Riley was on when he first told her about Shadow Guardians. She scanned through, but the page only described the werewolf myth throughout modern history, nothing about their true heritage or meaning. She muttered to herself, "What page was it on?"

Leila flicked to the next page, the page before it, the page after it. She turned to the index... but there wasn't a single notation about Shadow or Guardians... nothing about the mark... nothing about the Fallen.

"Riley?" She glanced up to see his head buried in his hands. She turned the book to the front again and scoured the contents section. Irish folklore, Greek gods, even the damn Nhang her mom loved was there, but nothing about any of what Riley read to her. Nothing.

"I got it!" Sebastian puffed, shoving his hand in front of her face. A line of blood marked his knuckle. "My fist *accidentally* found his face when I was passing the ball to Don. Let's do this thing."

Six of them huddled under the bleachers, rain streaming around them. A few sophomores sat nearby, playing a game of 'would you rather?' or something equally obnoxious. Sebastian stood over them, crossing his arms in such a way that both his biceps and cut knuckles were on display. He stared until they ran off. Turning back, he said, "Ready when you are, Bitsa."

They each held their breaths as he tipped his hand and blood dripped into the bottle. Leila put the lid on and shook it up. Darkened globs of deep red swirled within the white.

"Are you sure it doesn't work on those already transitioned?" Sebastian asked.

"I don't think so. But, you could try." Leila unscrewed the cap and passed the bottle to Gabby. "You first."

Gabby opened her mouth, as if to protest, but closed it again as she took the bottle. She shook her blazer off, undid the top two buttons of her shirt and bared her shoulders. Leila noticed her spiral was in the exact same place as Damien's. Gabby spread some ointment over the mark and held the bottle out.

Sebastian took the bottle and turned to Morgan. He helped her cover the mark on her waist and, with a trail of solution still left on his fingers, he shoved his hand down his top and wiped across his collar.

Leila glanced at Riley as she took the bottle from Sebastian. He hadn't looked at her since she found out the book had no information about Guardians whatsoever. She kept her eyes on him as she unraveled her bandage.

Riley looked then. "I thought you said the mark was gone?"

"It seems we both like to embellish the truth then, don't we?" Leila dipped her fingers into the bottle and rubbed the cream over her arm.

A slight quiver shook Riley's lips. "I wasn't embellishing the truth. I just didn't know how to tell you what I knew, without you asking questions about how I knew it."

"Well, you told me about your sister anyway. So, you could have led with that."

He leaned forward, holding the timber seat above for balance. "I'm sorry."

Everyone was quiet as they argued, but Leila was too upset to pretend anymore. She stepped away from him. "Yeah, well it's not happening to you, it's happening to me. Next time, the truth will do."

Beside her, Gabby stifled a laugh.

"Gabs," Sadie hushed, thwacking Gabby's shoulder with the back of her hand. "This is no time for laughter."

"Sorry. It tickles?" Gabby said, her voice lilting, as though it was a question. "How long does it take?"

"It should be immediate." Leila looked at her arm. Still marked.

"Uhh, guys?" Sadie pointed.

Morgan convulsed on the spot, grabbing both Riley and Sebastian by their shirts. Her body lurched forward. A scream bellowed from her mouth. Removing one hand from Riley, she clutched Sebastian for full support.

Sebastian gripped her as her knees buckled. "What's happening to her?"

"Is the mark gone?" Sadie asked.

Sebastian laid Morgan down, gently lowering her head onto the muddy ground. He lifted up her top, letting it bunch up underneath her breast. And, as though the mark was never there, he smoothed his hand across her bare untainted skin.

"It worked," he said, looking at Leila. He peered down at Morgan and combed his fingers through her hair. He repeated with a whisper, "It worked."

Tears streamed down Morgan's face.

Riley grabbed Leila's wrist and pulled her arm up to inspect it. He wiped the residual ointment out of the way. The faint glow behind her mark, grew brighter.

"Dammit," he said, under his breath, dropping her hand. He turned, took a few steps, and threw his fist into the bleacher. Peeling paint flaked sprinkles around them.

"Mine's still here, too." Gabby shrugged and picked her blazer up.

"Oh well," Sadie said brightly, looking between her two best friends. She bared her teeth in an over-done grin. "At least you weren't marked by Cap?"

For a moment, Leila felt numb. All hope had been ripped out from beneath her. Her safety net, gone. Then, she got angry. She thought about Riley's list. They had exhausted all possible people, the only ones left were her friends. One of them did this to her.

"I want your blood." She darted her eyes to Sadie. Turning to Riley, she continued through gritted teeth. "Yours too." She pointed from Sebastian to Gabby. "I want everyone's blood."

Sadie's mouth dropped. "Oh. It will be okay, you will be okay, we will find —"

"No!" Leila yelled, stepping out from under the bleachers into the rain. "No, I won't!"

And then, she ran — which seemed to be her thing now. She ran through the school's parking lot and down the wet road. She decided to run until she couldn't run anymore. Until whoever marked her, found her and turned her into the monster she was destined to be.

THURSDAY

afternoon

A few minutes into Leila's run, with rain soothing her heated temperament, she decided to go home. Tsukiko was her only chance now. She knew if she was going to become a Guardian, she may as well be a True one.

She swung the front door open and startled the two love birds, snuggling in the lounge room.

"How did you go, did it work?" Kale asked, standing up to smooth his shirt.

On her way towards the stairs, Leila twisted her arm in their direction, showing them her still in-tact mark. Without stopping, she stormed up the stairs and into her room, taking one last moment to be human.

She threw herself onto the bed and cried as though her heart was ripping open and the only thing to mend it was burning coal. In a house once full of bright memories and innocent dreams, darkness lurked. It inched closer, threatening to drain all the light that remained.

And right when Leila was ready to give into the depths of despair, an inconvenient buzz came from her pocket. Thinking it was Riley, she took the phone and threw it across the room like a Frisbee. Another buzz. She dragged a pillow over her face, and moaned, "Can't I wallow for one minute?"

In its resting place, just below her window, her phone buzzed again. Wiping the unshed tears still welling in the corner of her eyes, she swung herself off the bed and sauntered towards the phone. She picked it up, ready to tell him to leave her alone, but it wasn't Riley's name lighting the screen.

"Mom?" she sniffed.

Wasting no time for pleasantries, Aileen's urgent tone spilled through the receiver. "Leila, that spiral and Guardian thing you were talking about yesterday? I did some digging around, talked to a few people. You're right, it is real. What I want to know is how you know about it?"

Leila collapsed to the ground, and leaned her head back on the window pane. "I just... do. What have you learned?"

"It's about an angelic war, how a ton of people are being recruited and turned... I never thought Therianthropes could have been angels and demons, it's a remarkable theory —"

"Theory?" Leila interrupted, sitting upright. "I thought you said it was real?"

"Leila, have you been marked?" Aileen blurted.

"No," Leila replied too quickly.

"Has a friend?"

Leila thought of Damien, of Gabby, of Morgan, and Sebastian.

"Yes." It wasn't technically a lie.

"I'll be home as soon as I can. In the meantime, stay away from them."

Leila rolled her eyes and pulled herself up to sit on the edge of her window sill. "They are friends—"

"Friends? Plural? I swear to god if you don't stay the hell away from those monsters I will ground you until you're thirty." A scratching noise echoed through the phone, then a muffled, "Tate, it's hit Cedar Falls, this time we are leaving!"

Leila's heart sank. She couldn't keep the truth from her any longer. "Mom—"

"It's probably best if you go straight home. If your friends have been marked, no doubt others have been." Aileen was stubborn at the best of times. When she had an idea, nothing could get in her way.

Leila knew she had to be forceful to get her to listen. "Mom?"

"You need to lay low, stay to yourself, are you on your way home yet? Don't leave the house until I—"

"*Mom!*" Leila yelled.

"Mmm?"

"I *am* home, but it's too late."

"What's too late?" A brief pause followed by desperation. "Leila? What's too late?"

Leila sighed, and shifted on the window sill. Resting her forehead on the cold glass, she said, "I've already been marked."

"No! No, no, no!"

"Yes."

Leila glanced out the window as her mother kept repeating, "No."

An old red Honda pulled up on the curb.

"Oh baby, my baby," Aileen sobbed.

As her mother sat in her hotel room half way down the coast and cried through the receiver, Leila's boyfriend stepped out of his car, not fifteen meters away. The sight of Riley calmed her. Despite the fact she pushed him away, here he was, still willing to support her.

"I gotta go." Leila stood up, watching Riley approach the front door.

She threw her phone on her bed and ran to the stairs. The first thing she wanted to say to him was 'sorry'. She knew he was only trying to protect her. She knew he didn't want to scare her with stories of his sister. She knew he cared about her. But she also wanted to tell him what an idiot he was for following her home. Didn't he know the danger he was putting himself in, just by being near her?

Leila was half way down the stairs when she heard the open the door.

"William?" Tsukiko said, as though recognizing an old friend.

"It's Riley, now. I changed my name, like you said."

"And *you're* the boyfriend? Oh my god! Come in."

Leila slowed her pace. She didn't need to see their faces to know they knew each. But how? And why did she call him William?

"You know him?" Kale asked what Leila was thinking.

"Yes!" Kiko sounded delighted. "This is great news."

Leila stopped half way down the stairwell.

"Why is this great news?" Leila imagined Kale giving Riley a dubious glare as he spoke.

"My brother, Ren, turned him," Kiko explained. "The first cure didn't work on Leila because his blood wasn't in it."

"You think this guy marked my sister?"

Leila crouched down between the rails to get a view of the living room, in time to see Kiko nodding. Instinctively, Leila lifted her hand to her heart. She stared through the banisters as Kale stood up and towered over Riley.

"Uh, I..." Riley stepped back. He was wearing his maroon slouch beanie, a tuft of blond fringe fell out from the front. He looked so innocent.

Tsukiko placed a hand on Kale's shoulder, holding him back. She turned to Riley and said, "I'm curious, though. Why did you mark her and torture her for days without telling her? I told you to lay low, I thought you wanted out?"

Riley's eyes widened. "I did… do want out…" his head turned towards the stairs.

Leila froze. Their eyes met.

"Hey!" he called, running towards her.

Leila shook her head, heart lodged in her throat, and reversed up the stairs. Before Riley had even reached the first step, she'd run to the bathroom and locked the door.

She couldn't comprehend it. After all this time with him pretending to protect her, pretending to care about her, pretending to be innocent and human. He was… one of *them*.

"Leila?" Riley's voice echoed through the second floor.

With her lips pressed together, daring not to make a sound, she listened to him opening and closing doors, looking for her. It didn't take long for the bathroom door knob to shake.

"Leila? Are you in here?"

Digging her teeth into her bottom lip, she climbed into the bath, as though the porcelain would keep her safe.

"Let's get out of here," Riley said, tapping on the door. "Let's go somewhere, just the two of us. I know you said you want me to stay out of it, but I can't. I'm a part of it. You're a part of me."

Stepping onto the edge of the bath, Leila opened the window to get some air.

"We'll get out of this town, I'll keep you safe."

The wind hit her face and the freshness lured her out. Before she realized what she was doing, Leila had hauled herself through the small window.

"You and me against the world." Riley gave a tiny laugh. "Always together, despite all—"

She didn't hear the rest of his sentence though, as she slid down the roof and jumped to the ground.

Again, she ran.

THURSDAY

late afternoon

Winter had settled in. Snow stuck to the edges of the lake, the white frame signaling the start of the dark and cold months ahead. Leila sat on the icy ledge of the mountain, her legs dangling a thousand meters over Cedar Falls. She was thinking about Riley and his lies. Too many for her to count. The book, the list, his sister. The biggest one was the most confusing — he was a Guardian.

And he marked her.

This time she knew it was true.

Of course, other people had held her suspicions: Sebastian, Tsukiko, Cap, even Taj for a second. But when she heard Tsukiko ask Riley why he marked her, she knew it. Her whole body sang a resounding 'yes'.

Staring down at the bench were she and Riley shared their first kiss four days ago, Leila's body lifted and her heart sunk.

Four days.

That's all it took for the season to change and, along with it, her life.

The falling sun sent a golden reflection across the lake. Wondering what time it was, Leila checked her blazer pockets for her phone, but all she found was loose change. Five dollars to be exact. Riley suggested they get out of town together. And that sounded like a wonderful idea, up until the 'together' part. Five dollars. Enough for a bus ticket somewhere — it didn't matter where, just out of there.

She stood up decisively and began walking back towards town.

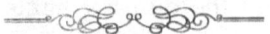

With the bus terminal in sight, Leila sped down the main street of town. She rushed past the owner of the boutique, as they hurriedly locked up their doors and made a dash to their car. A few people peppered the side walk, giggling as they entered cafes and restaurants, set for a good night out. Street lamps flickered on, signaling Cedar Fall's own purgatory — the time between day and night where half the town were afraid, rushing inside their homes before night could fall; and the other half were carefree, living their lives as though the news reports were from a place far removed. Leila never had the chance to decide which side she resided, already swallowed by the darkness while still oblivious to its danger, falling in love with the very thing the town fears.

Her pace slowed.

She fell in love with him.

She was still in love with him.

Her forehead wrinkled into her brow and she steamed toward the terminal. She knew then, which side she would have chosen had she been given the chance. Yes, she loved him. But she would have been with the half of town that hid from the dark… she would have chosen the light.

It didn't matter, though. She was already in the clutches of the night – it lurked on the edge of her skin in the shape of a spiral, waiting to sink into her blood.

Outside the Burger Lounge, a woman leaned against a lamp post, twisting her short hair in front of her eyes. Her face looked familiar to Leila, but she couldn't quite pinpoint where she knew her from. Pausing mid-twist, her eyes drifted to Leila. She instantly released her blonde tendrils and clutched at her phone. She furiously tapped the screen, walking fast in the opposite direction.

Leila watched her for a second, still trying to figure out who she was, until the dim fog lights of a speeding car brought her back to reality. She blinked and locked her eyes back on the bus terminal.

The car – a silver coupe – turned into the lane a few meters in front of her.

"Leilani Bel Money!" A voice called.

Leaning out of the passenger window, Taj held his hands up to his face pretending to hold a camera. Light from the rising moon hit the car's hood and reflected a shimmer across his face. For a moment, a silver glow lit up his eyes. Leila lifted her hand but couldn't quite manage a wave in return. Instead, she gave a quick smile and refocused her sights back to her destination. She needed to forget Cedar Falls and everything its shadows concealed.

She crossed the road and began to pass Jimmy's Italian Restaurant on the corner. The restaurant had a large glass window with navy blue awnings that backdropped the barren outside tables and chairs. Inside, it wasn't as busy as usual, most people were bustled in the booths at the back of the building. Only one lone customer sat by the front window, his face hidden by a menu. Leila rushed on, blissfully unaware of his presence. But, as she passed, he looked up and that faint, all-too common tug in the pit of her stomach rose.

She glared in through the window, her panicked eyes meeting his unsurprised stare. His hair was dark, and his fringe framed the left side of his face. Her heart leapt. It was Damien. He looked at her, his lips pressing together in a grim frown. As he stood up, she averted her eyes back to the bus terminal and continued on. Hearing a muffled "Leila!", her pace quickened. She shot a quick look over her shoulder to see the restaurant door swinging open.

Running, Leila took a hard right into the alleyway between the restaurant and the electronics store. The alley was clear, aside from a large dumpster, and doubled as a walkway to a parking lot. She ducked behind the dumpster and watched Damien rush past in search of her. Her forehead rested on the cool metal she hid behind, and she took a moment to catch her breath and thoughts.

Riley obviously had Damien waiting for her. She knew Damien was a True... her chin jerked up... *did Riley turn him?* That would mean Riley was a True. Of course he was, but that wasn't the point. The point was that he marked her without her consent. She stood up, determined. It didn't matter that he was True, it didn't matter that she loved him, it mattered that he lied.

She stepped out of the alleyway and, making sure Damien was out of sight, pointed her feet towards the bus terminal once more.

Another tug. Damien was calling for her.

Can't I leave this town? Leila thought right as the tug became stronger.

Grasping her stomach, she spun around. A barren sidewalk stretched out before her. The moon—full and bright—shone itself against the glistening pavement, still wet from the afternoon rain. Darkness lurked behind every parked car, down every alley, inside every empty store.

"Damien?" Leila asked, her voice timid and lost.

"Riley?" She was afraid of the answer.

"Kiko?"

298

The tug was different than any other she'd felt. It was laced with a tinge of, dare she think it, evil. Less of a magnet and more of a tear, like the butterflies inside her stomach had razor-blades for wings.

"Mr. Robertson?" She tried.

Laughter erupted behind her.

"Oh, my ethnically ambiguous Princess. You really are stupid."

Leila rolled her eyes to the sky — half clouded, half star-studded — taking a moment before facing him. She hadn't seen Cap since she found out who he was... what he was.

"You stole a Beta from me." Cap's voice was light and friendly yet had a raspy acidic undertone she'd never noticed before. Like she was hearing his true, or rather, Fallen, self for the first time.

Leila turned around.

Cap stood so close she could feel his breath through her eyelashes. His chin was lifted as he leered down at her and a subtle smirk had set on his face. His eyes were their normal shade of hazel, his skin still smooth, his shoulders still round and strong. Everything about him screamed confident school leader, who could be forgiven for having a small power-trip every now and then. There was nothing about him that could have given his secret away. But Leila knew better now. She knew what he was capable of.

"A Beta?" she asked innocently, trying not to aggravate him.

He pointed down the alley Leila had just hidden in. Brad and Don waited in the shadows, staring at Leila with heated eyes. In between them, under their clutching fingers, was Morgan, sobbing and weak.

THURSDAY

early evening

"Let's go for a walk, come on. Don't make a scene."

Leila struggled against Cap's strength. His claws pierced into her upper arm and pulled her into the alley. Her own newly discovered strength nowhere to be found. As soon as they were in the shadows, Cap let Leila go, leaving a row of puncture wounds in her skin.

"See this?" He pushed Don to the side and lifted Morgan's shirt, baring her skin where the mark once was. His unblinking eyes glowed red. "Do you know what biting someone without a mark does to them?"

Morgan was crying. Smeared blood curved around her face from a long scratch that started at her forehead and ended at her temple. Her breaths were shaky as she stared at Leila, silently begging for help.

Cap flicked his tongue quickly over his fangs, bent over and clamped his mouth around Morgan's hip. As Morgan screamed, Leila lurched forward. Like a bodyguard, Brad moved in to stop her. He clutched her shoulders and pushed, slamming her back against the brick wall. Pain seared down her spine as he fumbled at her sleeve, snapping at her uncovered mark.

"Wait!" Cap scolded, blood dripping down his chin. He let go of Morgan and she crumpled to the ground like a discarded candy wrapper. "God Brad, you turn one cheerleader and kill one tourist and you think you're a king. *I* am the Alpha." Cap shifted his eyes to Leila. "*I* turn her."

Hanging his head, Brad released her and cowered back into the shadows. At the edge of the alley, Don peered around the corner, darting his head up and down the street. It was then Leila realized that Morgan had stopped sobbing.

"Now, where were we?" Cap said, taking Brad's place in front of Leila. "Oh, that's right. You stole a beta from me. You want to take her place?"

"No." Leila peered around him, desperate to see Morgan make some kind of movement to prove she was still alive.

"Really? You could be a good fit for my clan. I saw the way you partied last night. To be honest, I didn't think you had it in you, you're always so straight-laced and boring." Cap feigned a theatrical yawn.

Taking advantage of his momentarily lapse in attention, Leila pushed against him. He stumbled back, surprised. Relieved to have her strength returned, Leila used the freedom to run. She'd taken two steps towards Morgan by the time Cap's fingers wrapped around her wrist. He growled under his breath and yanked her backwards. Leila crashed to the ground, her already tender back cracking hard against the pavement.

Cap dropped to all fours and climbed over her tensed body, stretching his mouth. Saliva dripped from his lips. He hissed, "You reek without that bandage wrapped around you."

Leila writhed underneath him, stretching her neck to get a better look at Morgan's chest, her eyes straining to see any sign of life. A breath—small and shaky, but still breath.

"Look at me when I talk to you!" Cap squeezed her cheeks, forcing her to meet his gaze. "I'll be your Alpha and you *will* obey me."

A ground-shuddering howl as fierce as a hurricane echoed behind them. Cap snapped his head up to the parking lot. His face dropped and panic flooded his eyes. Venom rolled off his lip and landed on Leila's cheek. She winced as he snarled—half-human, half-animal—still staring into the darkened space.

In no less than a heartbeat, a white blur flashed over Leila and took Cap with it.

Low growls echoed throughout the alleyway as Leila willed her eyes to adjust. Right beside Morgan's gasping body, a massive white wolf held down Cap in his half-shifted phase. Its large paws were placed on either side of Cap's head as it curled its top lip, baring four-inch fangs.

Leila shuffled back against the wall, staring. The thick fur, the size, even the smell of it—she knew instantly. It was the white wolf from the other night, the one that stalked and threatened her.

Cap seized his open mouth towards the wolf's neck, but his second phase of transformation was no competition for a Guardian in full shift. The wolf lifted its paw, swiping the side of Cap's face. His athletic body skidded along the ground like he was nothing but a rag doll.

Don growled, running from his lookout position at the edge of the alley. His eyes turned bright green as he helped Cap up. Together they shifted into sandy-colored cougars —Don a slightly a lighter shade than his Alpha.

Leila threw a hand to her mouth to muffle an involuntary gasp. Cougar attacks, that's what the reports were saying. Cap was responsible for so many deaths.

Brad took no time to shift into his Leopard form. He joined his friends and the three of them prowled in unison. Six illuminated eyes on the intruding wolf.

Every sound was amplified in that alleyway. Leila's hastened breath, Morgan's unconscious whimpers, the soft patter of paws hitting concrete.

The white wolf, snarling in defense, placed itself between Leila and the Fallen. Its body was larger than theirs, but still, it was three against one. The wolf moved forward, his blue eyes on the clan's Alpha, flexing his muscles with each step he made. As he directed Cap down the alley, Don and Brad set their sights on Leila.

While most of the town was tucked up safe in their homes, Leila cowered against the wall, in pain and confused. She had actively sought those with a mark for days, and now here they were, surrounding her. She looked at Morgan, writhing in her own blood, ashamed at the innate desire to run and hide.

A loud shriek rumbled from above, followed swiftly by a swooping eagle. Ruler-length talons spread out as it lurched towards the ground, making a bee-line for Brad. Together they rolled out into the half-lit parking lot.

The eagle's arrival barely made Don flinch. He continued towards Leila — and even behind his cat-like face she could have sworn she saw him smiling. Leila remembered cruelly deserting him in the classroom that time he kissed her. She shivered at the thought of his wet lips and grubby hands on her body and wondered if he would enjoy hurting her.

She balled her hands into fists.

At the edge of the alley, where the street lamps threatened to reveal what lurked in the shadows, the wolf urged Cap to step into the light. It had no interest in fighting though — glancing back down the alley, its eyes narrowed in on Leila. Abandoning Cap, it leapt from its spot, standing between Leila and her would-be assailant.

Leila jumped to her feet, her back suddenly not aching anymore.

Don's cougar growled. He sprung over the wolf. His paws hit the brick wall like a parkour pro, before landing at Leila's feet.

Without hesitation, the wolf lunged towards Don and sunk its teeth around his neck. A deep growl rumbled as its jaw clamped tight, teeth crunching through muscle and bone. After a few quick head shakes, it spat Don out like unwanted food. He rolled along the pavement and reverted to his dormant form. Human — yet lifeless.

The wolf turned back to Leila, licking its lips from blood. It stepped closer to her, nudging her foot with its nose. Neon blue eyes looked at her, hooded with concern.

Recognition hit. "Riley?"

Claws scratched the ground in quick succession as Cap hurtled towards them. His head slammed into the wolf's side, sending it skidding along the ground, stopping hard against the dumpster. Within a few moments neon blue eyes turned a warm shade of brown covered by black-rimmed glasses. Large paws became long slender fingers. And white fur was replaced by blond hair and a maroon beanie.

Cap leaned back, as though ready to make a final blow, but instead he turned to Leila. His paws lifted slow and predatory, red eyes glued to her arm. One small pounce was all it would take for him to be on her, and one bite to transition her. He leapt to close the gap. On his descent upon her, Leila squeezed her fist tight and swung her arm forward. Cap flew through the air from the blow, landing out onto the open street.

Leila released her nails from her palms, air streaming in and out of her flaring nostrils. She sat up on her knees, time and knowledge catching up to her. She glared at the bodies scattered around her.

"Is it bad to admit I enjoyed that?" Damien jogged

towards her from the parking lot. He had a cut on his cheek and teeth marks around his wrist.

"Morgan," Leila huffed, pointing behind the dumpster. "She's hurt."

Damien rushed to Morgan's weakening body and gently rolled her into his arms. As he rose, her head fell backwards, and her limp limbs sprawled downward. Blood poured from a deep gash across her torso.

"I've gotta..." Damien started.

Riley sat up holding his head. "Yeah, go. Go!"

Damien ran out of the alley and turned left towards the hospital.

Bringing his hand away from his head, Riley inspected the blood on his fingers. He wiped them over his blazer and gave a tentative smile to Leila. He winced as he shuffled closer to her.

"Are you all right?" she asked, checking her own wounded arm where Cap grabbed her with his claws.

"You're asking me that?" He shook his head.

Leila took a deep breath and rolled back off her knees, letting her whole body relax underneath her. She couldn't look at him as she said, "So, you were the wolf on Tuesday... the one who threatened me."

He reached forward, slowly, as if afraid a sudden movement might scare her away. His fingers found her mark. He let his palm cup her forearm, pressing hard against her skin. "You were bringing so much attention to yourself. I was scared. It was the only thing I could think that might stop you. It was desperate and selfish. I regretted doing it straight away..." He lifted his free hand and his knuckles barely grazed along her cheek. "I'm sorry."

A line of red slid down the side of his face. Leila reached for the small cut above his brow. "And what else are you sorry for?"

"Everything."

"Well, you don't need to apologize for *everything*," Leila teased. "Just the paranormal type things. Wolves and spirals and stupid fake books and... marking me."

"Leila, I swear it wasn't me." Riley's eyes flitted between hers, wide and fearful and earnest. "I didn't mark you. I never wanted you to see this side of my life. It's why I lied in the first place."

Tears sprung to Leila's eyes. She couldn't tell if she was relieved that he didn't mark her or if she was upset because she wish he did. She squeezed her lids in a long blink. "You swear on your immortal life?"

"I'm not immortal. But yes, I swear on my life." He lifted his hand from her mark and made a scout's honor sign. "No more lies."

Behind them, Cap moaned and stirred where he laid. It didn't matter who marked her anymore. Cap was after her, and there was one thing she knew. She wasn't going down without a fight. Actually, two things — she wasn't going to lose herself in the process, either.

No more desperation. Just Leila. Strong, defiant, carefree, and a little bit sarcastic.

Leila dabbed the corners of her eyes, willing the tears away. She jumped to her feet and crossed her arms. "Good, because I will drop your ass faster than I can leap out of a second-floor window. And let me tell you, it was fast. I jumped off those tiles like they were springs on a trampoline."

Riley gave a brief smile, then stood up, dusting himself off. "No time for jokes. I'm taking you home."

"Home?" Leila teased, following him to the parking lot. "I thought you wanted to run away together?"

He shot her a bemused look. One that said, "you're terrible," but also, "don't ever change". She took his hand and together, they rushed towards his car.

Climbing into the passenger seat, Leila asked, "Anyway, how did you find me?"

"Name your prize." Riley smirked, starting the ignition. "Damien. Odette. Plus, you don't have the bandage on, I can sense you miles away."

Leila pouted, covering the mark with her hand.

THURSDAY

evening

Leila had only taken one step into the house when Kale came barreling towards at her. "What the hell were you thinking, running off like that?" he screamed, veins rising on his neck. Then, when he noticed the puncture wounds on her arm, he lowered his voice, "You're hurt?"

"I'm okay, don't fuss." She brushed him off and sat on the sofa.

Kiko emerged from the kitchen, a small bottle held tight in one hand and a safety pin in the other. She walked straight to Riley, and without saying a word, lifted his hand and pricked the end of his finger with the pin.

Drops of blood fell into the bottle, sending swirls of dark red through a pre-mixed ointment. When she was satisfied she'd had enough of his blood, she slid in front of Leila and perched on the edge of the sofa. Still silent, she passed Leila the bottle.

Sighing, Leila took the ointment and rubbed it over the mark. The four of them stared at her, waiting for an instant reaction like Morgan had. Through the thick lathering of pinkish ointment, the glow behind the black spiral flickered slightly, like a bulb not quite attached to its socket.

Kiko eyed the mark, frowning at the abnormal reaction. "How do you feel?"

"I'm fine," Leila whispered. Half of her expected the traumatic reversal to begin at any moment, but the other half desperately wished against it—because that would mean Riley had lied.

A whole minute passed and the glow stopped flickering, settling into a constant stream of light—brighter than it had been before.

"I don't understand." Kiko sat back, dark brows falling over her eyes.

Riley said, "I told you, it wasn't me who marked her."

Leila sunk down, resting her head on the back of the sofa. She looked to the ceiling. The cure had failed again.

"I have to turn you," Kiko blurted, grabbing a hold of Leila's wrists. "It's the only way to assure you become a True. Whoever marked you obviously wasn't sired by Riley or me."

Leila sat up straight. She had come to terms with the fact she'd become a Guardian, but in that moment, it all seemed so sudden. Her eyes darted to Riley, who was standing in front of the window, a good five meters from everyone else.

Kiko stretched out Leila's arm, eyeing the mark.

"Wait!" Leila protested, pulling back.

She glanced at Riley, who immediately took a step forward, ready to object if Leila asked him to.

Leila turned back to Kiko. "So, every other Guardian out there is Fallen? We haven't tried your brother's blood, or any other True Guardian that might be out there somewhere."

"Honey, I'm sorry. It's better to be safe than sorry." Kiko reached for Leila's hand and squeezed gently. "From what's been happening, this town is becoming a Fallen hot spot. Cap, or whatever his name is, has been turning people at an alarming rate."

"What do you think?" Leila asked her brother.

Kale nodded, his face remaining stoic as he placed a reassuring had on her shoulder.

"Do you want this for me?" This time she asked Riley.

His eyes were hooded and dark.

"Riley?"

He raised his hands to his head. "I don't know... maybe."

With that, Kiko leaned forward. Making the decision for them, she twisted Leila's arm around. Her eyes flashed red as she wiped the residual ointment away.

It was a simple touch, a finger across a forearm, yet somehow more meaningful than either could have anticipated. Beneath the dark spiral, the glow brightened and the light tingle Leila had become accustomed to immediately turned into searing pain. She stared at her mark as though it was on fire, the pain intensifying with every millisecond that passed.

"It hurts," she cried, doubling over in distress.

Behind Kiko, Riley roared. He dropped to his knees, stretching his fingers over his shoulder. Fangs involuntarily grew, dripping a line of venom over his bottom lip that landed in a splat on the floor. His eyes were like saucers, switching between his normal brown to a blue neon glow brighter than his wolf's.

Leila screamed then, a noise that shattered through the house as though made by something not quite human. The glow on her arm continued to brighten, until a cylinder of rushing light shot out of it and beamed up through the ceiling.

All at once, the agony receded into a dull pressure, like it had been forced out by light.

"Oh my god!" Kiko exclaimed, throwing a cushion over Leila's mark. Rays of light still shone out beneath it. She rushed to the kitchen.

Riley's eyes settled back to brown and his fangs retracted. As his own pain ceased, he let go of his shoulder and panted on all fours. Looking up, he said, "What the hell was that?"

"We've come at this all wrong," Kiko declares, returning. She threw the cushion across the room. "You haven't been marked…" She wrapped a tea-towel around Leila's arm, careful to cover every inch of the mark. "You've been imprinted."

When the mark's beacon was contained under the towel, Kiko reached for Riley and scruffed him by the collar. She pulled him closer and pulled the back of his shirt down to reveal a spiral on his shoulder blade. She put her finger in the middle of the spiral and counted the lines that led out of it.

"One, two, three. Riley there's four of them now."

Riley craned his neck. "Four? Are you sure?"

"Did you see her mark before? Were there three rungs? Did you even count them?"

He shook his head, eyes widening.

Leila tried hard to understand, but it was a world beyond her own. "What does that mean?"

"It means." Kiko took a hastened breath. "That you are in more danger than first expected."

Kale, silent until now, raced to sit beside his little sister. "And what does that mean?"

"It means," said Riley, rising to his feet. He chewed on his bottom lip, dimples flashing in and out of sight. "I've made a huge mistake."

Kiko threw her arms in the air exasperated. She glared

at him. "What were you thinking?"

"I... I wasn't thinking. I didn't mean to." Riley tried to explain.

Kiko's eyes narrowed as she stepped towards Riley. "You didn't mean to? Or is it that you couldn't help yourself? I thought I taught you the dangers of imprinting someone. You can't just jump into it within a few months." She raised her finger, poking at his chest until his back hit the wall. "What? Did you take a look at her and think she was a nice piece of ass that you could keep forever by turning her?"

"No, of course not. I... I..." Riley stuttered. He pushed himself off the wall decisively. "I care about her."

"Back up!" Kale raised his hand in the air. "What the hell is going on here? What is an imprint? Why is my baby sister in danger?"

Kiko turned around, her irises glowing red. She closed her eyes and took a deep breath, when she opened them again her eyes were normal. "Okay, sorry."

She returned to Leila, and sitting on the coffee table, calmly explained, "An imprint isn't a normal mark. It cannot be removed. An imprint occurs when a Guardian falls in love. There are rules of course. The love needs to be completely mutual. It needs to be activated by an Alpha, in this case, me. And, the transition needs to take place on a full moon."

Riley placed his hand over his shoulder, sliding his fingers underneath his shirt. He looked at Leila, eyes dazed. "It's why you're strong already."

"She is?" Kiko asked. She nodded to herself. "I suppose that makes sense. Imprints make the strongest Guardians. But they are so few... I don't know of any. The Fallen are threatened by them, more so than they are with marked ones. They hunt them together—clans joining to eradicate the threat. Generally, once the Imprint's mark is activated, by the time the full moon comes around they are killed."

"Wait." Kale sat forward, wagging a finger at Riley. "It's a full moon tonight."

"Whoa, hang on." Kiko slid along the coffee table to face Kale. She placed a gentle hand on his. "Leila has to think about this. I can turn her and she would be a normal Guardian, not strong or imprinted. But if Riley turns her, life will not be normal again." Kiko reached her other hand to Leila's knee. "You will be called upon the Guardians of the Veil to destroy all Fallen, and at the same time you'll be hunted by those you seek to destroy. You will have five times the strength of normal Guardians, but you are not immune to death. It will seek you. Do you understand? The life of an Imprinted Guardian is not a light choice to make, you will constantly be looking over your—"

"Well then," Kale interrupted, the crease between his eyebrows deepening. "*You* turn her. Turn her now!"

"But how do you know that's what her life..." Riley cleared his throat, walking to the three of them near the sofa. "Our life will be like? You just said you don't know of any Imprinted Guardians. Besides, Damien and I defeated an Alpha and two of his minions, maybe we can continue to protect her without turning her."

Kale shot Riley an icy glare that could have frozen lava. "Hey! Dude. I don't think you should speak. You've done enough damage don't you think?"

"You're not the only one who cares about her," Riley snapped back.

Waving her hand high, Leila said, "Hello? I'm still here. This is my life we are discussing, isn't it? I get the final say, don't I?"

"Yes. Of course, yes." Kiko's calm voice waded through the growing tension in the room. "Now, you have all the information, do you want to be a normal Guardian or an imprinted one?"

"It's not only my choice though is it?" Leila said, looking at Riley. Blood drained from his face and heavy breathed he awaited her reply. "We should talk."

Riley turned to Kiko. "How much time do we have?"

Kiko nodded towards the stairs. "Be quick. The beacon was only shining for a moment but it will be enough for the Fallen to start tracking her, especially the ones already here in town."

Leila led the way, her walk turning into a run by the time she reached the stairs.

Back in the living room Kale asked Kiko, "Who the hell is Damien? How many Guardians has that kid turned?"

Leila charged through her doorway. She made a bee-line to her window, as if seeing the outside somehow released her from the prison she had found herself in. She sighed; her breath smearing fog across the glass.

Riley followed her into her room. He glanced at her dresser decorated in Polaroids and bold necklaces, and smiled painfully. He collapsed on the end of her bed. "I've ruined your life."

Leila lifted her hand to the cold window, clearing the view with her fingertips. Outside, dark clouds began covering the moon, the last remaining light being hidden by darkness.

"Would it be better for Kiko to turn me?" she asked.

Riley ripped his beanie off and clutched it between his hands. "I screwed up. I screwed up so bad. I'm so sorry Leila, I had no idea."

In one swift movement, Leila snapped her drapes shut and turned around. "At least I didn't get marked by a Fallen."

"How can you do that? Why do you do that?" Riley, look up. A tear sat in the corner of his eye.

Leila sighed and sat next to him. "Do what?"

"Joke. How can you be so positive?" He scrunched his beanie, soft wool moved around and around in his clenched fists. "This whole time I've been trying to protect you, but I never stopped to think you needed protecting from me."

Leila pulled his beanie from his grasp and looked at his hat-flattened hair. She opened her mouth to make a teasing comment about how he should keep it on, but took a long breath instead. Dropping the beanie, she ran her fingers through the lengths of his hair.

"How can I need protecting from someone who always makes me feel safe?" she said, feeling the smoothness of his shaved jaw. "I knew you'd show up last night, you know, at the falls party. I was acting like an idiot, but only because I knew you'd keep me safe. I knew you'd make sure I was fine."

Riley shook his head, gaze finding the floor. "I let it get out of hand. I marked—imprinted you, and I didn't even know I did it. But then to lie to you, about what I really am, this—thing? What kind of boyfriend does that? "

"Don't lie anymore, then." Leila twisted on her mattress to face him. "Tell me. Tell me everything."

He pinched the bridge of his glasses and slid them off. He placed them on top of the beanie on the floor like he was shedding layers of himself. "Truthfully? I don't even need these in the way most people do.

"After I transitioned, my enhancement was sight. I could see things so clearly a mile away. Insects, dust, everything. It was hard to function, always being on high alert from the smallest of movements. The glasses dial my vision back to normal." He looked at Leila, his eyes flitting between hers. "You say your eyes are hazel. But to me they're so much more. Light brown expanding into green. Flecks of blue highlight the left one—like droplets of water falling down a leaf."

Leila's breath hitched. "How lo—" she began, losing

her words. "When did…" She stopped and swallowed, resisting the urge to kiss him. "How long have you been like this?"

"Last year," he replied, eyes still fixated on hers. "After Tessa, I became just as obsessed as she did. Looking for her, looking for answers. Tsukiko found me and warned me to stop. She told me the difference between Guardians. I begged her brother to turn me, I thought having the ability would bring me closer to finding my sister. But all it did was bring me into a war I didn't want to fight in. That's why we moved here. To get away from it all." He stroked the side of Leila's face. "But it followed me."

Closing her eyes, Leila nuzzled into his touch. "What do we do?"

"I don't want to do anything. I don't want this for you. Ren says we are Guardian angels, but I know the truth, we're more beast than beauty." He tore himself away from her and leaned forward, resting his elbows upon his knees.

Leila leaned in with him, her hand finding the side of his head right behind his ear. "You're beautiful to me."

The moment he turned to face her, she forced her open mouth onto his. He didn't take long to reciprocate— his fingers in her hair, his tongue along her tongue. As she swung her leg over to straddle him, he lowered his hands to her waist. He gave a quiet moan as he peppered her neck with kisses.

"Leila," he whispered. "We don't have time for this."

"What if tonight is all we have?"

As soon as she said the words, Riley moved. He stood up with Leila still wrapped around him and spun around. Holding her weight, he lowered her slowly onto the mattress. Then, as he laid on top of her, Leila felt his hip bones digging into her upper thighs. But instead of touching and kissing her, he buried his head into the quilt beside her face. He breathed deep, clasping both of her hands over the top of her head. When he lifted his head back up, Leila startled. His brown eyes were neon blue, and glowed as bright as the sun. When he saw Leila's expression, he winced and razor sharp teeth popped out from under his lip. A low rumble came from the back of his throat and his mouth snapped shut.

"Ahhhh," he roared, tearing himself off her. He stood, hunched and out of breath, staring Leila down with his radiant eyes. "This is me, this is what I am... I don't want this for you."

Between sharp breaths, Riley growled. As the wolf threatened to take over, his arms remained at his sides. He was shaking as his claws dug into his thighs, blood dripping from the holes they created.

Leila gave a pained smile. He was right; on the outside, he looked like a beast. Yet, within his frozen stance and timid movements, she could still see *him*. She inched forward, not taking her eyes off his. As she got closer, he squinted, cowering back.

"It's okay," she said, reaching her hand. "I see you, Riley. You're still there. And I will be, too. Kiko will turn me, we don't have to worry about this imprint business. We can just be normal teenagers who have the ability to shape shift. That's all it has to be."

When she reached him, he straightened. She traced his arm, from his elbow to his wrist, and pulled at his hand to remove the claws from his leg. She did the same with the other arm and placed his hands on her cheeks.

He sniffed as a lone tear traced the shape of his nose. "I'm so sorry."

Leila ran her fingers through his hair again, fixing it up a bit. With a deep and calm breath, she looked him square in the eyes. "It's not your fault that I love you."

As she said the words, his face softened and the glow behind his eyes dulled. Fangs retracting, he said, "I love you, too... obviously."

Riley pulled her in close to him and planted his lips onto hers. In that moment, Leila was transported into a world where there was only love and happiness and peace. She forgot about angels and demons and werewolves and spiral marks. There was nothing else in the world that mattered to her than being caught up in him.

Riley moved her back onto the bed. This time he didn't shift—this time he stared into her eyes and held himself away from her with straightened arms, his hands on either side of her head. His eyes said what his voice couldn't, they said, *"not now, but forever."* Leila returned her own gaze that said, *"yes now, and forever."*

"Don't look at me like that," Riley whispered, a distant ache in his stare.

Leila tucked her hands under his shirt and rolled it over his head. He moaned, moving his hands from the bed to her body. His face changed then—serious, hungry, and wanting, yet still resisting. Leila grabbed his waist, begging him to close the gap between them.

And then, the door flung open and Riley fell on top of her.

THURSDAY

late evening

Kale barged into Leila's room. When he saw a shirtless Riley on top of her, like any good big brother, his face fell as though contemplating his next move. Leila wondered if he'd throw Riley out the window or continue with what he initially came in to do.

Slinking off with his hands raised, Riley retreated. "It's not what you think."

"Yes it is," Leila teased.

Kale cleared his throat and pointed between the two of them. "We're going to talk about this later." He grabbed Leila by the wrist. "But now, we're leaving."

"Why?" Leila asked, as he dragged her out the door.

Behind them, Riley rushed to keep up, threading himself back into his shirt.

Kale stopped at the top of the stairs and looked back at him. "They're here!"

As Kale pulled his sister down the stairs, a blur of white flew past them and leapt through a broken window. Leila had no time to see where Kiko was before Kale led her out the side door that was connected to their garage.

"Get in," he whispered, finding his Mustang keys on the hook by the door.

Leila hurried into his car. When he joined her, she looked at him with fear. "What's happening?"

Kale didn't need to reply when the roller door opened. Three men with glowing eyes waited on the driveway for them. Kale planted his foot to the floor without hesitation and two of them moved out of the way.

Leila winced as the car jerked up, and then down, rolling over a body.

On the front lawn, Riley and Kiko stood side-by-side in their animal forms, feigning off other Guardians. A coyote, dark brown with patches of white on its chest, jumped on Riley's back and dug its teeth into his arm.

"Riley?" Leila screamed as Kale turned out of the driveway. "Wait. Go back. *Kale!*"

She stared out the back window as the distance between them increased. Turning back to Kale with a tear drenched face, she begged, "Please, we have to go back, Kale. We need to help them."

"It's not about them right now, Leila. Kiko and Riley are distracting them while I get you the hell out of here." He glanced at her arm. "Make sure your mark is completely covered."

The tea towel on her arm was slightly unwrapped, releasing a dulled glow underneath it.

"*It probably slipped while Riley and I were...*" Leila choked on her own thoughts. An ache pulsated from her heart and shuddered through her body.

They passed the sign on the edge of town, a blurred salutation of: *You are now leaving Cedar Falls*. Leila buckled her seat belt as they sped along the windy road. Tall forest trees on either side hugged them as they drove.

Leila rested her head on the window pane. Above the flickering tree tops, clouds seemed to follow them. A small snowflake landed on the glass, splattering outward before sliding down. "Where are we going?"

"Kiko said that Riley's dad owns a cabin down near the border." He paused to glance in the rear-vision mirror. "If we get that far, that's where we'll meet them."

They turned a bend onto the longest stretch of road since the main street of Cedar Falls. The Mustang's headlights reflected off a rush of snow, now streaming from the night sky like falling stars.

Slowing down, Kale took a few short breaths and muttered, "I hate driving in this weather."

Leila watched the snow peppering from above, her head still hard against the glass. There was something familiar about it, something mesmerizing. "Just like my dream," she whispered.

Her stomach tightened, flames tearing through her as though her insides were being ripped out. She sat up straight, on high alert. "He's here."

A light-colored cougar stepped onto the road.

Kale pressed his foot onto the break but he wasn't quick enough, the animal disappeared underneath them — a loud clunk soon followed. The car stalled and silence surrounded them.

"Did you hit it?" Leila asked, hopeful.

"I think so." Kale twisted his neck, looking in all directions, desperately trying to find proof.

The road in front of them curved into the dark, and the long stretch of road behind them was completely bare. To their right, pine trees climbed up a steep hillside. Leila danced her eyes around them to see what the shadows were hiding. She clenched her fists, wondering why the strength she was becoming accustomed to felt too far out of reach. "Let's go, Kale. It's not safe here."

"I'm trying," Kale said, clicking the keys over. The car jolted once. He tried again. The car rumbled and then a loud crack resounded from inside the engine. He looked to Leila with despair.

She returned his gaze, but instead of despair her face was full of fear. Outside the car, beyond her brother, a figure stood.

Cap—not a cougar anymore—half-shifted. His red eyes glared in their direction, his lips rising into a smirk as he lifted the battery, torn out from under the car. He threw it onto the road and slammed his hands onto the driver's side door. And, as he stared at them with wild eyes, he pushed. Tires screeched from the bitumen and crunched along the gravel on the side of the road.

Panicked, Leila looked out her window, watching in disbelief as the trees got closer. *Is this how I die?* she thought. *Death by tree squash?*

"You have to get out of here," Kale commanded, snapping her out of her paralysis.

"What about you?" She spoke the words to her brother, but Cap was all she could look at. He snarled, baring blood-stained teeth.

Kale unlatched her seatbelt and leaned across to open the door. "He's not here for me."

The door flung open and before Leila had a chance to think, Kale pushed her out. She tumbled onto the bank, looking up to see her previous seat become occupied by a tree trunk. The next thing she saw was Cap's fist hitting the side of Kale's face and Kale falling out the open door onto the ground.

Cap roared into the air and began moving around the car towards Leila.

She stood up, fists still clenched.

"Hello again," he said.

Leaves rustled beside them. Brad emerged from the forest, holding onto a girl with blonde hair. Not Morgan though. This time, it was Sadie.

She looked up at Leila, her eyes swollen and wet. Her long hair fell in messy strands over her small shoulders, and hidden underneath, three claw lines cut across her collarbone.

"Nooo," Leila cried.

"This is how it works, *Lei-lan-i*." Cap articulated every syllable in her name. "You take a beta from *me*, I take a friend from *you*."

"Please, let her go, let's talk about this as humans," Leila begged, squeezing her fists tighter. She never knew when she would be strong. It came in waves and unexpected times. But if she could get him to relent, even a little, she had a chance to take him down. She had to take the risk, Sadie's life depended on it.

Cap bared his teeth and glared at her with glowing red eyes. "Oh, sweet thief, haven't you heard? I'm a Fallen; I have no conscience, no filter, no remorse. Your friend's cute but I don't care if she dies. It's not personal, not really. I wouldn't let anyone get away with what you did. Look at it this way, if someone stole a necklace from you, you'd storm into their house and take everything they owned." He laughed to himself. "Nah, probably not, you True's are so straight-laced and boring."

"So, this is about revenge?"

"What else would it be about? Why else would I pursue you? Here's a newsflash, you're not that great. Average, actually. Your whole mixed-race vibe is hot and I'd do you... but your personality is too..." he finished his sentence with a shiver.

Leila watched him recoil, her mind running in circles. Keeping her hope at bay, she asked, "You don't know what I am, do you?"

Cap frowned. "Riley's play-toy beta."

"Yeah, okay." Leila outwardly scoffed, but on the inside she was laughing. He had no idea Riley imprinted her—which means he wasn't hunting her out of fear for what she could become, he was hunting her out of revenge. Which meant one thing, he was led by his emotions.

She stepped closer, her hands raised in surrender. "Just let her go, we can talk about this."

Rolling his eyes, Cap sighed. "Ugh, fine. Here's a human offer. We'll let her go, if you take her place."

Brad let out a snort and said, "Yeah, you won't be Riley's play-toy beta, you'll be Cap's!"

Leila nodded, hoping her elusive super strength was back in full force.

"No!" Sadie yelled, "Don't do it.'"

Leila took one step forward, stopped, and pointed at her best friend. "Let her go first."

Cap lifted his chin to Brad, who immediately released his hold on Sadie. She stalled, looking between Leila and Cap as though contemplating the wisest thing to do. Predatory animals do like the hunt, after all.

Leila nodded at Sadie and mouthed, "*Run!*"

Sadie high-tailed it to the other side of the road and hid behind a tree. As soon as she was out of harm's way, Leila wrapped her knuckles against Cap's jaw. His knees weakened beneath him.

Brad lurched forward. Leila snapped her arm out, her hand finding his neck. Squeezing, she commanded, "Back off."

As he cowered backwards and ran into the forest, Leila returned to Cap. Before he could straighten himself fully, she grasped his shoulders and threw him backwards. She marveled at her own strength as he flew ten meters and skidded across the road. Marching towards him, she was determined to finish the job. Behind him, Sadie's chest pressed against a tree, her startled face peering out from around it. Watching. Waiting.

Cap struggled to his feet—but he didn't rise to face Leila, instead his eyes fixed on Sadie.

"Wait!" Leila called, running.

Cap lunged, mouth open.

Sadie's wide eyes filled with tears and terror.

Leila stared, helplessly urging herself forward. Deep down she knew though, there was no way she could be fast enough to reach him before his teeth were around her best friend's neck.

As Cap took his final leap and Sadie whimpered, "help me," an unfamiliar howl rose between them.

Sadie was proud of Leila. For everything she was and everything she was becoming. As soon as Leila told her about the mark on her arm, Sadie was the first to stand by her side and make sense of it all. It excited her, the unknown. There were Guardians who shape-shifted and she wanted to be a part of that magical world. Not to be one, of course. She was more a side-line watcher than participator. But to see it, to be around it, it made her feel alive in the most vulnerable of ways.

She watched Leila, an average seventeen-year-old girl, throw a senior jock across the road. Leila told her to run, but she couldn't leave—she was frozen by fear and a little bit of intrigue. The roughness of bark scratched at the cuts on Sadie's collarbone as she held onto the tree like it was protecting her, her gaze glued to the Fallen Guardian on the road in front of her.

Cap shook his head and forced himself to his feet, but instead of retaliating against Leila's attack, his eyes squared on Sadie. His face looked distorted, a mixture between man and monster, like his bones were in all the wrong places. He opened his mouth and flicked his tongue over his fangs. Sadie realized then, that she was about to be forced to participate, again.

Doubt crept in. This time it felt different. Final.

She looked to Leila, but she was too far away to help.

As Cap reeled in on her, she grasped the tree trunk tighter.

This can't be it, she thought. *I'm too young. I haven't graduated. I haven't decided what I want to do with my life. I haven't skinny dipped, or smoked a cigarette... dammit, I haven't even kissed anyone yet. And great, my last thought before I die is about how lame I am. Sorry Mom. And Dad. You thought Summer was the rebel, and here I am caught up in this mess. Here lies Sadie Sloan, she was such a great side-kick. Ever the flirt, ever the gossip, ever the —*

"Don't worry." A voice whispered into her ear.

Her head moved so quick it sent a sharp pain down her neck. Beside her was a boy. A senior. One who used to be kind but turned into a jerk. One with glowing blue eyes, like a bright neon sign. A wolf gone rogue.

"Help me," she whimpered.

The boy nodded, then let out a challenging howl.

There, standing in defense of Sadie, was Sebastian — half-shifted and ready for war.

Cap stopped, tilting his head like a confused puppy. And then, two bodies fully shifted. One sandy cougar, and one gray wolf. They charged towards each other, both leaping in the air. Colliding with an almighty crunch, they tumbled along the side of the road. Swirls of dust and gravel surged around their sparing bodies.

Sebastian snapped his teeth at Cap, piercing a small gash in his chest. Cap scrambled back onto the road, returning to his half-shifted phase. He touched the fresh cut and looked at his own blood on his fingertips.

Leila ran around them to Sadie, embracing her into a tight hug. "Are you okay?"

Sadie nodded, her eyes floating back to the fight.

Sebastian attacked again, this time Cap rolled to the side, avoiding the blow. "You're my beta, I command you to stop."

A shimmer of blue fell over Sebastian's wolf and he returned to human form. He looked down at Cap—lip curling, eyes still glowing. He lunged and swiped his claws down Cap's face. "Make me."

In the distance, headlights appeared. Leila took Sadie's hand and they rushed to the Mustang. Leila opened the door. "Sit," she told Sadie as she knelt over Kale's unconscious body. As the approaching car slowed down, she pressed her fingers to his neck to feel his strong pulse.

An old red Honda pulled up behind them and all four doors swung open. Riley charged out first. Leila jumped to her feet and barreled towards him.

"I didn't want to leave you," she said, crashing straight into his embrace. Tears welled as she wrapped her arms around his neck. Remembering the attack back at her home, she pulled away to study the bite mark on his shoulder. It looked tender but was already healing.

"It was a stupid idea." Riley held her tight. "We're stronger together, Kiko should have known that." He pulled away and looked over his shoulder. "I've brought back-up."

His back-up stepped out of his car: Mr. Robertson, Ren, Gabby, the girl with short blonde hair who Leila saw down the street before. That's why she looked so familiar, it was Riley's cousin, Odette.

Kiko stormed past them all. "Where's Kale?!"

"He's fine. Out cold, but fine," Leila said, pointing behind her.

Kiko rushed to Kale and dragged him onto the other side of the car, hiding him from the road. As Kiko returned, an eagle shrieked above them. Its wing span was as wide as the road, and the tips of its feathers shook soft snow off the trees as it landed.

Damien shifted to his human form. "Heh," he said, pointing his thumb at Sebastian and Cap. "That's unexpected."

Cap lay clutching at his own throat, gasping for breath. Sebastian stood over his Alpha, panting, blood all over him. He scowled at the audience. "What? I'm no one's lackey."

And as Sebastian ran off into the forest from where he came, Cap's struggle for air ended.

"Does that mean he's an Alpha now?" Mr. Robertson asked.

"Shhh," Kiko hissed. Her head tilted, one ear to the sky.

It was eerily quiet. Everything except the distant sound of foot prints, a lot of them.

"Quick." Riley grabbed Leila's hand and pulled her up the bank. "Up here."

Everyone followed them into the forest. They climbed the hill, stopping when they could only just see the cars through the trees.

"They're going to kill you." Kiko wedged herself between Leila and Riley. "We need to turn you... now!"

FULL MOON

before midnight

Kiko threw Leila against a tree. "Take off the towel, quick."

In the distance, resounding howls echoed through the forest and their accompanying footsteps grew closer.

Kiko bared her teeth, long and sharp, venom dripping from the canines. She made a hissing noise from the back of her throat. Her pupils had dilated so much Leila couldn't see them anymore, all she saw was glowing red.

Leila's heart pounded, and all the tears in her eyes couldn't show just how afraid she was. She held Kiko at arm's length. "Wait!"

If this has to be done, if I have to make this transition, then no one else can do this except...

"Him," Leila said, pointing to Riley.

Kiko's head lowered as she swung around to look at him. Riley's face contorted as though he was trying to hide his own fear, but it was written all over him. It streamed from his twitching eyes, from his quivering chin, from his clenched fists.

Kiko narrowed her eyes and stared at Leila as though trying to see if she meant it or not.

Ren, Kiko's younger brother, moved forward and touched her shoulder. He whispered, "Kiko."

The touched broke her out of her daze. Kiko blinked and smiled softly. "It is your choice."

Kiko stood up, stepping aside for Riley. He swallowed hard and moved forward. Everyone stood around them— solemn and expectant—beseeching for the best outcome.

"Are you sure?" Riley asked, kneeling before her.

Words refused to form, all she could do was nod.

Riley clutched her hands. "This changes everything."

She knew it. Strangely, knowing it was him that had caused it all, knowing it was him that will end it all—it gave her peace. Giving his hands a reassuring squeeze, she said, "It's okay."

He released one of her hands. He let his fingertips glide along her arm and up over her shoulder to rest on her jaw-line. His coarse thumb stroked her cheek, and the grooves on it made it felt like both sandpaper and heaven on her skin. He didn't take his eyes off hers as they changed from brown to bright blue. He kept looking at her as his teeth grew three times their normal size. Without a blink or a glance in any other direction, he lifted her marked arm and removed the tea-towel. The beam of light shone up through the tree tops. His other hand still cupped her jaw; his thumb wiping any tears that slid down her face.

"This may sting," he said, his voice as soft as a purr.

He lowered his head to cover the beacon that expelled from her mark, and as his mouth opened, a drop of venom rolled over his lip.

What Leila wouldn't have given to be anywhere else than there, where that mouth was about to kiss her instead of bite her. But there she was, with the clouded moonlight glistening on her face and his teeth piercing her skin. As they sunk over her mark, Riley averted his gaze to the ground.

Leila closed her eyes. It felt as though a thousand knives stabbed her. A spiral of darkness seeped from her boyfriend's teeth and dug into her flesh, making its way from the mark and burning a hole into her very core. Riley let out a low moan, and bit down deeper. She squeezed her eyes tighter, not wanting to see the mess he was making of her arm. She flung her hand out and clasped his shoulder.

"Stop!' she wanted to say. "Please stop!" But no words came out.

Riley's hand moved from her face to her elbow as his teeth slowly retracted.

Feeling as though she might pass out — die even — the darkness spun inside of her, growing with every hasty breath. It spread until it corrupted every inch of her body and there was no humanity left. She had nothing left. But then, a glow of light — like a firefly in a darkened forest. Then another appeared. And another. And soon, a billion glowing lights danced in a golden flurry throughout her aura. They replaced the darkness with an array of colors; bold and bright and beautiful. They replaced fear with love, and pain with strength. They replaced uncertainty with faith, and struggle with ease.

A noise rustled from the depths of her voice box with a thunderous crack; it was most definitely a war-cry — loud and deep.

A roar.

FULL MOON

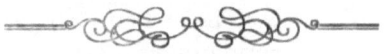

midnight

Leila opened her eyes.

Everything was bright, like a blank canvas. Spots of color in the shape of a tree began to form, as though an artist was painting a watercolor to life. Large brush strokes of light gold became dark green and gray/brown peppered in white.

As her eyes adjusted, she lifted her arm to see the damage Riley had done. There was no bite mark though, and the spiral remained—except not the same, there was no glow.

"That was quick," Riley said.

"It must have been the soul imprint," Ren replied.

Looking up, Leila pored over Riley. He was fully human, dormant as Damien explained. A wolf sat beside him, illuminated in blue and transparent, like a ghost. It gave a wink and bowed its head, a separate entity to Riley.

Leila blinked, looking behind them to Damien. He was human too yet engulfed in a yellow crystalline-like eagle.

It was then she realized. Guardians don't morph into animals; they were still themselves the whole time, but somehow when shifted, only the animal's form was shown to humans.

"You look amazing!" Gabby said.

The silver outline of a wolf stood by her side. She had an arm around Sadie—who seemed so small and fragile. There was no glowing animal near her at all, she was human and grounded. Leila sensed something different between her and Gabby, between her and the rest of them.

"You turned Gabby." Leila knew she said the words, but her voice didn't sound quite the same.

"Well, yes, technically." Riley glanced across to his cousin.

Odette swept the hair out of her eyes and raised her hand in a demure wave. On her shoulder—pale green and translucent—a barn owl ruffled its feathers. "Guilty of the marking," she said, before quickly adding, "But it was her choice."

Gabby glanced at Odette, smiled, then looked back at Leila. "I'll tell you the full story one day."

Leila took a deep breath. As her eyes floated from Gabby back to Riley, she caught Ren's stare. He clutched at his leather jacket and tugged it across his chest. His Guardian was black, like obsidian, a panther. He turned in haste towards the road and immediately winced.

A male voice cried out and Leila shifted her gaze. Kale was slumped against his car on the side of the road. Tsukiko leaned away from him, a glowing red fox surrounding her body. Blood dripped from her bite and streaked his arm in crimson.

"Hey!" Leila yelled.

Wiping her mouth, Kiko swung her head around and Kale's knees buckled underneath him. Within a few seconds, Kiko's fox returned to her side and her eyes stopped glowing. She sped up the hill, faster than any human should be able to run. "How do you feel?"

"How do I feel?" Leila repeated.

Her chest rose and fell, puffs of air running like a steam train through her nostrils. Her eyes, alert and on edge, darted from Riley to the trees behind him. They snapped to Kale as he struggled to stand, then back to Kiko in front of her.

Leila's ears twitched, which was a weird, new feeling. She heard leaves crunch under Mr. Robertson's feet as his weight shuffled between his legs, the green wolf beside him on high alert.

"I feel..." she began.

"They're coming." Kale called, running towards them. He slowed down when he saw Leila.

Kiko looked shocked at Kale's sudden appearance. "How did you get up so quick?"

He didn't have time to answer as the dark bronze bear that had ran by his side, moved across his body. It engulfed him and as they aligned Kale's eyes turned bronze. Teeth and claws grew simultaneously. Him and the bear were one. And then, the bear moved forward. Reaching out of Kale, its paws landed on the ground. And even though Leila could only see it's outline still, large prints indented the ground beneath it.

Sadie yelped.

"He won't hurt you," Gabby reassured her. "None of us will, okay? Do you trust me?"

"Of course." Sadie grinned, feigning composure.

Gabby closed her eyes. Her wolf moved across, aligning with her body, then it stepped forward. As her eyes opened, bright silver circles shone like spotlights.

Sadie took a few steps back. To her, a light brown wolf stretched its hind legs, like a dog that had just woken up. It bared its teeth, stance ready for war.

Damien shifted next, and then Riley.

"I'll keep a look out," Odette said, her feet rising off the ground.

On high alert, Leila moved her focus to the road as dozens of footsteps materialized into Guardians — some aligned, some fully shifted. They were there for her, but they were too late.

"They will still want to stop you both," Kiko said, letting her fox step forward. "Your power threatens their very existence."

Riley turned to Leila. His wolf was in front of him, yet he was able to move freely through it as he reached his hand for hers.

"How do I bring the Guardian forward?" As Leila stood, she looked down at her still very human feet.

Riley squeezed her hand. "You will it. It's easy, just like stepping through an open door."

Leila glanced back to Sadie, who'd crept back further into the forest. A line of sweat dropped off her brow as she saw her best friend half-shifted and surrounded by wild animals. "Stay here," Leila urged.

Leila stepped towards the road. She took a deep breath. *Just like walking through an open door.*

As she took another step, a rush of light expelled out of her. A fusion of calm and intense vitality soared through her body. Flashes of color zoomed past, as her friends made their way down the hill. Riley released her hand, and together they ran, jumping over fallen branches and shrubs as though they were merely stones.

They were on the road in a matter of seconds. The Fallen in front of them stopped, whispers rising amongst them. Around a dozen turn on their heels, following the bend of the road into darkness, away.

Riley turned his head to Leila and so did his wolf. He smiled as his wolf howled, and then together, they lunged. Her feet moved before she had time to think, instinctively following Riley as he went after the escapees. The rise of energy in her overtook any lingering fear. It was an innate urge to protect—but more than herself. She needed to protect Sadie, the school, heck, the whole town. This is what it meant to be a Guardian, to defend the weakened and vulnerable.

Everything became a blur of teeth and blood, claws and growls. They parted the crowd with ease, as though knocking down bowling pins. One down, two down, four, eight. And when they skidded out onto the empty road, at least ten bodies lay on the ground in their wake. The snap of a breaking branch cracked a few yards away as two Fallen fled into the forest. Riley chased them as Leila walked back through the carnage to see if anyone dared get up.

Kiko and Kale were equally as ruthless. They chased a handful of Fallen up the hill, returning a moment later, covered in someone else's blood.

The others fought one-on-one. Damien was careful not to hurt his rivals too much, picking them up and dropping them from non-fatal heights. Gabby was more reckless, her anger leading her into a frenzy of frantic bites. Ren was swift and accurate, knocking his opponents to the ground before they could even touch him. Mr. Robertson flailed underneath a Fallen's barrage of messy, yet effective attacks. Ren saved him with a single claw across a throat. Mr. Robertson sat on the edge of the road, muscles rippling under his blood-stained shirt. With heavy breath he stood back up and wiped his mouth, ready for the next one.

"Leila, look out!" Odette shrieked from above.

Fangs sunk into the place between her shoulder and neck, her knees buckled at the excruciating pain. Leila crumbled under the pressure. Using her strength, she forced them backwards until they both fell and a head cracked against the road. She swiveled around to see who had attacked her.

"Don't kill me," Brad begged, his eyes full of fear. "I'm just doing what my Alpha commands. I won't hurt you, I promise."

"Your Alpha?" Leila let her eyes find Cap's lifeless body. "But he's dead."

Brad writhed under her. Leila needed to push hard on his chest to keep him trapped. She was still stronger than him, but not strong like before... when Riley was with her.

"Tsukiko?" Leila yelled, looking around.

Close by, Kiko's fingers were digging into someone's cheeks — and mimicking her movements was her fox, claws grasping at a stag. Hearing Leila's plea, she dropped him to the ground and rushed over.

"It's Riley..." Leila puffed, pushing Brad's shoulder down. "We aren't as strong when we're not together. He's down that way."

Kiko's brow lowered in confusion. "But he'd have to be at least five miles away for your combined strength to waver... unless..." realization hit. She replaced Leila's hand with her own on Brad's shoulders. "Go to him, I'll take care of this one!"

Color drained from Brad's face. "Please, I'm sorry. I'll do whatever you say. Please don't kill —"

Kiko lunged forward and her fox's teeth drilled into his leopard's neck.

With no time to object or even contemplate that Kiko killed someone ready to surrender, Leila stood and ran.

What did Kiko mean when she said "unless"? She thought, dodging the scattered Fallen that she took out moments earlier. They lay moaning on the road, a display of Imprinted strength.

Unless... he's hurt?

Leila stood on the gravel, where the concrete turned into forest.

Unless...

"Riley?" she called, her ears pricked for any reply. *Unless… he's dead?*

Pine nettles scratched her as she tore through the forest, searching for the very thing she once ran from. A large wolf with thick, white fur and shining blue eyes. She found him in a small clearing barely half a mile from the road. Two half-shifted Fallen were hunched over his listless body, scratching at his chest as though digging for treasure. His wolf lay dormant at his side, a dull shade of blue.

"Riley!" Leila screamed.

The predators both twisted their heads, manic. One of them looked familiar, a senior from school, one of Sebastian and Cap's friends. Leila couldn't recall his name. His dark orange wolf sat around his body, aligned but not in full control. The other Fallen stood up, a tall wildebeest surrounding her. A gleeful smile spread across her face, and her eyes shone murky green, like a dying shrub. Leila knew her name. Crystal.

"They said Imprint Guardians were dangerous. You don't look all that special… *he* certainly didn't put up a fight." Crystal laughed.

Leila ran at her in full force, they clashed together in a fury of snarls and swipes. Even though she was close to Riley again, Leila still wasn't as strong as before. Crystal didn't have claws, but her fingernails scraped across the fresh bite mark on Leila's shoulder. As she cried out in pain, Crystal pushed and Leila landed on Riley. The wetness of his wounded chest seeped across her back.

"Two in one go," the boy snarled.

Crystal clapped her hands in glee. "Cap would have loved this. Our first kills. Which one do you want, Thomas?"

"You choose." Thomas grinned.

Rolling over, Leila grabbed an unconscious Riley by the face. "Now is *not* the time to nap... wake up, Riley. Wake up."

Fingers encircled her ankles and dragged her away from him, through leaves and dirt.

Leila looked up to see Thomas return to Riley, violently searching for his heart. New blood poured over old — flesh and bone in a tangled mess.

Leila screamed, digging her claws into the ground like an anchor. She flipped over in time to stop Crystal's advance with a foot to the stomach. Crystal stumbled back, winded.

"Nooo," Leila cried, scrambling back towards Riley and Thomas.

She grabbed Thomas by the wrist; a spiral curved the whole way around it. She pulled him off Riley and lunged forward without hesitation. Her jaw clamped hard around his left ribs. Whimpering, Thomas recoiled and shuffled back. Leila followed him, pushing him further and further away from Riley.

A cruel smile spread across his face as he looked beyond her. "Crush his skull, Crystal."

Leila turned around to see Crystal lifting her foot, the wildebeest moving forward. To Riley, in his human form, a hoof the size of that would kill him.

Leila ran and leapt, wrapping him up in her body. She closed her eyes and waited for the blow.

Crystal's boot hit the back of Leila's head, but no pain followed.

Instead, a loud rumble. A crashing of sorts. Like a bomb had exploded, yet there were no fragments, only light. A ripple of gold and blue circled out from the entwined two, like a pebble in a pond.

A shock so fierce it knocked Crystal and Thomas flying. Their Guardians tumbled even further as though ripped from their human counterparts. Their animal shapes dissipated as they rose through the trees and into the sky, shimmering until there was nothing left.

Stillness followed, as though everything that came before was simply a dream.

Underneath Leila, Riley shuffled, his hands finding her back.

She moved back and watched his eyes open—but they were not brown… nor both blue… one was gold and one was blue.

"Wow," he said, looking between her own eyes.

"What happened?" she asked, doing the same.

"I have no idea. One moment I'm chasing them and the next they jumped me. And, then… you."

Leila quickly scrambled off him to check his bleeding chest. His shirt was in tatters, pieces covering the ground around him. His chest didn't have a single scratch. She glided her palms all over, just in case her eyes weren't seeing what was really there. Next, she touched the bite on her shoulder but there was only skin, smooth and whole.

Her claws retracted and as she returned to her human form, she couldn't see Riley's wolf anymore.

"What was that?" Riley motioned to the air above them. "Was it… us?"

"I think so," Leila replied, glancing over her shoulder.

Crystal rolled onto her back and with gasping breath crawled towards Thomas. She rested her fingers against his neck, visible relief at the feeling of his pulse. Slowly, she lifted her thick sweatshirt to inspect her ribcage. "It's gone," she muttered, looking over to Leila. And then with apologetic eyes, she said, "Thank you."

"I think they're not-so-Fallen anymore," Leila stated, noticing the lack of mark around Thomas' wrist.

Riley sat up. He frowned, then smiled, then laughed. He buried his face into Leila's hair as his hands prodded at her back. "You saved me."

"Yeah, well, don't act like it's such a shock," Leila teased.

"I'm not shocked. It's..." He gave a smirk. "It really is just you and me against the world."

Leila grabbed his face with both hands. "Whatever it takes."

FRIDAY

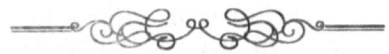

early

"What was that light?" Kiko asked. "After you ran for Riley, there was this shudder and then an explosion of light."

"I thought maybe you could tell us about that," Riley said, answering for Leila.

They sat on the sofa in The Belmonte's living room. Leila's legs were entwined over Riley's as his arm settled around her back, grateful they were both still breathing. Tsukiko and Kale were on the opposite chair, doing much the same. Ren, silent as he mostly was, stood by the boarded-up broken window, keeping watch.

"I've never seen anything like it." Kiko's eyes glistened as she spoke, her hand absent-mindedly making circles over Kale's buzz cut.

Leila smiled at how relaxed Kiko seemed since they'd fought off the Fallen. She thought back to the moment, remembering the fusion of gold and blue that surrounded them.

She said, "It was kind of like our Guardians combined somehow, creating a —"

"There's so much we don't know about Imprints..." Kiko interrupted, sitting up straight. She rested her chin on the side of her shoulder and looked at Kale. Smiling, he ran his fingers through her hair, tucking it behind her ear even though it wasn't on her face. Kiko blinked dreamily. "Damn, rare soul Imprints."

Ren turned around. "We know about Imprints, sister. Or shall I give you a refresher?"

An invisible rush of tension cracked through the room. From Ren's glare to Kiko's blithesome state. Her expression fell immediately, and she hissed, "We didn't know they could create an explosion that removed Guardians from their humans."

Riley raised his hand. "Uh, I'd like a refresher, considering I am one now."

The corners of Ren's lips lifted. "That you are, William. Just like the first ever Guardians." He glanced at Kiko before continuing, "I think the story goes that there were three of them, all siblings. They were given their abilities by the Guardians of the Veil, and tasked to create more Guardians, to protect humans from each other. One of the siblings happened to fall in love with a Marked one, creating the first ever soul Imprint."

"I find it odd that there aren't more Imprints, considering how easy it is to fall in love." Kale smiled at Kiko.

Ren sniffed, the smallest of twinges hitting his eyes. "It's not just love. It's real love, true love... rare love. As far as I know, there haven't been many Imprints in history."

Leila felt Riley's eyes on her and a rush of heat circled her heart. What they had was rare. She had to admit how damn amazing that was.

"It's dangerous love." Ren glared at Kiko and Kale, then shifted his gaze to Leila and Riley, his frown a warning. "The first Imprints were reckless and passionate. Somewhere along the way, one of them killed a human and they became the first Fallen. The other, blind with love, joined them. Together they started a new clan, one that reaches further than we can fathom. That's how they gained so much strength, they're the reason the war started."

Leila was afraid to breathe. She didn't want to make a sound. The first Fallen were Imprints. The thought made her feel sick.

Ren gave a tilted smile, as if he knew what she was thinking. He continued, "Together your power is strong… but remember it's also dangerous."

"Danger is overrated in this house." Leila leaned her head in the groove of Riley's shoulder. It wasn't that she wanted to make light of the situation, but the words flew out before she could think of anything else.

"It's not a joke, guys," Ren half-scolded. "You two and your newborn friends left a lot of Fallen alive back there. They'll be back, or at the very least spread the word about the Imprints in Cedar Falls. I'm just saying, don't let your love get in the way of your purpose."

Leila had often been told she was reckless. But she couldn't imagine neglecting her new-found responsibility, not even for Riley. In fact, the overwhelming urge to protect those weaker than her, felt stronger than their love itself. And that was saying something, because she was so desperately in love with him. Then, a thought flashed through her mind like a light bulb. Maybe they would be the reason the war would end. Leila sat up straight.

"We won't," she said in unison with Riley.

"Oh shoosh with your doom and gloom, brother," Kiko chided. "You look seventeen but act like an old man… but with the four of us — we'll be unstoppable."

Ren huffed, moving back to his lookout at the broken window. "I thought as much."

"Four of us?" Riley asked.

Kiko pulled down Kale's shirt. On his skin was a spiral with one, two, three, four rungs. She grinned with glee. "The Fallen fighting for power will become a thing of the past."

Ren glanced over his shoulder. With nostrils expanding he shook his head and quickly returned to his post.

"Don't be jealous, brother." There was a hint of spite in Kiko's tone. "You'll find love one day."

Oblivious to the sibling tension, Kale smiled, eyes on Kiko. "You know what? If being an Imprint means getting rid of psycho chumps like that Cap kid, I'm up for it."

"That reminds me," Riley whispered to Leila, digging his hand into his pocket. "I forgot to show you this."

He passed his phone to Leila. Across the full screen, a photo displayed.

It was Morgan and Leila at the Falls party.

"Oh, that's actually super cute." She held the phone with both hands. "I'm so glad she's okay."

"Yeah, but look." Riley pointed to a figure next to the fire behind the girls.

"Is that?"

"Yep."

"What?" Kale asked.

Leila thought of Taj's demands and smiled. "It's what I'd call a scoop."

The front door flew open.

"I have the cure!" Aileen cried, tumbling inside. Her arms full of plants and creams. "Salt, vervain, I've also got lavender and althea, you know, just in case. Oh, and well... we also need the blood of the person who marked you. It's that easy. Ha! I mean, it's gotta be someone you've come into contact with over the last few days. So, we'll write a list, I guess. How hard can that be, right?"

Tate followed her in, wrinkles deepened on his brow.

"Why is there broken glass all over my roses?"

Leila stood up. A flutter in her stomach erupted. It bubbled all the way up past her heart, through her mouth, and burst out as a laugh.

FRIDAY

morning

Leila stood outside of Taj's locker, contemplating whether she was making the right call or not.

A few lockers down the rumor mill began.

"I can't believe this is happening."

"It makes you scared to go outside, huh? Knowing there are killer bears and cougars on the loose."

Leila swung her backpack around and retrieved a small envelope from the top. On the front in bold black were the words, *Here's your paparazzi shot*. She stared at it, knowing the contents would cause more harm.

"I know. My dad is picking me up from school today, he won't even let me walk to the corner store."

"Can you imagine how sad Coach must be, most of his star players, just... gone."

Inside the envelope was a print of two teenage girls cheek to cheek. Beside a fire raging six feet high, a boy — Captain of the senior basketball team — was dropping dissoluble pills into two red cups.

"Apparently, Morgan Wakefield is in the hospital, she was one of the lucky ones."

"It's weird we won't get to see them again. Especially Cap, he was so nice to everyone. "

The hair stood on the back of Leila's neck. She held an image that said the opposite. A photo of her and Morgan at the party, of Cap in the background, spiking their drinks. She lifted the envelope up to a slit in Taj's locker.

"It's shocking. Bad things always happen to the good guys."

Without another moment of hesitation, Leila pushed the envelope with the incriminating photo inside the locker.

"Hi," a timid voice said behind her.

Leila jumped as though she'd been sprung cheating in an exam. She turned to see Crystal smiling softly. Crystal wasn't wearing make-up — which was a first — and Leila noticed how naturally pretty she was, freckles and all.

"Hi," Leila replied, then slowly added, "How are you?"

"Confused, disturbed, relieved." Crystal nervously kneaded her hands together. She took a hastened breath then met Leila's gaze. "Mostly, I'm grateful, you know? Like I've been given a second chance."

"And how do you feel? Fallen?" Leila prodded, making sure.

"What do you mean? Is that the term for someone who's not a shifter anymore?"

"No, it's…" Leila went to place a hand on Crystal's shoulder but pulled away at the last moment. "Hey, can you explain something for me, about last night? What made you want to hurt Riley and me?"

Crystal blinked rapidly. "Honestly, I don't know. Ever since Don bit me, there was this darkness around me, like every bad thought I'd ever had occupied my mind all at the same time. There was nothing else that mattered in that moment. I didn't really want to hurt you. It was just this need. Like sleeping or breathing, I *had* to."

She frowned, her eyes dropping to the floor. "I'm sorry, there's no nicer way to say it. And I don't really want to analyze it. The darkness is gone, you took it out of me. I just wanted to say thanks. So... thank you." Crystal nodded once, then turned on her heels and rushed down the hall.

"Ugh," Gab moaned, meeting Leila. "Gossip is floating through the school. Everyone is as vapid as ever."

Not everyone, Leila thought, looking at Crystal walk away.

"Hey killers." Sadie stood on her tip-toes and threw her arms up around both of their shoulders.

"Shhh," Leila hushed, looking around to see if anyone heard.

"Oh, relax," Gabby teased.

Sadie threw her thumb over her shoulder at Damien on the opposite side of the corridor. "He told me Morgan is okay. That's good, huh?"

Leila nodded but she wasn't paying attention. She was watching Sebastian walk down the hall—his shoulders back and chest risen as he stared everyone down. It still baffled Leila at how he was meant to be a Fallen, yet seemed to possess more self-control than they were supposed to have.

Sadie turned to see what Leila was looking at. In a beat, she bounced over towards him. Sadie wrapped her arms around him and nuzzled her head onto his shoulder. He stood still, eyes darting around as though he'd stepped on a land mine. It didn't take long for Leila to take another place at his side, hugging him too. Gabby finished off the group huddle with her arms stretching as far as they could go around all of them.

"Thank you," Sadie whispered, chin up.

At the sound of her voice, Sebastian exhaled and tilted his head onto hers. He spread his hand, pushing his palm against the arch of her back. "Anytime," he replied softly, his breath floating across her forehead. Two long seconds passed before he wriggled his shoulders.

"Ugh, get off me, can't a guy get some space?" He marched down the hall towards his remaining friends. Right before he reached them, in a moment of small humility, he turned back and smiled.

"Project Sebastian completed." Sadie gleefully held her hand up.

"Sort of, I guess," Leila said, snapping her palm against Sadie's. "But I'll take it."

Walking over, Damien held his hand up and Sadie high-fived him. He got one from Gabby and then, Leila. "What are we high-fiving?"

"Our clan," Gabby said.

Sadie cleared her throat. "And me?"

"You're already a part of our clan." Leila smiled.

Damien placed an arm around her and tugged her in close. "Yeah. You're the mundane to our hunter, the Stiles to our wolf pack, the Elena to our vampiness, the... nope, that's all I got."

Sadie nestled her head in front of his armpit and nodded, satisfied.

Speaking of hugs... Leila asked, "Where's Riley?"

"There," Gabby replied, pointing behind Leila.

She turned as Riley walked through the door. History books poked out the top of his bag, his toned biceps flexed as he held a rose in one hand and his backpack strap in the other. There he was, Guardian slash nerd slash hopeless romantic. He walked towards Leila with a smile as wide as the Atlantic.

"One second," he said to Leila, holding a finger up. The same hand slapped into Damien's, a rough shake in display of solidarity — a thank you without words. Next, he squeezed Gabby's shoulder — a quick nod of appreciation. And, then, he pushed through to Sadie, she looked tiny in his embrace.

Finally, he turned back to Leila. With his smile still firmly planted on his face, he stepped toward her. She fell forward, letting his arms circle her waist. Her feet left the floor as he spun her around.

Then, Riley Jansen kissed Leila Belmonte.

And, for the first time in a while, it wasn't a kiss burdened with what-ifs. It was soft-lipped and eager. A kiss between teenagers who wanted to be close, caught up in feelings they'd never felt before.

A chorus around them echoed: "Okay, that's me gone." And, "Looks like our cue to get to class." And, "Oh my god, they're the sweetest... all right, all right, I'm going."

When they came up for air, their friends were already walking away.

With her toes finding the ground, he passed her the rose. A smile bloomed as big as the flower in her hand. "Is this from my garden?"

Riley bit his lip, bringing his dimples to the surface. "Don't tell your dad."

She placed the de-thorned stem in through her loose top-knot. "Can I ask you something?"

"You just did." Riley gave a lop-sided smile.

"I'm being serious."

He smacked his lips together, trying to hide his smile, and nodded.

"What am I?" she asked.

His eyes lit up. "That's easy. You are beautiful and smart and funny but also so very brave."

"No," Leila chortled, gently hitting his chest. "I mean, what's my Guardian's animal?"

Riley grinned as if he knew that's what she meant the whole time. "The only thing you could've been."

"That doesn't help."

"Leilani," Riley said, sweeping a stray ringlet from covering her eye. "You're a lion."

Leila laughed. That was her, she guessed, wild and untamed.

EPILOGUE

FRIDAY

almost midnight

Gabby couldn't sleep. She paced across her bedroom floor, too excited to close her eyes. She was a Guardian now, an actual glow-inducing, innocent-protecting, shape-shifting Guardian.

Thanks to Odette.

Gabby bit her lip, too embarrassed to even smile to herself over the memory. She followed her. After Leila met Riley at the lake, she chased that girl.

"Hey!" she'd said, behind her.

Odette stopped and turned. She was smiling, as though she knew she was being followed and by whom.

"Do I know you?" Gabby asked, trying not to sound clichéd. It had to be better than, "So, you come here often?" though, so she went with it, albeit feigning confidence.

"I don't think so," Odette replied, a wry smile on her face. "I'm not from here."

"Right. How do you know Riley? He has a girlfriend, you know."

"Oh, you think I'm into him. No, he's my cousin, so... eww. Plus, he's not a female, so... not my type. And yes, I know he has a girlfriend, he won't shut up about her."

I knew it!

Gabby instinctively pulled at the ends of her hair. "Oh. Good. Yeah, she doesn't talk much about him but that's because she really likes him. Strange girl that one. But, what can I say, I'd die for her."

"You'd die for her?" A strange expression passed over Odette's face.

Standing in front of this beautiful creature sent goosebumps down Gabby's arms. Nervous yet relaxed at the same time. As if they were always meant to meet that day.

"Yeah, she's stubborn as gum on a boot but she has this way of looking past the B.S. people pretend to be. She sees people for who they really are. The good things, you know?" Whether she wanted them to or not, the words tumbled from Gabby's lips. "She saw me for who I really was, and I'll never forget it. Anyway, I don't know why I just told you that." Gabby cleared her throat. "Do you like coffee?"

"I *do* like coffee," Odette declared as if they found something rare in common. "But now I feel bad. Riley told me something... about your friend. I know you don't know me very well, or at all, but..." Another funny expression hit Odette's face. "Listen, Riley's stubborn too, so he won't ask for help. But he came to me because Leila's in trouble. I mean, he thinks she might be, but that's enough to be worried, right?"

Gabby leaned closer. "What kind of trouble?"

Without flinching, Odette whispered, "Can you keep a secret?"

Gabby looked her over, unsure how a stranger could ask something of another stranger like that. But it was about Leila and there was something about this six-foot goddess that made her blurt, "Yes."

And next minute she was face to face with a girl showing pale eyes that glowed green. Purpose flooded then, as though all meaning had arrived. She knew in her heart she was born for it. Destiny and all that crap.

And now Gabby couldn't sleep, because the night before she'd beaten a handful of Fallen and it was all she could think about. Justice was running through her bones.

She threw herself onto her bed. The very spot Riley turned her. Odette wanted to do it, and Gabby would have let her, too, but Riley gave her a look that no one would want to mess with. Gabby understood it after he turned her. He was in charge, a tiny string connected them, and what he said was just how it was going to be. Except with Leila.

Gabby smiled to herself. *No one could ever control that girl.*

The sound of breaking glass caused Gabby to half-shift.

From her room she could hear her brother, Benjamin, yell out, "Stop it, you're hurting her!"

Another voice, not quite human yet clearer than anything, "Save her, save her, save her."

Gabby fully shifted as she went, a flash of silver running down the hall to the kitchen. She found her mom slumped in the corner between the sink and the oven, broken glass surrounding her. Her eyes were closed as she struggled with breath. Gabby's step-father, Michael, knelt beside Rosie. He was stroking a large bruise on her cheek and repeating the word "Sorry" over and over.

"What did you do to her?" Gabby asked, not realizing her words were replaced by a light growl.

Michael startled, his eyes widening at the sight of a wolf in his kitchen. He shuffled back slowly, slithering behind the island bench. Gabby met him from the opposite side but instead of finding just one man, she found two.

Benjamin laid on the ground, a butcher's knife in his chest.

"Benji?" she whimpered. To Michael, the wolf let out a low howl, its light brown fur shuddering as it buckled at the knees.

"Here." Michael kicked Benjamin's hand as though he was an offering. "Take this one." He took a few slow steps back before escaping out the door.

Moving closer to Benjamin, Gabby's wolf sniffed at his fatal wound, and she collapsed by his side.

How could this happen? She was a Guardian, she was meant to protect people—especially her family. But even in her own home, her mother was abused and her brother…

She'd failed at her very purpose.

Gabby lifted her head to the heavens, and as she screamed, her wolf howled so fiercely the house rattled like an aftershock. When her lungs were out of breath, she bolted through the open back door, nose to the ground on the hunt for her brother's killer.

It didn't take long for her to find him, he reeked of alcohol and sweat. She killed him, Michael, her step-dad. As though he were made of marshmallow, she unceremoniously tore through his flesh only stopping upon hearing footsteps behind her.

"Gabby?" Riley asked, stepping slowly towards the wolf and its prey.

She looked up, wild eyes glowing in the night. Seeing him jolted her, an Alpha demanding his Beta to fall in line. Her wolf retreated, moving back to make way for her to return.

Human, she wiped her mouth with one hand and her tears with the other.

"Gabby?" Riley said her name softer this time, careful not to startle her.

He was afraid. Not for himself but for her. The lesson was clear; when a True Guardian killed a civilian, they would become a Fallen.

ACKNOWLEDGEMENTS

When a story called, I had to answer. My first thanks goes to *the Muse* for bringing me this idea. It started from a dream, where my husband was a werewolf and I didn't know it.

Jonathon (the husband), you probably won't read this book but I hope you know I love you anyway. If I was hunted by a pack of werewolves, you'd be the one I'd beg to turn me.

To my Alpha readers, Jasmine and Alicia—as always, your first thoughts drive me, and I thank you for that.

My beta readers, Kalli and Debbie, I'm sending you all my books from here on in.

Lindsay "cut the damn speech tag" Mead, thank you for your feedback. You've helped me make this book better and I'll be forever grateful.

Janet, editor and deadline meeter, thanks for all your hours.

To everyone who reviews… you rock.

Until the next book … Elle xxx

ABOUT THE AUTHOR

Elle Scott lives in the Huon Valley, Tasmania, Australia with her husband, two sons, three cats, and one big ball of fluff, Labrador.

Telling stories has always been a part of her. When she was young, it was her dream to be a famous actress, and she would spend hours playing "make believe" with her sister. Her wild imagination turned everyday moments in life into extraordinary events. A long bus ride became an adventurous trek on the back of a horse galloping on the beach; or days spent in her backyard became days in the African Safari! Her imagination took her from her warm bed into a world where humans can shift into animals. Her biggest thrill is taking her oddball dreams and making them a reality with words.

Elle also tells real stories for real people. She is a multi-award winning family photographer.

Elle hopes to one day run workshops for self-conscious women, to turn them from a wallflower into a wildflower and give them the confidence to chase their dreams with ferocity.

FOLLOW ELLE:

Instagram - @ellescott_author
Facebook - @ellescottauthor

JOIN ELLE'S VIP LIST TODAY

And receive the first book in the complete Incandescent
Series for free

RAY OF LIGHT follows three strong females as they find
themselves in the crossfire of a war over mysterious orbs.

www.ellescottbooks.com/freebook